TERRITORIAL INSTINCTS

A BARKER STREET BONES MYSTERY - BOOK 1

SANDY ST. JOHN

SOUTHPAW PRESS

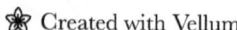

~

For my mom, who started taking me to the library before I could walk. You gave me my love of books, and so much more. My first and best audience —this one was always for you.

And for my dad, who really prefers books of intrigue and espionage. I didn't expect you to read this, much less like it. You loved it (probably because I wrote it), and I couldn't ask for more.

Your belief and support mean everything.
Love you, guys.

~

I really should have read my horoscope before getting out of bed. If I'd seen it was going to be a one-star day, I might not have gotten up. Although horoscopes are usually so vague. "Beam in more of what you want." What does that even mean? Now if it had said, "You're likely to find a dead body today," well, that would have been good information. I would have definitely stayed home and probably stayed inside.

But I didn't read my horoscope, and I probably wouldn't have believed anything I read anyway. My name is Jessie Gallagher, and I make gourmet dog biscuits for a living. Well, truth be told, I'm not actually making a living from my business yet. Heck, I'm not even making money, but I'm determined to make a success of this because the idea of going back to another corporate job makes my stomach churn.

It was October and I was up early, like every morning. I'd already walked my dog and was watering flowers in the backyard before starting the day's baking. A front had come through overnight and the heat that had gripped Houston for the past few weeks had finally broken. I leaned over to turn off the hose when I heard a rasp like a shovel scraping gravel coming from my neighbor's yard. As I stood up, a mound of something solid sailed over the fence, nearly hitting me in the head. Luckily, I have decent reflexes, and I dodged sideways automatically even before recognizing what it was. A second heap soared past and landed with a plop on my flagstone patio. The smell was a dead giveaway.

"Hey! What are you doing?" I shouted to the unseen person.

"Returning your crap." This must be my new neighbor. He'd moved in several months ago, but I hadn't had the pleasure to meet him yet.

"Whatever you have over there is not mine," I said, heat rising in my cheeks. I debated throwing it back, but it looked like it would have to be scraped off the stones first.

"I meant it's your dog's. Gah, what an idiot." His back door slammed.

Addie, the dog in question, poked her black-and-white head through the doggie door, nose twitching. She gave a disgusted look and disappeared abruptly back inside.

I clenched my teeth and pulled a couple of baggies from my pocket. Cleaning up dog poop doesn't faze me; in addition to my dog biscuit company, I also walk dogs to make ends meet. At least until sales pick up. So this is something I do every day, but the casual way he'd just lobbed the mess over my wall really rankled.

Determined not to let this ruin my day, I cleaned up and got to work. I love the rhythm of baking and I let myself relax as I gathered the ingredients for my liver cookies. Dogs go crazy at the smell of these, although I'm not sure why; I think they smell ghastly. In the beginning, I gagged every time I peeled the butcher paper back from the raw organs. Now, though, I was used to it. Taking my time, I measured dry items into one bowl while slopping the liver into the wide mouth of the Cuisinart. Hitting the switch, I watched the liver whirl around, hitting the plastic sides with a soft thwop, thwop, thwop.

The routine movements were soothing and the irritation over my neighbor receded. Halfway through rolling out my first batch, the phone rang. Wiping my greasy hands on a paper towel, I grabbed the phone before the machine could pick up.

"Hello, Barker Street Bones?"

There was a moment of silence on the other end of the line. "What?" A laugh. "Is this Jessie Gallagher?"

The voice sounded familiar, but out of context. A beat of silence, then it came to me and I nearly hung up. Dayna Burke, my old boss. Why was she calling me? First the poop-throwing neighbor, now this.

"Yes, it is," I said, using the tone I reserve for cold-calling-bogus-solicitors.

"Jessie, this is Dayna Burke. You remember, from Astor Oil." As if I could forget.

"Sure. Hey, Dayna, how're you doing?"

"I'm doing great! I heard you were walking dogs because you couldn't find another job. Is that true? You really couldn't find another job?" She sounded so happy to hear it.

"Actually, I started my own business making gourmet dog biscuits. It's doing quite well, although I do have some dog-walking clients. Was there another reason you had for calling?" Because Dayna would never just call someone to see how they were, not even if she'd accidentally run them over with her car.

"Yes, well, actually I'm calling about this 'business' of yours. The dog-walking part. I need my dog walked this afternoon."

Muscle memory in my neck kicked in and I began to tense up. But guess what? She wasn't my boss anymore.

"I'm sorry. I have all the clients I need right now."

"That's too bad. I was hoping you'd do it as a favor for an

old friend." A small gag choked my throat. "I have a meeting after work that'll probably go late, and my husband is out of town. But if you can't do it, then I guess Henry will just have to hold it till I get home." I gripped the phone until my fingers ached. *Hang up. Hang up*, I told myself.

"Henry is my new dog," she ran on as if I cared. "We got him about two months ago. But anyway, if you can't make it, I guess he'll be all right in his crate. Maybe that'll teach him to hold it."

She kept that poor dog in a crate all day? I gave a deep sigh of resignation and told her to hold on while I checked my schedule. I kept her waiting as long as I could, knowing how much she hated to hold.

"I might be able to get over there around four or so," I said.

"If that's the best you can do, I guess it's fine. Then if I'm really late getting home, he should be okay. You need to feed him while you're there too." I could hear another line ringing in the background. "I'll leave the key with Naomi. Just come by here and get it." And she hung up.

I'd walked out of my oil company job five months ago because of this woman. Already, I was regretting this. I hadn't exactly left on good terms, so why would she call me? Unless she missed degrading me. That sounded about right.

I steamrolled my way through three more batches of liver treats. How could one call trigger such anxiety? All I had to do was call her back and tell her I couldn't make it. Even as I thought it, I knew I would do it for the dog. I'm a sucker that way. By shuffling my schedule slightly, I could run by the office around lunchtime, and if I was lucky, Dayna wouldn't be around.

Grabbing my phone, I raced to get ready. I hit my friend Evan's work number as I rummaged through my closet. He's the only one from Astor Oil I still keep in touch with.

"Hey," I said when he answered.

"Hey, I was going to call you," he said. "I heard some good gossip today about your favorite person."

Evan loved the gossip around the office as much as the girls in the admin pool did. And he usually knew almost as much as they did.

"I got some news too," I said before he had a chance to continue. "Guess who called me today?"

There was a moment of silence while he thought about it. "I don't know. Who?"

"Dayna. She wants me to go walk her dog this afternoon."

"Get out of here. Is she going to pay you? Or does she think you're still working for her and she can just order you to do it?"

Geez, I hadn't even thought of that. So much for my unflappable business sense.

"Oh, well."

Evan laughed. "She's not gonna pay you. But, hey, maybe this will cheer you up." His voice dropped to a whisper. "Guess who Dayna did the dirty with? You're never going to believe it."

This was a harder question than you'd think. Dayna was not known to be super committed to her marriage vows. "I couldn't begin to guess."

"Naomi's husband." Naomi was Dayna's admin. Built like a brick, with the personality of curdled milk, Naomi spent much of her time trying to convert anyone she could corner. Convert to what, we weren't really sure.

"No." No, really, yuck. "Eww. As much as I usually believe all the bad things about her, no. Why would she have anything to do with Naomi's husband? That's disgusting. She likes power. And authority. And attractive men. He's none of those things."

"I know. I think she did it to piss Naomi off. You know

what a fanatic she is, and apparently, she's been making a lot of remarks about Dayna lately. Someone said they heard Naomi telling her the story about the whore of Babylon last week."

"Are you kidding me? What, so Dayna decided to prove her point? Does Naomi know?" Great, now I really didn't want to have to see her.

"Hard to say with her." He cut off suddenly and I heard a muffled rustling.

"Evan?"

"Yes, and I really need you to check those numbers. I've got to get this report out today," he said in his most professional voice.

"Gotta go, huh? Well I have to come down there and pick up Dayna's key from Naomi. I'll probably be there around lunchtime. Can you let me in?" I really didn't want to face Naomi alone after that revelation.

"Call me," he whispered, then he hung up.

Poor Evan, still a prisoner. Maybe we could grab a quick lunch before my first dog-walking appointment.

I made it downtown just before eleven. It was a little early for the lunch rush, but clots of smokers huddled in designated areas outside the high-rise doors. I drove down Louisiana, looking for public parking. I'd forgotten what a pain it was to find parking downtown, and after several passes I finally found a lot that wasn't full, about four blocks away. Naturally it was an all-day lot, so I had to pay the full daily rate. I kicked myself again.

Astor Oil occupies twelve floors of One Allen Center, and while the building does have security, the elevators still provide public access. Although, once you reach the Astor Oil floors, you need a security badge. I texted Evan to let him know I was on my way up.

I hit the button for twenty-three and checked my reflection

in the door. I felt as nervous as I had going into my first job interview. *You're fine*, I told myself. *What's there to be nervous about?*

Evan was waiting at the elevator reception area wearing his usual khaki pants and rumpled blue button-down. His blue eyes lit up when I stepped off.

"Wow, I haven't seen you this dressed up in months," he said, which was no doubt true.

He held the security door open for me and we made our way down the hall towards Naomi's desk. Not much had changed since I'd left, although for the first time I noticed how harsh the fluorescent lighting was. The furious clacking of keyboards hit my ears even before we turned the corner and entered the open floor plan. The desks were arranged in rows, with minimal privacy and maximum noise.

Hardly anyone looked up, and for that I was thankful. I was happy with the choice I'd made to leave here and pursue my dream, but I knew this floor was filled with power-hungry people who would view my choice as a failure.

Naomi's desk was empty. Her workspace looked Spartan compared to her neighbors': chair pushed in neatly, folders stacked, not a stray pen in sight. I glanced around, expecting to see her walking towards me with her little red insulated lunch bag. Funny the things you remember.

"That's new," said Evan, pointing to a paper that was tacked above her monitor. In bold letters it read: "A worthless person is one who walks with a false mouth!" I wasn't sure if that was scripture or a fortune cookie saying.

"Uh-oh," I said, "I guess she's heard."

"I guess so," he said. "But who would tell her something like that?"

"I can't imagine. Maybe she overheard someone talking about it."

"Maybe," he said. "Oh, here." Evan leaned across her desk and picked up an envelope. "I guess this is for you."

He handed me a thick envelope with my name written in bold black strokes across the front. It was sealed, and I tore open the flap, extracting the key. No note, no directions, just a key. Typical Dayna. Good thing I remembered where she lived from last year's Christmas party. At least I thought I did. I slipped the key into my purse and tossed the envelope towards Naomi's trash can. It landed with a flutter and balanced on the edge. Stepping forward to tip it in, I noticed another sign inside the trash can. I reached in and pulled it out, smoothing its crinkled edges as I read.

"All liars will go to the lake that burns with fire and brimstone, which is the second death!" I showed it to Evan. "She's scaring me a little," I said. "I think she's farther around the bend than she was when I worked here."

"No kidding," he said, shifting his feet uncomfortably and glancing around nervously. "Let's get out of here before she comes back. She really does creep me out. Anyway, I'm starving."

I threw the paper back into her trash can and followed Evan out. We headed downstairs to the food court that was in the tunnel under the building. The lunch hour was just getting started, and the lines weren't long yet.

"I'll meet you back here," he said, falling back into our old routine. We used to eat lunch together almost every day, and he always alternated between the Mexican place and the hamburger joint. I usually got a salad or a sandwich. I opted for a sandwich today, and when I got back I found Evan already arranging his lunch at a table near the wall. He was busy spreading packets of ketchup over a sloppy-looking cheeseburger, while a large container of fries spilled over his bag.

"You really need to start eating healthier," I told him.

"Yeah, I know," he said, taking a giant bite. "Maybe next week."

We ate fast, since I needed to get to my rounds and he needed to get back to work.

Around a bite of hamburger, Evan said, "According to Sue, Dayna was openly talking about it while she was on the phone yesterday. Sue's that new girl I told you about last week. She sits next to Naomi, right outside Dayna's office. Said Dayna was really laughing about it."

I pictured Naomi's husband and shuddered involuntarily. "I still can't picture it," I said, trying hard not to. "It seems pretty far-fetched that Dayna would go to that extreme just because Naomi was annoying her." Although even as I said it, I realized that nothing was too extreme for Dayna when she wanted to make someone miserable.

"I guess it happened here in the office a couple of nights ago."

"Here?"

"Yeah, Walter came to pick Naomi up. I guess Dayna had her working late, getting copies of some presentation ready. She made Naomi go down to the copy center and wait. So, there's Walter waiting at Naomi's desk, and Dayna decided to have a little fun. She invited him into her office and started hitting on him. I'm sure the poor guy's never had that happen." Evan stopped to take a drink. "Then, according to what she said on the phone, she started asking him about..." He paused. "You know." Evan's cheeks flushed and he looked away.

"What? Sex?"

"Well, you know. Kind of. Something I'm sure Naomi wouldn't approve of."

"Oh." Now I got it.

"Anyway. Can you imagine? The next thing you know, she takes care of him right there at her desk. By the time Naomi got back, the guy was done and didn't even know what hit him."

"Did Naomi know at that point what had happened?" I'd finished my sandwich and was working on the fries that Evan hadn't eaten yet.

"No. I guess neither one of them said anything. But her husband was so freaked out he, like, couldn't even talk."

"Do you think he told her what happened?"

"I don't know. Maybe. Maybe he needed to confess."

"Or maybe he didn't say anything, but she heard people at work talking about it."

"Either way, it's just not good," he said. "I'm trying to stay out of the way of both of them. Then again, that's nothing new."

He finished the last of the fries and we scooped up our trash, threw it in the bin and headed for the elevators. I was disturbed by that little story and wished I hadn't agreed to walk Dayna's dog. Oh well. I'd do it this one time and then I'd be done. The farther I stayed away from Dayna Burke, the better.

CHAPTER TWO

My dog-walking rounds went quickly; generally, when I'm hanging out with my doggie pals, time flies. Being that I only have eight clients, I've gotten to know each of them very well. I spend about thirty minutes a day getting each of them outside for a bathroom break, a little exercise and some company to break up their days while their owners are gone. The lunch with Evan had me running behind, but I wouldn't cut any time off my rounds. I would just shift everything back a little bit.

It was just past four thirty when I made my way north to Dayna's neighborhood. All of my regular clients live in the West University area, which is a lovely but pricey area around the Rice University campus. Dayna lives in a developing and eclectic part of Houston known as the Montrose area. Just outside downtown, it's a mixed haven for gays, yuppies and other offbeat souls.

I hadn't been in this part of town since her Christmas party the year before and was surprised how much had changed. A lot of the older homes were gone, replaced by behemoth townhouses that filled small lots to the edges and towered over the street. Other homes featured major renovations, proudly holding their own amongst grander neighbors. And still others continued to fall down board by board, abandoned and neglected.

Dayna's house was one of the smaller renovations. It was a Craftsmen style that seemed out of character for her. I always pictured her as a glass-and-chrome kind of person–basically cold and colorless. From what I gathered at the party, the house was her husband's project and she'd made it clear how bored she was by the whole thing.

I wondered briefly where her husband was. Daniel claimed to be some sort of documentary filmmaker, although talk around the office suggested that he'd never actually sold any of his films. My guess was that Dayna bankrolled them. Not a bad deal if you can get it. I was ashamed of myself as soon as I thought it. Who was I to judge? I'd been able to walk out of a job I hated because of a little trust fund my grandfather had left me. But at least I was working to support myself again with my own business. I wasn't getting rich, but technically, I already was rich.

A handful of pickup trucks lined the street in front of Dayna's house, and the rhythmic pounding of hammers beat through the air from a couple of doors down, where more giant townhouses were springing out of the earth. I pulled in behind a dented extended-cab pickup and cut the engine. Matching busty silver women winked out from the low-hanging mud flaps. Nice. Why do guys put those on their trucks?

I slipped Dayna's key into my hand and tucked my purse under the car seat. This shouldn't take long. I made a mental note to block Dayna's number from both my home and cell phones.

Dried leaves littered the small front porch, and a handful of flyers poked out from behind the door handle. It looked like no one ever used this door. I grabbed the flyers and slid the key into the lock. Belatedly, I realized that Dayna hadn't mentioned what kind of dog Henry was.

Turning the key, I pushed open the door. Immediately, a caramel-colored ball of fur flew past me and out the door. Dammit! She'd said he'd be in a crate. My heart flew into overdrive as he raced down the front walk to the sidewalk, never even giving a backward glance.

"Henry," I called, racing after him. "Henry!"

I couldn't tell what kind of dog he was; I only knew he was fast. Damn. She was going to kill me. I raced down the sidewalk after him, heading away from the construction workers, calling his name and running at top speed.

Dayna should have mentioned that he was an escape artist. Dammit. "Henry!" He turned near an abandoned house and I plunged into the yard after him, slowing down to avoid breaking an ankle on the debris in the yard. I picked my way as quickly and carefully as I could. "Here, boy. Here, boy!"

Why, oh, why didn't I have any dog treats in my pocket? Maybe because I'd given them all to my clients. I heard a scuttling sound ahead of me. He must have found his way into the house. Good, maybe I could corner him in there.

"Whoa, hey, little fella." I heard a surprised voice around the corner.

"Hello, there! Could you please grab that dog for me if you can?" I shouted out. *Please, please,* I was thinking.

A wrinkly little black man in tattered clothes ambled around the side of the house, holding a heavily panting Henry in his arms. Henry turned out to be a Norfolk terrier with spiky crème brûlée-colored fur, nicely accented by a whiskey-shaded beard. Frightened brown eyes peered at me for a minute before disappearing under the man's arm.

"Hey, boy," I said, holding my hand out towards him. The dog tried to burrow closer to his rescuer.

"Looks here like this little dog don't want to see you," the man said with a raspy voice. He bent and stroked Henry's side with a bony finger. "You okay, little one," he cooed. "You okay."

"I can't tell you how much I appreciate you catching him," I said.

The man kept stroking Henry, but turned his dark eyes on me. "What'd you do to him?" he demanded.

"Nothing," I said, taking a defensive step back. "I'm supposed to be walking him for my old boss. She said he'd be in a crate, so I wasn't expecting him to take off like that when I opened the front door."

"Hmph," he said, still not taking his eyes off me. Henry's breathing was starting to quiet and his sides slowed their heavy heaving, but he kept his head hidden. "How come he don't want to see you?"

"I don't know. I've never met him before, but dogs usually love me." This particular dog was starting to make me feel bad, and making me sound like a liar. "Henry?" I called softly, leaning in towards him. "Henry?"

"You not his owner?"

"No. I was supposed to stop by and walk him. His owner's a lady I used to work with."

"Well, I don't know that I want to turn this guy over to someone he don't like. He don't want to go with you in a big way. Maybe I'll just be keepin' him for myself." He took a couple of paces backward, holding tight to the dog.

Oh, great. "Are you sure you want a dog? They're a lot of work. Trust me, I've got one of my own." He dropped his head and looked at the ground.

"You think I can't take care a' this guy?"

"No, no. I didn't say that. You're obviously great with dogs. It's just that this dog already has a home."

He stroked Henry's head and cradled him gently. "Hey, dog. Hey. Looky here, this lady wants you to go with her." I watched his weathered face crinkle with concern. "I don't want you to do anything you don't want to do." Henry finally lifted his head and stared at the homeless man. "She seems nice enough even if you don't want to go with her." He glanced back at me. "Nice lady gonna take care of you. You don't worry none. And if you need to come runnin' again, I'm usually around here. You just come lookin' for me."

He shifted Henry a little. The dog probably only weighed about ten pounds, but this little guy looked like he was barely pushing a hundred himself.

"What's your name?" I asked him.

"Hudson," he said, shifting the dog again and holding out his hand.

"I'm Jessie." I shook his hand, his bony fingers as rough against mine as emery boards. "It's nice to meet you. I can't tell you how much I appreciate your help." I ran a quick mental rundown of my wallet's contents to see if I could give Hudson a little something for his trouble. "Maybe you could walk back with us and I can give you a little reward for catching him."

Hudson held Henry out and shook his head. "No, ma'am. That's okay. I don't want no money. I just want to make sure this little one is gonna be treated right."

I wished I knew that, but with Dayna as an owner, I couldn't swear to it.

"I want to make sure he's treated right too," I said.

I took Henry from him and the dog settled into the crook of my arm. His breath still came in little short pants, but he'd stopped struggling to get away. Hudson slowly melted back towards the abandoned house. I headed back towards Dayna's, carrying Henry like a football under one arm while I stroked his head with my opposite hand. His little body was muscular, and he felt tense in my grasp.

"It's okay, boy," I soothed him. "I'll get your leash and we'll go for a nice walk."

I glanced behind me once, certain I could feel Hudson's eyes on me, but I didn't see him; he had vanished into the shadows.

I passed my car, debating whether I should grab one of the spare leashes that I always carry, but I decided against it, as most of the ones I have are thick and heavy, designed for bigger dogs. I'd just grab his from the house. As I crunched across the leaves on the porch, Henry began to squirm and wriggle in my grasp. His sturdy little legs clawed at me and he struggled with his whole body to get away. I held him tight against my chest and went in through the door that I'd left open moments ago.

"Henry. It's okay. It's *okay*," I told him. I kicked the door shut behind me so he couldn't race off again and set him on the floor. He turned and began clawing frantically at the door. Fine flakes of paint rained down under the assault of his nails, and he whimpered in his throat as he worked. "Wooo, wooo, wooo." He must really have to go.

"Hey, no! Cut that out!" I scooped him up again, but he nearly cracked me in the nose with his thrashing head, so I set him back down. Leaving him to his destruction, I headed for the kitchen, hoping to find a leash fast. Dayna was not going to be happy with the mess he was making of her front door. The only thing I could hope was that this was something that he'd done before so she wouldn't blame it on me.

I raced up the hallway towards the kitchen, hoping a leash was somewhere in plain view. I needed to get that dog out before he grated all the paint on the front door into fine baby powder. Thankfully, I spotted one rolled up on the counter. As I grabbed it, I noticed the disarray: loose papers scattered everywhere like a tornado had ripped through the room, couch and chair cushions askew, even the pictures on the wall tipped at crazy angles.

"Oh, are you in trouble," I shouted towards Henry, who,

judging by the noise, was continuing to dig his way through the door. "No wonder you need to get away." Then I paused to consider the pictures. They were on the walls. Way up high on the walls. There was no way his stocky little body could have reached that height.

A slight feeling of unease crept along my spine, and I backed slowly away from the mess. I could still hear Henry woo-woo'ing in the front hall, determined to get out. Why was he so determined? This wasn't typical "I gotta go" behavior. Goose bumps rose along my arms and I stood frozen, listening. Aside from the sounds of the dog and my own heart thumping frenetically against my chest, I heard nothing else inside the house. Outside I could hear one of the construction workers calling to another in Spanish, and the rumble of a diesel engine as it revved and pulled down the street. But nothing else inside. Nothing to justify the fear that wormed its way down my legs, turning my feet into leaden lumps. Maybe this is how the house always looked.

The dog could hold it one more minute. Moving as quietly as I could, I followed the trail of papers, creeping along the wall like a TV cop. I hadn't been in this part of the house at last year's Christmas party, but I had to assume it led towards the bedrooms.

The first room on the right was an office. The blinds were drawn and I peered into the dimness, waiting for my eyes to adjust. The paper chaos continued in here as well. Who keeps this much paperwork? Good grief, buy a shredder already.

As my eyes adjusted, I could see that a bookcase had been tipped over and rested precariously against the desk. No way could the dog have done this. There must have been a break-in. I held my breath and listened again. The creepy feeling that I wasn't alone motivated me to move.

A quick check of the rest of the house and I'd be out the door with the dog. Dogs are sensitive, and if that dog was feeling anything close to the level of unease I was feeling in this house, it would be cruel to leave him here. As much as I didn't want to see Dayna again, maybe I'd just take the dog home with me, leave a note and bring him back when she got home.

I turned back towards the hall. Forget about checking the other rooms, I'd just grab the dog and go. I almost made it, but the hand sticking out from behind the desk stopped me in my tracks.

My own hand flew to my mouth as I tried not to scream. Oh crap, oh crap! I inched into the room, craning my neck farther around the desk. My flight instinct screamed at me to get the hell out of there.

Dayna lay on the floor behind the desk at an awkward angle. The hand that I'd spotted reached up over her head. The other one clutched at her throat. Her face looked bloated and bluish, and her bulging eyes strained at her eyelids, staring at me unseeingly. She definitely wasn't moving.

I stood rooted to the spot, unable to look away. My stomach finally took charge and I heaved and vomited over the papers on the floor. Oh my God. Dayna. I felt dizzy, and the edges of my peripheral vision started to close in. Black spots danced in my middle vision. I was going to pass out. I knelt on the floor for a minute, trying to gather myself. I could feel the wetness of vomit against my knee and I gagged again.

From a distance, I could still hear Henry trying to claw his way through the door. Pulling myself up and pushing the dizziness away, I lurched for the front hall, leash still clutched tightly in my hand. My fingers felt fat and uncoordinated as I tried to latch the leash to his collar. On the third try I got it, opened the door and we bolted out and down the walkway.

I had to get help. Call the police. We ran down the same path we'd followed only moments before, although it felt like a different lifetime. Call the police. I slowed my pace, trying to get a grip now that I was out of there and away from that horrifying face. We'd already passed my car. I stopped, but Henry was still running full speed. He twanged to a stop as he reached the end of his leash.

I picked him up and held him tight. His warm body comforted me. Poor thing. That's what he'd been so terrified of. Who could blame him? I'd all but pushed him out of the way trying to get out myself. My heart still raced at abnormal speed. I took a couple of deep breaths and returned to my car. Setting Henry on the passenger seat, I grabbed my cell phone and dialed 911.

I hadn't checked for a pulse. Maybe I should go back in and check.

"911, what's your emergency?"

"I just found my old boss dead in her house."

"Do you need police or ambulance?"

"I don't know. I think she's dead!"

"Ma'am, you need to calm down. Police or ambulance?"

"She's friggin' dead!" I shouted. "You tell me who you need to send!""Ma'am, you need to remain calm. What address do you need emergency response sent to?"

I peered out my window, trying to find the street number. I didn't actually know Dayna's street number.

"Ma'am? What address, please?" She was starting to sound a bit snippy.

"I'm trying to see," I snapped back. "It's Willard, just past Stanford. I don't know the number. Just send someone and I'll flag them down when they get here."

"I need a street address." I peered at the house across from where I was sitting.

"I'm sitting across from 409. I don't know the address of the house where the"– I paused, trying to get the word out. "Where the victim is."

"Okay, we've got someone on the way. What is your name?"

I glanced around the car for Henry. He'd disappeared into the backseat. I could hear crunching, but all I could see was his butt end sticking out from under the seat.

"Hey, stop that," I scolded him. "Get over here."

"Ma'am? Ma'am. I need your name."

I could hear sirens in the distance, but more immediately I could hear the dog choking on something. I twisted around over the console and tried to pull him out, dropping my cell phone in the process. "Hey, are you okay?"

His mouth opened wide as he hacked and choked trying to expel whatever it was that was stuck. Grabbing him around the middle, I hauled him into the front seat. I stuck a finger into his mouth and felt around the back of his throat. A jagged end of something stuck against his soft palate and I hooked my finger around it and pulled it loose. The 911 woman was going crazy on the other end of the line. All I could make out in the squawking was the word "name."

A white patrol car careened around the corner, lights ablaze and sirens at full blare. I deposited Henry on the passenger seat and opened the car door. Glancing back at him, I could see he had his ears pinned back against the noise, but was nevertheless going back to work on his unidentified object. Great. I scooped up my cell phone, disconnected and grabbed the goopy mess away from him before he could kill himself on it. Slamming the door behind me, I stepped into the street just as the police car whipped past.

CHAPTER THREE

The patrol car slid to a stop in the middle of the street, lights still flashing but sirens mercifully silenced. More sirens screamed in the distance, and I could see curtains being pulled back in the surrounding houses. People checking to see if they should come out and be nosy, or whether they might be injured in the melee. The construction noises stopped as the workers came forward to see what was going on.

I gave the officer a little wave and was suddenly aware I needed a breath mint or a stick of gum in a bad way. Oh well. These guys were used to disasters.

The responding officer was young and black, with muscular arms bulging under his blue shirt. He took a moment to adjust his gear-laden belt before approaching. His gun bulged prominently and his hand hovered at a measured distance from the butt.

"Are you the one who called in the complaint?" he asked. Dragging my eyes away from his gun, I turned toward cautious black eyes.

"Yes." I pointed towards Dayna's house. "I found my old

boss in her house. She's dead." I paused. "I think. No, I'm pretty sure."

He eyed me carefully, trying to assess my reliability as a witness. I could tell he'd experienced a lot of panic and false alarms during his budding career. Reliable or not, he had to check it out.

"That house right there?" he asked, pointing right to it. Sirens were coming closer.

"Yes. The front door is open. She's in the back, down the hall and around towards the bedrooms. I think it's a home office. At least, there was a desk and computer and files and of course all the paper. The paper is everywhere. I've never actually been in that room before, although I was at their house for last year's Christmas party. It was a lot neater then." I knew I was babbling, but I couldn't stop. He eyed me warily, and I could tell I was dropping fast on his reliability meter. "Anyway, she was blue and I'm pretty sure she's dead."

He waited for the next cop car to arrive, then motioned me to stay where I was while he walked over to the new arrivals. Two officers got out, one a woman, and the three of them huddled. She apparently lost the draw and was sent to babysit me. The other two drew their guns and approached the house. That was all it took for the peeping neighbors to come streaming out.

"What's going on in there?"

"What happened?"

A couple of kids on bikes began riding in wavy lines up and down the front path. "Get back!" the lady officer yelled, fixing them with an evil stare. The kids rode off through Dayna's yard and across one of the flower beds, crushing the late-season begonias. It was a good thing she was dead; she'd be furious.

The officer pulled out a roll of crime scene tape from somewhere on her body and began roping off the front yard. I edged toward my car, wondering how Henry was doing and whether he'd succeeded in choking himself yet.

Eagle-eye paused in her taping and pointed a finger at me. "Don't you go anywhere," she said.

I felt like dragging my toe along the ground and sulking. The adrenaline was wearing off and I was tired. I just wanted to go home and this looked like it might take long while.

"I just need to go check the dog. He's in my car," I told her.

"I'm sure your dog will be fine for a few more minutes," she said with a slight sneer. She deliberately slowed down her taping, watching me for a reaction. *Power trip*, I thought. *She's going to make me stand here because she can.*

An older woman, well wrapped in a bulky sweater and even bulkier tennis shoes, sniffed me out as someone in the know.

"I live next door to the Burkes," she said conspiratorially. "What happened? I saw you running with the dog. Is everything okay?"

I felt the eagle eye land on me, and before I had a chance to respond, she finished stringing up her tape and was bearing down on me. "I need you to step over here, please."

A third cop car pulled up and two more officers came forward and started moving the crowd back.

The older lady gave me a sympathetic look and edged away just enough to make the officer happy, but still close enough to hear whatever we had to say. The policewoman's badge read "Jones." She pulled a small notebook from a pocket, flipped it open, then noticed our hovering neighbor.

"Come with me, please."

She marched smartly through the crowd and I followed along like a delinquent first grader in her wake. I managed to sneak a peek into my car on the way past, but didn't see any sign of Henry through the tinted windows. That could be good or bad.

Officer Jones opened the back door of her patrol car and motioned me in. If I wasn't still feeling kind of woozy, I would have been hesitant to sit on that seat. It was sticky and smelled like body odor, old socks and French fries. Not that I smelled too great at this point, but still.

"Why don't you tell me exactly what happened here this afternoon?" she asked, standing just past the door. Upwind of me, probably.

Not sure where to start, I went into an abbreviated version of my new business, explaining that Dayna had called me unexpectedly this morning, asking me to walk her dog this afternoon. She asked a lot of questions while the buzz of activity continued on around us. At some point a detective joined us, but I barely noticed the shift in questioning. An ambulance pulled up and two guys with a stretcher wheeled up the walk. I think more police came, but as I talked, I focused less on what was going on around me, and more on remembering the details that they were asking for.

The detective asked me if I'd seen anything suspicious when I got to the house, or noticed anyone unusual in the vicinity. I had told Officer Jones about Henry running out the first time, and I repeated that for the detective, but didn't mention Hudson. I don't know why, I guess I felt like the way Henry ran to him and the way he was able to comfort the dog meant that he couldn't have had anything to do with what had happened to Dayna. Maybe that wasn't my call to make, but I figured one of the other neighbors would clue the cops as to Hudson's presence.

Just as we were wrapping up, a chilling thought came to me. What if the killer was still there the first time I opened the door? What if he'd been hiding in the kitchen? What if Henry hadn't bolted out past me?

For the first time, Officer Jones softened up a little. "Do you have someone waiting for you at home, or someone you can stay with?" she asked. "I know this can be traumatic. It would probably be better if you weren't alone tonight." The detective strode away, presumably in pursuit of more and better information.

"Will they be able to tell when she was killed?" I asked.

She paused before answering. "The coroner can usually determine time of death, but sometimes it's just a range. We'll be interviewing people to find out what her last hours were: who spoke to her last, where she was, like that. We already know that she told you she wouldn't be home until late tonight so we need to find out what changed and why she was home."

"What should I do with her dog?" I asked.

"Let me check with the other officers as to whether they've been able to contact her husband. Wait right here." The crowd had changed. More people had gotten home from work and joined the crowd, while the earlier arrivals had gotten bored and left. A headache began to throb along the sides of my temples, my shoulders ached with tension and a chill ran all the way through to my bones. I laid my head back on the seat, heedless of potential lice infestation.

I wanted to get home to Addie, but like Officer Jones had mentioned, I wasn't sure I wanted to be alone tonight. I could go stay with Frances, my grandmother, but she would want to know why, and since she lived in my parents' guesthouse, they would inevitably find out what was going on as well. I didn't think I was up to coping with that scene tonight.

I could call Evan to come over. He'd want to hear the whole crazy story anyway. I wondered if word had spread to the office. He had never stayed over at my house, but I did have a good-sized couch he could sleep on. Although that seemed weird to me too. Well, maybe he could just come over for dinner.

I'd closed my eyes and was drifting just a little bit, so when Officer Jones poked her head into to the open door and cleared her throat just a few inches from my ear, my already overtaxed nervous system jolted with alarm. I bolted upright, nearly giving myself whiplash with the quick move.

"We haven't been able to reach her husband," she said. "They suggested you could turn the dog over to me and I can contact animal control."

Animal control? Henry would end up in a shelter. He might or might not make it home again. They might even put him down. Houston shelters have a notoriously high kill rate.

"Can I just take him home with me until you can reach Daniel?" I asked. "I'll take good care of him. He'd be terrified being hauled off to a shelter." For the first time I felt tears prick the backs of my eyes.

"I think that would be a fine idea," she said. "We have your number, so if it's okay with you, we'll give it to him to contact you about getting the dog back as soon as we locate him." She paused, no doubt thinking about the fact that most people were killed by their nearest and dearest. "Or we'll have someone contact you about what to do with the dog in the next day or so."

"Thanks." I hauled myself up from the backseat and lurched to my feet. I felt stiff even though I'd only been sitting there for thirty or forty minutes. I moved as inconspicuously as I could towards my car. I didn't want to talk to anyone else. Two local news trucks had pulled haphazardly against the curb, blocking several driveways. Camera crews raced frantically around dragging wires and other pieces of equipment while the on-air talent primped in front of tiny mirrors. The timing was great, guaranteed to be The Big Story on the six o'clock news.

Luckily my car was not totally blocked in. I slid into the driver seat and found Henry curled in a ball on the passenger seat. He raised red-rimmed eyes in my direction, decided I wasn't a threat and curled back up. I couldn't tell if he was exhausted or depressed. I was feeling a bit of both myself.

I edged the car through the crowd to the first clear cross street and made my way towards Montrose. Rush hour was in full swing and traffic was at a crawl. It took me about twenty minutes to get home. Not until I pulled into the garage did I consider how Addie would react to another dog on her turf.

She was waiting at the door with her usual big welcome, tail wagging furiously, lips pulled back in a smile, leaping around with excitement. And then she saw the newcomer. Within seconds, her hackles rose, her tail stiffened and her lips pulled back in a snarl.

"Addie, no!" Henry cowered behind me, his day going from bad to worse. "It's okay. He's just here for the night." The rumbling continued deep in her throat and she continued her stiff-legged circling of us both. I leaned down to unsnap the leash, intending to let them work out their dominance issues, when Henry flashed his canines in a sudden move and Addie responded like lightning, her teeth snapping and nipping at his side, nearly bowling him over in the attack. He skidded into the cupboard and she backed away, hackles still stiff on her neck.

"Hey!" I screamed. "No!" Henry trembled on the floor and Addie threw herself down at my feet and rolled onto her side. I leaned over her and poked a stern finger towards her. "That is a *no*. You be nice. You will not kill this poor little guy. You will not even hurt him. Do you hear me?"

She hooked one paw over her nose and covered her eyes, exposing more belly. I knew I couldn't give in to the temptation to rub that belly, but it had been a truly horrible afternoon and the last thing I needed was to be yelling at my dog. I wanted to hold her and rub her and have a good cry into her soft fur while she nuzzled my face with concern.

Henry tentatively raised his head and began sniffing at his side, inspecting the damage. I didn't see any blood, which I took as a good sign. Of course, he could have internal injuries, but I doubted it. It had been quite a show, but I didn't think she'd actually touched him.

I needed a shower. I could use a drink. I wasn't really hungry, but some company would be good. Maybe Evan would be willing to pick up some takeout and come over. I put Henry in the bathroom for safekeeping before picking up the phone.

"Did they announce that Dayna's dead yet?" I asked without preamble when he picked up his phone.

"What?!" Obviously, the news hadn't made it to the office yet. I glanced at the clock. It was six-forty, and most people would already be gone for the evening. With the exception of Dayna's group. Most of them were probably still slaving away over their keyboards.

"I found her when I went to walk her dog. It was awful." I was horrified to hear my voice crack. Evan and I are buddies, and the only emotions we usually deal with are anger, irritation and occasional despondency, all usually caused by Dayna.

"Oh my God," he said. "What happened?"

I took a big breath. "I'm not sure exactly. But it looked like someone killed her. She was all blue and twisted, and her house was a mess."

There was a moment of silence on the other end of the phone. Evan must be as shocked as I was. "Well, in that case, I guess I don't have to finish this project tonight." Or maybe not.

Henry started to howl from his bathroom prison.

"What is that?"

"I've got her dog here, poor thing. First, he sees his owner murdered. Then Addie tried to kill him. And now I've got him locked in the bathroom for his own safety. I just don't know what else to do with him. I didn't want the cops to give him to animal control, and they hadn't gotten ahold of her husband yet when I left. So, I brought him here."

"Do you think her husband did it? What's his name

again?" He rushed ahead without waiting for a reply. "It had to be hell being married to her." I could hear the rustling of papers from his end.

"I don't know. I just can't stop seeing her face, the way it looked." Henry ratcheted up his howling, probably due to the proximity of Addie's nose at the crack under the door. "Hey, do you want to come over? I'm still kind of creeped out."

"Sure. Have you eaten? Do you want to go out?" He sounded eager to come by and get the full story.

"No, I hate to leave the dogs here alone. Can you pick something up on your way over?"

I wasn't sure what to do about Henry, but decided it was probably safer to leave him in his little powder room while I went upstairs and showered. Addie was torn, not sure whether she should follow me or keep an eye on the bathroom door in case the dreaded stranger escaped.

The shower felt wonderful; hot water pounded on my knotted muscles, making them loosen ever so slightly. Closing my eyes dredged up visions of the blue face with the staring eyes, so I kept them open, focusing on the soothing green sage of my bath towels. I'd just finished drying my hair when the doorbell rang.

Addie flew towards the door in full court greeting. Henry renewed his howls from the powder room, enhanced by frantic digging at the door. Great. New project: repaint bathroom door. I peeped through the hole and saw the dark top of Evan's head as he leaned towards the door, calling softly to Addie.

I opened the door and stood back while Addie assaulted Evan like a linebacker reincarnate. After one good body blow to the chest, Evan inched in, trying to keep her face from colliding with his nose while holding a white plastic bag out of reach. I shut the door behind him and we made our way towards the kitchen.

The howling from the powder room subsided to a sad little

whimpering. I felt sorry for the little guy. He'd had a really bad day and was no doubt scared and hungry. He probably needed to go out as well. Evan set the food down on the counter, and the smell of tomato and spicy sausage wafted up. Italian comfort food; I was feeling better already.

Evan pulled plates and silverware from the cupboards while I tended to Henry. Addie still wasn't happy about him being in her house, but the draw of food was stronger than her territorial instincts at this point, so she danced around Evan, hoping he would drop something. I took Henry out to my small backyard and let him sniff around at the unfamiliar scents. He finally made his way to the small patch of grass and squatted like a girl dog.

"Good boy!" I told him. He raced over to me, wagging his whole backside. I knelt down and he shoved his head up under my arm, pressing himself to my side. "Oh, you poor little thing," I told him in a jovial tone. He kept wagging and wiggling until he was nestled in my arms. I scooped him up and carried him inside.

Steam wafted towards Evan's face as he unwrapped the tinfoil from a loaf of garlic bread. Addie sat military upright at his feet, staring at the bread, eyes unblinking. She didn't even glance over when I set Henry down on the floor.

I rummaged around the refrigerator and found a couple of cold beers. I could have gone for some wine, but Evan is a beer guy, and at this point anything with alcohol sounded good. We sat at the small table in the kitchen. The warmth of the food and Evan's reassuring presence calmed me enough to bring back my appetite. He seemed really nonchalant about the whole thing. In fact, he was morbidly curious to hear all the details.

I ran through my afternoon's experience, leaving out little and embellishing the parts he really wanted to hear about. Suddenly I had an image of Evan in the break room, spilling all of this information to hordes of gawkers and gossip hounds.

"So, you really can't tell everyone at work about all this," I told him. "I mean, I don't know how much I should even be telling you."

"Did the police tell you not to discuss it with anyone?" he asked.

"No."

"Well, there you go. If it was all so confidential, they would have told you that." He twirled a baseball-sized wad of spaghetti around his fork and shoveled it all into his mouth at once.

"I guess so." It was probably a little late for me to worry about whether he would share all the gruesome details I'd just told him. I pushed the rest of my pasta aside but kept a tight hold on my beer.

The evening was taking on a surreal quality. We'd had dinner in my kitchen countless times, and on the surface, tonight felt like all those others. Except for the intrusive image that kept flashing through my head of Dayna's dead face. I wasn't sure if I was more disturbed by that, or by Evan's utter lack of concern at Dayna's death.

I cleaned up the kitchen while Evan played with the dogs. He had his hands full trying to manage the jealousy issues.

"So, what if the killer was still there when I went in the first time?" I asked Evan, trying to squelch the little flutter of fear that percolated in my stomach every time I thought about it.

He leaned back against the kitchen wall, legs stretched out in front of him, separating the two dogs. They seemed content for the moment, each ignoring the other. I knew that would end as soon I brought out the dog food.

"Okay, let's go back to what you saw and heard when you first went in the house," he said. "Maybe you'll remember something that didn't seem like a big deal at the time."

I thought back. "I remember thinking that they must not come in and out of the front door much because the leaves were all piled up on the porch and there were flyers." I paused, trying to picture the scene. "Then I opened the door and the dog raced out and I ran after him. That's about it." My brain was still sifting through images. The sound of construction nearby. The cars lining the road. What? What might I have noticed?

"Did you see Dayna's car in the driveway? Or anyone else's car?"

I visualized her house: driveway to the left, a stockade fence, and the garage around to the back where I couldn't see it. "I don't think I saw anything in the driveway. But I doubt the killer would just park so casually right out in the open like that."

"Unless it was Daniel," he said.

"And unless he wasn't planning to kill her. If he was planning to kill her, he would have hidden his car." I put away the last dish.

"He could have killed her in a fit of rage," he said, absently stroking the dogs. "She could drive you to it. You know she could."

Working for Dayna had been hell. She was as cold and uncaring a person as I've ever met, although it was more her cheap shots and dirty fighting that inspired the rage. She was a master at hitting people in the most hurtful places. Nothing was too personal or painful to be used as a weapon. I'd even seen her berate someone in a meeting for not being attentive enough, when we all knew his wife was battling cancer and he'd been spending every night at the hospital. Yes, she could drive you to it.

"Did I tell you about the meeting I was in Monday?" Evan asked.

"No. What happened?" I knelt down to see Henry, but

Addie was having none of that. She leapt to her feet and shoved between us, settling on her haunches and lifting an appealing paw. Henry took advantage of the opportunity to crawl up into Evan's lap.

"I've been working on this presentation she asked me to do for about two weeks, putting it together the way she told me she wanted it. Then Monday morning, about three hours before the meeting, she came by my desk and told me that it was all wrong and she wanted me to redo it another way. I couldn't believe it." His voice was rising and getting higher-pitched. "And the changes she wanted were totally wrong. So, I told her that I thought it was right the way I had it, but she got like she does." He paused. "Or did. You know, real quiet, eyes staring through me, and told me if I knew what was good for me, I'd make the changes and stop questioning her.

"So, I made the changes and I went to the meeting." As long as I've known Evan, I've known that he hates speaking in front of groups. He's really good one-on-one or with just a few people, but put him in front of a crowd and his fair skin turns blotchy and he loses his ability to think on his feet. I was already dreading the rest of the story. "She'd invited all of the accounting managers, the credit guys, and some of the commodities traders who were in from New York. I mean, in addition to everyone that was supposed to be there." Red streaks started running across his cheeks.

"Uh-oh."

"Yeah. So, I go through my new presentation, which by the way I had no time to practice. And the room was totally quiet and I feel like an idiot because I know this is wrong, only it's what she told me she wanted. I get through the whole thing and no one says anything. They all just sit there. And they're sitting there thinking this guy is a total moron if this is what he thinks our business is."

"Uh-oh."

"Yeah. So, what does Dayna do? She sits there for a few minutes, letting the silence stretch out, doodling on her pad, and finally she says, 'What the hell was that?'" His cheeks reflected the crimson I knew they'd been at the time. "So, I said, 'This is what you told me this morning that you wanted it changed to.'" He was staring hard at the kitchen floor tiles. "And of course, in front of everyone she denied that, apologized profusely for having wasted their valuable time, and explained how difficult her job was when she had such halfwits on staff."

I felt terrible for him. I also felt a small measure of relief that I hadn't been there to witness his humiliation.

"I wish I had the guts you had," he said, shifting Henry off his lap and rising to his feet.

I rose too. "Look, it wasn't guts. If I didn't have the trust fund thing, I'd still be there with you. It makes a big difference."

"I guess so," he said. "I wonder what'll happen now that she's dead."

"This is a terrible thing to say, but it's got to be better without her."

A smile lit his face for a minute before fading. "Unless they give her job to Chip." Chip Vermuellen had started just a few weeks before I quit, but I'd seen enough to know that he was as ambitious as Dayna, if just a little smoother in his backstabbing.

"I'll keep my fingers crossed they don't," I said.

With a final pat for the dogs, he was gone before I had a chance to remember that I was still worried that the killer might have seen me.

CHAPTER FOUR

The temperature had dropped and the wind blew a damp breeze in behind Evan as he shut the door. I busied myself getting the dogs fed, no easy task since Addie was determined to make things as unpleasant for the newcomer as possible. I finally shut Henry in the powder room with a cereal bowl full of Addie's food and fed her at her normal spot in the kitchen. I felt like a mother whose toddler was throwing a temper tantrum when confronted with the new baby. Torn between wanting to assure Addie that her place in my heart was secure, and still comfort this poor little scared dog, I could only hope that Daniel would call tomorrow to get him.

I puttered around the house, killing time and trying to calm my mind until it was time for bed. On one hand, Evan's visit had helped, but on the other, I felt his callousness over Dayna's death rather disturbing. I hadn't liked her either, but I certainly didn't wish anyone dead. Well, maybe he hadn't wished her dead. Or maybe if I'd been in his place and was forced to put up with her abuse on a daily basis, I would wish her dead too. I didn't know. What I did know was that I really needed some sleep.

So really, I shouldn't have watched the ten o'clock news, because of course, Dayna was the lead story.

"A local business woman was found slain in her home near downtown this afternoon. For the latest, let's go to Susie Arrayno in the Montrose area." The picture switched from the studio to a petite, dark-haired woman in a formfitting suit standing in front of Dayna's darkened house. The crime scene tape that Officer Jones had strung up still fluttered in the wind, and a handful of smiling kids waved frantically at the camera from behind the reporter's back.

Susie gave one last pat to her hair, remembered that this was a serious story and ratcheted down the wattage on her smile. "Police confirm that longtime businesswoman, Dayna Burke, was found murdered in her home just outside downtown earlier this afternoon. Neighbors were shocked by the news and frightened that something this terrible could happen on their street." Footage filmed prior in the day began to roll, panning the crowds gathered on the sidewalk outside Dayna's house. I spotted the nosy little neighbor in her sweater and tennis shoes, waving gaily at the camera. The reporter on the scene cornered a young woman with blue hair and multiple facial piercings and shoved a microphone in her face.

"This is terrible," she said. "I mean, I really didn't know her, but you know, to have something like this happen so close to home, it like, really gets to you." She batted her black-lined eyes and looked appropriately sad. We went back to Susie. "Police have little to go on at this time, but are continuing to look for anything or anyone that might lead them to the murderer of this wife and successful business leader. Susie Arrayno reporting for Eye-Witness News."

I flipped off the set. That wasn't very helpful. Nor did it give me what I was hoping to hear—namely that police had a suspect in custody. I told myself again that the killer probably hadn't been there when I was there. Dayna had probably been dead for a while before I got there. Right?

I hustled the dogs outside one last time and headed up to bed. I shut Henry in my bathroom just in case the unfamiliar food disagreed with his stomach, or Addie accidentally killed him while I was sleeping. Random thoughts of the day raced through my mind. It seemed like forever ago that I was worrying about what to wear to pick up Dayna's key at the office. Hard to believe that was just this morning.

I tossed and turned for what seemed like hours before finally drifting into a fitful sleep. A little after one, Henry began to howl and whine in the bathroom. Addie curled tighter into her bed and ignored him. I tried to do the same, but after five minutes of that racket I got up. I took him out in the backyard, but he just sniffed around until I got annoyed and carried him back inside to his bathroom quarters. As soon as I shut the door, the whining started again.

"This is not going to work," I told him. "If I let you out, will you be good?"

I opened the door and he bounded joyfully out and onto my bed. In a flash, Addie was on her feet, chasing him off. He ran under the bed and she raced side to side, snuffling and growling, but couldn't reach him.

I was too tired to referee this battle, so I crawled back into bed. "Addie, don't hurt him." I rolled over and pulled the pillow up over my ear.

At five thirty I got up to walk the dogs and start my morning baking. It appeared that Henry had spent the rest of the night under the bed. In fact, he refused to come out. I couldn't blame him. Addie crouched by my side, pulling her lips back so he could see her teeth. But every time she saw me looking at her, she'd drop her lips and wag enthusiastically as if to say, "Just kidding!"

It wasn't until I shut her out of the room that Henry inched forward on his belly and poked his nose out from under the dust ruffle. He was a sweet little guy, but it was obvious that Addie was too set in her only-dog ways to accept a newcomer. And Henry already had a home. Hopefully Daniel would call me today to pick him up.

We made it through breakfast and a walk with no bloodshed, and I took that as a sign that my day was going to be okay. I whipped out an additional four batches of doggie salmon snaps on top of what I had planned for the day, and still managed to hit the road for my dog-walking rounds on time. I wasn't sure how the dogs would do without a referee, so Henry went back to the powder room. He seemed resigned and settled quickly on the rug, nose between his paws. He wouldn't even take the fresh-baked biscuit I left him.

At twelve forty I stopped back by my house to check on the dogs and grab a little lunch. There was one call on my answering machine, and I hit the playback button before releasing Henry from his confinement.

"Yeah, I got this number from the police." Long pause. "They told me to call you; you got my sister's dog." It was a woman's voice, thick accent dragging on the words. "I want it back. You need to give it to me. I'll be over to her house today gettin' some stuff, and you can give it to me there."

That was it. No name. No time when she would be there. Nothing. I disliked the voice and told myself not to be judgmental. Her sister had just been killed, so she probably wasn't at her best. I'd never even known that Dayna had a sister. In fact, I didn't know anything about her background other than the fact she'd graduated from Louisiana State University and had slashed and burned her way to where she was. Or where she'd been. The accent threw me a little too. Dayna had a slight twang, but nothing like this woman. Her sister sounded uneducated. She also sounded accusatory, as if I'd stolen her dog.

The lack of sleep from the night before was catching up to me, and I felt sluggish and heavy-headed. I brewed a strong cup of tea to perk myself up and made a little salad while the dogs explored the backyard. Keeping watch out the window, I ate standing up. Henry loped around, nose to the ground, following unseen tracks. Addie watched him like he was crazy. Twice I saw him sashay over to where she stood and bump her legs with his butt before galloping away. He was warming up to her and wanted to play. She seemed less enchanted, but at least she was keeping her teeth to herself.

The humidity had picked up again, and in spite of the slightly cooler temperatures, it was feeling sticky. I spent a little extra time with each dog on my afternoon rounds. Nelson was one of my favorites, a stately old golden retriever, always dignified and quietly friendly. He seemed to want to amble a little more slowly today, and I certainly wasn't going to rush him. I had the impression that he allowed me to join him on his walks, never that I was walking him. In my current state of melancholy, I wanted to spend even more time with him. When we got back to his house, he lay down immediately on the cool tile floor, and I stayed to pet his soft fur and make sure he was okay.

The springer spaniel brothers knew I was late, and were hanging over the back of the couch at the window, tongues lolling out. As I came up the walkway I could see their brown-and-white heads bouncing up and down, tangling up in each other's legs in their rush to get to the door. Whereas Nelson was stately, these guys were clowns. They had the ability to cheer me up no matter the situation, and my time with them today was no different. We walked for twenty minutes, then spent another fifteen playing with their toys in the den. One would set a ball rolling and the other would chase it and bring it back. They loved having an appreciative audience and I figured that they spent the mornings coming up with new routines.

My cell phone rang as I was leaving the spaniels. It was Evan.

"Things are crazy around here," he said. "Everyone's speculating on who could have done it. Naomi is the favorite right now because she left early yesterday, and you know that whole thing about Dayna and her husband."

"Really?" I tried to imagine Naomi choking the life out of someone, and even though she was smaller than Dayna, surprisingly, it wasn't hard for me to picture.

"The police have been here interviewing people. They haven't wanted to talk to me yet, and I don't know if they will. Should I tell them I know you?"

"I don't see why that would come up, but I guess it can't hurt anything if it does. I mean, they know I worked there. They'll just probably ask where you were yesterday and all that." I thought about the humiliation Dayna had dealt him earlier in the week and felt sure someone would mention that meeting. Although if the police were to take time following up on every grievous wrong that Dayna had inflicted, they'd never get anywhere. "Her sister called me this morning. She wants me to bring Henry over to Dayna's house and give him to her."

There was a small silence on the other end. "Oh. I thought maybe no one would want him."

"He's a sweet thing," I said. "I'm sure he'll be a comfort to them." I thought about the voice on my machine. I didn't want that person to take Henry. I wanted him to go to someone who would love him.

"I gotta go. Here they come," he said, slamming the phone down with a bang.

"Good luck," I said to empty air.

My next visits with Klaus (German shepherd), and Jenny (yellow Lab) were good but uneventful. I wondered what the police were asking Evan about. Lord knows Evan can turn on the gossip when he wants, and I hoped he'd have the sense to just answer their questions and not add a whole lot of additional commentary.

I t was almost four when I got back to my house. Both dogs were happy to see me, and with the exception of an occasional growl on Addie's part, peace continued to reign. The light was blinking on my answering machine. Same voice. "Yeah, I hope you don't think you're keepin' that dog. I'm under the understanding that that is a purebred dog. It's worth some money and that dog rightfully belongs to me now, so you bring him on over here. The cops say I can have it." What about Daniel? Surely, he wouldn't want to give away his own dog. Had he been arrested? Was that why the sister was taking the dog?

"Okay, boy. We're going to go in the car and take you to your new owner. I'm sure she'll be nice and you'll be happy with her. She sounds really nice." In my heart, I knew lying to a dog was wrong. Henry's tail whipped around like a rotor blade when I mentioned the word *car*. I held him tight against my chest for a minute, trying not to feel attached. She was probably nicer than she sounded on the phone.

Since I hadn't brought any of Henry's belongings with me, it didn't take me long to pack him up. I did drop a couple of Addie's old toys in a plastic bag to go with him. Once in the car I tried to secure him with Addie's seat belt, but he crawled right out of the harness and jumped into the front passenger seat where he sat perfectly straight, although he had to strain his neck a bit to see out the window.

I took the side roads to get to Dayna's, telling myself that it was safer for Henry, being that he wasn't belted in, but really, I was just dragging it out, not wanting to hand him over. Even with all the stalling, I eventually pulled up in the same place as yesterday. He'd begun to wag and whine when we got within a couple blocks of his house, happy to be home. The construction was still going on a few doors down, and pickup trucks still lined the sides of the road. I lifted Henry out of the car and set him down on the ground. He pulled on the leash and headed for the driveway and the back door. I let him lead me that way rather than going to the front door.

Henry squeaked and wagged as he ran. I rounded the corner, where the kitchen door stood open. My heart began to thud a little faster and I realized suddenly that I didn't know who the voice on the phone really belonged to. Maybe Dayna didn't really have a sister. They hadn't even left a name. Maybe the killer had seen me and was luring me over here to get rid of a potential witness.

Before I had a chance to run, a dark-headed woman poked her head out the door.

"Enrique!" she said, with a soft Spanish accent flavoring the name. A smile lit up her face, and she knelt and opened her arms to the wiggling mass of fur. "Enrique!"

This clearly wasn't the sister. Henry was beside himself with joy. His tail wagged in wild circles, and he wriggled in and out of her arms, jumping to shower her face with wet, wild kisses. She was getting tangled up in the leash I had dropped, and she laughed and collapsed on the step outside the door.

"*Querido! Qué buen muchacho. Mi Quique.*" She looked up and smiled at me, trying to extricate herself from the leash. I held out a hand and helped her to her feet.

"*Gracias,*" she said, brushing at the back of her pants. Henry continued dancing around her feet, whimpering with joy. She took the leash, and the smile ran from her face as she glanced towards the kitchen. "*Señora,*" she whispered and nodded her head towards the kitchen. "*La señora está allí.*" My Spanish was more than just a little rusty, but I was pretty sure she was talking about the sister. This must be the housekeeper, hence Henry's fabulous greeting. She was obviously the one who'd been taking care of the dog.

She stood back and allowed me to enter before her. The kitchen was empty, but peering around into the family room, I glimpsed a wide bottom sticking out from a cabinet under the bookcase.

"Hello?" I said, aware of the housekeeper fading into the background.

The head attached to the bottom whirled around and faced me. Sensing her vulnerable position, she lumbered to her feet and planted her hands on her hips.

"It's about time," she said. "I guess you're the one as took the dog."

"Yes, hi," I said, stepping forward and extending my hand. "I'm Jessie Gallagher."

She stared at my outstretched hand like she wasn't sure what to do with it. Finally, she grasped my fingertips with her clammy sausages and gave them a little shake. "I'm Shurlin," she said, wiping her hand on her pants, as if my fingers had been the nasty, damp ones. I fought the urge to do the same.

"Shurlin, it's nice to meet you. I'm Jessie Gallagher."

"No, it's SHUR-Lin," she said fixing me with little piggy eyes.

"Oh, sorry, SHUR-Lin."

She gave a big sigh, irritated by the idiot. I glanced toward the kitchen, but the pretty little housekeeper had faded against the wall like a gecko. I wasn't sure why we were having this big debate over her name, but it was obviously important to her. And while I couldn't see much of a physical resemblance, there was something about the attitude that was a lot like Dayna's.

"C-h-e-r-i-l-y-n-n," she proceeded to spell it, spitting out each letter for me.

"Okay, got it," I said. "Sorry."

"Cherilynn Lott, Dayna's sister."

"Yes, you mentioned that in your message. I didn't even know Dayna had a sister."

Cherilynn made a "pfft" sound and turned back toward the cupboard. "Didn't nobody know Dayna had a family. We wasn't good enough for her hifalutin friends." I wouldn't consider myself a friend of Dayna's, but perhaps now wasn't a good time to split hairs. It seemed she'd been in the middle of extracting all the things out of the cupboard and was now proceeding to shove them all back in. Stacks of old magazines, some artsy-looking books and a stack of DVDs were making their way back in, I suspected not in the same order that they'd come out.

"I'm sorry about your sister," I said. Another "pfft," came my way. The DVDs were falling back out, and she shoved the door shut, trying to keep them in.

"Did ya bring the dog?" She turned her attention to the next cupboard. I glanced around the room, remembering how it had looked yesterday. It looked much the same today, papers still everywhere, pictures still askew.

"Um, yes. About that. I was wondering. Is Daniel coming back soon? Because I'd have thought he'd want to keep the dog." I'd only met Daniel once, but he seemed much more a dog guy than this woman. I didn't like the look of her mean eyes. Apparently, Henry didn't either, because he was cowering behind the housekeeper's legs, alternately whimpering for her attention and growling at Cherilynn.

"Daniel ain't here. I'm not sure when he's coming. But that dog was my sister's dog and it rightly belongs to me now." Her rear end was back in the air as she started pulling things out of the next cupboard and strewing them across the floor. It looked like an assortment of notebooks and file folders. She swept the last of them onto the floor, sat back and began picking through them.

"Do you already have a dog?" I asked.

"No."

"Have you ever had a dog?" I asked, wondering about what sort of life Henry was going to have with this woman. I could imagine it a little too clearly.

"Oh, we've had dogs here and there. Most of 'em run off or was hit by cars." She dumped a file folder upside down and spread the contents across the floor like a card shark spreading his deck.

"I'd hate for you to be burdened by Henry," I began again. "I think if Daniel doesn't want him, I could certainly find a good home for him."

She pounced on a document, held it close in front of her face and scanned it, lips moving as she read.

"Huh? Burdened? Wha'chu talking about?" She dropped the document and continued her perusal.

"The dog, Henry. That's his name," I said. I considered picking him up and running with him, because I was pretty sure I could out run this stumpy-legged woman. But she did have my phone number, and the police knew I had the dog and they had my address.

"Dumb name for a dog," she said with a grunt for emphasis.

I glanced over at the housekeeper, not sure how much, if anything, she understood. I could tell she was frightened by Dayna's sister, but I wasn't even sure if she knew Dayna was dead. I walked back to the kitchen and knelt beside Henry. He put his paws on my knee and reached his head up for a kiss. I was feeling sick to my stomach. There had to be something I could do.

"Are you the housekeeper?" I asked.

"*Yo soy, Consuela*," she responded. And then she was off and running in Spanish, words flying together until I couldn't tell where one ended and the next began.

I finally had to stop her. "*No habla espanol*," I said. Okay, habla un poco espanol, but only if spoken very slowly and the words are one of about fifty that I know. She was way out of my league.

"Oh," she said sadly. "*No hablo inglés.*" I'd pretty much guessed that by now.

I searched my brain. "*Señora Dayna es morte.*"

She looked puzzled. "*Morte?*"

Wasn't that right? No, not *morte*. "*Señora Dayna es muerto.*"

Her hand flew to her mouth, and she gave a quick sharp intake of breath. I guessed I'd hit it this time. "*Muerta? No, no. Señora no puede estar muerta.*" Her eyes filled with tears and she clutched her knuckles to her mouth. "Oh, no!"

"I'm sorry," I told her, patting her awkwardly on the shoulder. I touched Henry's head, lowered my voice to a whisper and pointed towards Cherilynn, who continued to trash the place. "She wants to take him."

"Enrique?" she whispered. "*Ella?*" She pointed discreetly towards Cherilynn.

I nodded my head. "Yes, she wants to take him."

Tears began to roll down her cheeks and she lifted him to her chest. "*Mi querido. Que pobre muchacho.*" She was sobbing now, tears rolling off her dark lashes like a downpour. I felt terrible.

"Have the police talked to you?" I asked.

That made her head snap up. "*Policia?*" Her eyes widened in alarm. "*Policia? No! No, policia!*"

Oh dear. No doubt a green card issue here, but surely they would just want to question her as to whether she had seen or heard anything that seemed amiss. I doubted the homicide investigators would care about her immigration status. But then again, you never knew.

"Okay, okay," I said. "*No policia.* Although they might want to talk to you about Señora Dayna."

Consuela held Henry close to her chest and buried her face in his fur. Well, if the cops hadn't shown any interest in questioning her, who was I to quibble with them?

Cherilynn appeared to be finished with her search of the family room and joined us in the kitchen.

"What's with her?" she asked, pointing a meaty hand toward Consuela.

"She didn't realize that Dayna had been killed," I answered, wondering why it was the housekeeper in tears and not the sister.

"If she'd learn some damn English, I coulda told her a' couple a hours ago. Instead she's just been sittin' here staring at me like I'm some kinda crook or something." Ambling down the hall, she muttered over her shoulder, "I hope she don't think she's getting' paid for sittin' around here today."

I wondered again what was going on with Daniel. Cherilynn was acting as if this house and everything in it was already hers, but this was Texas, a community property state, which would mean everything went to the husband. Maybe she'd knocked him over the head and had him hidden in a trunk somewhere until she was done pillaging.

There didn't seem to be a reason for me to stick around, although in spite of her demands for me to bring the dog over, Cherilynn had shown no interest in him. Maybe if I left the kitchen door ajar, he might follow me out.

"Hey, you got any food for that dog I can take with me?" she shouted. "I don't want to have to spend my money buying that mutt anything."

I followed her into the living room where she was looking under the couch cushions.

"You know, again, I really wouldn't mind taking him and finding him a good home. Dogs can be expensive to take care of. And they're a lot of work. I just hate for you to have to take him on at a time like this."

She snorted. "How much work can he be? Throw some food out the door. Real hard." She threw the cushions down on the sofa and walked away, leaving them helter-skelter. I followed behind her, pushing them into place and straightening the edges.

"I really wouldn't mind keeping him another night till Daniel gets back," I said.

"You seem awful hot to keep that dog," she said, her voice rising. "I already told ya, he's mine and he's comin' with me. You ain't takin' it from me."

"I'm not trying to take him from you. I just want to make sure this is what's best for everyone."

She walked towards me a couple paces and I noticed that she was taller than I had originally estimated. She was definitely a solid woman. I took a step back.

"Who are you again? And don't tell me Jessie whatever-your-last-name is, I ain't stupid, I heard that part. But who are you? Police told me you had the dog but didn't say how you got it."

"I used to work with Dayna. Now, I've got a dog-walking business now. Dayna called me yesterday to come over and take care of Henry."

"People pay you to walk their dogs?" She let out a big guffaw at that one. "Dumbest thing I ever heard. Just like Dayna to throw money away. She never appreciated nothin'."

I had thought Dayna to be in her early forties. Her sister looked older than that, although looking past the lines worn deep by unhappiness, she may actually have been close to Dayna's age than I'd originally thought.

"So, you the one that found her?" she asked, now studying me like she'd not seen me before.

"I was," I said. Visions of the bulging eyes floated in my head but I pushed them resolutely away.

"Did you see who done it?"

"No. Henry ran out the door when I got here, and I ended up chasing him down the street. The killer was probably already gone by then." At least I hoped he was gone by then.

"But he coulda still been there? Maybe if you wasn't so busy chasing after that mutt you could have kept my sister from bein' killed." She turned her tree trunk body away from me in disgust.

"Do you have any other siblings?" I asked, trying to take the spotlight off my failings.

"Nah. Just the two of us. I think Momma couldn't have any more kids after me. I don't know why. But Dayna was always puttin' on airs and thinkin' she was better than all of us. It used to make Daddy so mad the way she'd talk down to him like he was nothin' but a dog."

See? There it was again. Not a good sign for Henry.

Her eyes swept past me to the window. "It was better after she went off. I don't know where she got the money to go to school. She didn't get it at home. There was talk when I was in high school as to how she was screwin' one of the teachers. Maybe he gave her the money. Just a whore. That's all she was."

I thought about my family. I wasn't that close to my parents, but I knew they loved me and wanted the best for me. Okay, sometimes they were a little too concerned about image, but overall, they were good people. It sounded like Dayna's family pioneered dysfunctional.

"Well, I wasn't very close to Dayna," I said. How do you respond to someone calling their dead sister a whore? The things they don't cover in prep school. "She was obviously driven in her career."

"She just wanted to get as far from where she came from as she could. Never told no one about her family, she was that ashamed of us." Her eyes strayed to the corners of the room, but there didn't seem to be anything else for her to pick apart.

Again, I tried not to be judgmental, but I could certainly understand Dayna not parading these folks around the office. Assuming the rest of the family was like the sister.

"Are your parents okay? This must be really hard for them."

"Oh, they're long gone. Momma ran off, musta been twenty-five years back. We think she found a trucker going out the interstate and she just went out with him. Never did look back. And Daddy died a couple years ago. Smokin' finally got his lungs ate up," she said.

"Well, I'm sorry to hear that," I said. Hers was a terrible story. I was really out of my league how to respond, although she didn't seem like it was a big deal to her at all.

"So, you got any food I can take with me for that thing?" she asked.

The bonding was over. I guessed I didn't have any recourse at this point for keeping Henry. Had I known what this woman was like, I never would have brought him over here. I would keep trying to reach Daniel, but beyond that, I needed to let it go. Dogs are tough. Just because all owners don't treat their animals with the love and respect I lavish on Addie, doesn't mean they're abused. Right?

"Let me see what I can find," I said, heading back to the kitchen. Consuela was still on the floor with Henry cradled in her arms. He was as limp as a shoelace, his head rolled over her arm and eyes rolling with delight as she stroked his belly. He might as well enjoy it now because I had the feeling he wasn't going to be getting any belly rubs where he was going.

I went to the pantry to look for Henry's food. If we didn't have the communication problem, I would ask Consuela, but it seemed easier to just look around myself. It also gave me an excuse to take a peek around. I hated to admit it, but Cheri-lynn's poking around was triggering my nosy instincts. The pantry was stocked with boxes of garbage bags, a few cans of soup and several rows of cleaning supplies. There was an opened bag of dried dog food on the floor. I peeked inside—about half gone. There was also a box of dog treats that I pulled down and put next to the food.

His bed was in the family room, halfway covered with sheets of paper, a sock sticking out from beneath the cushion. I removed the papers but left the sock. Maybe the smell would give him some small comfort wherever he was going. I put the bed next to the food, and Henry took a small hop off Consuela's lap onto its soft cushion. I retrieved the bag of Addie's toys that I'd brought for him and added it to the pitiful pile. I felt like I was packing him up for an extended stay at a reform school boot camp.

"Okay, I have all his stuff over here," I shouted in the direction I'd last seen Cherilynn.

"Whatever. Just make sure you leave the dog too." It sounded like she'd moved to the study. I wondered if she knew where her sister had been killed.

I knelt beside Henry, rubbed his neck and kissed his shaggy head. He wagged happily at me from his bed, oblivious to his approaching departure. "You be a good boy," I said. "I'll keep calling Daniel for you. I promise." Tears stung my eyes as I gave him a final rub and rushed out the back door. I caught one last glimpse of his sparkling eyes and wagging tail before I rounded the corner.

I cried all the way home.

CHAPTER FIVE

By the time I got home, darkness had engulfed my house and the temperature had dropped several degrees. I made myself a cup of tea and pulled on a sweatshirt before joining Addie on the back patio. Just outside the back door, the smell assaulted me. Piles of dog poop covered my wrought-iron table.

Today was not the day for this. Storming into the house, I grabbed a potty-bag and did what I could to scrape as much as possible from the open-weave tabletop. The rest would need to be hosed down and scrubbed. I took what I had and marched next door.

The man that opened the door to my angry knocks appeared to be in his mid-twenties, with tousled brown hair and arrogant eyes.

"Yeah?"

I shoved the bag at him, but he pulled his arms quickly behind his back. His white button-down shirt was rumpled and hung long over gym shorts and dark socks. His breath smelled of beer and salami.

"I believe this is yours," I said, shoving the bag against

his chest.

"What are you doing?" he screeched, taking a step back and thrusting the door at me in self-defense.

"You left your shit in my backyard." I dropped the bag with a plop inside his doorway, and since I hadn't tied it, it fell to the side and a small dog turd rolled out on his tile entry.

"Oh my *God*! I can't believe you did that! I am calling the police."

I turned around and stomped back across the driveway to my front door.

"You can't leave this here," he said, his voice rising. "I am calling the homeowners' association right now."

I went in and slammed the door. My heart was beating with fury and I could feel a vein pulsing in my temple. My quiet evening on the patio was ruined, so I set the tea aside, grabbed a bottle of wine, a juice glass and a box of crackers and curled up in a miserable little heap on the couch. Addie, sympathetic to my mood as ever, curled herself in a matching little heap on the opposite end. Two large glasses of wine later, I was finally feeling more relaxed if not more cheerful. Evan had called midway through my liquid dinner to let me know about his police questioning, which had been rather routine and unexciting. I gave him an update on Henry, and influenced by the wine, I immediately got choked up and maudlin about his future. It didn't help that I felt like Evan was blaming me for Henry's predicament.

"You didn't have to take him over there," he said.

"Well, how was I supposed to know what a bitch she was?" I asked.

"She's Dayna's sister. What did you think she'd be like?"

He had a point. I'd been foolish to think that maybe her sister would be broken up over Dayna's death and that maybe the dog would bring her comfort.

I stored the wine bottle in the fridge, gave Addie her

belated dinner and dragged myself up the stairs to my small study. Surely Daniel would want to keep Henry. I searched my memory for what I knew about Dayna's husband. He made documentaries, none of which had supposedly ever sold. He had been pleasant when I'd met him at the Christmas party, although after a couple of drinks he'd gotten quite flirty. With his dark, ruffled hair and casual way of looking directly into your eyes when you talked, I could see how some women might fall for his act. But flirting back with Dayna's husband would be like teasing a pit bull with a steak bone. Not something I'd ever wanted to try.

I dug through my desk drawers for an old Astor Oil employee telephone list I knew I had somewhere. Pay stubs, benefits statements, 401(k) information, miscellaneous spreadsheets that I once worked on, healthcare coverage, and other random documents filled two manila folders, but I couldn't find the employee phone list. Addie brought over an old rawhide bone she'd been hiding somewhere and plopped down against my leg to work on it. I knew I had Dayna's number somewhere.

F ifteen minutes later, I found the invitation to Dayna's Christmas party, complete with RSVP phone number. That would work.

The phone rang seven times before the answering machine picked up. Belatedly I looked at my watch—nine-fifty. "Hi, this is Dayna. Daniel and I can't come to the phone. Leave a message." Beep. Dead Dayna still answered the machine. I left a message, probably a little more rambling than I intended, conveying my concern over Henry's fate and asked Daniel to give me a call as soon as he could. Just before hanging up, I remembered to tack on my condolences for the loss of his wife.

The teasers for the ten o'clock news featured a headshot of

Dayna. "Tonight, an update on the murder of a Houston area businesswoman. Was there a witness to this grisly crime? Watch Eye-Witness News at Ten to find out. And what can we expect weather-wise for the rest of the workweek? Trudy has you covered with the latest weather."

Was there a witness? Had someone else been in the area who saw something before I even got there? The hope that the police were hard on the heels of the killer lightened my mood considerably, and I admitted to myself how frightened I was by the idea that the killer might have seen me, while I'd been oblivious to his presence.

"Addie, did you hear that? They might have a witness to who killed Dayna!" Addie danced around, jacked up by my tone. "That's good, yes, that's good!" I told her.

She ran down the stairs and returned proudly carrying two of her squeaky toys. One landed at my feet as she teased me with the other, squeaking it, then pulling it just out of reach as I grabbed for it.

"Good evening. Tonight, on Eye-Witness News..." *Squeak. Squeak. Squeak.*

"Shhhh. Shush, Addie," I said, cranking up the volume. *Squeak. Squeak.* I grabbed the toy, ripped it out of her mouth and threw it out of the room. She raced after it, tail waving behind her.

"Eye-Witness News has learned that there may be an eyewitness to the murder of Houston businesswoman, Dayna Burke." The view switched to the front of Dayna's house. The crowds of yesterday were gone, the camera instead focused on Dayna's sister. She was wearing the same outfit I'd seen her in earlier, and judging by the fading daylight, this had been shot after I'd left.

She patted her hair self-consciously, smacked her lips together, then looked directly into the camera. "Dayna was my only sister. I can't tell you how hard this is havin' her ripped from our family this way." She bent forward, and for a moment I thought she was going to throw up. Instead she lifted Henry up and held him in her arms, crying piteously for the camera. "This is all I have left to remind me of her. I know we can't bring her back, but I just want whoever done this to pay the price." The out-of-sight reporter jiggled the mike a little closer, and Henry sniffed it politely, then pulled back his lips and smiled a full-tooth smile for the camera, tongue hanging sideways, giving him a rakish, goofy air.

"Didn't you say earlier there may be an eyewitness?" the voice prompted her. Addie was back squeaking away on her plastic carrot. I upped the volume again and ignored her.

"Oh yeah. The dog walker walked right in on the murderer while he was killin' my sister." Her beady little eyes stared straight into the camera. "Whoever it was that done this, I want you to know she saw you and she's gonna lead the police right to you."

My heart rolled over and landed with a thump on my breastbone. What?! What was she doing going on television telling a killer I saw him? I hadn't seen anything! "This is not true," I said out loud. Only my dog was listening.

Sleep was impossible. Ordinary house sounds took on ominous tones, and I bolted upright with every whir of the refrigerator or bang of the hot water heater. At ten after two, I heard a car slow in front of my house, idle for a few minutes, then peal out with a squeal of tires. I popped out of bed and ran to the window, expecting to see a Molotov cocktail smoking against my front door, but saw nothing.

Addie seemed restless as well, picking up on my nervousness. She paced the upstairs, dropping with a sigh first in front of the windows, then moving to the top of the stairs, ears pricked and alert. Instead of comforting me, her watchfulness compounded my fear. She never acted like this, and generally slept all night without moving. She probably sensed the killer waiting outside for his moment to strike. With luck, he would get the address wrong and kill my neighbor.

Dawn finally arrived, finding me sluggish and unwell. Pain radiated behind my eyes and my stomach felt sour. No epiphanies had come to me during the night other than a resolution to call the police to try and find out how much danger I was in. And I'd decided to track down Cherilynn Lott and see if she'd let me buy Henry from her. I suspected money might hold more weight with her than sentiment. What I would do with him if I got him, I didn't know, but I did know that I could not let her keep him. Daniel hadn't called, but he still might. Maybe Evan would take him. If not, surely I could find a home for him amongst my many dog-loving contacts.

Tea was not going to cut it this morning, so I packed Addie into the car and headed for the bagel shop up the street. A tall hazelnut coffee and a chocolate chip bagel might make me feel better. Early-morning commuters, in their casual business attire, crowded the store. I felt like a bag lady in my rumpled sweatshirt, shorts and ponytailed hair topped by baseball cap. I got my order to go and used the change for a *Houston Chronicle*. Addie was going to have to miss her walk this morning as I was barely up to walking my paying customers.

Back at home, I opened the blinds for Addie and slumped at the kitchen table with my bagel and coffee. The streaming sun cast a happy yellow glow across the room, and the caffeine began to infuse life into my blood. Natural optimism and logic returned slowly. Cherilynn hadn't mentioned me by name. There must be hundreds of dog walkers in Houston. Thousands, probably. I wasn't even a true dog walker, in the sense that my business was primarily dog treats with a little dog walking thrown in on the side. And Dayna hadn't been a client, she had just been a fluke. A good deed for which I was being punished.

No one could track me down based on what Cherilynn had

said. I settled back and perused the paper. A car chase in north Houston overnight, a car bomb in the Middle East, early autumn storms across the Midwest, all very normal stuff. It wasn't until page six that my newfound calm gave way.

Next to a half-page ad for Gallery Furniture, the headline read: "Sister of Murder Victim Demands Justice." My eyes skimmed the page. "Dayna Burke, Houston businesswoman," blah blah blah. "Found murdered Tuesday afternoon in her Montrose area home," blah blah blah. "Her sister, Cherilynn Lott, is demanding justice for the killing. 'I don't want any other families to go through what our family is going through. No one should have to suffer this way. Please, if you know anything that can help catch this killer, please come forward.' Ms. Lott also indicated that a dog walker, Jessie Gallager, found the body when she came to walk the Burkes' dog, and may have seen the killer."

I dropped the paper onto the table and took a couple of deep breaths. She needed to be stopped. How could she keep saying this and getting away with it? I saw no such thing. I didn't see anyone but the back end of the dog running out the door. It was a small point to mention, but they hadn't even spelled my name right. I was also pretty sure that Cherilynn's quote had been cleaned up by the grammar police at the paper.

This was negligent reporting. They had to know they were putting me in danger. Boy, was the *Chronicle* going to hear from me. I scanned the byline—Angela Crampton. What else did Angela Crampton have to say? "Police have not confirmed that there were any eyewitnesses, only that their investigation continues. They're asking anyone with information to please contact the Houston Police Department." Swell. So, the police didn't confirm it, but neither did they deny it.

Anger and fear rolled around my stomach. I was jittery from the coffee and edgy from lack of sleep, but I wasn't sure what I should do. I wanted to call Angela Crampton and have a little discussion about fact checking, and the minor issue that she was putting me in danger. But that would take a lot of energy that I didn't have. I could call Officer Jones and ask for police protection, but I didn't really think they did that unless you were going to testify against the mob. And frankly, the whole Witness Protection Program just had a lot of drawbacks.

I glanced at the clock and calculated how much time I had before I needed to start my rounds. Roughly enough for at least a couple batches of dog cookies, but even that seemed too much trouble. I moved to the couch and curled up. I'd never felt unsafe before. Not truly unsafe, and I was having a hard time wrapping my brain around it.

I must have drifted off, because when the phone rang, my heart shot against my rib cage so hard I thought it must have bruised itself. It was still hammering wildly when I answered.

Evan had seen both the TV news and the paper and was worried for my safety.

"You should come stay with me for a few days," he said. I thought about his frat-boy apartment, complete with particle board furniture, shag carpeting and rowdy band of cockroaches, and decided I'd rather take my chances home alone.

"That's really nice, Evan," I said. "But I think it'll be okay." Actually, I didn't think it would be okay, but I'd take an unknown killer over a known cockroach any day. My other line beeped and I told him I'd call him later.

"Jessica, tell me that's not you I see them referring to on the news." It was Frances, my grandmother. Who knew she watched the local news?

"It's not as bad as you'd think," I tried to reassure her.

"You discover a dead body belonging to a boss you despised, you see the killer who has not yet been apprehended, and they advertise it on every channel in Houston. Please tell me how that is not as bad as I thought."

It wasn't like Frances to sound so snippy. "I didn't actually see anything," I told her. "Except the back end of a dog running out the door. That was it."

"So, they are completely misrepresenting the facts on every channel and in print. I am going to call Charles as soon as we are finished." Charles had been my grandfather's solicitor for decades, and when he passed on, his son Charles had picked up where the original Charles left off, continuing to provide every imaginable assistance to my grandmother after Granddad died. I tried to think what Charles could accomplish that I could not. Nothing sprang immediately to mind.

"You and Addie must come stay with me," she said. I hesitated. It wasn't that I didn't enjoy staying with Frances, but the downside was that she lived twenty-five feet from my parents in their guesthouse. I was too tired and too beat up to face them.

"Thank you, but I'll be fine. Evan said I could go stay with him."

"And are you going to stay with Evan?" That woman knew me too well.

"No. But I'm sure I'll be fine here. I have Addie. She'll protect me."

I heard a ladylike exhale, bordering on a snort. "You know I love Addie," she said. "But I'm not sure I'm willing to trust her with your life. You should come stay with me. I'm sure you'd be much safer over here."

"Frances, really. I'll be fine. I'll be careful. I promise. Look, maybe we can have dinner tomorrow night. How's that? And maybe I'll stay there for the night after dinner, but I still have work to do. You know I have clients, and I've got a lot of baking to do for Halloween. Seriously, I'll be fine."

She didn't sound convinced, but she finally agreed to dinner. In a weird way, having everyone worry about me was bringing back a bit of my own confidence. Surely it wasn't nearly as melodramatic as it all sounded.

CHAPTER SIX

The message light on my answering machine was blinking frantically when I got home after my dog-walking rounds. My mother had called to see if I was okay. Apparently, someone at one of her clubs had seen the news and inquired as to whether I was the same Jessie Gallagher that was mentioned in the story. It undoubtedly caused my mother no end of embarrassment, since it highlighted the dog-walking aspect of my life. I'm relatively certain that my mother is very vague about what I do when her friends ask, focusing instead on my brother, who is making quite a name for himself on the West Coast as a software designer.

The second message was from Daniel Burke, who sounded entirely too chipper for having just lost his wife. He wanted to let me know that he was unable to take Henry. I felt a flash of irritation at his callousness. It didn't bother me that he wasn't mourning Dayna—that was understandable—but rather that he was so selfish that he couldn't even take responsibility for his own dog. He finished by telling me to give him a call and maybe we could meet for a drink sometime to talk about what I thought would be best for Henry. Yeah, right.

Finally, there was a call from Angela Crampton. She sounded irritable and out of breath.

"I tried to call you, you know. Before we went to print." Again, yeah, right. There hadn't been any calls on my caller ID that could have been her. "Anyway, *sorry* if you weren't happy about the story. You could always give me your side of it, you know." I could hear distinct gum smacking between sentences. "Call me on my cell and I'll meet you." She gave her number and hung up without saying goodbye.

Quite a collection of calls there; all very disappointing in their own way. At least my mother was concerned about me. I guess.

The thought that maybe Cherilynn could be persuaded to part with Henry for a small fee had been simmering since this morning. I knew she'd professed that she wanted him to remind her of her dear departed sister, but I also knew that to be the load of poop that it was. Although now that Daniel had rejected the poor dog, it would mean having to find a home for him since Addie wasn't going to share her territory. A good home. I riffled through names in my head, not quite lighting on any one in particular, but no worries—I was sure I could find someone to take a sweet little guy like him.

I booted up my computer and went to my favorite people-finder website. Cherilynn Lott. How many could there be? There were none, actually. And there was only one C. Lott. I checked the address, but I had no idea what part of town she lived in. She might not even be listed as herself. She could be married and listed under her husband's name. I took off the C and just typed in Lott, Houston. One hundred and fifty-nine hits. This was not very helpful.

Daniel would know. I went through another search for Dayna's number, same pile of paper, same difficulty finding the Christmas party invitation. Finally, I found it and dialed the number.

"Hello!" said a jaunty voice.

"Daniel?" I asked.

"Yes, it is," he said, dropping from jaunty to sultry in the space of two seconds. "Who is this?"

"This is Jessie Gallagher. I got your message about not being able to keep Henry and I wanted to talk to you about that."

"Well, Jessie, it's good to hear from you. The police told me you were the one that found Dayna. I'm sorry you had to go through that. Are you okay?"

His voice held an odd mix of concern and flirtatiousness. He was the one who had lost his wife, and I felt I should be asking him if he was okay, but yet it seemed superfluous.

"I'm fine," I said. "But I'm worried about Henry. Your sister-in-law insisted I hand him over to her, and to tell you the truth, after meeting her, I'm really sorry I did." So much for tact.

He sighed into the phone rather dramatically. "I'm sorry I wasn't here. I can't keep a dog. Hell, I travel too much. They're too much work, and they need someone who's going to actually think about their needs. But you're right. Cherilynn definitely shouldn't have a dog. It was bad enough Dayna got him, although to her credit, she did treat him pretty well."

He trailed off, and I could hear him swallowing noisily into my ear.

"Why don't you come over? We could have a drink and talk about it."

Good Lord, was he hitting on me?

"Oh, sorry," I said. "I'm going out tonight and I'm in a bit of a rush. But I was hoping you could give me Cherilynn's phone number or address. I want to check with her and make sure Henry's doing okay."

"I'm sure the dog's fine, but let me see if I can find it."

He kept me holding for several minutes while he looked for

Cherilynn's number. His breathing into the phone was so loud and labored that I started getting uncomfortable. He finally came up with the phone number.

"I don't have her address handy," he said. "I've only been there once. Can you say red-neck?" He drew out the red-neck into multiple syllables. "Hard to believe she and Dayna were sisters. Anyway, it's east of town, out I-10 a few exits."

"Thanks, I appreciate it," I said.

"No problem," he said. "Although you've really got me feeling bad." I could hear a little pout when he said "bad," like he was really thinking naughty. His inflections were getting on my nerves. "I wasn't even thinking when the police asked me about the dog. I was devastated by Dayna's death, as you can imagine, and trying to get home as fast as I could. The shoot was at a critical stage, and I knew I couldn't deal with everything else, much less a dog. It just never crossed my mind where he'd end up, although it should have." The "shoot." Listen to Mr. Big Producer here.

"Yes, well, I just hope he's okay." I sounded frosty and prissy even to my own ears.

"If I can help you out in any way, just let me know."

"You could call Cherilynn and tell her you want him back. I'll see about finding a good home for him," I said.

There was a moment of silence. "Oh gosh," he finally said. "That's my other line. I really need to take it. It's probably the film critic that wanted to interview me. Sorry to run." And with a click, he was gone.

What a jerk. I pictured Cherilynn working diligently to clear out his house before he got home and wondered how far she'd gotten. I wasn't sure which of them I disliked more. Then again, anyone associated with Dayna was bound to be unpleasant.

At least I had Cherilynn's phone number. Back online, I resumed my search for the Lotts. I really didn't want to call and check on Henry; I wanted to see him in person. If I called and warned the sister I was coming, she probably wouldn't let me see him out of pure spite.

I did a reverse search on the phone number. Lonnie Lott. I copied the address and immediately googled directions. As Daniel had said, they lived east of town, just past the Beltway in Channelview, approximately twenty-two miles from my house. Accounting for rush-hour traffic, I estimated it would take about thirty to forty minutes to get there.

An unaccountable pang of anxiety twirled in my stomach. Either I was nervous about what I was about to do, or I was coming down with a stomach virus. I shut down my computer and told Addie I was going out.

As I suspected, rush hour was in full swing, and I crawled along the interstate with hordes of irritated drivers. Sightseeing east of Houston was somewhat limited: acres of tractor-trailers for sale, slabs of empty concrete, and shabby little motels with adult video stores mixed in for fun.

The air hung heavy with the acrid scent of propylene, ethylene, or whatever other cancer-causing compounds floated out of the refineries. I checked to make sure the air ducts of my car were closed, although that was about as helpful as taping down aluminum lawn furniture in a hurricane.

I almost missed my exit, swerving at the last minute to catch Sheldon Road heading south. Houston's lack of zoning laws was well evidenced here by a random mix of industrial and residential, with a handful of abandoned railcars thrown here and there. The stacks of a refinery were visible to the south over squatty scrub trees that seemed to thrive in this area, and an orange flare burned high into the sky.

I drove slowly, taking in the feel of the neighborhood. Numerous body shops lined this stretch of road. In the front window of a hair salon, hand-painted letters proclaimed "Joleen's House of Hair and Beuty." Attached to the salon was

Moe's Insurance. A stack of used tires blocked the parking spaces in front. It seemed incredulous that Dayna had sprung from this area.

The houses off Sheldon were small, set back on huge lots. I had the sense that this was low ground and probably flooded every time a thunderstorm rolled through. Some of the houses were well kept with tidy lawns, neatly trimmed bushes and fresh paint, but the majority looked like they were on the downside of prosperity.

I found the Lotts' property a few blocks farther south. It sat so close to its one neighbor that it appeared as if two houses had been built on one parcel of land. The house on the right had a realtor sign propped against the mailbox, nestled in amongst knee-high weeds. The Lotts' sat to the left of a shared dirt drive that extended into muddy patches of lawn. The house was small, with a sagging front porch, peeling white paint and a roof that buckled in worrisome ways.

A movement to the left drew my attention, and I saw a flash of pale brown fur. Henry was tied to a stake between the house and an even more run-down outbuilding. The tether was only about five feet long, and he was turning in circles, trying to find a dry place to lie that was out of the mud. My heart turned over as I pulled in the driveway. No way I could leave him here to live this way. There wasn't even a water bowl in sight, although there were plenty of rusted-out car parts scattered everywhere. Perhaps they thought he could survive on rusty rainwater.

Filthy black screens covered the windows, so I couldn't see if anyone was watching my arrival. An old Chevy van sat between the two houses and I wasn't sure if it belonged to the Lotts or their neighbor. I pulled my car to the left, closer to Henry, and got out, shutting the door softly behind me. My first instinct was to grab him and run, but before I could even reach him, the front screen door squealed open and snapped back shut with a shotgun bang. Cherilynn's short, fat legs stumped towards me at a remarkable speed.

"Whatchu want?" she shouted at me, still motoring in my direction. I took a step back towards the safety of my car.

"Hi," I said with false brightness. "How's it going?" Henry had jumped up when he saw me get out the car, and his little bottom wriggled so hard I thought he might dislodge a vertebra. He pulled at his restraint and began barking in high-pitched yips as he jumped on his hind legs. I started towards him. "Hey, boy."

"Don't you go near that dog," Cherilynn shouted at me. The sun was behind me and she squinted her eyes and raised a hand to shield them. At the same time, she kicked her foot in the dirt towards Henry, spraying pebbles in his direction. "Shut up!"

I put on my best conciliatory look. Not that she could see it with the sun in her eyes, but it was the same look that had usually worked with her sister. "Now don't get upset," I said. "I just wanted to make sure that things were working out with your new dog." I glanced over at him and saw the mud-caked legs and crusted tail. It didn't look like it was working out to me.

"It's working out just fine," she said. "Shut up!"

I walked over to Henry and knelt down beside him. He squirmed towards my face, front legs wrapping around my neck and back legs jumping on my thighs. His little pink tongue lapped at my chin. I rubbed his neck and cooed at him.

"See, he's fine," Cherilynn said moving closer to keep an eye on me.

"He doesn't have any water," I pointed out trying to keep my tone neutral.

"Well, he did." She looked around at the junk in the near vicinity. "Right there." She pointed to an overturned plastic Cool Whip container. "Stupid thing knocked it over." She ambled over and picked it up, groaning as she straightened. "I can't be spending all day babysitting him," she mumbled. "Ain't my fault he's too stupid to keep his water in the bowl."

The rumble of a diesel engine roared from the street. An extended-cab pickup pulled into the drive, partially blocking my car.

"Great," said Cherilynn. "Now my husband's home. He ain't gonna like you poking around here."

Henry's jumping became more frantic than happy, and his tail tucked between his legs as he hid his head under my arm. I stood up, cradling him in my arms, not wanting to face the husband from a kneeling position. The short rope kept me within a couple feet of the stake.

Lonnie Lott stepped down from the cab and stood staring at me from a distance. Luckily, he had the same problem with the sun that his wife was having.

"Cherilynn, who's that?" he asked, as if I were incapable of understanding that he was talking about me. He was built like a grizzly bear, tall and thick with arms that looked powerful enough to smash me to smithereens. Dingy gray coveralls strained against the pressure of his stomach and rode high up his ankles over a pair of steel-toed boots. A hard hat would have completed his outfit, but instead he had an orange-and-brown baseball cap with a deer head and a rifle emblazoned across the front. I didn't feel at all vulnerable.

"It's that girl that had Dayna's dog," she said.

"What's she doing here now?" he asked.

It was very strange being the subject of this conversation. I felt the need to pipe up.

"Hi, I'm Jessie," I said, not bothering to hold out my hand as I really didn't want him getting that close to me, nor did I want to run the risk of having him break all the bones in my hand. Furthermore, his hands looked filthy. "I just wanted to check that everything was going okay with Henry. I know when

I talked to Cherilynn yesterday, she said you hadn't had a dog before."

"I've had dogs before," he said. "But I don't know what business it is of yours."

Henry trembled in my arms. He was obviously terrified of this man.

"Well, actually it's not," I conceded in my most diplomatic voice. "But I grew pretty fond of this guy while I was taking care of him, and I just thought that if you didn't want him, or he was going to be too much trouble or anything, I would be happy to take him off your hands."

"See, I told you, Lonnie, she wants to take him," said Cherilynn. "That's a pure-breed dog and he's worth some money. You ain't taking him from us."

"I was going to say I'd buy him from you," I said. "I'm sure we can work something out."

Lonnie stood riveted, staring hard at my face. He wasn't even blinking. It was rather unnerving, really. Cherilynn stamped her foot and flapped her arms against her sides like an overweight bird unable to lift off. Her lower lip poked out and her eyes narrowed. "That is one of the only reminders I have of my darlin' sister. You think you can just come in here and offer us a couple a' dollars and you can take it away from me?"

It appeared she was trying to work herself up into tears, but they just weren't coming.

"I know it's not just about the money," I said. "I just thought it would only be fair to compensate you for him since he probably is purebred."

"Get out," said Lonnie. His tone was low and menacing, and fear ran up my back, tickling the little hairs under my ponytail. Henry pressed closer against me, and my heart broke for him. "Put that dog down and get out," he said. Cherilynn stopped flapping and turned her pouting face towards her husband.

"She didn't even tell us yet how much she'd give us for him," she started.

He whirled to face her faster than I'd have thought a big man like him could move. He was at least a foot taller than she was, and he leaned his face towards her. "Shut up," he said to her. I shot her a look, hoping that maybe she and I could work something out if only he would go into the house. But one look at his steel-toed boots planted in the dirt and I knew he wasn't going anywhere until I was gone. I glanced towards his pickup.

"I'm not sure I can get out. I think you might be blocking me a bit."

He just stood and stared. I held Henry up to my chin and kissed his head. "I'm so sorry, boy," I murmured to him. Tears pooled in the corners of my eyes and spilled over onto my cheeks. Henry turned and licked at them with his soft pink tongue. I could feel his heart beating against my palm. The dread of leaving him here even for a night was overwhelming. My brain frantically darted around, trying to come up with a plan, but the best I could come up with was calling the Humane Society and seeing if I could get someone out to take him. Even as I thought it, I knew how long something like that would take. Maybe I could reach out to Cherilynn when her husband wasn't home. I'd offer her enough money that she wouldn't be able to resist it. Then she could just tell him that the dog ran away.

I set him gently on the ground and walked away. He ran after me until the rope brought him up with a hard snap. I could hear him choking as he pulled and strained to reach me. His whines followed me to my car as I opened the door.

"Look, how much do you want for him?" I asked, my voice choking with emotion.

Lonnie Lott just stood staring at me, his dark eyes boring into mine. This guy was not right in the head. I knew I wasn't going to get anywhere with him, but I couldn't understand it.

They obviously didn't want the dog. If they kept treating him the way they were, he wasn't going to be worth anything if they tried to sell him. Surely Cherilynn could be persuaded to sell him. Then again, maybe she was too afraid of her insane husband to risk it.

I executed a twenty-nine-point turn to get my car out of the driveway and past Lonnie's truck. I'd have driven across the yard except I was afraid of the debris puncturing my tires. I even considered driving into that big stupid pickup truck, but the damage would be entirely worse for my car, and possibly for my body as well if I was any judge of character.

I took one last look at Henry as I pulled into the street. He was choking himself at the end of the rope, his front legs waving in the air after me. His cries and yelps followed me as I headed down the street, and they continued to echo in my head long after I'd made it home.

CHAPTER SEVEN

A ddie sniffed me all over when I got home. I slid down on the kitchen floor next to her while she licked the tear tracks from my cheeks and rested her head on my shoulder. Dogs are one of God's greatest earthly comforters. Unfortunately, even with the best of Addie's care, I still couldn't shake the misery that the memory of Henry's little face wrought in my heart. There had to be something that I could do to help him. I slogged up the stairs and started water running in the tub. Perhaps a glass of wine and a bath would help. I shuffled back downstairs, filled a large glass, fed Addie and headed back to the tub.

Soaking in the hot water with the jets pounding away at my stress, I contemplated what I could do to save Henry from those horrible people. I needed Daniel to call Cherilynn and tell her that he wanted his dog back. That would be the easiest and most direct action. I would even go pick up Henry and find a good home for him myself. Daniel wouldn't have to do anything but make the phone call. But Daniel hadn't exactly stepped up when I'd talked to him earlier. He'd made it pretty clear he didn't want anything to do with his in-laws. I couldn't really blame him, but nevertheless, this was not a big thing I was asking him to do.

I could call the Humane Society or another rescue agency. But I couldn't prove that the Lotts were abusing Henry. Just tying him to a stake didn't constitute abuse in the eyes of Texas law (although I could debate that law with you all day long). It wasn't extremely hot or cold, so I couldn't cite cruelty there. And not too many agencies would take my word for it that I had a "bad feeling" about them. It would also take a long time, and I wasn't sure Henry had a long time to wait.

The water was cooling around me and my wine was almost gone when I faced head-on the thought that had been flitting around in my brain since I'd first seen the rope around Henry's neck. I could take him. I knew, even as I thought it, that this was really my only option. I couldn't leave him there to live his life out at the end of a rope. While the weather was nice now, it was going to get colder soon, and if he survived the winter, he likely wouldn't survive the Texas summer out there without even a hint of shade. If the upside-down Cool Whip container was any indication, he'd probably die of dehydration before the week was out.

I got out of the tub and into the softest, baggiest pajamas I owned. The pressure in my chest had eased a bit since I'd decided on a course of action. Addie stood by the side of the tub, watching with fascination as the water drained away.

Pulling on my slippers, I started working out plans in my head. I could go out there tonight, but Lonnie and Cherilynn would be on high alert after my visit today. I dreaded leaving Henry there for one minute longer than I had to, but I needed this rescue mission to be successful on the first attempt. Definitely tomorrow. I couldn't stand to leave him there any longer than that.

Lonnie had shown up a little after five today, so it was probably safe to assume he worked a typical eight-to-five day. The question was Cherilynn. I had no idea if she worked or not. If she was home, that would be a problem because it wasn't as if Henry was the quietest dog in the pack.

Padding to the kitchen, I poked my head into the refrigerator. Not a lot besides the liver I had thawing for tomorrow's baking. Gross. I pulled out eggs and found some mushrooms and a pepper in the produce drawer that didn't look too old, and diced those up. I was just pouring the eggs into a heated skillet when the phone rang. I grabbed the cordless handset and jammed it against my shoulder still holding the skillet.

"Hello?" The phone slipped from its tenuous position and crashed to the floor, little plastic pieces breaking off, scattering across the floor and skittering under the stove. Shoot. I picked the phone up and held it to my ear.

"Hello?"

Nobody there. If it was important, they'd call back. I pressed the largest pieces back together and hoped it wasn't completely broken. The eggs were beginning to brown along the sides when the phone rang again. I glanced at the caller ID —Unknown Number.

"Hello?" I didn't hear anything so I held the phone away from me, trying to see what, if any, parts were missing. I couldn't tell, so I listened again. "Hello?" Still nothing. I gave the phone a little bang against the counter. No one there.

I threw the mushrooms and peppers into the skillet and started getting drooly like Addie before her dinner. The phone rang again. Unknown Number again. A normal person would let the machine pick it up, but I had an unhealthy fear of something happening to my family members, and a solid conviction that the one time that I didn't answer, there would be an actual emergency.

"Hel-*lo*?" I was getting a little annoyed. Silence. Sometimes telemarketers call you and leave you hanging while they daydream or talk to their boiler room buddies, but generally you can hear noise in the background. I didn't hear any boiler room noise. Instead I heard breathing, or maybe it was the noise of an oscillating fan in the background. I listened harder but couldn't really make anything out. Another minute of listening and I was fairly sure it was breathing.

"Hello?" I repeated, a little note of fear creeping in despite my best attempts to keep it out. The breathing got a little louder. I hung up and slid the phone down the counter away from me.

The eggs were burning now, but I'd lost my appetite as a sliver of unease worked its way in. I'd been so hung up on worrying about Henry that I'd almost forgotten about the crazed killer on the loose. The crazed killer who had probably read my name in the paper today, and was now checking to see if I was home so he could come over and kill me.

Why waste a trip if I wasn't there?

The rational part of my brain tried to reassure me. Everyone gets crank calls from time to time. Right? But I was freaked out. The truth of the matter is that I'm a chicken at heart. Oh sure, I like reading mysteries (so long as they're not too graphic) and once in a while I watch a thriller (ditto on the graphic thing), but for the most part I prefer my life to be like a chick flick: some light humor, an occasional romance and a few Hallmark moments thrown in here and there. The idea of a crazed psycho killer was not my idea of a good time.

I ran around the house, turning on all the lights, but realized that would just make it easier for someone to watch me. I crept to each window and door, checking to make sure they were all locked, but that just made me notice how flimsy windows really are. Anyone could bash right through one. How had I never noticed this before?

I looked around for a weapon to defend myself. No gun. In spite of living in Texas my whole life (minus the couple of years at boarding school), this was the first time I'd ever even thought about it. I wondered if it was too late to run out and get one tonight. Wait, I seemed to remember something about a waiting period. Was that here or another state?

I studied the knives on the counter, then imagined all the things a lunatic could do to me with them. I immediately hid them in a cabinet behind the crock pot.

My nonstick skillet caught my eye. I swung it through the air like a baseball bat, while little pieces of egg rained down on Addie. It was heavy and sliced cleanly through the air. Yes! This could crack someone's head right open. Addie was eyeing me with a look that said she was beginning to doubt my sanity.

They say that dogs make good deterrents. Maybe against burglars, but I'd never heard how they were against homicidal maniacs. Judging from how well Henry had protected Dayna, they weren't all that effective.

The phone rang again, and I nearly leapt out of my slippers. I could feel evil pulsating from it with every ring. I snatched it up.

"HELLO?" I shouted into the mouthpiece.

"Geez, Jess! Damn, why are you screaming?" asked Evan, barely speaking above a whisper himself.

"I'm sorry," I said. "I've been getting these calls tonight and they're freaking me out. What's up and why are you whispering?"

"I'm at the office and I wanted to see if you'd like to come down and go through Dayna's office with me."

I glanced at the clock and saw that it was only eight twenty. I'd thought it was much later. Anything was better than sitting here as killer bait. And mostly I didn't want to be alone. Strength in numbers, right? I told him I needed to change and I'd be right over.

What do you wear to ransack a dead woman's office? I settled on black jeans and a black hoodie. What to do with Addie? I knew she'd probably be fine at home. After all, if someone really was out to get me, they were out to get me, not my dog. Still, I wasn't willing to take any chances.

"What took you so long?" Evan hissed when I finally reached the office. He jammed at the elevator button with unnecessary force.

"I had to run Addie by Frances's," I said. "I didn't want to leave her alone."

Evan was too irritated to care about why I needed my grandmother to babysit my dog. We rode up in silence.

The floor was eerie when it wasn't populated with disgruntled workers. Fluorescent lights cast a yellow glare over empty desks, and the white noise that was barely noticeable during the day sounded loud and annoying like radio static.

"Why are we doing this, and what are we looking for?" I asked in a muted whisper.

"I don't know," he answered, hurrying down the row. I rushed to keep up, feeling like a delinquent breaking into a school. We paused by his desk, which was just two down from Dayna's darkened office. Up to this point, we hadn't done anything wrong, and we were both reluctant to make the first move towards the door. I rubbed my head where a small headache was forming behind my eyes. These lights were horrible. Or maybe it was the wine. Whatever. Suddenly Dayna's dark office held some appeal.

"I would like to see her calendar," I said. "I'd like to know what meeting she had the night she asked me to go take Henry out. And I'd like to know why she was home when she was."

"I don't know what the police have taken or what they've left," Evan replied. "But go look. And hurry," he said. "I don't know what time the cleaning crew comes. I imagine they could be here any minute."

Go look? He had said, "Do you want to come look through Dayna's office with me?" What had happened to the "with me"? He was standing hunched over his computer screen, legs positioned like they were ready to run.

"Aren't you coming with me?" I snapped.

"You go." He waved a hand at me. "I'll keep an eye out."

"And what? You'll hoot like an owl if anyone comes?"

I stomped towards Dayna's office. Fine.

The blinds across the glass were open and light streamed in through the open door, so I didn't bother with the lights. I headed straight to Dayna's desk, which was unfortunately barren. Either Naomi had cleaned it up, or the cops had taken everything, because Dayna's desk was generally a mess. That didn't bode well for my search. Anything meaningful was no doubt already gone. I pulled out her chair and sat down, hunching over the desk drawers while keeping a furtive look out the door. Evan was still bent over his computer, his head swiveling from side to side like an off-balance bobblehead doll.

The central drawer held the usual assortment of office bric-a-brac: paper clips, highlighters, plastic forks, ratty cracker packages, and dozens of half-used yellow sticky pads. Feeling around towards the back of the drawer, I found what felt like a picture frame and pulled it out. It was a snapshot of Henry looking straight into the camera, ears pricked and mouth open in a wide smile. Aww. I set it on the desk to take with me. It surprised me that Dayna would have something that sentimental at work. I'd never seen a picture of Daniel here.

The side drawer was locked. Rats. I wondered if it had been locked before or after the cops had searched. I felt around in the middle drawer again, trying to find a key, but no luck. There wasn't anything on top of the desk, so I turned to the file cabinets behind. The top drawer opened easily, but only contained folders with pricing information, company publications and old annual reports. The bottom drawer held a battered pair of running shoes and a blue sweater.

I poked my head towards the window to see if Evan was

still standing guard. He was in the exact same position, still swinging his head periodically towards the elevator banks.

"Evan," I whispered.

He turned towards me. "What?"

"I need to find the key to her desk drawer. Go look on Naomi's desk and see if it's there."

He furrowed his brows at me. "I have to keep a look out. You go."

I made a mental note to never burgle another office with Evan.

Naomi's desk was immaculate. There wasn't a paper in sight, unless you counted the one tacked to the board next to her monitor. "Vengeance is mine sayeth the Lord!" That was interesting. Did she think it was God who had struck Dayna down, or had she given Him a little help? I was pretty sure Naomi was nutty enough to snap, do something horrific, then believe it was God's divine will that had directed her to do it.

All the desk drawers were locked, so I peeked under her phone and her small page-a-day calendar. Nothing. An extensive collection of porcelain angels populated her cabinet. Angels are supposed to be good and comforting; these guys gave me the willies. With eyes that stared out from hooded lids and lips that twisted into arrogant sneers, these guys didn't seem religious at all. I began turning each one over, not expecting to find anything. But under the purple robed one, I found a key taped to the bottom. It was small like a desk key, so I grabbed it and hurried back to Dayna's office.

It fit right into the lock and turned smoothly. Yes! I crouched over the drawer, peering in. File folders jammed the drawer. They were wedged so tight I could barely fit my finger in between them. Grabbing some files from the middle, I pulled up, lifting everything at once. I grabbed one and flipped it open. A resume caught my eye—Hank Mecklinberg. I'd heard the name, but didn't know him personally. I think he retired several years ago. There were copies of all his reviews, papers from human resources showing salary history, hand-written notes outlining personal items: he'd divorced in 2002—wife left him for an insurance salesman; son arrested for DUI in Rhode Island while at school; out for doctor's visit—possible heart problem. Geez, this was so personal.

I grabbed another file. Naomi Silva. Same things: resume, HR documents, salary history, handwritten notes. Naomi had gotten married in 2004 and honeymooned at a Bible retreat in Arkansas. Another note questioned what her husband did, followed up with an update indicating he was the manager of a grocery store. Yet another paper referred to Naomi's dedica-tion to her religion and questioned whether her husband was allowed to have sex. What the heck? Why did this matter to Dayna? It was creepy how much stuff she had stored. Not everyone she worked with was represented. I wondered how she had selected her targets. I restacked the files I had and went to look for my own. They weren't in alphabetical order; hard to tell what kind of filing system this was. There it was—Jessie Gallagher.

I'd just opened the file when I heard Evan shout, "Hey, Chip! What are you doing up here so late?"

"Jesus, Petty. What are you screaming for?" Ugh, Chip Vermuellen. This guy's sole goal since his first day had been to move up the ladder. No doubt he viewed Dayna's early demise as a premium opportunity.

"You just surprised me, that's all," Evan said, still shouting. "I didn't expect to see anyone else up here tonight."

I clutched the loose stack of folders against my chest, jammed the rest back into the drawer and turned the key as silently as possible while sliding into the kneehole of Dayna's desk. Shoot, I'd left Henry's picture on the desk. Oh well, hopefully Chip wouldn't come in here. I pulled the chair in as far as possible and willed him to keep going.

"Yes, well, I had a couple of things I needed to take care of." I could hear him moving closer to the door.

"Wait!" Evan yelled as I saw the lights flick on overhead. "Since you're here, could you come look at this spreadsheet for me? I'm not sure I've got the calculations right."

The light stayed on, but I could hear Chip's feet scraping against the carpet as he moved towards Evan.

"Shit, Petty, I didn't come up here to help you with your stupid problems."

I looked around, trying to figure out what to do. The sides of the desk didn't go all the way to the floor, but they went down far enough that I didn't think Chip would see me unless he came all the way around and saw me behind the chair. What if he was planning to sit down at the desk? How would I explain what I was doing? At best, this could be extremely embarrassing; at worst, he might call the cops and have me arrested for trespassing. Evan would no doubt be fired, and he didn't have a trust fund to fall back on.

I could hear an argument ensuing at Evan's desk, but I couldn't catch the words. I poked my head out just a little and took a quick look around the far side of the desk. A lone corn plant stood in the corner, and even though I'd lost about five pounds in the past few months, I was pretty sure I couldn't hide behind that tiny trunk. No handy closets or wardrobes for me to slip into.

I pulled my head back just as I heard Chip saying, "You're an idiot, Petty. And what kind of pathetic life do you have if you're up here trying to figure out something like that at nine o'clock at night?"

Evan had come closer to Dayna's office, because I could hear him clearly. "I guess it's about as pathetic as yours, since you're here too."

"I forgot something," Chip said. "Otherwise I'd be out actually living. Unlike you."

A silence ensued, and I couldn't hear footsteps or talking or anything else but my own breathing, which was beginning to sound loud even to me. A cramp knotted the arch of my left foot, and I was afraid that I would have to leap up to relieve the pressure. Where was Chip? And where was Evan? You'd think he would come in here and let me know if the coast was clear.

Finally, I heard footsteps. I stopped breathing. It was Evan.

"You can come out now," he said, switching off the overhead light. "He's finally gone." I pushed the chair back and crawled out like an old woman who'd been left in a box overnight. The files were still clutched to my chest.

"You should see these," I said to Evan. "She's got files on everyone. Really personal stuff." I grabbed mine and opened it, trying to see what sort of dirt she had on me. Glancing through, still keeping an eye on the door in case Chip came back, I saw all the regular stuff, then tons of news clippings. Stories about my father and his law firm, cases he'd won, benefits he'd been to. There were articles on my mother, all her charity events, galas and society luncheons. It looked like there was more in there about my family than there was about me. Finally, I came to the handwritten notes.

"Influential family. British nanny, prep school, sorority girl. Thinks she's better than everyone." *I do not!* And how did she know I had a nanny? Another page: "Has no idea what it's like outside River Oaks. No boyfriend or real personal life. Health nut." I'm not a health nut, and I do have a personal life. "Hates working late. Find projects that make her stay late." My hackles were going up. *You've got to be kidding me.* Evan was reading over my shoulder and I could feel his breath on my cheek.

"Wow. Am I in there?" he asked, pointing at the drawer.

"I don't know. I haven't had a chance to look."

"Unlock it," he said, pulling on the handle. I handed him

the key. He started pawing through the files as soon as he pulled it open.

"Here it is!" He opened it and started looking through. I peeked over his shoulder, but he stepped away, holding the side of the file up so I couldn't see. "Do you mind? It's personal," he said.

Sheesh. "You saw mine."

"Not all of it," he muttered, already engrossed. I tried to take a peep over his shoulder, but he turned away. His face got red and he slammed the folder closed and tucked it under his arm.

"What are you doing with that?" I asked. "You can't just take it."

"Watch me," he said.

I looked at the remaining folders, wondering what other malicious items Dayna had collected. Maybe she had something in there that was motive for murder.

"Okay, fine, so what about the rest of these? Do you think it would be all right if I took them home and read through them? Maybe there's something in here that can help us figure out who killed her," I said.

"Probably everyone in there would have liked to kill her," he said, his cheeks still flaming. "I don't care if you take them."

"Do you think anyone would notice?"

"Like who?" he countered. "As far as I know, the cops are done here. Who else is going to care?" We debated the point for several more minutes, but the only one we thought might notice would be Naomi, and what would she do? The sound of laughter came floating to us from the elevator bank, and I startled like a pheasant being flushed. Evan and I grabbed the folders and Henry's photo and shot out of the dark office into the light of the open space. We were only steps away from Evan's desk when the cleaning crew came around the corner. I held my hand over my heart trying to slow down the beating.

"Let's get out of here," I said. "Do you have a bag or something I can put this all in? I feel like I look guilty."

Evan dug around, but was only able to produce a plastic grocery bag that he'd brought his lunch in. A wilted piece of lettuce was stuck to the side and he picked it off.

Good enough. We packed everything in and left together.

CHAPTER EIGHT

F rances is probably as cool a grandmother as anyone could ever have, but even she has her limits. I wasn't fooled by the calm demeanor as she sat sipping her tea when I swung back by her house to pick Addie up.

"So, did you have a nice outing?" she inquired politely.

"Yes, thank you," I responded, thinking perhaps the less I said and the faster I departed, the better this would be all around.

She set her teacup down and poured a bit more from a lovely bone-china teapot that looked as if it belonged in the queen's favorite sitting room. She hadn't offered me a cup, which was unusual, and she was sitting quite straight without her back even touching the chair. I, on the other hand, slouched in a way that would have gotten me expelled from boarding school, and was too tired to care.

"I assume you did not feel that Addie would be safe at home alone this evening," she said without meeting my eyes.

We were sitting in her living room, a room I've always loved for its comfortable elegance, with its overstuffed floral-print chairs and chintz love seats. Addie was lying on the floor, leaning against my legs, no doubt leaving smears of dog hair along the black denim where she rested.

"No. No," I said, my voice rising to highlight the lie. "She's fine at home alone. I just don't like to leave her by herself sometimes."

"She seemed quite tired this evening," Frances said. "I would have thought she would have just slept at your house much like she did at mine." In spite of the mild words, I could sense an underlying anger.

My grandmother and I have a relationship that is separate and apart from my parents. Sometimes I forget that she's related to them at all. Well, related to my mother, at least. Frances is my mother's mother, but aside from a similar set to the mouth, and the same blue eyes, they couldn't be more dissimilar.

I sighed. "Fine. You're right. She would have been fine with me leaving her alone. And I'm sure she would have been fine at my house. I'm still just a little, and I mean just a little"—I illustrated by holding my forefinger and thumb a quarter inch apart—"freaked out by that whole thing with my boss."

She finally looked up and met my eyes. The worry in hers was obvious, and I felt guilty for causing her that concern.

"Are the police any further on uncovering who's responsible?" she asked.

"Not that I'm aware of," I said.

"Perhaps they could be persuaded to send additional patrols past your house," she said, running a finger along the handle of her teacup. I might feel better with additional patrols, but this wasn't Mayberry, and I doubted the HPD would find it in their hearts and their budget to babysit me.

"I'll be careful. I promise," I said, heaving myself to my feet. Addie hopped up and pranced in circles. Frances leaned down to give her a quick pat and neck rub.

"Take care of Jessie," she murmured to the dog. I walked

over and pulled her into a hug. She put her arms around me and held me tight against her bony frame. "It's just that I love you so much, Jessica."

"I know," I said. "I love you too." I thought about my plan to rescue Henry the next day. "I'm not sure I can make dinner tomorrow," I waffled. "I want to, but something might be coming up. How about I call you?" She wasn't thrilled, but as always, she was polite.

The night was dark and my body felt heavy with fatigue. I buckled Addie into the backseat before backing down the drive. She immediately assumed her standard navigator position, front paws on the console and head thrust toward the windshield. The bag I'd thrown onto the passenger seat quickly caught her attention, and she spent so long with her head buried in the plastic bag, I worried she'd suffocate. I pushed it onto the floor in front of the passenger seat, out of her range.

Traffic was light and it didn't take me long to get home. Fragmented thoughts crashed through my head, but I was too tired to settle on any one thing. For the second time that night, I dragged myself up the stairs when I got home. I threw the bag full of Dayna's desk items into the hamper in my bathroom and covered it with dirty socks. I felt like I needed to hide it without being sure exactly why. I was too tired to look through the papers tonight, and I fell, exhausted and vaguely depressed, into bed.

I was awakened by shouting outside my window. It took me a few seconds to fight past the grogginess that enveloped my brain. Glancing at the clock, I saw it was already six twenty. Dang! I must have forgotten to set my alarm.

Bounding out of bed, I cracked a slit in the blinds and observed the scene outside. My crazy neighbor appeared to be accosting a woman walking an Australian shepherd. *Wow, he is nuts.* I left the two of them to work out their drama and headed for the kitchen. I was definitely behind on my cookie making now. *This is your business,* I reminded myself. *You've got to stop getting distracted and start being serious about it.* Pulling my bowls out and gathering the ingredients together lifted my spirits. I did love this. I was so much more satisfied creating my tiny doggie empire than I could ever be in the corporate world.

I didn't have much time to walk Addie this morning. Maybe I'd drop her at daycare for the afternoon to work off some energy. And if all went according to plan, she'd be tired tonight and she would be nicer to Henry. That, of course, was if the stealing of Henry went well.

Motivated by the memory of Henry's terrified reaction to Lonnie, I whipped together two batches of liver treats and two batches of salmon treats, forming the dough into adorable little bone shapes. While the first batch was baking, I took a quick shower, planning my day as the warm steam swirled around my head.

I could shift my schedule by an hour without upsetting any of the dogs' routines too much. I was also behind on delivering dog cookies to my daycare distributors and was no doubt missing out on sales. Perhaps I could fit in a few quick deliveries before my first dog walking. And I still hadn't found out if Cherilynn worked or stayed home. How in the world would I get Henry if she was home all day?

Well, I'd deal with that when the time came. The morning flew by in a blaze of activity. I dropped Addie at daycare, delivering several batches of cookies to the owner of her daycare at the same time. This was one of my primary distribution channels, and it was heartening to see that there was only one package left. I'd calculated that there should have been at least eight to ten still sitting on their shelf. Maybe people were buying them for Halloween. Running to a half a dozen other daycares and doggie spas, I delivered the last of my inventory. I was going to have to do some serious baking tonight and probably straight through the weekend as well.

It was a beautiful October day; the humidity was down and the sky was a clear blue. The sludge that so often darkened our skies was gone for the time being, replaced by wispy white puffs of clouds that swirled and danced in an unseen wind. All of my clients were friskier today, refreshed as I was by the weather.

By three forty-five, I'd finished my dog walking, picked Addie up from daycare and was barreling along Interstate 10 East towards Channelview. I had dog treats in my pocket, gardening clippers to cut the rope, a water bottle and a plastic bowl, and my running shoes tied tight. I still didn't know if Cherilynn was home—nothing had occurred to me on my dog-walking rounds to figure that part out. The best plan I'd managed to come up with was to slip into the yard, cut the rope, and run with the dog without being seen. This required Henry to be quiet, and for me to escape unnoticed. I know, not the best plan, but the only one I had.

Clouds had increased during the afternoon, but I kept my sunglasses on in a weak attempt to disguise myself. I also wore an Astros baseball cap pulled low with my ponytail sticking out the back, and a black windbreaker. The whole disguise wouldn't even fool my mailman, who only saw me in person maybe once a year, but then again, he seemed a bit brighter than Cherilynn and Lonnie, although not nearly as tough.

I made the exit and meandered towards the Lotts' house. As I got closer, my heart increased its pumping activity up towards my target exercise rate, and my palms broke out in a sweat. I cruised slowly down the street trying to determine if Cherilynn (or Lonnie, God forbid) was home. If he was home, I was going to have to come back and try this again later.

Two doors down, a group of children were playing what looked like a version of tag that involved the boys chasing after screaming girls with something dangling from the end of a stick. I couldn't make out what it was, but I thought if someone chased me with that thing, I'd scream too.

The Lotts' yard looked quiet. Lonnie's giant truck wasn't there, and there weren't any other cars in the drive either, although there was one poking out from behind the house that appeared to be up on blocks. Hopefully that was an extra one, not Cherilynn's waiting for some attention.

Next door on the other side sat a cable truck, but I didn't see anyone outside. I continued down the street, trying to decide the best place to park for an optimal getaway. I needed to be close enough that I could get to my car at a dead run, but not so close that I drew attention to myself.

I continued around the block to see what was behind the house. Maybe there was somewhere on the block behind that I could park. The lots were deep and I wasn't familiar enough with the neighborhood to know when I was behind the Lotts' house. The houses on this street seemed to be even farther apart, and there were more wooded areas. About a block from the main street was a greasy-looking Chicken Shack with a gravel parking area that ran along behind the restaurant. I pulled into the lot and backed into a spot towards the far side of the dumpster.

It seemed like a good enough place to leave my car. There weren't any windows in the back of the restaurant, so unless someone came out to throw something away, no one would even see my car. I pocketed the clippers and my keys and got out, feet crunching loudly on the gravel. Maybe I should go in and buy something so they wouldn't tow my car if they noticed it. A lot of places were pretty strict about parking being for paying customers only. But then again, this wasn't prime down-town property. I was just being ridiculous. And delaying my real mission because I was nervous.

I crunched my way to the street and began walking at a good clip in the direction of the Lotts' property. A low chain-link fence ran along the street surrounding a ramshackle trailer. I was pretty sure I needed to go a bit farther. I continued past the trailer, looking out of the corner of my eye to see if any of the neighbors were dialing the police to report a suspicious person. I definitely felt like a suspicious person. I didn't see any activity, so I kept moving.

The chain-link fence ended in a falling-down heap and a brushy, wooded lot loomed ahead. I must be somewhat close to the Lotts', so I ventured off the street and into the high weeds. *Lord, please don't let there be any snakes,* I prayed fervently. I hadn't considered that possibility and was ruing the decision to wear running shoes. Those snakes would have no problem biting my skinny little exposed ankles in these shoes. I should have worn my cowboy boots.

I picked my way as carefully as I could through the bramble. A path of sorts led into the trees and I followed it, passing discarded packs of cigarettes and flattened Budweiser cans. This must be where the local truants passed their time when they were skipping school. Thorny bushes snagged at my jacket as I pushed deeper into the lot, and a thick muck sucked at my shoes. The shade from the canopy of the trees forced me to pull my sunglasses off so that I could see where I was going.

Over the buzz of late-season mosquitoes, I could hear low voices and I stopped, trying to hear which direction they were coming from. Up ahead and to the left of the track, piles of dirt broke through the underbrush. It looked like someone had built an off-road bike track that was slowly being reclaimed by nature. I crept forward slowly, trying not to snap any twigs or crunch any leaves, but in this overgrown mess, I sounded more like a buffalo on a rampage than a stealthy scout.

"What was that?" I heard the panicked whisper coming from behind a dirt pile. Damn. Should I run? But then I'd have to plan this whole escapade over again. The thought of Henry spending another night at the end of that rope kept me rooted.

A tousled red head poked itself around the nearest pile of dirt, and frightened blue eyes stared at me from a dirty face. He looked to be about fifteen, but a scrawny fifteen, not fully grown. We stared at each other, neither saying a word, like shoplifters catching each other mid-theft.

"Hey, man. What are you doing? Is something over there?"

A black-haired kid joined the first one on the dirt pile and stared at me with the same frightened look. They must not get a lot of strangers around here.

"Hi," I said, waving one hand awkwardly, like perhaps they didn't understand my English. They continued to stare at me blankly. "Okay, then," I said, peering past them, trying to see if there was anyone else with them. They appeared to be the whole tribe.

The dark-haired one started whipping his hand back and forth, dropping a glowing cigarette onto the ground.

"Damn," he said, blowing on his fingers, then sticking the burned tips straight into his mouth. His friend looked over at him with a pitying glance.

"Idiot," he mumbled. They both turned back to me. I felt obligated to say something or run the risk entering an all-night staring contest.

"So, uh, I was trying to get to the Lotts' place," I said, trying to decide which way to play this. "They have a new dog that they're thinking about getting rid of. I was going to see if I wanted him."

Red-hair flopped back down on the other side of the hill, and Dark-hair, still nursing his burnt fingers, moseyed over to stand next to his buddy.

"Wouldn't catch me goin' over to that crazy dude's place for nuthin'," said Red. They definitely knew Lonnie then.

"How come?" I prodded, relaxing and acting as if it was perfectly normal for me to be strolling through these woods.

"Dude's crazy," the other one confirmed.

"Mean sonvabitch," intoned the first. They weren't telling me anything I hadn't already figured out. "Hope they let you have Little Dude. I feel sorry for him."

"Yeah, me too," I said. "So, you wouldn't happen to know if his wife works, would you?"

They exchanged glances and shrugged bony shoulders at the same time. "Don't know. She used to work at the Sack-N-Save, but I don't know if she still does."

I glanced at my watch. I needed to get moving before Lonnie got home.

"So, if I keep going this way, am I going to get to their house?"

"You'll come out behind the aunt's house. They're just to the right. Although I wouldn't let Crazy Dude catch you near his workshop. He gets really mad about that."

They both laughed, but it was a fearful sound. "What's in the workshop?"

Red-hair picked up a twig and started swirling it in the air. Dark-hair kicked at a weed. At first, I thought they weren't going to answer.

"Doesn't seem like much," said Red. "Just some tools and stuff. An old TV and some beer. You know, shit like that."

"Woulda thought he had something really amazing in there, as mad as he got when he saw us lookin' in the window."

"What'd he do?" I asked.

"Freaked out."

"Came after us with a shotgun."

"Fired at us too."

Lordy. This man was insane. "You're kidding! Geez, he must be crazy." I started kicking at a weed myself. Maybe this wasn't such a great plan I had. I needed to get Henry out of there, but I didn't want to get killed doing it. "Well, that doesn't make me feel much better."

"Sorry," said the dark-haired one. "I hope you get the dog.

It would be better for everyone." He looked me straight in the eye, and I was struck at how beautiful his eyes were: a warm brown, with eyelashes to die for.

"Thanks. If you hear shots, call an ambulance." I gave a nervous laugh and continued on my way.

The faster I did this thing, the faster I'd be done. Snakes didn't hold the terror for me that they had just moments before, and I crept forward through the dense brush. The path petered out at a stand of dense bushes, but I could see a clearing through the branches. I stood quietly, trying to get my bearings. Directly in front of me, about twenty yards away, was the house the kids had told me about.

The windows had heavy blinds drawn across them, and just outside the back door was the car on blocks that I had seen from the street. It had a desolate air, as if no one lived there. The kids had called it the aunt's place. Whose aunt, I wondered. I felt strangely comforted knowing that those kids were in the woods behind me. Perhaps they'd come save me if Lonnie peppered me full of holes. Then again, they'd probably already packed up their ciggies and headed home for dinner.

To the right was the back of the Lotts' house. I couldn't see the whole driveway from this angle, so I worked my way through even heavier brush farther along the yard. Twigs snapped under my feet, and I froze as I heard Henry set up a frantic barking. Shoot, he'd heard me, but he didn't know it was me.

Be quiet! Be quiet! Be quiet, I thought sending him frantic brain waves. It didn't work. He continued to bark. If anyone was home, they were obviously alerted to my presence now. I crashed a little more quickly along the back, wanting desperately to see if there was a car in the drive. Cherilynn was probably loading up the buckshot right now.

I finally worked my way to a point where I had a clear view of the driveway. Nothing but Henry and his rope. I hesitated only a second before dashing forward towards the little ball of fluff. As soon as he recognized me, his bark went from watchdog low to high-pitched squeal.

"Shush! Shush!" I said, kneeling down beside him. He jumped on my legs, crawled up my chest, and almost knocked me over in his excitement. His legs were getting tangled in the rope and he fell off me into the dirt. I tried to slip the rope over his head, but they'd tied it too tight.

I glanced over at the house to make sure there wasn't a shotgun aimed at my head, but so far so good. The kids two doors down had given up on their tag game, or maybe the girls had just stopped screaming over the dangling thing, because I couldn't hear anything from that direction either.

I needed to get Henry out of here. The other end of the rope was tied to a metal pipe that curved out of the ground. The knot on that end was secure as well. I pulled the clippers from my pocket and went to work on the rope. It was thicker than I'd expected, and I worked frantically, desperate to get him out of here before either of the Lotts got home. Henry wasn't making it easy for me—he kept wrapping his front paws around my neck and trying to crawl up my chest with his back paws. His back feet found purchase on my cutting arm and kept kicking me away from my task.

I'd just cut through the first strand of rope when I heard a car coming down the street. I plunked him back on the ground and raced towards a shed about ten yards away. This must be the shed Red and Dark had warned me about. Oh well, nowhere else to hide. Henry ran with me until the rope ran out and he twanged harshly backwards, choking himself as he fell. I made it around the side of the shed just as the car pulled into the driveway. It was Cherilynn coming home.

CHAPTER NINE

True to form, Cherilynn didn't look like she was in a very good mood. She slammed the car door with excess force and stomped across the rocky patch of yard to the front door, which she entered and slammed with the same degree of force she'd used on the car door. I suspected the car was built better and would stand up longer to this type of abuse. The house was questionable.

At least she hadn't even spared a glance for Henry. He was still straining at the rope, trying to get to me. If she looked out a window, we were done for sure. She would surely come out and look to see what he was after. I did a careful study of the side of the house. Two small windows overlooked this part of the yard, one blocked by a window unit air conditioner. The other was towards the back of the house, and I had no way of knowing what room it was in. Hopefully not the kitchen. The window was so grimy and dark that I couldn't even see if there were curtains across it.

I didn't have a choice but to keep trying to cut through the rope that was holding Henry. A quick glance at my watch urged me forward. I had to be gone before Lonnie got home. Cherilynn might have been one of the meanest women I'd ever met, but she didn't frighten me in the primal way that Lonnie did. He made me understand how Addie felt when she raised the fur along the back of her neck.

The piles of junk presented a new challenge for me, and I picked my way around rusty paint cans, abandoned tires, pipes of all sizes and even dented realtor signs, careful not to kick anything inadvertently and advertise my presence. Henry was so overjoyed to have me back that I was terrified he'd start his joyful yowling again. I clamped an arm tightly around his neck, trying to keep him still while I sawed viciously at the rope. He must have sensed my fear, because he remained silent, hiding his head under my arm.

My heart hammered almost out of control, and droplets of sweat collected under my windbreaker. The gardening clippers had been a mistake. What I needed was a serrated knife. I thought about all the junk surrounding me, wondering if there was something that would do a better job, but I was afraid to waste any more time.

Sawing, chopping and pulling at the rope finally got me most of the way through it. I was down to the last strand when I heard the rumble of an approaching diesel engine from about a block away. Damn! Lonnie.

Holding tight to Henry, I gave a final jerk on the rope. It didn't break, and I frantically pulled and tugged trying to break it free. Standing up and holding the dog under one arm, I pulled harder, ignoring the rope burns cutting into my fingers. Henry began to struggle and whine, feeding my frenzy.

I heard the front door bang open as the diesel engine came closer.

"You, girl!" Cherilynn spotted me and her shoes slammed against the rotting porch boards as she came towards me. I didn't bother to look up. "You get away from here! I told you to leave that dog alone."

Grunting now, I sliced and pulled at the final thread. It finally broke loose and I turned to run with Henry. I just wanted to be out of sight before Lonnie saw me.

"Here," I shouted tossing a hundred-dollar bill behind me as I started to run. I'd been planning on leaving that behind, maybe tucked behind a rock so that it seemed more like I'd bought the dog rather than stole him.

Cherilynn was no fool. She knew exactly what was floating in the air, and she shut up right away. I ran around the side of the shed and sprinted towards the neighbor's yard, hoping to make it into the back woods before Lonnie pulled into the drive. I was also hoping that Cherilynn would pocket the money and tell him the dog had just gotten away, but I couldn't count on that. She could conceivably pocket the money and still send him after me.

I tucked Henry under one arm like a football and crashed through the row of bushes into the blessed cover of the trees, using my other arm to brush aside branches that threatened to poke my eyes out. I didn't care how much noise I made, I just cared about making tracks out of there. The path was hard to spot, since I'd entered the undergrowth from a different angle, but I pushed forward, forging my own trail. My breathing was so loud that I couldn't hear if anyone was coming after me.

The fear of a shotgun blast made me glance over my shoulder to see if Lonnie was coming. I didn't know why they were so fired up about keeping this dog when they obviously had no interest in him, but sitting down to discuss their motivation probably wasn't going to happen.

Dead leaves covered the ground, and I never even saw the tree root that snagged my foot. I flew forward like a wide receiver headed for the end zone, football firmly clutched in one arm. Even as I fell, I knew I had to protect Henry. If I fell directly on him, I would hurt, if not kill him. I twisted in midflight and braced my free hand in front of me to break my fall.

A branch raked across my face, and I landed heavily on my hand. A sharp pain radiated up my wrist and the skin peeled back from my palm. My knee hurt too, but as far as I could tell, Henry hadn't even touched the ground. I got back up and kept running. I had to get to my car. Hair from my ponytail was coming loose and falling into my eyes. I realized that I'd lost my baseball cap somewhere along the way, but there was no time to look for it now. At least it was just a plain Astros cap, one of millions in the city.

I passed the overgrown dirt piles, not bothering to see if the boys were still there. Shouts of "Way to go, dude!" cheered me on. I guessed they were still there and approved of my purchase. The trees thinned as I got closer to the street and I slowed down. Lonnie could have easily driven around the block and might even now be waiting for me. Conflicting thoughts raced through my head. I wanted to run straight to my car, get in, head back to the city and never come this way again. But what if he was waiting? I couldn't lose Henry now.

I crouched behind an overgrown crepe myrtle that had never been trained as a tree. Its thick foliage provided a good cover, but at the same time, I couldn't see past it very well. Holding my breath, I listened for the roar of a diesel engine. Nothing. Henry's tail thumped against my hip at the same time a twig snapped directly behind me. I whirled around and clutched the dog to my chest with both hands, ready to defend him.

"Dude," said the red-haired kid. "Sorry. Didn't mean to scare you."

His dark-haired shadow nodded in agreement.

"You scared the hell out of me," I said in a raspy whisper.

They both crouched a little closer. "Why are you whispering?" Dark-hair crept closer. "You didn't really buy that dog, did you?" he asked.

"I sort of did," I said. "I took him and I left them money."

"Works for me," said Red.

"Hey, could I get you guys to do me a favor?" I asked. I glanced towards the street but still couldn't see past the crepe myrtle. Henry was wagging furiously in my arms, straining his neck as far as he could, trying to reach the nearest boy. They both held out their hands and let him sniff them.

"Little Dude," the one said, stroking his side gently. "Good getaway."

"Yeah, that's the thing," I said. "Mr. Lott was just pulling into his driveway when I got out of there. His wife saw me, but I'm hoping the money'll keep her quiet. But I'm not sure. I need to make sure he's not waiting out there on the road for me. Could one of you, like, casually walk out there and see if anyone's waiting for me?"

They exchanged glances.

"You could just walk out there, see if he's there. If you see him, keep walking. His wife saw me take the dog, so it's not like he's got any reason to stop you. And if you don't see anyone, just come back and let me know."

They looked at each other again, and at the same time balled up their fists for an impromptu game of rock, paper, scissors.

"One, two, three, go!" they shouted at the same time.

Red smacked his fist with rock, and Dark opened with paper. Dark smiled.

"I won," he said, then clouded over with uncertainty. "But does that mean I stay with her or go?"

"You win," said Red. "You get to stay with Little Dude and the rescuer." He took a deep breath. "I'll go." Squaring his bony shoulders, he strode forward out from the shelter of the trees. I could see the yellow of his t-shirt through the branches, then that disappeared too.

His friend was nervous for him, and he snapped a branch off the crepe myrtle, twirling and picking at it, the whole while never taking his eyes off the departing back of Red.

"What's your name?" I whispered.

"Todd," he answered in a similarly muted whisper.

"And your friend?"

"That's Shaun," he said. "We've been best friends since we were like two."

"I'm Jessie," I said, even though he hadn't asked. I suspected he wasn't being rude, just distracted.

"Oh, yeah. Nice to meet you," he responded, flummoxed and ill at ease with my adultness for the first time.

"I really appreciate you guys helping me out," I said. Henry was being very calm in my arms, happy to be away from his stake. "I just couldn't stand to leave him back there."

Todd ruffled Henry's silky ear. "Yeah, we felt sorry for him as soon as he showed up there. But we never thought about trying to get him. We figured Mr. Lott would kill us if he knew we touched something of his."

"Do you really think he'd kill you?" Maybe the police wouldn't have to look any farther for Dayna's killer.

We saw the yellow shirt coming back towards us and we crouched lower until Shaun came around the side of the bush to give us an update. Henry wriggled and thumped his tail in greeting, but stayed silent.

"I don't see him anywhere on the road," he whispered, his eyes straying nervously to the shadowy brush behind us. It took an effort for me not to turn and look over my shoulder. Todd didn't make the effort, because his thin neck whipped around to look behind us. We all stopped breathing at the same time, listening for stealthy footsteps or the cocking of a shotgun. "Do you want us to go with you to your car?" he asked.

I did. I did want them to come with me to my car, and perhaps ride along with me until I was safely out of here. "No, that's okay," I told them. "If I do run into Lonnie, I don't want him to see me with you. I don't want him thinking you guys had anything to do with this." From the looks they exchanged, they didn't want him to think they had anything to do with this either.

The sun was sinking, and shadows lengthened down the street and out of the surrounding yards. I crept forward out of the protection of the brush and started down the street at a brisk walk. Okay, it was more of a trot, but I just wanted to get to my car. My ears buzzed with the effort of listening, but all I heard was the crunch of my own shoes on gravel and the hum of highway traffic in the distance.

Around the bend, I could see my car, wedged in next to the dumpster, just as I'd left it. At the last house before the Chicken Shack, I heard a truck rolling slowly up the street behind me. Without looking behind me, I dashed up the driveway. If I could make it around the back of the house, whoever was in the truck wouldn't see me. It might not even be Lonnie, but at this point, I was spooked.

The driveway was pitted and weedy as if seldom used, and angled up to the house at a slight incline. I ran as fast as I could and hoped we weren't going to run into someone's guard dog. As I raced around the back of the house, I heard the truck stop out front. The back screen door opened slowly, and a short, round woman with gray hair and a loud-print house dress beckoned me in.

"Come on," she hissed. "Come on."

Ignoring all childhood training, I raced right into this stranger's back door. I barely had time to register an outdated kitchen before she hustled Henry and me down a dim hallway and into a back bedroom.

"Stay right there," she instructed in a husky whisper. Someone was pounding on the front door, shaking it on its frame. "Well, hold on there," she shouted. "Give an old lady a chance to get there, will ya?" Her frantic race to get me down the hall slowed to a sedate crawl as she ambled to the door, slippers scuffing along the wood floor. By the time she reached the front door the pounding had stopped. She began calling out, "Hello? Hello?" The screen door banged shut behind her as she stepped outside, still calling.

As small as Henry was, he was starting to get heavy, and my arm muscles were getting fatigued. I shifted him to the other arm, wincing at the pain in my wrist. I glanced nervously around the small room, wondering if I'd made a good move or if I'd trapped myself. One small window overlooked the back-yard, and I made my way over to it. Based on the thick paint surrounding the edges, if I had to get out this window, I'd have to bust through the glass.

A moving shadow drew my attention through the window to the yard. A large hulking figure was moving briskly around the backyard, swinging a two-by-four towards every bush he encountered and poking it into the dark spaces of overgrown brush. He was wearing the same coveralls he'd had on the last time I'd seen him, and if I had to guess, I'd say he had the same dangerous-looking steel-toed boots on too.

"Lonnie Lott, what are you doing in my backyard beating my bushes? You stop that right now." My rescuer, nearly two feet shorter than her trespasser, advanced on Lonnie like a general in full charge. I halfway expected her to grab him by the ear and hustle him away, but she stopped short of that. He stopped swinging the board and mumbled something I couldn't hear. Henry started to whine.

"Shush," I murmured. I wasn't sure how good the insulation was in here, and in spite of her bravado, I wasn't sure that little old lady could protect us. I'd dropped down on the floor to the side of the window, but now risked a little peep through the glass. Lonnie was mumbling something and swinging his board back and forth.

"I don't see any dogs running around back here."

"Well, I saw someone run up your driveway just a minute ago." He was getting agitated. Not a good thing.

"I've been sitting by that front window all afternoon. I think I would have seen if someone was running around my driveway." She paused and shoved her face towards his, trying to make eye contact, but his head dropped and bobbed to the side. He started mumbling again, then pulled a rope out of his pocket and held it towards her. Squinting through the streaked window, I could just make out that it was probably the rope that had held Henry.

My rescuer took it in her hand and held it close to her eyes to examine it. "Well, dogs shouldn't be tied up. You should know that," she scolded. "I wouldn't blame him if he chewed through it. Now go home and have a nice dinner with Cheri-lynn. She's probably still busted up over her sister's death."

Lonnie glanced towards the house, and I dropped back down under the sill. Hopefully it was too dark for him to see in. The shadows were getting darker and I could barely make out the surrounding lumps that were furniture. I heard more mumbling on his part, and a softer feminine response, but the voices were moving farther away.

The floor pressed hard against my tailbone, my arms were tired, my knee and wrist were beginning to throb and fatigue washed over me like a thick heavy wave, pinning me in place. I needed to get up. I needed to get home. I wanted to go to bed. Henry settled against my chest like a warm pillow, happy to be held, and it seemed like entirely too much trouble to get to my feet.

The screen door screeched and slammed at the same time Lonnie's truck roared to life on the street. He was gone. Thank God. The slippers shuffled down the hall and a form loomed in the doorway.

"He's gone," she said. "You can come out now."

I hauled myself to my feet, once again picking up Henry. Surely, he must be getting tired of being held by now, but he seemed content. My left leg had fallen asleep and I limped on it as hundreds of ghostly needles shot through my foot.

"Thank you so much," I said as we made our way back down the hall towards the kitchen. She hit the switch on the wall and the kitchen sprang to life in a warm yellow hue. "I really appreciate you letting me in." She went to the sink and filled an old-fashioned teapot with water, then shuffled to the stove and turned on the burner.

"Well, you looked like the demons were after you, and when I saw Lonnie's truck, I figured in a way, they were." She smiled up at me and reached out with gnarled hands to pet Henry's head. "He's a sweet boy, isn't he?" Henry wagged in agreement. "You can put him down if you want, I don't mind."

I wondered vaguely about when he might have last tinkled, but decided not to worry about it. My elbow was stiff from holding it in one position for so long, and I flexed my arm after setting him down.

"I'm Melba, by the way," she said, patting her gray curls. *Melba toast*, I thought. "Like the toast," she said, smiling, obviously having heard that probably a million times before.

"I'm Jessie," I said, smiling back. "Not like anything I can think of offhand."

"I have a sister Lorna," she said. "Like the Lorna Doone cookies. Mother certainly liked her snacks." She bent down with some difficulty to pet Henry. "And what's his name?"

"Henry," I told her.

"That's a fine name for a fine dog," she said. Henry stood on his hind legs and stretched up her house dress towards her face. He opened his mouth in what looked like a wide grin and let his little pink tongue loll out the side of his mouth. "Oh, he's a character," she said, obviously taken by his charms. "Reminds me of my Prince. Lord, how I loved him." She straightened back up and retrieved two mugs from a cupboard over the stove. "Cup of tea?" she asked.

Darkness was falling fast and a chill seeped into the room from the back door. I wished I was home, curled up in my reading chair with Addie warming my feet on the ottoman. But looking at Melba's sweet face, it seemed unkind to say no. She had, after all, taken me, a total stranger, into her house and hidden me from Lonnie. In so doing, she had also saved Henry.

"That would be really nice," I said. Henry was happily sniffing his way around the floorboards, tail wagging and back end sashaying along with a wiggle. At least it didn't seem like he'd been hurt or abused in his short time with the Lotts.

Melba shut off the teakettle just as it started to scream, and poured the steaming liquid over two Lipton tea bags. We sat down at a black-and-white speckled Formica-and-chrome kitchen table that looked like it had been sitting there since the fifties. It probably had. I curled my fingers around a thick white ceramic mug that said "Welcome Friend." Melba's pale blue mug proclaimed "Knitting Queen."

It had been a long day, and the adrenaline rushes that had kept me going this afternoon were fading away, leaving me feeling flat and tired. Melba sipped her tea quietly, watching me curiously over the rim of her cup.

"Henry belonged to my former boss," I began, feeling I owed her an explanation in return for her hospitality. "She called me the day she was killed and wanted me to go walk him. I found her dead." I took a sip of my tea, blocking out the unbidden image of Dayna's dead face. "I didn't know what to do with Henry. Dayna's husband didn't want him." Henry, breaking from his exploration of the kitchen, trotted over for a petting. "He really is a sweet little guy. Then Cherilynn called and said she wanted him. Well, being that she was Dayna's sister, of course I took him to her." I paused, not sure what this woman's relationship was to the Lotts.

"It must have been hard finding Dayna like that," she said. "It's a terrible thing that happened. I've known Cherilynn and Dayna since they were kids." She paused, staring off into her memory. "Their aunt Edith and I were best friends from way back. She pretty much raised them after their momma ran off. She did the best she could with them. It wasn't easy for her." She took another sip of tea and leaned back in her chair.

"Dayna. Well, Dayna always did think she was too good for this place. And Cherilynn, well, I know how she probably comes off to strangers, but really, she's a good person. Edith set Cherilynn and Lonnie up in that little house next to her after they married. And once she got sick, Cherilynn took care of her. She couldn't have taken better care of Edith if she had been her real mother." I was having a hard time reconciling this picture of Cherilynn, but then I'd only seen a part of her. Admittedly not a flattering part.

Henry finished his exploration of the kitchen and sprang up into Melba's lap, settling into a tight little ball. She gave a pleased little laugh and began stroking his fur with methodical strokes.

"So, you took this little guy to Cherilynn, and yet here you come today, running away with him and Lonnie hot on your heels." Her eyes were bright and alert, like a child who couldn't wait to hear the end of the story.

"I love dogs," I said. "In fact, I started a dog biscuit business a few months ago." Henry perked his ears up and watched me like he too was engrossed in my story. "The day I handed

Henry over to Cherilynn, well, you're right, she didn't make that great an impression on me. Mostly it seemed like she didn't know anything about having a dog or taking care of one. Yesterday I showed up at their house to check on him and see how things were going." And found a sweet house dog with a rope tied too tight around his neck, no water, no shelter.

"Well, I know for a fact that Cherilynn's got no real experience with animals," said Melba. "As for Lonnie, I don't know, but I'm willing to bet you dollars to donuts he doesn't have the patience to take care of an animal."

"Henry was tied to a rope in the yard. He didn't have any water, no food, there wasn't even shade for him to lay in. I know it's not that hot now, but if that's how they were planning on keeping him, I couldn't leave him like that. It's just not right. And he seemed terrified of Lonnie. I don't know if he hit him or kicked him, but Henry cowered as soon as he saw him."

Melba gave a sad little sigh. "I like to think the best of people," she said. "But he does have a temper. And it's usually bad. I hope he's not treating Cherilynn poorly. She wouldn't tell anyone if he was. She's too proud. Lonnie's a regular bully. He backs down if you stand up to him, but I don't know that I'd push him too far." She leaned over and kissed Henry's head. "Anyway, I'm glad you got this little one out of there. Are you going to keep him?"

I thought of Addie waiting at home, and the jealous streak she had. "I've already got a dog who runs my house," I said. "But I'll keep him until I find someone who'll take good care of him." Maybe Evan. If not, I'd check with my contacts at the doggie daycares and spas on my next round of biscuit deliveries. I'd take Henry along with me. Once they saw his cute face, he shouldn't be hard to place.

I still didn't have a leash for Henry, so once again I had to carry him. My arm was going to be sore tomorrow. Melba walked with us down to the end of her driveway and watched all the way down the street until I made it to my car. The streetlights were far apart out here, but there was one in front of Melba's house, and I could see her standing in the glow of yellow-amber light. As I opened the door and let Henry into the backseat, I saw her give a little victory punch in the air with her arm.

CHAPTER TEN

The ride back to the city seemed long, and my eyes were fatigued from staring at headlights in the rearview mirror, trying to determine if anyone was following me. I'd maneuvered abruptly away from at least four pickup trucks that I thought might be Lonnie, causing other drivers to stare at me like I was drunk or crazy. I wasn't drunk, although at this point I wasn't sure how far I was from crazy.

Once we reached speed on the highway, Henry began digging at my backseat upholstery, trying to incise a little nest for himself. I told him to knock it off, and he complied by throwing himself down with a loud sigh. I guessed we were both feeling a little frayed. The dashboard clock showed it was only a little past six. I'd thought it had to be at least eight o'clock by now. Maybe I'd call Evan when I got home to see if he'd take Henry for a couple of days. My gut told me it would be better if Henry wasn't at my house, in case Lonnie or Cheri-lynn came looking for him. Then I could truthfully say I didn't have him.

The windows of my house were dark, and I felt a jab of guilt at having forgotten to leave any lights on for Addie. She hated being left in the dark, and on top of that, here I was bringing Henry into her house again. My headlights cut a swath of light across the driveway, picking up two figures standing just outside my neighbor's front door. I hit the button on my garage door remote and waited impatiently for it to go up. I wasn't up for the dog-hater tonight. One of the figures waved at me, and I squinted into the darkness, trying to make out why it looked familiar to me.

It was a woman wearing a skirt that came just past her knees, and what looked like a sweater almost as long. My neighbor's porch light was behind her, putting her face in shadow, although I could make out a pair of glasses that had reflected my headlights.

Henry bounded up in his seat, paws against the window and began barking in loud, high-pitched yelps towards the figure.

"Oh my God, you have got to be *kidding* me!" my neighbor shouted when he heard Henry. "Tell me you are *not* bringing another damn dog home!"

"Young man! Do not take the name of thy Lord in vain!"

Of course, it was Naomi.

"And that language! You should be ashamed of yourself. Didn't your parents teach you not to swear?"

I took advantage of the diversion to pull into my garage and contemplated closing the door behind me. I was definitely not in the mood for a visit from Naomi. And what the heck was she doing here, anyway?

I could hear her still squawking at my neighbor when he slammed his front door. It was the first decision he'd made that I agreed with, but alas, Naomi was still standing in my driveway, and I'm afraid I was raised better than that.

I got reluctantly out of the car, pulling an even more reluctant Henry with me. Addie began barking inside, and Henry kept up his high-pitched yelping at Naomi, although now that he didn't have the protection of the window, he'd stopped his lunging. The noise of the two dogs combined was maddening.

"Shush," I said to him, holding him tightly against my chest.

Naomi edged into the garage and eyed him as if he was something disgusting I'd just pulled out of a clogged pipe. Her lips were moving in silent words and she moved a hand up along her already slicked-back hair. Maybe she was saying a special blessing for one of God's creatures, but I doubted it. Maybe she and my dog-hating neighbor had more in common than I would have thought. I waited for her to explain why she was here. We weren't friends when I worked with her, and beyond her telling me that sinners get what they deserve when Dayna fired me, we hadn't spoken since.

"Jessie, it's nice to see you," she said, sounding prim. Her stubby fingers moved away from her hair and began picking at the folds of her sleeves; her wide nose wrinkled as if she smelled something bad. I took a quick sniff of the cool night air but only smelled the lingering exhaust of my car.

"You too, Naomi." I generally try not to lie, but manners are manners.

"I guess you're wondering what brings me to your house," she said. She straightened her shoulders and sucked in a big breath. "I understand that you were the one who found Dayna, and I was concerned for your well-being." Her eyes darted around the garage, never settling on any one thing for more than a second. She looked everywhere but at me. If I didn't know better, I'd think she was on drugs.

The garage light clicked off, plunging us into darkness. Henry went silent against my chest and I kicked a leg towards the sensor, triggering the light to come back on. In that split second of darkness, Naomi had moved a few paces closer and I backed away reflexively. I don't like most people in my personal space, particularly when they creep up into it.

"I'm fine," I said, backing slowly towards the door. Addie was whining inside, wondering why I wasn't coming in. I had no intention of inviting Naomi into my house. "Thanks for coming."

She took another step closer and Henry started to growl low in his throat. His whole body vibrated, but I was afraid that Naomi couldn't hear him. I shifted him up a little, hoping to make him sound louder, and hoping he'd start showing teeth soon.

"It must have been very traumatic for you," she said softly. Her eyes were on me now, and I was wishing they'd start darting around the garage again instead. I'd forgotten what a pale shade of gray they were, as they peered at me from behind gold frames. "Do you want to tell me about it?"

"No, not particularly," I said. "I already told the police all about it. I think that's enough. But again, it was nice of you to check on me. It's been a long day, though, and I need to feed the dogs."

I waited for her to take the obvious dismissal, but she continued to stand rooted.

"I've missed you around the office," she said. Well, that was a news flash. I was pretty sure she'd despised me as she did most of the others there.

"Yes, well, I'm happy with my decision and it definitely turned out for the best." I inched backwards towards the door. If she would just step back out of the garage, I would hit the button and close the door. Instead she inched closer again. I could smell her breath, which wasn't pleasant, and I was beginning to get irritated.

"God wants what's best for His children," she said. "And I want what's best for you too."

I was tired. Physically tired. Mentally tired. I wanted to put Henry down because my arm was beyond tired. And crazy

Naomi wouldn't leave. Crankiness churned inside me, wiping away good manners.

"How's your husband?" I asked, thinking mean-spiritedly about what Evan had told me about her husband and Dayna. Naomi stiffened like she'd been shot with a thick needle.

"Why are you asking about him?"

"Just being polite," I said with a small shrug. She continued to stare at me without blinking. "Anything else I can do for you?" I asked.

"No. I was just trying to be nice, coming here to see if I could offer you the comfort of God's word." She turned around and stomped out of the garage.

I felt a little bit guilty, although it confirmed that the rumor was true, or at least Naomi believed it to be true. Closing the garage door, I let myself into the house. Addie leaped to her feet as I swung the door open, wagging furiously. She'd been lying pressed up against the door, but as soon as she saw Henry, the wagging stopped. Her mouth closed with a snap and her hackles started rising up along her back. And I'd thought maybe she'd missed him.

"Addie, be nice," I said as I set Henry down on the floor. He cowered behind my legs, refusing to make eye contact with her. Good move on his part. I moved into the kitchen, turning on lights and glancing at the answering machine. Henry rolled over onto his back, acknowledging her superiority. She circled him, staring intently and sniffing him over to assert her dominance. His tail made little thumping noises against the tile. Finally appeased, Addie turned back to me and gave me a lukewarm wag. I guess she was placing the blame for his presence with me, which was accurate.

"He's not staying forever, sweetie," I told her. "Hopefully not even tonight. I know you're an only dog. He's just going through a rough patch right now and I need to find someone nice to take care of him." Addie listened thoughtfully to all this, head cocked and ears perked. I don't know exactly how much she understands when I talk to her, but she seems to have a good grasp of English.

The light on my answering machine was blinking and I hit the playback button.

"You have one new message. Message one," said the mechanical voice.

"Hi, Jessie. This is Monique over at Urban Play Pals. I know this is short notice, but one of my customers was wanting to pick up twenty bags of your liver cookies tomorrow. She wants to give them as party favors for her Maltese's birthday party. I've only got two in stock, so I wanted to see if I could get the rest from you by tomorrow. Please let me know so I can let my customer know. Thanks!"

Oh boy. I really need to get another oven. I ran back out to the garage to check whether I had enough ingredients in the freezer. Running through what I needed in my mind, I calculated that I would need to make at least nine batches. If everything turned out perfectly, I could probably get by with eight, assuming none of them broke or turned out funny looking. Now if I only had enough liver on hand.

Poking my head into the freezer, I counted how many packages of raw liver I had. I kept the liver on one shelf and the salmon I used on another. Luckily both were fully stocked, although I'd have to add extra time for the thawing. As I pulled the bags from the shelf, I heard a scraping at the garage door. What was that?

I hadn't turned the overhead light on, and I slowly closed the freezer door, extinguishing even that small bit of illumination. The scraping sounded again. Moving slowly, still carrying the frozen liver, I made my way towards the sound. It sounded like someone was trying to slide something under the door. There was a rattle as someone grasped the handle on the other side and jiggled the door.

Lonnie! I wheeled around and headed for the kitchen, feet scraping against the concrete, not caring how much noise I made. Slamming and locking the door behind me, I dropped the frozen liver into the sink. The dogs ran over, startled by my sudden actions. I pushed past Henry's wagging butt, grabbed the cordless phone, and headed up the stairs, taking two at a time.

There weren't any windows in my house that gave a good view of the front garage area, but if I looked out my bedroom window, craned my neck as far to the left as it would go, and pressed my face against the pane, I could see some of that area. The dogs, convinced we were playing a chase game, jockeyed to get closest to me, Addie growling a warning at Henry to back off.

I pushed open a little slit between my blinds and took an initial peep out the window. Nothing. Opening the slit a little wider, I pressed my face closer to the window. The closest streetlight was burned out, and I'd forgotten to turn my porch light on, so the whole front of my house was shrouded in darkness. I watched and waited until my eyeballs began to hurt from being turned at such an awkward angle, but there were no shadows moving that I could see. The dogs had jumped onto the bed and settled down behind me, waiting to see what we'd be playing next.

I sank down on the edge of the bed and Addie scooted over towards me, placing herself between me and Henry. She dropped her ears back into their relaxed position and rolled slightly sideways exposing her belly for me to rub.

"I know I heard someone out there," I told them. Henry wagged but stayed where he was, careful not to infringe on Addie's domain. Someone had definitely been trying to lift my garage door. I'd assumed it was Lonnie, but how would he know where I lived? He probably didn't even know my name unless by some stroke of luck Cherilynn had remembered it. I hadn't heard that big diesel engine, but he could have parked farther down the street.

Maybe Naomi was out there. Somehow the thought of her creeping around was even more disturbing than that of Lonnie with his silent, dark anger. Why had she come by tonight? I flopped back on the bed, hunger pangs gnawing at my stomach, but fatigue winning out. Naomi had always set off my uneasy-meter with her fanatical ways and intolerance of pretty much everyone. It surprised me that Dayna had put up with her for as long as she had. But in spite of Dayna's forceful management style, perhaps she'd been afraid to let her go in case it was viewed as religious discrimination. Although if you asked me, I'd say it was Naomi creating a hostile working environment, not the other way around. I thought of the note I'd found in her trash the day I went to pick up Dayna's key—something about liars burning with brimstone and fire. That was the sort of thing that kept people from asking her to do things that she should have been doing. No one wanted to get close to a looney.

If Dayna really had been inappropriate with Naomi's husband, I could only imagine what Naomi would do about that. Would she divorce her husband? Would she kill Dayna? Naomi wasn't as tall as Dayna had been. I would have thought she wasn't as strong either, but she was stocky, and who knew what someone in a crazed rage could do? If she took Dayna by surprise, she could have knocked her over and dazed her. I thought back to the bluish face. I'd spent the past few days trying to forget it, and I didn't want to start thinking about it now, but it looked to me like she'd been strangled. Of course, I'm no expert in death, nor did I want to be, but it didn't take a forensics expert to put together the blue face together with strangling. The police would know the cause of death by now, but I hadn't seen any reports of it on the news. Maybe Dayna had already had her fifteen minutes of fame and everyone had lost interest. Everyone but her family and her killer.

The cordless phone I'd dropped on the bed, shrilled next to my head, nearly causing me to wet my pants. It was Evan. I told him I had Henry and arranged for him to swing by and pick him up. He agreed to take him for a few days if I would come by and walk him while he was at work. Worked for me.

I roused myself from the bed and took another peep out the window. All was still quiet, although from the swaying tree branches, it looked like the wind had picked up. I needed to get started on my dog cookies if I was going to get them done tonight.

I called Monique back to let her know I could have the cookies ready, but got voicemail. Urban Play Pals had someone on staff twenty-four hours to stay with the dogs that were boarding overnight. They even offered cage-free sleepovers for dogs who didn't like to be confined, with a person sleeping on a Murphy bed amongst the canine pack. No doubt the on-staff person was in the back, working on the dogs' dinners. I left a message to call back if they had any questions, otherwise I'd see them in the morning.

Back in the kitchen, I started the hot water running in the sink to speed the liver-thawing process and gathered all my other ingredients. Henry jumped on his little back legs, trying to reach the wonderful smells coming from the counter. Addie, normally used to this routine, was thrown off by Henry's antics. She kept cutting between him and me, knocking him off balance and finally chasing him out of the kitchen altogether.

When the liver was almost thawed, I put the first package in the Cuisinart and started it spinning. Unfortunately, neither my food processor nor my mixing bowls were large enough for me to combine batches. Oh well, I'd just have to take one at a time.

The dogs alerted me to the doorbell, which I couldn't hear

over the whirring, by running to the door and barking at top volume. I flicked off the Cuisinart and followed them. Peering through the peephole, I realized I didn't have my front light on yet. I hit the switch and saw the top of Evan's dark head bending forward.

I grabbed Henry by the collar so he wouldn't slip out the open door.

"What are you doing?" I asked as I saw Evan bending forward and peering at the bottom of his shoe. Then the smell hit me. "Oh, you've got to be kidding me." A patty of dog poop was sticking on the sole of his shoe, the remainder of the pile smooshed against the walkway.

"I'm sorry," I told him. "It's my neighbor. The guy's such a jerk. He keeps throwing dog poop over here because I have a dog. He acts like I'm responsible for every dog that does its business in his yard."

"Well, that's real nice," he said holding his foot up.

"Here, take it off and I'll clean it for you." Addie wandered out the door and around the front towards the driveway. "Hey, get back here," I warned her, but she kept going. Scooping up Henry and dumping him into Evan's arms, I chased after her. She was in the driveway sniffing the ground in front of the door. Bending close beside her, I looked along the pavement but couldn't see a thing. "Come on," I coaxed her. "Let's go see Evan." Her tail swooped up in a graceful curve and swished through the air as we headed back.

Evan was already inside sitting on the couch fussing over Henry, shoes left outside next to my mat. "Who's a good boy? Who's a good boy?" he asked in baby tones. Addie ran over wagging madly, but Evan was too busy being charmed by the new guy. I went back to the kitchen, determined not to be up all night baking, and gave Addie a tiny bit of liver to make up for Evan's slight. The Cuisinart quickly drowned out the cooing going on in the living room, but I could still see Evan's head bobbing up and down in front of Henry, lips puckered as if he'd moved on to kissy noises. It was good that he liked Henry, although I wasn't sure if he would take him permanently. He'd always said that he wasn't ready for a dog, but once he got used to the routine, I had no doubt he could do it.

The liver was still being pulverized when I saw Evan pick up the cordless phone I'd left on the couch. I switched off the processor.

"Helloo?" Evan said into the phone. He looked over at me, put a hand over the mouthpiece and whispered, "I think someone's there, but they're not saying anything." He held the phone out to me.

"Hang up," I hissed back.

He put the phone back to his ear and kept listening. Probably two minutes went by without either of us saying anything. Finally, he hung up. "They hung up," he said. "What's up with that? Is that your neighbor too?"

I hadn't considered that. I'd thought it was the killer trying to find out if I was available for being killed. It was good that Evan had answered. Maybe now the killer, if that's who it was, would think I had a big strong husband or boyfriend who wouldn't tolerate anyone harassing or killing me. Although that singsong *hellooo* of Evan's didn't inspire images of brawn.

"Check the Caller ID," I said.

"Unknown number."

"I think it's Dayna's killer calling me," I told him. Even to me that sounded slightly ridiculous in this well-lit room with two dogs and both of us. However, it had seemed perfectly reasonable to me last night when I was here alone.

Evan got up from the couch and leaned against the counter, watching me work in the kitchen. "What is that?" he asked, pointing to the pink, blobby mass in the food processor. "That's more disgusting than what was on my shoe."

"Liver biscuit batter," I told him. "I've got to make eighteen bags of cookies by tomorrow." Grasping the plastic work bowl, I scraped the contents into a waiting glass mixing bowl and began blending in the dry ingredients. It was rather disgusting looking at this point. One of the secrets of making biscuits that sell well is not just using high-quality ingredients, preferably stinky ones that dogs will love, but also making them into cute, non-gross-looking cookies that their owners will appreciate.

"Why would Dayna's killer be calling you?" he asked, reverting back to our original thread. The beauty of talking to Evan was that we could jump around topics like caffeinated kids on a trampoline and still follow each other's trains of thought.

"So that he can know when I'm home and come over and kill me."

"Has anyone tried to kill you today?" he asked with some degree of seriousness.

"I think Lonnie would have if he'd seen me take Henry. Oh, and Naomi was here right before you came over."

"Naomi? What did she want?"

"Said she wanted to make sure I was okay after the trauma I must have experienced finding Dayna's body."

"Right, like she's not happy Dayna's dead," he said, coming into the kitchen and plopping into a chair. "She's been all Miss Sunshine the past couple of days. It's really annoying."

I looked at him trying to picture Naomi as Miss Sunshine. "I just can't imagine that."

"Yeah, I don't think anyone else was prepared for it either," he said. "Chip had to ask her to quit singing because it's annoying everyone around her."

"Have they figured out who's getting Dayna's job yet?"

"They haven't announced anything, but we're all pretty sure it'll be Chip." He groaned. "I need to win the lottery. I don't think I can take it much longer. Dayna was horrible, but

Chip's going to be just as bad." He thumped his head against the kitchen table in despair.

"You can always go find another job," I told him. We'd had this conversation dozens of times since I'd left Astor Oil, and yet Evan never actually got motivated enough to do anything different with his situation. I loved him dearly but sometimes got frustrated by his lack of action.

In order to prevent another turn around the same old topic, I launched into the tale of how I'd gotten Henry. Evan was incredulous at my audacious undertaking. Thinking about it, I was too.

"So, is this Lonnie guy going to come looking for me?" he asked. I could sense him preparing to back out of our deal.

"No. He doesn't know for sure I have Henry, and he doesn't know anything about you." I pounded out another batch of dough, smacking it against the floured counter. "Besides, they don't really want the dog, they just think he might be worth some money."

"What if they think he's worth more than a hundred bucks?"

That was true. I was still afraid Cherilynn would just keep the money and tell Lonnie I'd stolen the dog. I needed to find a good home for him, and I needed to get him out of my house in case they came looking for him.

Evan made himself useful by ordering a pizza and feeding the dogs. He tried to act nonchalant, but the questions he began throwing at me indicated how nervous he was about taking care of a dog. By the time the pizza arrived and we'd eaten most of it, he'd begun repeating all my instructions, over and over as if preparing for a test. I promised him he'd be fine, then freaked him out farther as I ran through the litany of household dog killers, from chocolate to antifreeze. By the time I got around to reminding him how fast Henry could get out a door, both hands were running wildly through his hair like he was trying to stop his head from exploding. I decided to lay off the additional warnings I'd been planning on. Maybe after a couple of days he'd be ready for more.

He stayed through three batches of liver cookies before calling it a night. I packed him up some of Addie's food, dog treats, potty bags and an extra leash. Anything he didn't have, we could get tomorrow.

"So, uh, how do you get the poop into the bag?" he asked, bending over to pat Addie goodbye and not making eye contact with me. His cheeks flushed pink and I held back a laugh. His earnestness made me answer seriously.

"It's easy," I said, pulling out a bag to demonstrate. "You just stick your hand in it like this." I shoved my hand into the bag like I was trying on a glove. "Scoop the poop." I made an exaggerated motion of ladling a giant pile. "Pull the other ends of the bag up so it's going inside out. Then tie the handles together—I'd recommend tying them in two or three knots—it cuts down on the smell. And voilà. There you go."

He was watching intently like I was showing him how to perform a lifesaving technique. The dogs watched as well, looking for all the world like if they only had thumbs they would be taking care of this themselves. I could see Evan rehearsing this in his mind.

"Okay?" I asked.

"Yeah, okay," he said. He grabbed the plastic grocery bag loaded with Henry's goodies and buckled the leash onto his collar. "Oh, by the way. Dayna's funeral is tomorrow. I wanted to see if you'd like to go with me. They told us we could take off from work to attend."

He overlooks mentioning this until now? He said the service started at eleven-thirty, at a church I'd never heard of before. If I rearranged some of my dog-walking clients, I could go, but I certainly couldn't stay long. We made our arrangements and Evan left with a prancing Henry by his side.

CHAPTER ELEVEN

The next day dawned unfortunately warm and humid for October. I had been hoping to take care of my first couple of dog-walking clients prior to Dayna's service, but I could already tell that that walking dogs in this weather would turn me into a sweaty frizz-ball. Well, I had no choice. I could maneuver my schedule to some degree, but I couldn't expect an elderly dog to hold it, just to keep my hair looking good. My best bet would be to wear something appropriate for a funeral that also hid sweat stains.

Addie got an abbreviated walk before I got ready for the day. My mind flew from one thing to another as we trudged through the dark, moist morning. How had Evan fared with Henry? Was Lonnie still looking for whoever had taken him? Did he think the dog had run away? Did he know I'd taken him? Who would come to Dayna's service? She had been horrible to most of the people she'd known—was that what they'd remember, or would they remember her better points and mourn her passing?

The streets were slick with moisture, though it hadn't rained, and my rubber-soled shoes skidded as we walked. The humidity must have magnified the street smells, because Addie stopped to sniff at every little thing. I was feeling vaguely cranky, the adrenaline rush of yesterday gone, replaced by a dull lethargy, so I pulled her along on her leash, jerking her away from bushes, lamp poles and manhole covers.

I didn't want to go to Dayna's funeral. In spite of being skittish from the crank calls, I'd been fairly successful in pushing the reality of her death out of my mind. Occasionally I'd picture her face as it had been in death, but it just didn't tie to the Dayna I'd known. The dead woman had looked pitiful and fragile. Those were things that live-Dayna never would have been. Live-Dayna had been aggressive and domineering with mean streaks thrown in for good measure. But she hadn't been invulnerable. Someone had killed her.

I'd never suffered the delusion that I was invincible. If anything, I tended to think of the worst thing that could happen and then picture it happening directly to me. I couldn't watch medical shows on television because within two days, I'd develop symptoms of every rare disease they'd showcased. Escaped convicts were no doubt heading straight to my house, carjackers were waiting for my Honda, and I'd be lucky to live to forty (even though the women in my family generally ran well into their eighties or nineties). When I'd worked with Dayna, I'd second-guessed everything I did. She'd effectively wiped out the confidence I'd worked hard to build up through my years of school and work.

And if I went to her funeral, her death would be more real. Thoughts of her killer would be pushed to the front of my mind. Right now, it was kind of like a story—something I could talk to Evan about over lunch, and we could laugh over in a "what a ridiculous thing" kind of way. But someone had killed her. And I was getting anonymous calls, and the news had said that there was a witness that could identify the killer, and all in all, that seemed like a dangerous and vulnerable position to be in.

Not to mention, Cherilynn and Lonnie were surely going to be there, which could be a scene in and of itself if they decided to make an issue of me stealing their dog. Anger bubbled to the top of my churning emotions. They were the ones mistreating a dog. I didn't have proof, but Lonnie had probably been abusing him. If they wanted to make a scene, I'd make one right back. I wasn't going to hide from bullies like the two of them.

Resolutely, I marched Addie through the rest of her walk. This was something I needed to do. I needed to face Dayna's death head-on. I needed to go to this funeral and prove to myself that I was imagining that someone was after me. Killers stalking potential witnesses happened in made-for-TV movies, not real life.

I delivered twenty bags of cookies to Urban Play Pals, ran to Costco to pick up more dry ingredients, and walked my first two clients, all while wearing a black nylon dress with tennis shoes. The humidity had increased since this morning, if that was even possible, and I sat in the car after my second dog walk, trying in vain to make my hair look like I hadn't been chasing squirrels through the bushes all morning. I finally pulled it back using a black ponytail holder in deference to the next stop on my agenda.

Evan had given me the name of the church where the service was being held. I'd never heard of it, but with the number of churches Houston has, that wasn't surprising. I made my way towards downtown, dodging lunchtime traffic. Just past Montrose I found the right street and headed north, driving slowly while scanning both sides. My stomach growled loudly, and I cursed myself for not thinking to bring a Powerbar or peanut butter sandwich with me.

Ahead on the right, I saw a low-slung red brick building

with a squatty white spire on top. This must be the place. I drove past to make sure the sign said the Church of the Kingdom of Kaffe. Yep, this was it. A mini traffic jam clogged the streets near the church as people looked for parking. Groups of Astor Oil employees were picking their way down broken sidewalks towards a frosted glass door.

I circled the block, found a dirt lot behind the building, and squeezed my CR-V into a tight space between a large black Suburban and a telephone pole. Slipping off my tennis shoes, I wedged my feet into a pair of closed-toe pumps, and negotiated the pitted parking lot towards an uneven sidewalk. Hopefully Evan was waiting for me outside. I didn't feel like venturing into the heavily weighted Astor Oil crowd alone. Not that there were any hard feelings with any of them. I'd gotten along with just about everyone, with the exception of Dayna. And her sidekick, Chip.

"Hey, Jessie."

Chip Vermuellen. Great. "Hi, Chip." I glanced at him but had to turn back and watch my feet in order not to break an ankle. The glance revealed that he was decked out in a spiffy black suit with a subdued gray tie. He looked like the classic mourner, although the gleam in his eye was a clear giveaway that he was delighted at Dayna's demise.

"I thought that was you. I heard you were the one to find Dayna. I'm sure that must have been very difficult for you." I'd forgotten how smarmy his tone always was.

"It wasn't my best day," I told him, eyeing a group ahead and praying I'd see Evan.

"So, have you found another job yet?" he asked. "I always thought your work was pretty good. If you need me to, I could see if we can find a spot for you in our new organization." He actually sounded as sincere as was possible for him.

"I appreciate that, but I've started my own business and I'm doing quite well." We made our way around the corner and I was relieved to see Evan approaching from the other direction.

"Jess!" Evan shouted. Then he saw who I was with and stopped midstride.

"Ah yes, your little friend Petty," said Chip. His upper lip twitched to one side like a dog at the first sign of an intruder. "If only he had half the brains you do, I might be able to work with him." He turned to me and gave me an unexpected kiss on the cheek, sliding one hand around my waist and pulling me close to him for a brief moment. "It was good to see you. Don't forget, if you need anything, you know where to find me."

He turned and walked away from me, completely ignoring Evan as he approached. Chip was better looking than I'd remembered. His butterscotch-blond hair was expensively cut. He was dressing better (although perhaps that was just for Dayna's funeral). And he was carrying himself with an air of confidence that was new. But I knew what kind of spirit lurked inside that package, and it wasn't good.

Evan, by contrast, was looking decidedly rumpled this morning. Dark circles smudged the fair skin beneath his eyes, and his thick, dark hair fell with a weary droop over his forehead.

"What was that?" he asked in low tone through clenched teeth. He seemed uncharacteristically on edge this morning.

"Just Chip saying hello," I said, feeling defensive. "Geez, what's the matter with you?"

He ran a hand through his hair, pushing it away from his forehead, but it fell right back where it had been. "Sorry," he mumbled. "It was a long night. When are you going to find someone to take Henry?"

Uh-oh.

"Well, I haven't even started thinking about it yet," I said. "Why? Is everything okay?"

People around us were moving quickly towards the door. I glanced at my watch and saw that it was 11:30.

"I guess we should go in. You can tell me about it after."

There was a logjam as everyone tried to squeeze in through one glass door. It seemed a weird setup for a church, but maybe they had a small congregation. We finally made it through into the dark interior. I expected traditional rows of pews, but instead small tables were scattered throughout the midsized space. Instead of an altar at the front, there was a counter with twin espresso machines, glass jars full of coffee beans, stacks of cardboard cups and a glass-fronted cabinet that would normally hold an assortment of pastries and bagels. Although currently the shelves were barren, having been stripped of everything but a smattering of crumbs.

Looking around the room, it appeared the early-comers were the ones who had emptied the shelves. The tiny tables were full, and almost everyone had a large coffee and some type of pastry crammed onto the table in front of them. Evan and I made eye contact in a "what the heck is this" kind of look.

He placed a hand at the small of my back and directed me to a table shoved behind a pillar towards the rear. It appeared to be the only one not taken. Other people were leaning against the walls. Standing room only for Dayna.

We made our way down a narrow aisle to the cramped table. Wedging myself into a chair, I realized that this table wasn't taken because you couldn't see past the pillar to the front of the room. I scooted my chair as far out as I could, halfway into the aisle, forcing Evan to shift farther back into the recessed space. By bouncing up a little in my chair, and craning my neck around, I could just make out the rest of the room.

What I hadn't noticed when we'd first come in, was the large mahogany coffin on rollers to the right of the counter. A large picture of Dayna was propped on a tripod in front of the coffin and draped with flowers. It looked like an old Glamour Shot that someone had dug out and had blown up.

The noise level was quite high for a memorial service, or even for a coffee bar. Who'd ever heard of having a memorial service in a coffee bar? Especially one where the body was present. Surely there were laws against bringing dead bodies into eating establishments. Or at least local ordinances. I made a mental note to never actually eat here.

I looked around for people I knew. There was a large contingent from Astor Oil, including some of the vice presidents from other departments. They were all dressed like Chip, spiffy and expensive. I spotted most of the people who had worked directly for Dayna, dressed a little more casually. One woman even had on a festive pink dress with polka dots. Their expressions ranged from surprised shock, to downright happiness. What a tough crowd.

Cherilynn and Lonnie overhung a couple of tiny chairs at a strategically placed table in the front, nearest the coffin. I could just make out the back of Lonnie's broad shoulders as he hunched over the table. Cherilynn's matted hair was visible past his right arm. At least they couldn't see me from where they were unless they turned around and searched me out in the crowd. I felt a little more comfortable having the advantage of anonymity.

A tripod with a video camera was set up towards the far wall, aimed at the coffin, although no one was manning it. I wondered what that was for.

The oversized clock on the wall showed eleven forty. Time to get this show on the road. Evan tapped his foot in an annoying manner against the table leg, causing the whole table to jiggle. I gave him a poke and hissed at him to knock it off.

Finally, the lights began to flick on and off like an intermission warning at the symphony. A dark head crouched over the video camera and I could hear someone blowing sharp breaths into a microphone. The crowd began to quiet.

"Thank you all for coming," boomed a voice from a loud-speaker just on the other side of the pillar. I hadn't noticed the speaker, and nearly screamed aloud as it blasted into my ear. I held a hand to my heart as if that would slow the beating.

"We are here to honor the life of my wife, Dayna." Judging from the direction all the heads were facing, Daniel was speaking from the front of the coffee bar in the direction of the counter. I pulled my chair even farther to the side, crashing into Evan, who gave me a look and scooted as far away from me as possible. I could see Daniel now, holding the microphone in one hand and resting the other on the edge of the casket. The camera was pointed directly at him.

"That life was cut short by a vicious killer." The collected group grew even quieter, as if everyone was holding his breath. "I hope the killer is brought to justice soon, and I shall pray for forgiveness for that person's soul. But today, I wanted to gather those closest to Dayna and celebrate her life and the memories she left behind. As you might have noticed from the location in which I decided to honor Dayna, I wanted this to be an informal occasion. One where we can all share our memories with each other.

"We are all complex individuals, and those around us each get to know parts and pieces of us, but rare is the person who fully knows another."

Here there was a long pause as he looked around the room, letting his gaze rest on individual people for several seconds at a time. As people saw his gaze approaching, they began looking down or away like kids unprepared for a pop quiz. I felt my hands go damp at the thought of having to get up in front of these people and say something about Dayna. I wracked my brain trying to think of something—anything—nice to say, but it was coming up blank. So, like any sane person, I slid a little farther back behind the pillar and out of sight of Daniel's wandering eyes.

Judging by the silence around the room, I wasn't the only one caught off guard. A lady at the table next to us eyed my position behind the pillar enviously and shifted nervously in her chair.

Finally, from the front of the room I saw movement as someone stood and made their way through the tangle of bodies towards Daniel. Daniel took this opportunity to seize the camera off its perch and with one hand hold it up and sweep it across the crowd. Chip Vermuellen took the microphone, bowed his head and had his own little moment of silence while Daniel captured every moment. I knew he made documentaries, but surely, he wasn't creating a documentary out of his wife's funeral.

Chip was silent for several more seconds. I wasn't sure if he was showing respect or had forgotten what he was going to say.

"Dayna Burke was an inspiration to me," he began.

"Oh, please," said Evan not even bothering to keep his voice low.

Chip's head turned in our direction.

"I believe many people misunderstood Dayna. Dayna strived to bring out the best in each of us. She pushed us to excel. She delivered superior results and expected no less from everyone around her. Nothing distracted her from doing the best she could every day.

"I learned more from Dayna in the short time I worked for her than I did in all my years of school. I'm going to miss her." He handed the mike back to Daniel and shifted his eyes to the knot of vice presidents like a gymnast looking for a score.

Daniel was now in front of Cherilynn.

"For those of you who don't know Cherilynn Lott, Cherilynn was Dayna's sister. She knew Dayna from the time she was born and probably knew her better than any of us. Cheri-

lynn, would you like to get up and share some of those preco-
cious memories with us?"

I popped up in my chair, trying to see over the crowd of
heads. Cherilynn just sat there. Daniel stuck the microphone in
her face with one hand and trained the video camera on her
face with the other hand. I would have batted them both away
and kept on smacking. I felt a moment of pity for Cherilynn,
which surprised me. Obviously, Daniel hadn't filled her in on
this impromptu plan either. And perhaps she was intimidated
by the crowd. Shoot, looking at this well-heeled crowd, I would
be intimidated if it was me.

After a moment, she heaved herself to her feet and took
the microphone. She was wearing a navy-blue, polyester
dress that hung in lumpy folds around her wide belly.
Without looking at anyone, she turned to the halfway mark
between the room full of people and her sister's coffin. Then
she stared at the floor, visibly composing what she wanted
to say.

"Dayna was my older sister," she began in a voice that was
thick and raspy. "I used to look up to her when we was kids.
She was the smart one. The pretty one. And I wanted to be like
her. But she didn't never want me around." She gave a sideways look at the closed lid. Daniel bobbed and weaved in front
of her with his video camera like a paparazzo on speed. She
turned away from him.

"We didn't have what you'd call a good childhood. Our
momma ran off, and Daddy was what you'd call mean. I guess
Dayna got her mean from Daddy. 'Cause she could be mean, I
can tell you. Always thought she was better than where she
come from."

The room was silent as Dayna's coworkers tried to recon-
cile this sibling and the background she was describing with the
powerhouse they had known. I was still struggling with that
shift myself. Dayna hadn't sounded at all like this semiliterate

woman. She'd been well-spoken, confident and quick as a rattler.

"Dayna was awful smart," Cherilynn continued, finally venturing a peek at her audience. Noticing how rapt they were appeared to give her a little boost. She drew her shoulders a little straighter and continued.

"I never saw her studyin', but she always got pretty good grades. Got herself a scholarship. I was real proud of her. I never told her that." She ducked her head, and I saw what seemed like the first sign of real grief. It quickly vanished.

"Soon as she got outta high school, she was gone. We didn't see much of her after that. Came back when Daddy passed on. Didn't even tell us she'd gotten married. Guess she was afraid we'd show up at the wedding.

"Anyway, I'm kind of surprised to see this many of you today. Maybe she changed. Maybe we just never got to see it, but I personally think she was just out for herself right up till she died.

"I know she's been screwing me and my family over, and I'd be surprised if she hadn't screwed some of you over too."

Lonnie grabbed her by the wrist and pulled her down into her chair with enough force to leave a mark. She dropped the microphone and it hit the floor and rolled, causing a loud whomp to emanate from the speakers. Everyone jumped. Daniel pushed the camera in Lonnie's face and left it there until I began to fear for his safety.

Finally, someone began blowing into and tapping on the microphone. Everyone shifted their gaze to see who was next, including Daniel and his camera. I have to say, I'd never been to a memorial service quite like this before.

Naomi stood firmly on her stocky legs facing the crowd. There was a murmuring amongst the crowd from Astor Oil as they realized who was facing them. I had to guess that most of them had heard the rumors about Dayna and Naomi's husband. I hadn't seen Walter, but he could easily blend into the crowd.

"As most of you know, I am Naomi Silvana. I worked with Dayna for the past couple of years. And I must start by saying that it is *blasphemous* to have a memorial service in a den of iniquity such as this." She glared directly into the lens that Daniel had trained on her face, then gave the camera a little smack with the microphone. He jumped a bit, looking wounded before using a sleeve to rub the camera lens clean of any marks. He took a step back before lifting the camera towards Naomi again.

"I am a good Christian woman, and I try to do the will of my God. It's not always easy, but I am strong and I will do what I need to do to bring as many wayward souls into the light as I can."

At this point, there was a great deal of shifting and shuffling as people gave each other stricken looks, recognizing that they were in the clutches of a self-proclaimed preacher who was seldom blessed with such a captive audience. A few people shot looks towards Cherilynn as if they hoped she might take the stage again.

"I strove to be a role model for Dayna. I lived my faith loud for her. I turned away from her ridicule and scorn and showed a cheerful face for the Lord every day in her presence."

A cheerful face? Who was she kidding? I glanced over at Evan to see what he thought of all this, but he had slumped down in his chair, stretched out his legs and was studying his shoes as if he'd never seen them before.

"But sometimes the devil has too strong a hold." Naomi dropped her voice and leaned forward. "Sometimes he takes aim at the righteous. That's when we have to *hold fast to our faith*," she thundered. I stuck a finger in my left ear, trying to keep the eardrum from rupturing as the words blasted out of the nearby speaker.

"We must do whatever we have to, to stop the devil." Several heads popped up, including my own, at these words. Had Naomi stopped Dayna-the-devil from performing any more sinful acts on her husband? I looked around the room again for Walter, but I didn't see him. Other people were obviously looking for him as well. Remembering what a meek little man he was, I rather hoped he wasn't here; I couldn't see him standing up well to such a public scrutiny.

"It's too late for Dayna. She doesn't have any more time to make amends for her sins. But you"—she waved a finger wildly around at the room— "you have a chance to turn from the sinful path you're on. I just hope it's not too late for you too."

With that, she shoved the microphone at Daniel, withering him with a look that indicated it was indeed too late for him, and stomped out of the room. The crowd gave a collective sigh of relief. I stole a glance at my watch. It was only twelve. With all the tension we'd been treated to, it seemed like it should be much later.

"Jessie Gallagher," said Daniel from the front of the room. I looked up from my watch, shocked to hear my name and to see him staring at me from his position next to the coffin. "Jessie is the one who found my beloved wife after the life had been taken from her. Jessie, would you like to come forward and say a few words to Dayna's friends and associates?"

I sat bonded to my chair with my mouth hanging unattractively open. What was I supposed to say? It seemed like the last two speakers had pretty much covered it. She was a terrible sister who was out to screw everyone, and she was rapidly approaching her destiny in hell. What could I possibly add to that?

"I really hadn't prepared anything," I stammered, remaining in my chair. "Perhaps someone else would like to say something." The microphone was being passed hand over hand in my direction, and Daniel had his stupid video camera, red light on, pointed in my direction. He picked his way through the crowd towards me, camera still trained on my face.

"Come on, Jessie. Just a few words. I'm sure everyone would like to know about Dayna's last few moments."

The microphone was poked into my hand by a balding, flabby man that I vaguely remembered from the accounting department.

"You saw her as no one else here ever did," he said in a creepy, silky voice. "You saw her with the life gone from her body." He crouched in front of me now, and I could see the glint in his eyes as he focused on me, convinced he had some good footage coming.

I grabbed the microphone, anger surging through me.

"What is wrong with you? This was your wife, you sick bastard. This isn't some twisted, fictionalized documentary. This was the woman you married. Who was killed!" I stood up, staring down at him.

"It's pretty sad when the only one who's got anything nice to say about someone is Chip Vermuellen."

"Hey, c'mon now," I heard Chip chime in from his perch amongst the Astor Oil executives.

"Naomi was at least right about one thing," I continued to rant. "This isn't a memorial service. This is some creepy circus you orchestrated trying to drum up drama. Well, don't drum it up using me," I shouted. Throwing the microphone at him, I grabbed my purse, pushed through the crowd at the back of the coffee bar and stomped my way towards the door.

To my surprise, I heard a smattering of applause that grew into a more confident wave. I didn't stop. I just wanted to get back to my next dog client. A client who had no guile or duplicity. The more I see of people, the more I appreciate dogs.

CHAPTER TWELVE

My dog clients have always been top-rate when it comes to cheering me up, but in spite of that fact, I spent the rest of the afternoon trying desperately to rid myself of the feeling that I'd been a part of something perverse. Like having inadvertently caught a glimpse of something nasty on the internet, I just wanted to shake off the feeling that Dayna's "memorial service" had left on me.

It didn't help that I spent the day wearing a black dress and sneakers to walk my dogs. I welcomed the dog hair and the slobber onto the dark nylon as if that could banish the morning's memories, and added an old baseball cap I found under the passenger's seat in my car to my ensemble. The sweat that dotted my chest and back, causing the dress to stick to me, just added to the mood. No worries, I was going to throw this dress out as soon as I got home.

My cell phone rang several times while I was in the car between clients, and I finally turned it off without looking to see who'd called and popped it in the glove compartment. I was in no mood for people. I spent a little extra time with each of my dogs, happy to be in their cheerful company. In spite of the humidity, I got them each walked, then spent extra time petting and loving on each of the big babies.

Blue, the Alaskan malamute, finally got me out of my funk. Blue tends to be reserved, and even after six months of my walking him daily, he generally regards me with a serious look in his beautiful eyes, as if he's not sure how I ended up so goofy. I wasn't feeling particularly goofy this day. Instead, I quietly leashed him and took him for his walk. He trotted along beside me, ever obedient, but today adding an occasional glance up at my face. Every time he looked at me, I said "Hey, Blue, you're a good boy," but he already knew that. We finished a quick circuit of his neighborhood and returned to his house.

Blue lives with a young guy who has impeccable taste. Their one-story gray stone house feels like it should be out in the country instead of in the middle of West U. It's furnished in a tasteful country style and there's never anything out of place. Blue has an L.L. Bean dog bed placed near the fireplace and a basket full of toys that I've never seen disturbed. I believe they're for show.

I unleashed him and went to check his water bowl. From the kitchen, I could hear his nails click-clicking on the hardwood floor in the family room. He returned carrying a mashed, plush ladybug toy between his powerful jaws. He gave a muffled woof, and as soon as he was sure I was watching, he proceeded to toss the ladybug high in the air and catch it on top of his nose.

It was so unexpected from this dignified creature that I laughed out loud. He sat there balancing the obviously much-loved toy on his nose for another minute before giving it a shorter toss and catching it in his teeth. His mouth split wide in a dog-smile, the first I'd ever seen from him, and I ran over and gave him a rough hug.

"Thanks, Blue. I needed that."

He patiently let me finish my hug and I gave his thick coat

a last ruffle before he trotted back to the family room to replace the ladybug in the toy basket, his mission complete. Wow. I might be able to teach Addie to catch something on her nose, but it would be even better if she'd learn to put her toys away.

I left Blue an extra biscuit as thanks for his performance, and continued on my rounds with a lighter heart. Thankful once again for my new life away from the corporate jungle, I finished my rounds and headed home to my own dog. She deserved a long walk too. After that I would spend the rest of the day getting a jump on my next cookie orders. If I could squeeze in a few extra batches here and there, I could increase sales at my current outlets, and maybe find a few new places to sell my gourmet dog delights. It felt good being in charge of my own destiny. I wanted to forget about Dayna's death, and all the unpleasant people who had known her.

The light on my answering machine at home blinked in rhythmic red pulses, and I thought of my cell phone sitting silently turned off in the glove compartment of my car. My standard worry over family member well-being warred with my aversion to hearing from anyone related to today's debacle. Unwilling to lose my Blue-induced good mood, I left the machine blinking to itself while I changed into shorts, a baggy t-shirt and my New Balance running shoes.

Addie danced around the bedroom in delight as she saw me change my clothes. She understands what various outfits mean to her; these clothes meant "Addie run." She bounded from the bed to the floor and back again, tail waving frantically back and forth. Mindful of the warmer temperature and higher humidity, neither of which went well with Addie's double coat, I vowed to keep the run short. Just enough to get her some much-loved exercise and clear the final dredges of the morning off my mind.

The newest pile of dog poop near my front door nearly derailed me. Seriously, what was it going to take to make my crazy neighbor stop his infernal obsession and constant bombardment of my property? I considered the homeowner's association as I started my warm-up walk. But from the few meetings I'd attended, I didn't hold out much hope that they would be of much assistance. Surely there was a law against throwing excrement onto someone else's property. But even if there was, I certainly couldn't picture myself calling the police over this.

We broke into a slow run, Addie loping along just to my left down the tree-lined street. I banished thoughts of my neighbor. I pushed away images of Dayna. I even refused to think about who had been calling me and whether they would just go away and leave me alone, or break into my house in the dead of night and smother me with a pillow.

I concentrated instead on my breathing and the heavy, rhythmic thuds as my feet hit the pavement. Thump, thump, thump, breathe. Thump, thump, thump, breathe. Beads of sweat popped out on my forehead, and Addie began to pant as she quick-stepped her way by my side. This was going to have to be unfortunately short. What had happened to the cooler weather of the past couple of days? Just when everyone else in the country was pulling out their jackets and sweatshirts, Houstonians were still tootling around town in shorts and flip-flops.

A horn blared directly behind me, startling me and sending me careening into the curb, which I promptly fell over, twisting my ankle and landing again on my sore wrist. What the heck? I rolled over, checking first to make sure Addie was okay before hauling myself to my feet to confront the driver. Addie was fine. She'd side-hopped lithely onto the grass and was jumping up on me to check my status. As her tongue caressed my skinned palm, I turned to the street.

A black sports car with tinted windows idled in position.

"What are you doing?" I shouted at the darkened window.

A hand with a lone raised finger shot up before the car

peeled away, roaring down the street. Nice, real nice. So much for a relaxing run. I limped my way back to the house, took a long shower, and tended my wounds with ice and antibiotic cream.

It was too early to go to bed, although that seemed like my best option. Still ignoring the answering machine, I logged on to the internet. Maybe some mindless surfing would take my mind off the day until I could respectably go to bed.

Waiting for my computer to boot, I made myself a creamy peanut butter sandwich on soft white bread. Just like Frances used to make for me and my brother when my mother was off at one of her ladies' clubs. When I got back to the monitor, I saw my instant message program blinking at me as insistently as my answering machine. *Oh, why can't they leave me alone?*

It was Evan.

"I know you're there. I can see you online," came his accusatory message.

I sighed. "I'm here. I was working."

"Yeah, whatever. I've been trying to call you."

"I was out on my rounds, then I took Addie for a run and nearly got run over," I typed.

The phone rang. Checking the caller ID, I saw Evan's number at Astor Oil. I picked up.

"Did you even listen to my messages?" he shrieked without preamble. I swear, I need to work on that high-pitched thing that Evan's been leaning towards lately. It's just not attractive in a guy.

"No. Aren't you even going to ask me if I'm all right?" I snipped back.

"What do you mean? Oh," he said,, obviously reading his instant message. "Are you okay?"

"I twisted my ankle and I skinned my palm, and the same wrist I fell on yesterday got it again today. Other than that, I'm fine," I said, actually beginning to feel sorry for myself and surprised that tears were pooling in the corners of my eyes.

"Okay, good," he said, obviously not concerned or curious about how I had almost gotten run over. "Anyway, it was crazy after you left today. Everyone just got up and started storming the doors, bitching about what a joke that whole thing had been. I was going to come after you, but I got stuck in the crowd, and by the time I got to the door, I realized there was a scene going on behind me. So I kind of hung back, and that's when I saw Dayna's sister's husband just really going after Daniel."

"What do you mean going after him?" I asked as he paused to take a breath.

"He had him by the front of the shirt, and he was shaking him and banging him into the wall. Kept saying something about how his wife had taken some of their stuff and he wanted it back."

"You mean Dayna had taken some of Lonnie and Cheri-lynn's stuff?"

"Yeah. He was pissed. I thought Daniel was going to wet his pants. He even dropped his camera. It sounded like it broke."

"I wonder what stuff he's talking about," I said while my mind contemplated what Lonnie would do to me for taking his dog, which I was sure he also considered "his stuff."

"I don't know. Daniel kept saying he didn't know what he was talking about. It wasn't till Dayna's sister saw me watching them that she got her big lug to let Daniel down."

"Did anyone else see this?" I asked.

"I don't know. I think the guy that works there was keeping an eye on things. He probably has a shotgun or a baseball bat behind the counter."

To calm down all the jacked-up coffee drinkers.

"What did Daniel do when Lonnie let him go?"

"He kind of fell on the floor, but then he acted all cool like he was picking up his camera."

I was having a hard time picturing never-ruffled Daniel being manhandled like that. I'd only met him a couple of times, but he always seemed very conscious of how he presented himself: hair always styled just so, perfect five-o'clock shadow, wrinkled jeans but crisp New-York styled shirts—like a wannabe model who thinks he's a cut above the average guy. That would have been a tough scene for him to play off.

"Shoot, I wish I'd hung around." Although if I'd had been there, I probably would have been next on Lonnie's grab-and-shake list.

"Oh, hey! How's Henry doing?" Even with as crazy a day as it'd been, I couldn't believe I'd forgotten to inquire about the sweet little thing.

There was an ominous moment of silence.

"And what are you still doing at work? Who's watching him?" I asked.

Another few seconds of dead air was filled only by Evan doing a couple deep breaths.

"Well, remember we'd talked about you going by to let him out and walk him while I was at work?" Evan finally asked very slowly. "I realize that we never actually finalized that, but I was assuming you were going to do it."

Now there was more silence.

"Oh," I finally said. "I guess I forgot that part. So, you mean to tell me he's been alone in your apartment *all day*?" Uh-oh. "Um, did you at least put him in the bathroom? Or maybe the kitchen?" My voice was doing a little squeaking thing. But aside from the obvious problem of the dog needing to relieve himself, I was conjuring up all the toxic, dangerous dog-killer things that Evan probably had around his apartment.

"You didn't leave any chocolate laying around, did you? Or electrical wires?" Oh Lord, I could just picture poor Henry electrocuted and lying alone on Evan's floor, which was probably dirty.

"No, I did not leave any chocolate laying around. And I hate to point this out to you, but everyone has wires. You didn't tell me anything about wires. You also didn't tell me that that dog is crazy. He was a mess last night. He wouldn't stop crying. *All night.*" He didn't have to sound so accusatory, like that was my fault.

I tamped down my temper and ran through options in my head.

"Look, I can get to your apartment in probably ten minutes. Why don't I go over, check on him and take him out?" Now that he mentioned it, I guess I had told him that I'd go over and take care of Henry. I also had to guess that I'd need to start looking for more permanent arrangements soon. Evan was not sounding like an enthusiastic dog person.

The drive to Evan's took about twelve minutes. I worked myself up into quite a state during that time as I pictured all the horrible things that Henry could have gotten into. Maybe he was just sleeping peacefully on the couch, worn out from his night of crying. Or maybe not.

When I reached the stairs, I could hear high-pitched wailing coming from his apartment. His neighbors were not going to be happy with that. I called to Henry through the door as I fiddled with the lock.

"Hey, boy, it's okay. It's me."

The door across the landing flew open hitting the back wall with a bang, and a slim girl, maybe nineteen or twenty, barefoot and wearing a skimpy tank top and baggy pajama bottoms, stood glaring at me. She would have been cute if it weren't for the expression on her face, which was really quite hostile. Evan hadn't mentioned his cute neighbor, but maybe she was always hostile.

"Is that your dog?" she asked, spitting every word out with very precise diction.

"Well, not really," I hedged.

"Okay, I don't really care whose dog it is, I just want it gone. Like now." And she stormed back into her apartment, slamming the door hard enough to vibrate the iron railing that I was holding. Some people are so intolerant.

There was a lull in the whining when Henry first heard me, but it quickly resumed when I stopped to chat with the neighbor. I jerked past the lock and raced through the door, hoping to calm him down before that scary little woman came beating on the door. Henry switched from wailing and whining to an even higher-pitched yipping as he jumped at my knees, clearly delighted to see me.

"Shush, shush," I said, kneeling down to hug his squirming little body. He wriggled against my chest, trying to smother my face with kisses. Over the top of his head I saw mountains of white puffy clouds strewn around Evan's living room. Uh-oh.

"What did you do?" I asked him. He glanced nonchalantly towards the puffs, then resumed his attack on my face. I stood up, afraid to see how bad the damage was. Maybe it was just one pillow, although it looked like an awful lot of stuffing to have come from just one pillow.

Henry ran straight into a cloud, joyfully pulling at the fluff, tearing off a bit, then shaking it wildly back and forth as if trying to kill it. Looked like fun. I stepped carefully around the living room, noticing the fabric from a couch pillow near the window. It looked like it had gone through a meat grinder. The couch itself wasn't looking so hot either. The back cushion, which was attached to the frame, had a large section missing from the top corner, stuffing exploding out. Scratch marks snared the upholstery, and the arms had smaller bite marks as if Henry had been testing it out to find the tastiest area. Evan was going to be furious, although truth be told, I'd always thought this sofa was kind of ugly.

I shuffled along the carpet, unable to see my feet through the mess. My right toe hit something hard, and I brushed the stuffing away to find what looked like a trophy of some kind. I picked it up to examine it more closely. A gold plastic runner was breaking out of the blocks atop a wooden base. At the bottom, a small brass plate proclaimed "First Place Division 1A 100-yard meter." Oh dear. This must go with Evan's oft-told story about how he'd won some big race at a high school championship track meet. Well, really the bite marks along the base weren't that bad. Okay, maybe if I touched it up with some brown shoe polish, it wouldn't look so bad. Better yet, I thought, tossing it onto the couch, maybe Evan needed to do something new and noteworthy.

It struck me that perhaps I should take Henry out to relieve himself. He'd been alone all day and he'd gotten quite excited when I arrived. And yet, he didn't seem interested in going out. He was too busy prancing through the destruction, showing off the work of his day.

I decided to risk a quick look in the kitchen and bedroom. The kitchen seemed relatively unscathed. Besides an over-turned food bowl and a few scatterings of polyester fluff, it looked good.

The bedroom hadn't fared quite so well. At the doorway, I stood and gasped. Henry had the grace to hesitate, as if eyeing his handiwork in a new and more negative light. His tail drooped a little and he sat down sadly by my side in a scattered heap of feathers. It appeared that Evan, unfortunately, preferred feather pillows on his bed.

It's amazing how many feathers can come out of two pillows. I went to the window and opened the shades in order to better survey the damage. It looked like Sherman's army had marched through in a bad mood.

The ceiling fan whirled around overhead, doing a spectacular job of circulating the gray feathers around the room. Unable to resist, Henry snapped at a few as they floated past his nose. I flipped the switch off.

Lamp shades tilted sideways, socks and underwear scattered across the floor and shoes spilled from a partially opened closet. A line of books had tipped out of a bookcase, and the cover on the top one had been eaten clean off.

How quickly could I get this cleaned up? I should call Evan and tell him not to come home. There wasn't much I could do about the couch, but I could run out and get the pillows replaced, vacuum up this mess and get it back to some semblance of order before Evan saw it. Maybe then he wouldn't have the meltdown I felt sure was coming.

The good news was that Henry was okay. That was the important part, right?

I was still wondering what to do with the little demolition artist when I heard a key turning in the lock. Uh-oh. Evan must have decided to come home.

Henry raced me to the door and greeted Evan with wild abandon: tail whipping the air, body wriggling wildly. He obviously had no compunction about how he'd spent his day.

"Holy shit," said Evan.

There wasn't much I could add to that, so I just stood there watching him survey the damage.

"Holy shit," he said again. Henry danced on his back legs pawing the air in front of Evan, like, hey buddy—here I am!

Evan made his way to the sofa and caressed the gaping hole.

"What did you do?" he asked Henry, that screech thing making itself heard again. It finally dawned on Henry that perhaps Evan was not appreciative of his efforts and his wagging began to wane.

"Seriously, what did you do?" Evan asked him as if he might actually receive an answer.

"It's not really as bad as it looks," I started to say when I glanced over and saw Henry squatting like a girl dog and urinating all over the rug.

"Holy shit," said Evan.

I really should have seen that coming. I scooped Henry up, spotted a leash on the coffee table and ran him out the door. Obviously, it was too late. He no longer needed to go.

CHAPTER THIRTEEN

I n the end, it turned out better than I'd thought it would. By the time I got back with Henry, Evan had regained his composure and was busy filling a large black trash bag with sofa stuffing. A wad of paper towels was soaking up the urine, and actually, with the exception of the feather pillows and the half-eaten book, Henry hadn't touched anything; Evan's room apparently always looked like that.

I didn't even need to take Henry home with me; Evan said he would keep him another few days. The biggest problem would be keeping him quiet when he was alone, and keeping him out of trouble. The three of us made a trip to the nearest Petco. We decided that the best plan would be to confine Henry to the kitchen when Evan went to work, then I would come by twice to let him out and give him a couple of short walks.

I also convinced Evan that he needed to get up and walk or run Henry before he went to work, until he was tired. That would do more to keep him calm while he was alone than anything. At Petco, we loaded up with Bitter Apple spray to keep him from chewing on anything in the kitchen, two rubber Kongs that could be filled with treats, and a selection of dog toys that would hopefully give Henry an outlet for his energy.

I left the boys to their evening of cleaning and bonding and headed home once again to my own sweet Addie. My answering machine blinked with more messages. I hit the play button.

Daniel was first, apologizing for putting me on the spot this morning. He wanted to make it up to me with dinner and drinks. I'm sure he would. There were a couple of messages from Evan, giving a brief highlight of Lonnie's manhandling of Daniel, then a reminder that I was going to check on Henry, right? Whoops. Guess I should really listen to my messages in a more timely manner. Two hang-ups, a call from Chip letting me know there was still a place for me at Astor Oil if I wanted it, and finally a message from Frances, inquiring when might be a good time for me to have dinner with her. Shoot! I'd forgotten to call her.

I am total scum.

That was the only call I returned.

I'd just hung up the phone when a scuffling sounded at my front door. Addie cranked into watchdog mode, her barks nearly deafening. I'd just put my eye to the peephole when something crashed into the door, scaring me backwards.

"Hey," someone croaked from outside, thumping on the door from ground level. "Hey, you gotta help me out here."

I flicked on the porch light, my heart racing as I tried to figure out what I was hearing. What if this was one of those scams, where you hear a baby crying near the side of your house and as soon as you open your door to check it out, the home invaders force their way in? I'd seen that on the news just a couple of months ago.

"Hey, open up. It's me."

Who was "me"? It was a male voice, and it sounded vaguely familiar, but who? I stood leaning my ear against the door, wanting to pretend I wasn't home. Only I'd just turned the light on.

"Sorry," I shouted through the door. "I don't know who you are."

"Dammit." A loud groaning came through the door, followed by a scrabbling against the door. "It's Larry, your neighbor. Let me in."

Oh, right, it did sound like him. Still, better safe than sorry. Before opening the door, I picked up a silver candlestick from the closest bookcase. Maybe it was a ploy and he had a buddy out there, or maybe I'd just bash him over the head for flinging all that dog poop into my yard.

I unlocked the deadbolt and cracked the door open. Addie stood braced and growling at my side in a convincingly menacing manner. Larry pushed past me in a half crawl, half run. He was bent over at the waist, clutching his stomach theatrically. My first thought was "what a drama queen," but then I took in the sweat beading on his forehead and running down the sides of his pale face. His hair was plastered to his forehead, and his dingy gray t-shirt stuck to his chest.

Addie looked as lost about what to do as I felt. Her growling changed to an uncertain whine.

"What's wrong with you?" I asked, frightened by the possibility he might throw up in my house. This fear was compounded by the brown, chunky residue that ran down the side of his shirt and halfway down his baggy sweatpants as well. My hand flew to my nose to try and block the nauseating stench that emanated from him.

He groaned and clenched his teeth as if in pain. I could hear vile noises coming from his stomach, and I all but danced in place, trying to figure out how to help him without getting too close, and wondering how I could get him back outside. My mind raced with thoughts of horrible viruses being let loose in my house. This was probably one of those horrible Ebola type things. Maybe he'd been traveling recently. Luckier for me if it was just food poisoning. Not contagious.

Dragging himself forward, he collapsed on the couch. Addie began sniffing at some of the brown chunks that had dislodged from his t-shirt onto the carpet.

"Addie, no!" I screamed at her, lunging for her collar and dragging her away. I ran her up the stairs and shut her in my bedroom, the sounds of groaning following me all the way. I could not deal with seeing her even sniff at something so disgusting. I was going to have to have my couch taken away and burned.

By the time I got back, which couldn't have been more than twenty seconds later, Larry had burbled up another puddle of revolting brown chunks all over the rug next to the couch. The rug would have to be burned too.

I ran towards the kitchen for a bucket, but barely made it to the sink before I threw up too. I don't know how nurses or mothers do it.

"Hey," he called weakly from the couch. "What are you doing? I need help over here."

"Sorry," I said, unable to keep the sarcasm from my voice. "I'm not good with vomiting people."

"Great," he said. "You can clean up after a dog, but a sick man puts you out of commission. No wonder you're not married."

Now that hurt. My marital status had nothing to do with cleaning up after vomiting men. Larry needed to shut up, I thought. Particularly if he needed my help, and most particularly after ruining my couch and rug.

"Look, do you want my help or not? Because as far as I'm

concerned, you are not really my problem, and I don't exactly appreciate you barging in here and throwing up all over my house."

This was greeted by more hacking noises, which made me put my hands over my ears so I wouldn't have to listen to any more retching.

"Do you need me to call 9-1-1?" I shouted at him.

"Just take me to the emergency room," he moaned.

Damn. Now he was going to ruin my car too.

"Can I take you in your car?" I asked. He was looking even grayer, and for the first time I actually began to worry about him. I didn't like the guy, but I certainly didn't want him to die in my living room. "Right, never mind. Can you make it to the car?" I asked.

He made an effort to get to his feet, but slipped off the couch and landed knee-first in the brown gunk. Struggling upright, he resumed the half crawl, half run that he'd employed on his entrance. I ran to the garage door and opened it so he could get out, then raced ahead of him and opened the back car door. I'd hoped to line the whole thing with old towels, but he threw himself in too quickly. Scooping up some dirty towels from the garage floor that I used to clean my clients' feet on rainy days, I threw them in on top of Larry. He moaned and made some noises about smelling like nasty, dirty dogs, but I thought he deserved at least that for all the dog poop he'd flung in my yard. If he lived, he and I were going to have to have a talk about that.

I lived just minutes from the medical center, but I'd never deposited someone at the emergency room before. When I inquired as to what hospital Larry would like to go to, he said he didn't care, so I made my way towards the medical center and planned on finding the first emergency entrance I could.

The groaning gave me hope that he would make it to the

hospital, and when he began complaining about the cold (I insisted on driving with all the windows down to minimize the odor in my car), I was convinced he would be okay. Anyone who could complain that much couldn't be that sick.

Traffic was light in the medical district. The bustle of scheduled appointments and daily business were over, and the lull of the evening would be broken only by emergencies. An ambulance hurtled past me, sirens blaring through the windows and lights creating a strobe effect against the seats. I saw an "Emergency Entrance" sign, but missed the turn and had to circle the block, going slower this time around so I wouldn't miss it again. It was encouraging that Larry hadn't thrown up again, and hope was rising that I wouldn't need a new car, although I'd surely have to have the inside cleaned by professionals.

The emergency drive was empty as I pulled up, parked, and ran around the side of the car to extract my passenger. I thought I was at Methodist Hospital, or maybe it was St. Luke's. Oh well, it didn't really matter to me. Larry was still a startling shade of gray, and I was thankful when an orderly pushed past me and helped him into a wheelchair. He trundled off with Larry, who had resumed moaning anew, apparently refreshed by a new audience. I stood in the bright entry lights, wondering what I was supposed to do now, when an overweight security guard in a white shirt and black pants hollered at me to move the car.

The temptation to get in the car and go home warred with the thought that I should go in and check to make sure my neighbor was okay. I drove slowly away from the emergency entrance, half-heartedly looking for a parking space. Larry could be waiting in there for a very long time. And I had gotten him here, where he could get help. Did I really need to sit and hold his hand too? I thought of all the dog poop he'd flung at me in the past week. The guy really was a jerk. Not to mention the fact that I'd left Addie locked in my bedroom. What if she needed to go out? The idea of going home to her and settling in for the evening appealed quite a bit.

Half a block away, a large Suburban was backing out of a wide street-level parking space. Shoot. I sighed loudly and pulled in. The evening was cool and damp. Risking car theft, I left all my windows down, hoping the lingering smell of Larry would fade away into the night.

The quiet of the street was broken as soon as I walked into the emergency room waiting area. Glaring lights blazed down on the chaos, and the noise almost made me turn around and walk out. Overriding everything was the high-pitched wail of a baby. He looked to be about a year old, and from the intensity of the screams, I expected to see him missing a limb or two, or maybe be covered in terrible burns. But outside of the frighteningly red face, he seemed healthy enough. The young Hispanic woman who was holding him seemed deaf to his cries. Her eyes were focused, unblinking, on a spot on the floor. Around them, the chairs were full of family members sporting the same vacant look of the young woman. They all seemed immune to the racket.

Competing with his cries, a middle-aged black woman was yelling at one of the nurses behind the desk. "I will not sit down! I've been sitting down! You need to tell me when we will be able to get in to see a doctor. We've been here before a lot of other people you've been letting in. I want to know why you letting in those other people and we still sitting here?"

My eyes roved the crowd, looking for Larry. Hopefully they'd already taken him in and maybe even checked him in for the night. Then I found him. The orderly had parked him at the edge of the crowd, between a pillar and rolling cart. He was slumped dejectedly in his wheelchair, his chin falling down on his chest, a small blue basin cradled in his hands. Damn.

I made my way over and stood before him.

"Uh, hey, you okay?" I asked.

He didn't move.

"Larry?" A feeling of horror coursed through me as I considered he might be dead. "Larry!?"

People nearby turned and looked over, a mildly interesting event in an otherwise long evening for them. The nurse behind the desk shot a bored look my way, years of experience showing in her weary eyes. Even if he was dead in his chair, it wasn't going to move her one way or another.

Larry finally lifted his head. Everyone turned away, disappointed. Vultures.

At least I was alert now. The moment of fear had triggered a healthy dose of adrenaline, and as usual, the adrenaline made me irritable.

"Geez, what's wrong with you? You scared me half to death," I snapped at him.

His head rolled back down on his chest. "I need a bathroom," he moaned.

"You've got your little bucket there," I said, swinging a finger towards the basin.

"I don't think that's going to cut it," he said. Over the din of the room, I could hear more ominous rumblings from his intestines.

"Oh." I looked frantically around for an orderly or a nurse. Failing that, I ran over to the nurses' station.

"Hey, my neighbor over there needs to get to a bathroom," I said frantically trying to make eye contact with either of the nurses sitting there. Neither one of them looked up. One continued her slow shuffling of paper, the other reached for a ringing phone. "Excuse me," I said to the shuffler. "He seems to be having some sort of intestinal thing, and I think it's about to be a real problem."

She pointed a red-painted nail down the hall. "Bathrooms are that way."

I ran back to Larry, who was leaning forward over his lap, clutching his knees tightly together. He didn't look like he was going to be able to walk to the bathroom, so I darted behind his chair and gave him a push. It took several precious seconds to figure out how to get the brakes off, but once I did, we shot down the hall in the direction the nurse had pointed. An older woman with her hospital gown flapping leaped nimbly out of our way as I shot right past the restroom sign.

It took a few yards to slow the careening chair and turn it back around. The sign indicated that it was a handicap restroom, which was good since Larry was looking pretty handicapped at this point. I opened the door and shoved him in, pulling the door shut behind him. There was only so far I was willing to go to be helpful here.

I leaned against the wall outside, trying not to listen to the volatile and explosive noises coming from within. When I couldn't stand it anymore, I ambled back to the waiting area to see if a chair had opened up. No chance. I contemplated what my responsibilities were here. I'd let Larry in when he showed up at my door needing help, at the expense of my sofa and rug. I'd brought him to the hospital, where he could get the medical attention he obviously needed, and finally, I'd gotten him to a bathroom when no one else could be bothered. Okay, maybe I needed to let someone know where he was, but after that, I thought I was free to go.

The harsh lights near the nurses' station, combined with the hospital smells, were making me woozy. Not to mention the army of wounded and sick who were waiting for attention and watching me with miserable eyes. The nauseating scent of Larry seemed to be stuck in my nose, and I could feel germs flying at me from every direction, seeking a fresh victim. I needed to go home. I needed a shower. I needed to disinfect myself.

The same nurse hunched behind the counter as I approached.

"Hi," I said trying to get her attention. More paper shuffling. "Okay, I just wanted to let someone know that my neighbor needed a bathroom, and I put him in the one down the hall. He really is sick. I think maybe someone should check on him. It doesn't sound good."

She glanced casually up at me, but didn't say anything.

"Okay?" I asked. "Because I have to go, and I just wanted someone to know where he is." She kept looking at me. "Okay?"

"What's his name?" she finally asked.

"Larry." This time I netted an eye roll.

"Larry what?"

"I don't know. We're not exactly close," I said. "He just showed up at my house tonight, throwing up all over." I was feeling oddly close to tears. I am not good with this kind of drama.

"Fine. Larry is in the bathroom," she said and went back to her papers. I stood there another minute, but she had tuned me out. Great, now what? Was that good enough? I wanted to feel like someone else had picked up the Larry burden.

I shuffled slowly down the hall back towards the restroom. The door was still closed, and even from ten feet away I could hear sounds. Well, at least he wasn't dead. An orderly pushing a loaded cart ambled my way, and I waylaid him, planting myself directly in his path.

"Hi, I'm sorry to bother you," I said with my most winning, albeit pitiful smile. "My neighbor is in there, and I need to leave. Is there any way you could maybe check on him and make sure when they finally call him, he doesn't miss his time with the doctor?"

The sounds were beginning to fade slightly, and I began backing slowly down the hall towards the exit. The orderly had kind eyes and he looked resigned. I felt bad. Worse actually for him than for Larry.

"I'm sorry," I said. "I really need to go."

He sighed. "I'll check," he said.

With a small wave, I turned and fled into the blessed cool of the night.

CHAPTER FOURTEEN

I spent a restless night and woke up cranky. Friday nights are usually my best sleeping nights, but guilt over leaving Larry at the hospital, a throbbing wrist, sore ankle and sympathetic pangs of nausea conspired to ruin my sleep. I'd returned from the hospital to the mess in my living room and had attempted to clean it up, but mostly I spent a miserable half an hour racing from the living room to the bathroom gagging as I ran. Every time I approached the mess, my stomach would flip over and my gag reflex would kick in. How was I ever going to raise children if one nasty pile of vomit caused this much nausea?

I finally emptied a can of Lysol along Larry's trail and covered the whole mess with an old paint tarp I found in the garage. Tomorrow I'd call professionals who specialized in biohazard cleanup, or maybe I'd see if I could get someone to haul the whole thing away.

Addie found the tarp intriguing. She alternated between growling at it with hackles raised and sniffing from a distance, body stretched and ready for flight if the thing should try and attack.

She and I had gone out for an early walk as I tried to walk

away my guilty feelings. Surely, I was not responsible for a grown man. I was sure he was fine. I'd peered closely at his house as Addie and I walked by, but it looked as it always did, blinds down, old papers collecting on his stoop. Maybe later I'd go over and check on him.

I took a quick shower after our walk and realized that I really needed to get baking today if I had any hope of keeping up with my orders. Halfway through a batch of salmon snaps, my doorbell rang. As guilty as I'd felt earlier, now a wave of irritation washed over me that it might be Larry again. Good grief, I had work to do.

I whipped open the door with a little more force than necessary and was surprised to see two uniformed officers standing there. One was standing several feet back, arms tensed and slightly bent, as if preparing to tackle me if I should flee, while the other one smiled at me cheerfully and twirled a pen between his fingers.

"Hi," I said for lack of anything else. It flashed through my brain that they were here to arrest me for Dayna's murder. I should call my father. He would come get me and have one of his associates represent me, although this kind of publicity would not endear me to him. This was going to ruin my mother's social standing, no doubt. And Addie. Sweet Addie. I'd have Frances come get her. Addie loved Frances.

"I'm sorry to bother you, ma'am," said the pen-twirler with a heavy drawl. "We need to talk to you about your neighbor. Could we come in for a couple of minutes?"

Oh, good, it was only about Larry. Oh wait. If the cops were showing up at my door, it probably meant he was dead.

"Yes, of course. Please come in," I said, standing aside to let them in.

Addie, ever the wild-eyed greeter, bounced joyfully in front of the uniforms. Up and down. Up and down. She didn't actually touch them, she just jumped up to take a look at their faces and catch a sniff of their breath.

"Sorry about that," I said. "I haven't been able to convince her that people don't like all that jumping."

"Incredible height from a flat-footed jump," said the tall one with a note of admiration. "I don't know that I've ever seen one get that much air. Except when you see those Frisbee dogs on TV."

I shut the door and noticed the surly one had already made his way into the living room and was studying the tarp-covered sofa.

"What's going on here?" he asked, waving a hand in the direction of the tented couch. My heart flipped over with anxiety. What if Larry really had something contagious? It could already be too late for me. Then again, if that was true, I'd expect guys in white hazmat suits, not cops.

"My neighbor came over last night and was really sick. I didn't get a chance to clean it up yet."

He lifted a corner of the canvas and dropped it immediately, whipping his head around to the side and covering his nose as the smell assaulted him. Maybe it hadn't been such a good idea to cover it all up; it seemed to have fermented overnight.

"Is he all right?" I asked in a voice that was just slightly shaky.

"Yes, he'll be okay," said the nice one. I peered at the badge on his shirt. Officer R. Neal. "But we do have a few questions for you, if you don't mind." He pulled a small spiral notebook from his pants pocket that looked as if it had been rescued from a garbage bin. Flipping it open, he began tapping his pen against it.

Ever mindful of my manners, even if the other officer wasn't (now he was poking rudely around my kitchen, where he had no business poking), I asked them if they would care to sit down. Naturally I indicated the kitchen table, since I assumed they would rather I not uncover the couch.

They did not care to sit down. I followed the shorter cop into the kitchen, where I stepped between him and my bowl of salmon snap batter, but not before he'd stuck his head into the bowl and taken a sniff. This time his cheeks puffed out as he tried to control a gag.

"What is that?" His nostrils were moving erratically like he had no control of them.

"It's batter for dog biscuits," I said, sliding the bowl away from him down the counter. It wasn't that bad. What a baby. His badge said "S. Ramey." I turned and checked the batch that was in the oven. Damn, they'd burned around the edges. Punching the off button, I pulled out the cookie sheet and dropped it in the sink.

The two of them exchanged glances and Officer Ramey continued his inspection of the kitchen while Officer Neal distracted me with questions.

"So, do you do a lot of cooking, then?"

I squinted my eyes at him. I wasn't sure if that was a polite question or if there was a point behind it. "If you call making dog biscuits cooking, then yes, you could say I do."

"You make them for your dog?"

"It's my business. I make and sell gourmet dog treats."

Officer Ramey snorted. I didn't like him much. Addie settled down on the kitchen floor with her chin on her paws. She was down, but not relaxed. She'd picked up on my negative vibe and was no longer wagging or looking very friendly.

"Really? Do you make gourmet treats for people as well?" His tone was neutral but I was on my guard.

"Not really. I cook for myself and sometimes I have people over for dinner. But I'm not sure what you're getting at," I said, watching Officer Ramey scoot open my pantry door with his shoe. I repressed the urge to slam it on him.

"Your neighbor said he was poisoned by some of your brownies."

I was speechless. I'd gone out of my way to help that jerk last night. I'd my evening spoiled, my living room ruined and my car contaminated, and now he was telling the police that I'd poisoned him with brownies. I realized my mouth was hanging open and I was staring stupidly at Officer Neal. Ramey took this opportunity to stick his head under my sink.

"Do you mind," I snapped at him. "I don't appreciate you poking around my house without my consent." Perhaps not the direction I should go, but now that I was being accused of poisoning someone, I felt the need to shut down his uninvited investigation of my house. He planted himself about a foot away from me and crossed his arms.

"I never made him brownies," I said, looking back at Neal and trying not to feel Ramey in my personal space. I inched away in spite of myself. "The guy's a total jerk. He throws dog poop into my yard all the time. Why don't you talk to him about that? Surely there's some kind of law against that?"

Neal started taking notes. "So, you two don't get along very well?"

"I don't even know him," I said, trying to ratchet my tone back to dispassionate. "He only moved in a couple of months ago. I never even saw him until this past week, when he began throwing dog poop over the fence into my backyard as well as onto my front walk."

"Why would he do that?" asked Neal.

"She probably lets her dog crap in his yard," said Ramey. "Makes me sick when people do that. I'd throw it back too." I closed my eyes, trying to control my temper. I wasn't sure what kind of grievance this cop had with me, but he was making me nervous.

"My dog does her business in my yard. And I clean it up. Every day. If she ever did go somewhere else, I would clean it up then too. I always clean up after my dog," I said, unable to stop the clipped tone. Addie started to whine. She didn't like this.

Ramey fixed her with a stare, trying to dominate her. Addie is uber confident and doesn't get dominated easily. She stared right back at him, narrowing her eyes slightly. I left them to their staring contest and turned back to Neal.

"I did not make my neighbor brownies, poisoned or otherwise," I said.

"If you two don't get along, why did he come to you for help last night?"

"I have no idea."

"But you let him in even though he throws dog droppings in your yard?"

"He was sick. He needed help." The pen flew along his tiny notebook. A glance at Addie and Ramey showed they were still locked in a staring match. A slight strain was beginning to show on Ramey's face. Addie can go a long time without blinking.

"I don't know why he would say that I gave him poisoned brownies," I said. "I really don't."

"Actually, he said that he ate your brownies. Brownies that were left for you."

"You said I poisoned him!" I said.

"No. I said he was poisoned by some of your brownies. Brownies that were meant for you."

My mouth dropped open again and a chill ran along my spine. Someone was trying to poison me. The fear I'd been feeling with the anonymous calls came thundering back.

"It appears that someone left a container." He consulted his notebook. "A Tupperware container, full of brownies on his doorstep. There was a sticker that said 'Jessie' attached on top. He said he didn't know who Jessie was, so he decided to help himself."

That at least sounded authentic.

"It seems that your neighbor has a bit of a sweet tooth, because he said he ate most of them all at once." A polite way of saying that he's a pig. That kind of behavior could account for the sagging gut he was getting. "At first when he started feeling sick, he thought that he just ate too many too fast, but he said that he knew pretty quick that something else was wrong."

I was trying to concentrate on what he was telling me, but I was severely hung up on the fact that those brownies were intended for me. Had I found them on my doorstep, would I have eaten them? I liked to think I wouldn't. I do have an innate sense of paranoia that until this time had been for naught. But really, who eats food from unknown sources that just shows up on their doorstep?

"So, Blondie," piped up Officer Ramey. "Who's got it in for ya?" He'd given up on his staring contest with my dog. I suspected she'd won, and he now turned his dark eyes on me. There was no friendliness there. His look suggested he hoped there was a whole host of people who had it in for me.

I wasn't sure what to tell these guys. If it had just been Officer Neal, I might have broken down and gone into detail about all the creepy feelings and the anonymous phone calls I'd gotten since my name was published as a witness to Dayna's murder. But I didn't like the way Officer Ramey was looking at me.

"I don't know," I said. "Do you have the container? Maybe I could tell something from the writing."

"It was typed," said Officer Neal. "We'll be taking the whole thing to the lab for testing." That might or might not be a good thing. It's not like the Houston crime lab has the best reputation.

Their remaining questions were administrative type things that I would have expected at the beginning: name, phone numbers where I could be reached, etc. Officer Neal told me to give him a call if I thought of anything else, and gave me his direct extension.

After they left, I sank down on the floor to digest what this all meant. Addie positioned herself close by my side. Running my hand absently over her soft fur, it struck me what seemed wrong with this picture: I'd thought that Dayna's killer, and consequently the person who was calling me, and maybe out to kill me, was a man. But baking poisoned brownies just seemed so girlie. Not for anything could I picture Lonnie baking brownies and delivering them to me in a Tupperware container. Cherilynn maybe, but not her husband.

The barely controlled anger and sheer power of Lonnie had convinced me that he could have easily killed Dayna. I'd been feeling that if there was a threat to me, it would come from him, so I'd assumed that if I didn't hear his diesel engine anywhere in my vicinity, I would be safe. This just blew the door off that assumption.

This had to be tied to Dayna's murder. Didn't it? Up until I'd found her body, my life had been cruising along in a fairly ordinary manner. It was only since I'd found her, and they'd announced in the newspaper, albeit erroneously, that I was a witness to her murder, that these things had been happening. Now someone was trying to poison me. Had to be tied.

My mind flitted over all the people who could have murdered Dayna: Daniel, Naomi, Naomi's husband, Walter, Lonnie, Cherilynn, an unknown stranger, someone from work, someone else in her family. I wondered how the police investigation was going. Not that they would tell me, but Daniel might be privy to their progress. Perhaps I should get together for a drink with him. It was one thing to leave the cops to their investigation and go about my business when someone wasn't trying to kill me, but last night's events put a whole new spin on it for me. I needed to protect myself, and I needed to know from what direction the threat was coming.

The clock on the wall caught my eye and I leaped to my feet, startling Addie out of a dream. The morning was ticking away; I needed to get back to work.

CHAPTER FIFTEEN

The more I thought about it, the more I was convinced that Naomi could easily be the brownie poisoner. Lab tests would show what kind of poison had been used, but I just couldn't see Lonnie baking and delivering poisoned brownies. The one hitch in my logic was the fact that Naomi knew where I lived. Why would she leave them on the wrong door step? I pondered this while I scouted through my closet for something cooler to change into since the afternoon had really warmed up. The day had flown by in a whirlwind of baking, and I was pleased with how much I'd gotten done. Settling on a short skirt, flat sandals and a cropped cotton blouse, I flounced back downstairs no closer to an answer.

And really, who would eat homemade food that just shows up on your doorstep? Okay, obviously Larry would, but he didn't appear to be an intellectual titan. If Naomi had left the brownies, she had no way to control who would eat them or when. I wondered how she would act if she saw me up and about and obviously well. Perhaps I'd pay her a little visit. I could tell her I felt bad about how our last conversation had ended and wanted to set things right.

After looking up Naomi's address online, I left Addie shut in my room with a peanut butter-filled Kong. She'd been exhibiting too much interest in the mess in the living room, and the last thing I needed was her licking up the leftover poisoned vomit. She wasn't happy, but she had her Kong, my bed and the window to look out of. What more could a dog want?

Naomi and Walter lived southwest of the city towards Sugarland. Traffic was heavy but moving well as I made my way down 59. The neighborhood was an older, well-kept subdivision of small to midsize houses, most of them in cookie-cutter brick with front-facing garage doors that dominated the elevations. I was willing to bet that at least once, someone had come home drunk and ended up at the wrong house. Every third lot housed a mature live oak that spread its heavy branches over the yards and driveways. I was guessing there was a militant homeowner's association here; not one house or yard was out of compliance with some arbitrary code. All flowerbed borders were of the same black molding; there were no lawn ornaments or statuary of any kind; all the bushes were trimmed with military precision and the flowers were either red or white with an occasional pot of yellow mums thrown in on a step. The only flags showing were of the American variety, no Halloween or crafty kinds; there were no kids' toys scattered anywhere, no basketball hoops, no bicycles, and no skateboards. Very neat, but a little unsettling.

I drove slowly down the street, looking for the correct house number. There wasn't much activity for a sunny Saturday afternoon. In fact, the only person I saw at all, was an older lady strolling with her overweight Sheltie. Naomi and Walter's house was second from the corner, two blocks into the development. A car idled in the driveway in front of an empty garage, and as I cruised past, I caught sight of a man in the driver's seat, fumbling with the pocket on his shirt. I didn't get a good look at him, but felt fairly confident that it was Walter.

He didn't look up, and I rounded the corner before turning into a convenient driveway where I could still see his car in my rearview mirror. Within seconds, he had finished whatever he was doing to himself and backed slowly out of the driveway, closing the garage door with his remote. Naomi's car hadn't been in the garage, and on a whim, I decided to follow him. I waited a few more seconds before backing out of the drive. I had to give the guy credit—he certainly was a careful driver. It's not easy to follow someone going ten miles an hour. I could only hope he'd pick up speed once we reached a main road. Otherwise I might as well announce on a loudspeaker that I was following him.

I didn't know what I hoped to accomplish by this little jaunt. It was curiosity as much as anything. There was a certain fascination with someone as meek, timid and religious as Walter falling prey to such a deviant plot of Dayna's. Although, knowing Dayna, the plot had not been planned; she had just taken a random circumstance and twisted it to her will. Maybe the rumor about them wasn't even true. It could have been totally fabricated. But then again, the grapevine at Astor Oil tended to be remarkably accurate. Sometimes the stories were inflated, but for the most part, there was truth behind the gossip.

We meandered through the neighborhood and made our way slowly towards Gessner Road, where we turned north. Once on Gessner, Walter moved to the middle lane and picked up speed. I let several cars slip between us so that I could still keep him in sight but not be so easy to spot. I had never tailed anyone before and was surprised at how much thought it took. I found myself trying to second-guess where he was headed and when he might be turning so I could position myself appropriately. We continued under I-59, past the Westpark Tollway and on toward Richmond. He was probably going to work, or grocery shopping or something. Didn't he work at a grocery store?

At Richmond, he carefully signaled and moved into the right-hand lane. I followed, still two cars behind, and just barely made the light as he turned east in front of a crush of cars waiting at the light. We stayed in the right lane, going so slow that cars behind me were alternately riding my bumper, then almost taking it off as they veered around to pass me. By now I was directly behind Walter, but he didn't appear to be interested in what was behind him; he was too busy leaning over the passenger seat and peering out the side window. We passed a row of restaurants and bars, wide parking lots less than half-full at this time of day. Maybe he was going out for a late lunch and deciding where to eat.

At a ratty little strip mall, he signaled and turned into the lot. I hesitated, not sure if I should follow him or continue on. Too late to make the turn, I shot past the driveway. Braking hard, I turned into the next drive, cringing as I caught sight of the car behind me in my mirror, looking like he was going to plow into my back side. He laid on the horn with the hand that wasn't clutching his cell phone and managed to shoot me the finger between blasts of the horn. So much for being discreet.

I pulled into a parking space to calm my nerves and looked around for Walter. He was idling about twenty yards away, seemingly oblivious to my near collision, intent instead on smoothing his hair back in the driver-side mirror. I took a quick look around at the storefronts to see where he might be headed. There was a pawnshop, a newsstand and a nail salon. He didn't seem like a manicure kind of guy, but what did I really know about him?

The parking lot was in dire need of repair. Potholes the size of pizza pans dotted the surface, begging to take out an axle. Walter was still examining himself in the mirror, but he'd moved from his hair to his teeth and was vigorously rubbing a finger up and down against the front ones. He couldn't have done this at home?

The street behind me was crowded with midday Saturday traffic, and a small crowd milled around the bus stop on the corner. A busty woman in a short, tight skirt broke away from the pack and began ambling slowly up the sidewalk past Walter's idling car. She flung her hips in hard, wide circles, causing her skirt to ride up even farther. Another few steps and we were all going to be subjected to an unfortunate view. I watched, fascinated as she gave Walter a little wave with her pinky. I could only assume she was a working girl and immediately realized that this was his intended destination. Walter didn't respond to the wave. Instead he swung his head around and pretended he hadn't seen her.

Rolling the car into drive, he slowly advanced up an aisle towards the pawnshop. When he reached the end, he turned around and headed back in our direction. On impulse, I tucked my purse under the seat and hopped out of my car. Adjusting my own short skirt, I walked nonchalantly along, pretending I was just sauntering down the sidewalk on a hot October day.

Walter drove a slightly beaten green sedan, with a long front end and pointy corners. I could smell the exhaust from thirty feet away and wondered how that thing ever passed inspection. The rumble of the engine was getting closer, and I peered down the street like I was looking for the bus.

"Excuse me?" a harsh female voice shouted directly behind my head. She was so close I could feel her breath on the back of my neck, and I nearly fell off the curb. Before I could even turn around, the woman moved swiftly in front of me. "I said ex-cuse me!" Bursts of garlicky breath hit my face, and I took a quick step back. She stood with strong-looking hands on her ample hips, glaring at me. Her eyes widened so far that the whites gleamed against her dark skin. The effect was frightening to behold.

A quick glance around revealed the bus stop crowd was delighted by this turn of events. A young Hispanic guy leaned against a street sign and crossed his arms, getting comfortable to enjoy the show. I had to hope one of them might step in to save me if things turned physical. Chances were, I'd have a hard time defending myself if she was determined to beat me up. If I wasn't wearing these stupid little strappy sandals I could probably outrun her, but in them it would be a toss-up.

"Uh, yes?" I asked. Walter's car made another circuit of the parking lot.

"What do you think you're doing?" She bobbed her head side to side with each word for emphasis.

"Waiting for the bus," I lied. Just then the bus pulled up with a squeal of brakes. Our audience filed on, saddened that they were going to miss the beating. I edged towards the bus, only I didn't have my purse on me, or any money for the fare. The driver snapped the door shut and lurched away from the curb.

"You not waiting for the bus. You drove here," she said. I cupped my hand around my car keys and tucked them behind my back.

"So what? It's not like it's a crime to walk down the sidewalk," I said. "And anyway, I was just going to get my nails done." I edged away, debating when I should make a break for it and run for my car. She squinted her eyes at me. Thank God the whites diminished to a normal circumference. That bugeyed look did nothing to improve her appearance.

"This here is my block," she said, scooting forward to close the distance between us.

"You can have this block," I said, glancing around at the shabby buildings, heavy traffic and broken pavement. "Really."

Walter stopped the car about twelve feet away and rolled

down the window for a better look at the drama unfolding before him. Through the open window, I could see him more clearly. Judging by his orange tint, it appeared that he'd been experimenting with a tan-in-a-can product and had missed a swath of skin along the side of his face, which stood out in stark white relief next to the carroty color around it. He pulled back his lips and smiled at me in what I assumed was supposed to be a sexy smile, but was, in fact, a sickly leer.

"You don't seem to understand what I'm saying," continued Working Girl. "That there is exactly what I'm talking about."

"That guy?" I asked. "You want that guy?" I was feeling sick at the thought of this whole thing.

"He a good customer." She looked over and gave him another pinky wave. "Okay, maybe he's not much to look at, but he comes around a lot." She peered a little closer at me. "That's not your daddy, is it?"

I don't believe I'd ever been more insulted. "Oh my God!" I said. "Does he look like my father?" Tilting her head to one side, she gave me a good once over.

"I don't know. I guess you're better looking, but really, you all look pretty much alike to me."

I gave an involuntary shudder. "Blech. That's disgusting," I said.

"So, then what you doing here?" she asked. "I think you following that man. I saw you follow him into this lot in that fancy S-U-V of yours." She did the head wag again when she said SUV. She might be territorial, but she was observant. Maybe I could get a little info from her. I turned my back to the simpering Walter. He apparently thought we were fighting over who was going to perform favors for him. Another shudder shot through my body. I really didn't want to get into the whole story with her. For all I knew she'd turn right around and spill it to Walter as soon as she got in his car.

"Well, I work with him, and we've been wondering where he runs off to all the time," I said, trying to create something plausible. "I mean, like, he just up and disappears and no one knows where he goes." She looked like she believed me and was giving me enough eye contact that she appeared interested. "So, we thought it would be fun to follow him to see what he's up to."

"Okay. So, you want me to tell you what exactly?"

"I don't know. But you're right. I did follow him here. We've got some bets on what he's doing," I said.

"What's your bet?" she asked, leaning back and relaxing her stance.

"To tell you the truth, he kind of gives me the creeps. The way he looks at us sometimes, I think he's a bit of a perv." Too late, I realized that I was probably insulting her. Her business revolved around guys with different instincts. I guess. I'd never actually talked to a prostitute before. I couldn't imagine her world, but it was too late to back down. "I put my money on him going to dirty movies." She laughed.

"He's past the dirty movies, honey. That man's obsessed," she said.

"Really? Obsessed with what?" I hated asking because I feared I really didn't want to know, but thought it might be relevant to finding Dayna's killer and my stalker.

"He obsessed with gettin' head." She'd lowered her voice as if she was giving away client's secrets, which in a sense she was. "Normally it's the young ones obsessed like that. He's kinda old if you ask me. But I can make a lot of money on that kind of obsession." I wondered if he'd had this obsession before Dayna or if Dayna had set it off.

"How long has he been coming around?"

"Not that long, maybe a couple a' weeks. But he's coming 'round here a couple times a day. And like I said, he's not young, so really, this free money for me if you know what I mean." She winked at me, and I was convinced I would have nightmares for months.

"Yes, I think I do," I said. I glanced over my shoulder. Walter was still patiently waiting although I feared his car would overheat if he didn't turn it off soon. "Do you think he's just new to your block and he's had this obsession for a while? Or do you think it's a new obsession?"

"I don't know what set him off." She pondered the question seriously. "I see a lot of stuff in my business. If I had to guess, I'd say that he's probably always had this interest, but maybe he's never been allowed to act on it. Probably has a snotty wife thinks that's nasty or something." I was willing to bet she was right on the mark with that statement. "But when he showed up here a couple weeks ago, he was a hot mess. He was scared to death to do what he did. Even talking to me nearly brought him to a nervous breakdown. Thought maybe I was vice or something. Figured out I wasn't and he's been coming back ever since."

We both shot a glance at the car, causing Walter to nearly swoon with excitement. I don't know what he was thinking would happen. Maybe he thought Working Girl was going to bring him a friend today. He was pathetic, really. I was concurrently disgusted by him and sorry for him. It couldn't be easy living with Naomi, but if he had any backbone, he would have left that marriage a long time ago. Looking at his hopeful eyes, I didn't see a killer. There wasn't nearly enough gumption there. Although Working Girl said he was obsessed, and obsessed people don't always act rationally, so I couldn't totally rule him out. I did move him farther down towards the bottom of my list though.

Naomi, on the other hand—if she knew what his encounter with Dayna had triggered, she would no doubt find herself justified in killing that Jezebel. If she found out about Working Girl here, I worried for her safety as well.

"I've met his wife," I said. "She's crazy, I think. If you see someone with fanatical eyes and thin, frizzy hair, I'd get the heck out her way." She nodded and smiled at me. "Thanks for the tip."

As I headed for my car, I couldn't help but watch as she went over to Walter's window. He looked slightly forlorn that I wouldn't be joining them but perked right up as she moved around to the passenger side. What a horrible life for both of them, I thought.

I drove home feeling disgusted. I should have never followed Walter. Now, not only would I be haunted by Dayna's dead face, but I couldn't stop imagining what was going on in Walter's car right now.

Hoping a quick walk with Addie would distract me, I hooked her to her leash and headed out the door as soon as I got home. The smell from the tarped area was seeping out in the warm air. It was reaching a point where I was afraid to move the cover at all. I might just have to move.

We walked slowly past Larry's again, but still no sign of life from within.

That was just as well. In spite of our evening together last night, I wasn't encouraged that he and I could ever be friends. Hopefully, though, the poop throwing would stop.

I was getting ready for my dinner with Frances when the phone rang. I hadn't heard from Evan all day and thought it might be him.

"Hello?"

I heard a small intake of breath. Pressing the phone closer to my ear, I listened without saying anything. A sharp click reverberated in my ear as they slammed down the phone. Had that been a woman? I'd assumed all the other times that it had been a man on the phone, but just that small sound had made me think female. In a strange way, I was comforted by the notion of it being a woman. I couldn't think of any woman I knew who was a frightening as Lonnie.

Not knowing where Frances might feel like going for dinner, I went with a versatile combo of black slacks and a pale yellow sweater. I even made the effort of matching my ponytail holder to the sweater. Quite presentable, I thought. I fed Addie her dinner before I left, and at the last minute decided to bring her with me. Frances always loved to see her, and I felt better about leaving her at Frances's place than at mine.

The sun had already started its rapid descent as I left the house. Addie was delighted at the last-minute invitation and stood planted on the console beside the driver's seat, her seat belt keeping her from leaning all the way to the windshield as she would like. Traffic was heavy, a carryover from the Saturday afternoon shoppers colliding with the early Saturday night revelers, and it was almost six twenty before I reached the brightly lit guesthouse behind my parents' house.

Addie raced out of the car as soon as I freed her from her seat belt and ran straight for Frances's door. Too polite to bark, but too excited to remain silent, she settled on something that sounded like a cross between a yodel and a growl. Frances opened the door only to be nearly mowed down by the wagging, writhing beast on the step.

"Addie! How nice to see you," Frances said, wisely grabbing on to the door frame to keep from being knocked over.

"Addie, stop that," I said to her as I made my way over. She raced ahead into the living room, nose to the floor as she ran. "Sorry about that," I said, giving my grandmother a kiss on her soft cheek. "She doesn't understand that people don't like being knocked over."

Frances laughed, holding me at arm's length. "That's all right, dear. How could anyone not like being loved like that?"

"There are some crazies out there," I said, following Addie

into the living room. "Sorry to bring her unannounced. I just hated to leave her by herself on a Saturday night."

"Don't be silly," said Frances. "You know I love seeing her. I love seeing you both." A bubble of guilt rose in my stomach. Usually I spend more time with Frances, visiting during the week or at least checking in by phone. She and I have always been close, even more so after my grandfather passed away. She had her friends, and she was active with the church and various activities, but I knew she loved spending time with me the most. The events of the past week had thrown me off stride in more ways than one.

"I love seeing you too, Frances. I'm sorry about missing dinner the other night. This week has just been a little hectic." She gave me a look but didn't respond.

After getting Addie settled with a Kong, we headed to Ouisie's Table for dinner. This was one of our favorite dinner places. Somehow, we always ended up with a cozy corner table where they let us linger as long as we wanted. The mix of high ceilings and slow-moving fans, big brick fireplace and a mouth-watering menu was Southern comfort at its best.

Tonight, I settled back into my corner seat with a glass of sauvignon blanc, and realized that, ensconced amongst the hustle and bustle of the other diners and restaurant staff, I felt safe for the first time in days. The civility of this scene chased away the tension that had hounded me since seeing Dayna's swollen face. Actually, since she'd called me. If I hadn't agreed to go walk Henry, it would have been some other hapless soul that found her.

Frances and I relaxed into our usual chitchat. How was my business going? Was I enjoying my walking clients? How were her friends? Did she have any trips planned? Could I handle my baking business with my current equipment or did I need to upgrade to more commercial-grade appliances? How were my parents doing? Did Mother have any new charity events coming up that could involve me in any way? And on along those lines throughout a bottle of wine, our dinner and into dessert and coffee.

I halfway expected Frances to bring up the events of the week, but surprisingly enough, she didn't. All in all, it was a very enjoyable evening, and I felt as if we'd moved past the breach that had overhung us earlier.

So relaxed was I that when I finally made it home with Addie, I didn't even notice the broken-out window on my back door until the glass began to crunch under the cute black boots I'd worn for dinner.

CHAPTER SIXTEEN

C ould be I didn't notice the window was broken because the house was dark. Belatedly, I realized that the floor lamp in the living room, which was normally on a timer, was dark. It shouldn't have turned off this early. A glimmer of light shone through the kitchen window from a nearby streetlamp, but it only turned objects near the window into varying shades of gray.

Addie had already trotted off towards the living room by the time I registered that the crunching underfoot was due to the smashed-out glass from the back door. The smell of dog poop assaulted my nose, too strong to be coming from the tied-up disposal bags on my patio. Anger flashed over the fear. If Larry had broken in and thrown dog feces into my house, I was calling those cops back and having him arrested. Surely even Officer Ramey couldn't condone that.

My little moment of bravado over, fear surged back to the forefront, and I bit down on my knuckle, trying not to cry out in fright. This wasn't Larry, I was almost positive of that. Crouching down behind the counter, I ran through my options.

If it weren't for Addie, I would race out the garage door and haul ass for the police station. But I couldn't risk leaving her.

It also struck me at some level how unconcerned she'd been about this attack on our home. What kind of watchdog was she, anyway? I listened hard. For footsteps. For the sound of a door closing. Or opening. For Addie's jingle of tags. Surely if someone was in the house, she'd have cornered them by now.

I heard nothing. Realizing that crouching in the kitchen overtop shards of glass wasn't going to get me anywhere, I felt around in the dark for my trusty skillet once again. It wasn't as good as a gun, but it could crack a skull if I needed it to. I tried desperately to be quiet, but the glass on the tile crunched and scraped under the soles of my boots. Feeling my way into the cabinet, I found the handle of the skillet and pulled it towards me. Too late, I remembered the mixing bowl I had set on top of it earlier. With a crash, the bowl joined its relatives from the window on the tile. I might as well blow a trumpet to announce my arrival.

The crash at least brought me something. Addie came running down the stairs at full bark. If anyone was in the house, they were fully aware of my presence now. I snatched up the skillet and flicked on the overhead light. Outside of the glass, the kitchen looked mostly untouched. The living room did not. The tarp had been pulled back off the couch and the cushions were scattered (adding to the ripe aroma of the room), books were tossed on the floor randomly like wood shingles in the aftermath of a tornado, and my neat little stacks of junk mail had been thrown against a wall. And if that wasn't enough, dotted throughout were wet smears of fresh dog doo.

Addie paraded happily through the mess, sniffing avidly at each unexpected item. She seemed to enjoy "ransacked" as a decor. Snapping my fingers at her to stay behind me, I crept to the bottom of the stairs. I doubted anyone was there, but if they were, they were waiting silently for me. I stood for two long minutes, trying to get up the nerve to check it out. The wind brushing a branch against an upstairs window decided it for me. I grabbed the cordless phone from its base and dialed 911.

When the patrol car arrived, Addie and I were waiting in my car with the windows up and the doors locked. I was still clutching my skillet and the phone. I'd reopened the garage door, figuring I could always run over anyone who tried to come near me, but with the car facing forward, I'd developed a crick in my neck from whipping my head back and forth every time I thought I heard something.

The officers who responded this time were yet another pair I'd not met this week. I don't know how many cops Houston boasts, but I guess the odds are such that I wouldn't keep getting the same ones. And what a sad thought it was, that I was getting to know so many of Houston's finest.

These two were young and black and approached the darkened garage warily. The overhead garage light flicked on as the first one crossed the sensor's field, and I opened the car door at the same time, startling the second one, who reached for his gun with such speed that I immediately threw my hands in the air, cracking the back of my knuckles against the door frame.

"Damn," I shouted, stuffing the battered bones into my mouth, as if licking them could make the pain subside.

"Step outside. Now!" shouted the skittish cop from the driveway. The first one had rounded the far side of the car and was taking inventory of who else might be in there. Addie, freaked out by their uniforms and the unusual events of the night, lunged at the window, fangs bared and hackles up. She looked rabid and I slammed the door before she could launch herself at one of them. The gun-happy one pointed his gun at Addie, which only incited her to more frantic decibels. Panic surged through me as he leveled his gun and stared down the sight at her.

"Don't!" I said, terrified that he would shoot her even though she couldn't get to him. "Please don't. She can't get out of there and she's scared. Please."

His partner rounded the side of the car and touched him on the arm. Turning to me he said, "Officer Wilson. This is Officer Lebaron. You reported a break-in?"

Addie was still barking, flecks of spit flying against the windows. I moved several feet out into the driveway, hoping to draw the cops out with me. I wasn't convinced the one wouldn't shoot her just for fun.

"Yes," I said. "I got home and someone had broken the window on my back door and trashed the place. Well, they trashed the downstairs. I don't know about the upstairs, I was afraid to go look."

Waves of exhaustion washed over me, and I rubbed my eyes feeling close to tears.

"Do you want us to check it out, ma'am?"

"Yes, please," I said, embarrassed by the quiver in my voice. I wanted Addie near me. I wanted, needed, to run my hands through her fur. I needed to soothe myself with her comforting warmth, but I couldn't risk bringing her out of the car. As soon as they disappeared through the door into the kitchen, both with guns drawn, Addie stopped barking and settled into a worried whine.

"It's okay," I told her through the window. "It's okay."

It only took a few minutes for them to reappear, holstering their weapons as they came through outside.

"There's no one in there," said Officer Wilson, motioning me to join him inside. "Lebaron is going to take a look around outside."

Hoping Lebaron wouldn't come back into the garage and shoot my dog, I followed Wilson into the kitchen.

"Is anything missing?" he asked.

"I don't know," I said, looking over the counter into the

mess in the living room. The TV was perched in its normal spot in the corner, the paintings still hung on the walls, and my crystal candlesticks graced the dining table. With all the clutter, it was difficult to tell offhand what might be missing. I didn't have a lot of electronics, but I did have some nice jewelry upstairs as well as my computer. Any burglar worth his salt would surely grab those items first. "Do you mind if I take a look upstairs? I've got some jewelry that my grandparents gave me…" My heart lurched at the thought of someone taking the earrings and necklace that my grandparents had given me for my college graduation. They'd taken the stones from pieces that had been in the family for years and had them reset by a jeweler into an original setting they designed just for me. It suited me perfectly. My grandfather had passed away not long after that, and I treasured their gift more than anything else I owned.

Taking the stairs at a full run, I raced for my bedroom. Why did I keep my jewelry in a jewelry box? It was like posting a neon sign for burglars: Jewels Here! My bedroom was nothing short of a disaster. All the drawers had been pulled from the dresser and the clothes dumped in little hillocks all around the room. My jewelry box wasn't on the top of the dresser, and a little sob caught in my throat. I was aware of Officer Wilson watching me from the doorway.

"I guess something's missing?"

Please be here. Please be here, my brain shouted as I ignored his question and scrabbled among the debris for signs of the box. I heard the creak of his belt as he shifted his weight and took a couple tentative steps into the room. Flinging garments wildly aside, I ran my arms along the floor under the mess. Finally, under the third pile I hit something hard and square. It was my jewelry box, but more than likely the creep had pulled the jewels out and just left the box. Holding my breath, I cracked open the lid. Everything was there. Right where it should be.

I blew out a breath of relief and patted a hand over my cheek to calm myself down.

"It's all here," I said, looking up at a surprised Wilson.

"You're kidding, right?" I guessed they didn't see many burglaries where the burglar didn't take anything.

"Let me just check my study." I was feeling more confident. If they hadn't taken my jewelry, they probably wouldn't have wanted much in my study except my computer.

I kicked through the piles of clothes that had been strewn almost all the way down the hall. The smell of dog poop was not as pungent up here, but an occasional burst of scent wafted up to my nostrils, bringing to light the enormity of this cleanup effort. All of these clothes would have to be washed or taken to the cleaners. Three feet from the study door, the clothes gave way to piles of paper. All of my file cabinets had been emptied, just like the dresser in the bedroom, and the floor of my study was completely covered with paper.

But in the middle of the chaos sat my computer, unmolested and undisturbed. Weird. It was creepy knowing that someone had looked through all my personal paperwork. I could see the copy of the last report my doctor had sent me, detailing the results of my blood work and pap smear. Credit card receipts, car repair bills, tax documents, all mixed in a gumbo and poured on the floor. It would take forever to get this back in order. If anything had been taken, I'd probably never be able to tell.

"You'll probably need to contact your credit card people," Officer Wilson volunteered. "And the credit agencies. We've been seeing a lot of identity theft going on."

He made his way as carefully as possible through and around the mounds of my personal items and headed back down the stairs to the kitchen. I followed more slowly, noticing how odd my things looked out of context. When I reached the kitchen, he pulled out a notebook, and began scribbling a series of shorthand marks that I couldn't make out. Or maybe that was just his handwriting.

Wilson was a man of few words, and he ran me quickly through my complaint. His concentration and complete lack of emotion made it easier for me to regain my own composure and tell my story without a single self-pitying tear. Halfway through, his partner joined us (thankfully, I hadn't heard any shots from the garage), and he poked curiously around my house, throwing out an occasional question. Most of his questions seemed to be of the more personal kind, such as: do you live here alone, do you have a boyfriend, might an old boyfriend be holding a grudge? At first I thought he was hitting on me in a roundabout way, but then it finally struck me that they were looking at this as the revenge of a disgruntled lover.

Wilson focused on the details of what I had seen, heard or noticed that might have been unusual. Lebaron seemed more interested in motive. Neither one of them made eye contact with me, and through the haze of exhaustion and the conviction that I was momentarily safe with these two burly cops entrenched in my house, I found my brain drifting off on its own trails. In spite of the dog poop, I knew this had nothing to do with Larry. It took some guts to break into someone's house, and Larry tended towards cowardly throwing from behind the safety of his bushes. My gaze traveled around the living room. This had to be the work of someone looking for something.

Start at the beginning, I told myself. The beginning of this nightmare was Dayna. The newspaper reported I'd seen someone when I found her body, but I hadn't. And that wouldn't account for someone breaking in and looking for something, unless they were breaking in looking for me. A chill ran along my core at that thought and I shivered.

"We'll be through here in just a few more minutes," said Lebaron. Maybe he was more observant than I thought. I hadn't brought up the whole dead Dayna mess. As with the cops from this morning, I was surprised that my name hadn't popped up on their radar as "Witness 1—Burke Homicide" or something along those lines. And while I had no idea how the inner workings of the police department flowed, it was apparent that I was probably buried in a homicide file on the desk of some overworked detective.

"Aren't you going to check for fingerprints and all that?" I asked.

He snorted, probably amazed as always by the density of the general public. "We haven't got the resources to fingerprint every break-in gets reported."

I watched him poke around a little more. "There are no old boyfriends that would do this," I said. "I think it has something to do with the murder of my old boss. I found her body, and ever since then, weird things have been going on." A stillness seemed to come over both cops, and if the cartilage in their ears was as flexible as Addie's, I think I would have seen them prick at full attention. They shot each other a look, some nonverbal communication that I didn't catch.

Lebaron appeared to win the lead. "What murder are you talking about?"

I gave them the quick and dirty version, skipping over most of my speculations as to who could have killed her and why, focusing instead on all the creepy things that had been happening to me since finding her. Wilson skipped out the door while I was in the middle of my discourse, no doubt to radio in for confirmation that there had been a murder in which I'd starred as the body-finder. Lebaron started taking his own notes on the back of a paper that he'd pulled from his pocket.

"So, huh, you probably have some ideas as to who killed her, huh?" he asked nonchalantly, relaxing his buff muscles into an at-ease position.

"A lot of people hated Dayna." I said. "I just don't know who hated her enough to kill her."

"But you say you worked for her, so you probably have a better idea as to who that someone is than, say, myself, who never even met her." His interest in this was almost palatable. Maybe he and Wilson hoped to land a case that was more challenging than your standard breaking and entering or domestic dispute.

"I quit there almost seven months ago. A lot changes in seven months."

"Maybe so, but it sounds like she was a witch to work for. Sometimes that's enough to trigger someone."

I thought back to my days of living hell working for Dayna Burke. I'm a fairly stable person, and even I finally quit. What if I hadn't had the financial security I did? What if I had to have that job to support a family? What if she was threatening to fire someone who had nothing to fall back on?

"She was horrible to work for," I said. "But imagine if she was that terrible in the office, what she might be like at home."

"You think her old man did it?" His dark eyes bored into mine as if trying to read what was really in my head. "I'm sure the detectives have been taking a look at him. They always look at the spouse. Lotta spouses decide they don't like being married."

I considered Daniel as the murderer yet again. If I had been married to Dayna, I might have killed her, and yet, while he struck me as a giant sleazeball, he seemed more parasite than predator. Dayna made a lot of money that supported his financial black hole of documentary making. But occasionally the parasite kills its host. Maybe she'd been threatening divorce. Divorced, his cash cow would stop producing, but widower, he was at least left with the current estate.

"Maybe," I said.

"Who's your money on?" he asked.

"Off the record?" I surely wanted this maniac caught, particularly with the unwanted attentions I'd been getting from him or her, but I didn't want to send the police beating on someone's door who had nothing to do with it, just because I thought they might.

"Just between you, me and Wilson," he said, giving me a wink as Wilson shoved back into the kitchen from the garage. "Jessie here's gonna give us the lowdown on what scumbag she thinks did the kill."

Wilson consulted his notebook. I wondered what he'd found out.

"Have they caught anyone yet?" I asked, reluctant to give away my opinions if they already had someone at the station being read their rights.

"Nope," Wilson said, tapping his pen against his notebook and looking over at his partner. "They don't have anyone on the hook for this one." They both turned and stared at me.

"So, let's hear what you think."

I told them about Dayna's brother-in-law and how frightening he was. "I don't know why he would have killed her, but knowing Dayna, she probably went out of her way to make him feel ignorant or low-rent."

They both wrote his name down as well as the Lotts' address even though this was "off the record." I felt a little better when Lebaron mumbled something about it being out of their range.

"The thing that bugs me, though," I continued, "are those poison brownies... I totally can't see that guy making brownies. He probably doesn't even know how to turn on the oven."

"Maybe the sister's in on it too."

"Maybe." Cherilynn didn't strike me as much of a baker either, but I guess it doesn't take much skill to open a mix, add a little oil, an egg and some garden-variety poison, and pop it in the oven. But outside of a bad case of sibling rivalry, what could induce Cherilynn to want Dayna killed? None of these scenarios felt right.

Suddenly aware of how long Addie had been trapped in the car, I glanced at the clock, anxious to check on her. At the same time, Wilson's radio crackled to life and they turned in unison towards the door. Wilson gave me the number at the station where I could reach either one of them, and urged me to call if anything else happened.

"I guess you're still not going to fingerprint, huh?"

They laughed, and I followed them out the garage door. Addie was crying softly from her perch in the backseat. She stood when the cops passed close by the window, but she didn't bark. Maybe she thought she was being punished for her earlier outburst. I hit the button to close the garage door as soon as they'd left, and hurried to get her out. I never punished her for being protective of me, and I certainly didn't want her to start second-guessing herself on that now. If anything, I'd rather she overdo it.

She raced around the garage, tracking everywhere they'd walked. I left her in the garage while I grabbed a broom and a dustpan. I didn't want her to cut her pads on the glass shards in the kitchen. In fact, I needed to check her feet as soon as I was done and make sure she hadn't already done so.

Wilson and Lebaron had taken the edge off my fear, but as soon as they were gone, it began to creep back in, like an insidious fog that seeps through the chinks in your weather stripping. The glass from the mixing bowl had shattered in large fragments, but the glass from the window was more the splinter-into-a-thousand-pieces-per-inch kind that I would probably still be getting stuck in my bare feet for months to come.

The door would have to be replaced, but there was no way that was going to happen until tomorrow at the earliest. I felt vulnerable with this big gaping hole in my back door and the maniac who had put it there still on the loose. I swept up the glass, vacuumed and then used a wet sponge to try and get the final shards. Dismay washed over me as I surveyed the dog poop that had been tracked over the living room floor, up the carpeted stairs and onto my clothes and papers. The cleaning of that would have to wait until tomorrow too.

I let Addie back in and she ran in frantic circles around the house, sniffing and whining. She tracked an invisible trail up the stairs and I followed her, wondering what that incredible nose told her about this. She did a quick run through my bedroom and bathroom, moving like a drug dog hot on the scent of heroin, then veered off for my study. The study seemed to stump her, and she ran in tight little circles all around the room, whining and crying with each whirl. She kept coming back to my file cabinet. It had been emptied, the mahogany-stained drawers left hanging, dejected and bereft of their cache.

So it appeared, at least by Addie's calculation, that the person had spent a good deal of time with my files. I would have to go through my papers carefully and see if I could determine just what was missing or what they had been looking for.

I tried to rationalize that I was lucky. My prized jewelry was still here, and it appeared that most of my other property was too, if not in its normal place. This could have been much worse. Addie could have been here when the person had broken in.

My blood ran cold at the thought of what could have happened to her. What if I hadn't taken her with me to Frances's tonight? Tears that had been threatening all night finally spilled over at the thought of anything happening to my beloved dog. I sat down hard on the study floor and buried my head against my knees. When was this going to stop? Seeing the tears, Addie came over and nudged her nose under my arm, working her face up towards mine. She licked away the hot tear marks that ran down my face, then began licking my forearm with slow, comforting strokes of her tongue.

We couldn't stay here tonight. I wasn't sure when I'd be comfortable staying here again. I felt vulnerable and violated and terribly, terribly tired. And under the fear and exhaustion, anger flickered to life. The fear of what could have happened to Addie sparked it. Whoever was doing this, had better watch out—they'd just crossed a very personal line.

CHAPTER SEVENTEEN

Exhaustion finally worked its magic, and I slept. Hard. When I woke, quiet surrounded me, broken only by a periodic unfamiliar whirring. My brain felt addled. What was that noise? As soon as I opened my eyes, furry lips nuzzled my face and a happy tail thumped the bed beside me.

Light blazed through a chink in heavy purple curtains, and the prior evening's events rushed back into my head. Oh yes, the break-in. Glancing at the clock, I saw that it was almost eight. I hadn't slept this late in years. Running my hand along Addie's side, I watched the fur fall in a little pile on the butterscotch bedspread. Housekeeping would not be pleased.

I'd checked into the downtown Doubletree the previous night. They'd given me a look when I'd waltzed into the lobby with Addie, pointing out that their pet policy limited dogs to twenty-five pounds or less, but judging by the lack of traffic in the lobby, Saturday night was not one of their busiest, and they relented. Well, they should. A hundred-dollar nonrefundable pet fee should entitle Addie to a gourmet breakfast and her own chaise lounge.

Last night, I had deliberated where to turn. I'd considered

calling Frances, Evan, even my parents, but mostly I just wanted to disappear. So I had, right into downtown Houston, which tends to be a ghost town on weekends. I'd settled on the Doubletree mostly because of the warm chocolate chip cookie that greets you on your arrival. Although, not having a reservation apparently meant that the right people hadn't been tipped off, so I was quite disappointed to find my room with no cookie box. Within fifteen minutes of my checking in, however, a cookie was delivered. Addie, already freaked out by recent events, barked furiously at the door when housekeeping knocked. By the time I opened the door, the poor staff member had made a break for it, and I found the cookie box still warm on the floor.

Paranoia only goes so far, and after one fleeting thought that maybe the cookie was poisoned, I realized that this had been a snap decision and no one knew where I was. I ate the cookie.

Even though the hotel wasn't crowded, I still felt safer having a buffer of valets, front desk clerks, and unseen security personnel. Our room was on the sixth floor, high enough up I wasn't worried about someone shooting me through the window, but still within reach of the fire department ladders if the building burned down.

Addie had never been in an elevator before, and the moving door had frightened her, causing her to cower low to the ground. She cowered even lower as we rose the six flights and raced out the door as soon as it opened. I would have to see if we could take the stairs down today without setting off any alarms.

I stretched my feet towards the cool, smooth recesses at the bottom of the bed, planning my day: conduct major cleaning of house; replace smashed window in back door; find crazed killer before he or she found me. Sounded like a pretty good plan. Oh, and if I had time, resume baking dog cookies before

I ran out of inventory, alienating my customers and ruining my business entirely.

A hot shower further revived me, and I felt a bit more self-possessed than I had last night. Addie also seemed refreshed, rested and decidedly less skittish. We skipped the elevator and made our way down the stairwell. Only once did I pause when I heard a door open several flights up before telling myself that no one besides the front desk clerk and my credit card people knew I was here. The lobby was completely empty, and I pulled Addie, nails slipping and scraping, across the slick marble floor, past the darkened bar towards a door that led outside.

We were at the back of the hotel, between high rises that stood empty this early on a Sunday morning. Later in the day there might be a small number of dedicated and lifeless employees making their way in with their smart-badges and rolling laptops, but right now the area was deserted. I pulled Addie past neatly flowered landscaping and shade-loving bushes and out onto the next block. A small grassy park across the street nestled next to an equally small church. The sun was bright and glistened off the glass towers nearby.

Addie spent a few minutes sniffing the strange smells before we headed back to the hotel. I let the front desk clerk know that I needed to extend my stay at least one more night. I doubted I would find anyone to fix my door on a Sunday, but was hopeful that I could get someone to repair it first thing Monday morning. After retrieving my car from the valet, I buckled Addie into her seat belt and headed off to find coffee and a bagel. I drove down Allen Parkway, where the Sunday morning fitness buffs were out in force, running and walking along the bayou park. Addie sat ramrod straight, her eyes riveted out the window, looking for cats and squirrels. There was an Einstein Bros. bagel shop on Shepherd, and I picked up a large coffee and two chocolate chip bagels. I had a lot of work to do, I needed the fuel.

My street looked peaceful, but I found myself driving slower and slower as I approached my house. The bright sunlight and my renewed energy helped, but they didn't totally dissipate the pinging of fear that clicked at an increasing pace like a Geiger counter approaching radiation. I wondered if anyone had noticed I had been gone overnight or if anyone was watching even now. No. I was not going to let this fear wear a pathway into my neurons, I had to banish it now. And the first step was getting my house back in order and getting on with my life.

In front of my house, everything looked the same as I had left it. No cop cars waiting out front, no hatchet-wielding loonies waiting behind my bushes. Larry's blinds were still down, and a hefty Sunday paper had been added to the pile on his stoop. Perhaps I should check on him today. Maybe the hospital had released him too soon and he had died at home. On second thought, I had enough problems of my own and only so much energy.

I pulled into the garage and closed the door behind me before letting Addie out of the car. She had obviously forgotten about the visit from the cops last night, because she wheeled around the garage, tracking their scents all over again as if it was brand-new. Once in the house, she continued her tracking. Every time she comes home, she runs through a routine of checking out the house to make sure everything is in the same order in which she left it. Judging by the frantic whines and considerable snuffling, things were definitely not in order.

Things were not in order for me either. The high humidity had seeped in through my inexpert patching job on the door, emphasizing the odors that brewed under the tarp. The house reeked like a Bourbon Street gutter the morning after Mardi Gras. Putting my bagels and coffee in the refrigerator so they wouldn't be contaminated by the smells, I pulled some rubber gloves from under the sink and dragged the tarp out the front door, depositing it near Larry's walkway. Addie was showing entirely too much interest in the nasty stains on the rug, so I chased her up the stairs and shut her in my room. Next, I started dragging the sofa towards the front door. It slid fairly easily across the hardwood, and I didn't even care that I might be scratching the floors. This biohazard had to go.

Once at the front door, I realized that no matter how much I pushed, pulled, twisted, pleaded and cursed, I couldn't get the couch through the door without help. Frankly, I couldn't see how it was going to fit through that door even with help. A breeze blew in, raising a small stink from the cushions. I would take a power saw to the thing if I had to. The rug I could remove with no help, although it was heavy and awkward to drag. More awkward because I didn't want it to touch me directly in any way. Addie watched the proceedings from my bedroom window. I wondered if anyone else was watching.

When the rug was out, I got Addie from upstairs and my breakfast from the refrigerator, and took them both outside to the patio. No poop on the flagstones and no poop on the table. That was either a good sign that my kindness to Larry Friday night had changed his ways, or a bad sign that he was indeed dead. Either way I was starving. I scarfed down both bagels, pausing after the first one to bring Addie's breakfast out too. Closing my eyes and warming my face in the sun, I could almost forget the mess still waiting for me inside.

Almost, but not quite. Glancing at my watch, I saw that it was almost ten. I'd get started on my cleaning before calling Evan and enlisting his help with the sofa. I wanted to get as much of my upstairs cleaned as possible before Henry came over. He was still young and playful enough to consider flinging my underwear around an amusing pastime.

I kicked my way through piles of clothes on the way to my

bedroom. The thought of some unknown person going through my underwear gave me the willies. I could never wear those things again, they would have to go. I gathered all the underwear into a throwaway pile. That reduced the mess by about fifteen percent. Socks went straight into the washing machine while the rest went into piles based on color. I would be doing laundry for days. Maybe I should just drag it all to a wash-and-fold place. I felt better already.

Next was the study. Unfortunately, there weren't any services I could think of that would come restore order to this mess. I wanted to utilize the same strategy of sorting everything into relevant piles before refiling, but first I just had to gather the whole blasted jumble up off the floor. Addie, tired of snuffling the clothes, came in and began sliding clunky feet all over my papers, wrinkling them even more. I retrieved a new beef-basted rawhide for her, and let her get to work on that while I concentrated on the cleanup.

What was the point of this destruction? Was someone looking for something, or were they just making a point that they could get to me? As I sorted, I tried to determine if anything was missing, but unless it was something big and noticeable, like a tax return, I probably wouldn't be able to tell. By noon my neck and back were sore from hunching over. Spread out before me, my life looked pretty boring. Addie had given up on the rawhide and was napping on the farthest pile of bank statements.

Getting stiffly to my feet, I did a quick series of stretches, trying to work out the kinks. I needed a break. I hadn't even started to clean up the dried dog doo that had been trampled all over the floors, nor had I started rescuing the scattered and damaged books from their injurious positions all over the floor.

Evan answered on the third ring.

"Hello?" he chirped and immediately began to giggle in a weirdly feminine manner.

"Evan?" I asked, wondering what was wrong with him.

The giggling accelerated into rapid panting. I considered hanging up, pretty sure I'd interrupted something obscene. Maybe that cute girl across the hall was visiting him, being friendlier than I would have thought possible. Just as I was about to hit the button and disconnect, he slowed down his breathing, gave a final chuckle and said, "Sorry. Whoa. Jessie? Is that you?"

"Uh, yeah. Sorry to interrupt whatever that was I was interrupting." My tone was infused with curiosity in spite of myself.

"No, no. I was just playing with Henry." He said something muffled and laughed again.

"Really?" I tried to sound like I believed him.

"He really loves that stuffed rabbit we got him. I hide it and he goes crazy looking for it. I was laying on the floor and I hid it under myself. You wouldn't believe how much his whiskers tickle." He laughed again. He was kind of getting on my nerves.

"Oh, that's nice." What was wrong with me? I should be jumping for joy that they were doing so well together. It dawned on me that I was jealous of his carefree weekend. Meanwhile my life was on the line and I was living in hiding. *Settle down, drama queen*, I told myself. *You* want *Evan to fall for Henry. Henry needs a good home.* Surprisingly, all of a sudden, a little demon popped up on my shoulder, and I wasn't sure I wanted Evan to have Henry.

"What's the matter?" Evan asked, picking up on the negative waves radiating through the phone line.

"I've had kind of a crappy weekend," I said, trying to get a handle on my sudden pity party. "My neighbor got poisoned by some brownies that were meant for me. My downstairs pretty much got ruined by that disaster, and if that wasn't enough, someone broke in while I was out with Frances last night and trashed the place."

There was silence for a minute while he digested that.

"Is Addie okay?" In an instant, he was forgiven and my negative thoughts towards him evaporated.

"Yes, luckily I took her with me and left her at Frances's while we went out."

"Do you want me to come over? I can help you with whatever you need."

He said he'd be right over and I went back to cleaning, happy to be getting backup. I had been reluctant to keep Evan in the loop mostly because of his penchant for gossip, but I needed to tell someone everything that was happening. That way if I ended up dead, at least there would be someone who could explain the madness. The police had multiple pieces of my story, but like puzzle pieces put away in different boxes, they weren't likely to get assembled into anything meaningful.

When Evan arrived, Henry flew through the door, ran a quick circuit around the downstairs, leaping and cutting over the mess on the floor, then launched himself at Addie, completely forgetting that she didn't have the same warm feelings for him that he had for her. She stood stock-still against the play attack, the only sign of her displeasure a faint rumbling deep in her chest. I led Evan through a quick tour of my personal disaster area. He was uncharacteristically quiet, merely taking it all in without comment. Finally, he turned and stared at me, his face dead serious. "Jessie, I'm scared for you."

"I'm scared for me too."

"No, really. I mean, before it seemed, I don't know, kind of like a game or something." Well, Dayna was dead, but I knew what he meant. "But this is real. What if you or Addie had been here when this nut broke in?"

"I know."

"You're not staying here." My play-pal Evan looked suddenly adult.

"I'm not. I checked into a hotel last night, at least until I can get this window fixed."

"More like until this freak is caught." He sounded angry, but I knew it was fear as much as anything. I didn't comment, because realistically it could be a long time before they caught this guy, and too much time at the Doubletree would quickly eat through all the profits from my fledging business and right on into my trust fund. Not exactly part of my financial plan.

We didn't talk much as we threw ourselves into the cleanup effort. Evan seemed lost in thought, and I raced around trying to get organized as quickly as possible. I needed to be back in operational mode tomorrow, so that I could get back to my baking and spend some much-needed time reconnecting with my cookie distributors.

The first thing we did was tackle the couch. Evan manfully declined the rubber gloves I offered him. He'd be sorry when his fingers slipped into the gooey gray matter that crusted the cushions. In no time at all we were able to maneuver the couch through the front door with only one smashed finger (mine), and three chips out of the door frame. We bumped and scraped the wooden feet all the way down the driveway, leaving the smelly, stained thing near the curb for big garbage to come take away. I wished I had a biohazard label to stick on it to warn the garbage handlers.

My living room looked unfamiliar and barren without the couch and the rug, but it made it easier to race through the remaining piles of debris. Once again without benefit of gloves, Evan took a bucket and sponge and went to work on the potty marks. I found myself mentally reviewing how often I saw Evan actually wash his hands, disturbed by his cavalier attitude towards filth. Fortunately, when I thought about it, I realized I saw him washing his hands quite a lot. More than most guys, anyway.

Within two hours, the place looked a lot better than it had when I'd arrived, and we collapsed in the kitchen with a drink. There was still a lot of sorting I would have to do in my study, but the main part of the house looked livable again.

"I can't help but think someone was looking for something," Evan said between sips of a Diet Coke. "Do you have anything of Dayna's that might mean something to her killer?"

"I still have her house key. I guess I should have given it to Daniel, but I haven't seen him except at the service, and you know how that went." Not to mention I had forgotten I had it until now. "I'm planning on getting together with him. Maybe he knows something."

"Maybe he did it," Evan countered. "I don't think you should see him. You don't know anything about that guy." He sounded slightly jealous, and I squinted my eyes at him, trying to figure out where he was coming from.

"Okay, even if he killed Dayna, what would be the point of breaking in here to steal back his house key?"

"So you can't get in there and search the place while he's not there."

"He could just change the locks."

"Oh, right." He took another sip of his drink. "Well, I couldn't blame him if he did kill her, but my money's still on her crazy brother-in-law. That dude really has issues."

I couldn't quibble with that. My money was on Lonnie too. "We need to figure out if he did it, why he did it. Then maybe the cops would have something concrete to arrest him with." The truth of the matter was, Lonnie scared the crap out of me. I figured he'd be happy to kill me for taking Henry away from him, much like an aggressive pit bull would react if you snatched its bone. Having to rely on Cherilynn to keep her mouth shut about what she had seen, only increased my unease. "So how do we pin it on him?"

Evan finished his drink and stifled a small burp. "I don't know."

I grabbed a notebook and fished a pen out of my purse. "Maybe we should start making a list of everything we know. You know, things like who has a motive, where people were at the time she was killed; stuff like that. Maybe something will come to us." I wrote down some names, leaving plenty of room to make notes around them. "Lonnie Lott."

"Lunatic," said Evan. I wrote it down next to Lonnie.

"Anger problems," I continued. "Based on what Cherilynn said at the funeral, probably thinks Dayna was screwing them over somehow."

"Okay, what about Cherilynn?" asked Evan. "She sounded pretty pissed off herself."

"Yes, she did," I said as I scribbled next to Cherilynn: "Thinks Dayna screwed her over," I wrote. "Bitter about their childhood."

"I wonder where they both were when Dayna was killed," said Evan.

"I'm sure the police have checked that out," I said. "But that doesn't help us any."

"Okay, who else?"

"Daniel, maybe," I said. "I gotta tell you, that whole funeral filming thing he did really freaked me out. That was so not normal. Did you hear how he was talking to me? Asking me what it was like seeing her dead?" I was getting all wound up again just thinking about it. Stabbing the paper with the pen, I wrote "sick documentary bastard" next to Daniel's name.

"He was totally getting off on the whole thing," Evan agreed. "I never liked that guy. And speaking of getting off, what about Naomi or her husband? There's two more not-so-normal people." Evan grimaced and I felt my own features twisting into a matching one just thinking about Walter and Dayna alone in her office.

"Yuck," I said, debating how to phrase that in my notes. Might as well say it like it is. "Dayna blows Walter," I wrote. "So, let's think about that," I said.

"I'd rather not," said Evan in an offended voice.

"No, seriously. Okay, I can see Naomi going off her nut and killing Dayna over that, can't you?"

"Well, yeah."

I wrote down Naomi. "How about Walter? Do you think Walter could kill her?"

"Walter couldn't kill a dust bunny. You've met him. He does what Naomi tells him to." He did seem pretty spineless.

"Oh my God! I didn't tell you what I did yesterday!" I gave him a condensed version of Walter and the hooker. The whole time, Evan's mouth hung open in astonishment. I don't think he blinked once. "What if Naomi told him to kill Dayna as retribution for his sin?" I threw out the question, visions of Naomi, inches from Walter's face, ordering him to do it.

"Well, if she had him kill Dayna, she'll have him kill this hooker too, if she finds out about it."

I added Walter to the list. "And then there are all those other people who hated her that we don't even know about."

"Like anyone who's ever worked for her," said Evan, turning slightly pink.

"Do I need to write you down?" I asked, sort of kidding but sort of not.

"No. I was at work. Remember?" He looked away, uncomfortable.

"Yeah, I didn't think so," I said, snapping my notebook shut. "I guess there's not much we can do about checking out all those unknown people who may have hated her."

"Then let's check out the people we know about. I got an idea."

"Okay, what?"

"Let's go pay a condolence call on the Lotts." I stared at him to see if he'd lost his mind. He looked normal, but he must have been at least partly insane to think that was a good idea. "We'll bring a nice plate of brownies," he continued. "And maybe some flowers if we have to," he said misinterpreting my silence.

"What are you, crazy?!" Even as I asked, I couldn't help but image Cherilynn's face as we handed her a plate of brownies. Assuming she was the poisoner, it would be priceless. Following hard on the heels of that thought came a vision of Lonnie cocking the barrel of his shotgun and blowing Evan and me off the porch. "I don't think it's a very good idea," I said.

"Why not? If they refuse to eat the brownies, then we know they're the killers." His fair cheeks flushed with excitement. Evan watches too many cop shows at night.

"And so there we are, sitting in their house, staring down the barrel of Lonnie's shotgun, going 'Aha! Gotcha!' What's to stop them from killing us right there and burying us in the woods behind their house?"

He blew out a disappointed breath. "But I really like the brownie idea."

I liked the brownie idea too. In the end, we decided to leave a plate of brownies on the doorsteps of all our suspects, starting with the Lotts.

CHAPTER EIGHTEEN

B efore we left, we had to decide what to do with the dogs. I thought they'd be fine if we left them alone, but Evan was convinced that Addie would kill Henry long before we returned. We considered putting them in separate rooms, but Evan worried about someone breaking in again. In the end, we decided to take them with us.

The afternoon had warmed up considerably, and we cranked the air conditioner in Evan's Mustang to high. Addie stood firmly planted between us, back feet braced on the backseat, front feet on the console, knocking Henry off the seat every time he encroached on her prime perch. He finally gave up and sat forlornly staring out a small side window.

We made a quick stop at Kroger, where I ran in and picked up two bags of bite-sized brownies from the bakery, some plastic plates and a roll of Saran Wrap. Ten minutes later we were flying down the highway.

Evan cranked up the radio almost as high as the air, and the blaring of hard rock not only made conversation impossible, but endangered the hearing in both my ears. Addie flattened her ears as far against her head as possible in self-defense, and Henry sat hunched in the back, being blasted by the speakers. I turned the volume down by half but still couldn't carry on a conversation. I would have to have a word with Evan about caring for Henry's hearing even if he didn't care for his own.

We made it to Channelview in record time (thanks be to God), and I turned the radio down to a bare whisper as we exited I-10. A ringing in my right ear portended a hearing aid in my later years. I tried to ignore the annoying high-pitched sound.

"So, uh, what exactly are we going to do now?" I asked. I had arranged the brownies nicely on the plate during the ride over, but how they were going to get from my lap to the Lotts' front door was another question.

"Well," Evan said, drawing it out into three syllables. "I'm not really sure."

The panting in the backseat increased into a whine as Evan turned right at my direction. Or maybe it was still the ringing in my ears.

Evan drove slowly, checking out the houses as we passed. He seemed as struck by the disconnect between his vision of Dayna's background and the reality of it as I had been the first time I'd seen it.

"I cannot believe that this is Dayna's hometown," he said. "The way she acted, you'd have thought she was from freakin' Beverly Hills."

"I know. Wait till you see the house where her sister lives. I just can't picture Dayna growing up here."

We cruised the back way around the block, past the wooded lot where I'd met Todd and Shaun. I wondered if they were there today, snuggled up in their hillside. I slunk down in my seat as we got closer to Cherilynn and Lonnie's place. From the backseat, Henry sent up a cry that made chill bumps rise on my arms.

"What's wrong with him?" asked Evan, slowing down even further as he turned to look in the backseat.

"Look out!" I shouted as the car drifted rapidly towards the swale at the side of the road. Evan spun back around, correcting our course before we went into the ditch. The last thing we needed was to end up stuck in a ditch fifty yards from the Lotts' with their stolen dog in the backseat. The stolen dog ratcheted up his cries as we got closer to the house, and Addie, upset by his distress, added a low whine to the chorus.

"Seriously, what's wrong with him?" Evan asked with alarm.

"He knows where he is," I said. "Maybe he thinks we're taking him back." The dirt drive that stretched between the Lotts' and the aunt's house next door was empty. Lonnie's big-ass truck was nowhere in sight, nor were any other cars visible. Sunlight drifted through the far neighbors' pines, dappling both houses with yellow streaks. With Evan driving, I was able to get a better look at the two houses. I'd hardly noticed the aunt's house on my last visit, intent as I was on the dog rescue. Now I took the time to look and was saddened by its air of neglect. Tall weeds ravaged the yard, hell-bent on taking over the house as well. Dirt and dust lay like a shroud over the small dwelling. It looked like no one had lived there for decades, although Melba had said their aunt had recently passed away. A For Sale sign was propped against the porch, and another one had fallen into a weed-choked ditch near the road. I couldn't imagine anyone buying the place.

"That's their house," I pointed out to Evan. He didn't look as jaunty as he had when he'd suggested this trip. He slowed to a crawl as we passed, leaning over the console to get a better look. The rope that I'd cut through to free Henry still lay in a heap, snaking among the junk piles in the yard. I was happy to see that no other poor dog had taken his place. The shed that Henry had been tied next to looked threatening even in the bright sunlight. Lonnie's angry energy seemed to dominate the area with menace.

"Doesn't look like anyone's home," he said with visible relief. Henry didn't care that no one was home, he wanted to get away from here. Based on his cries, he wanted to get far away from here. It probably hadn't been the best idea to bring him along. I should have known he would remember the place where he'd been so ill-treated. "What next?" Evan asked.

Before I could answer, a malodorous wind drifted forward from the backseat.

"What is that?" Evan cried, lowering his window. I threw my arm over my nose, breathing deeply the scent of my lotion in an attempt to block out the other, worse smell.

"I think Henry is really upset. You need to get somewhere that we can take him out before he ruins your backseat."

We raced up the street away from the Lotts'. Henry's cries turned from anxious to frantic as he continued to blast us with gas. Even Addie pushed her head past Evan's towards the open window, drinking in the warm, fresh air. Okay, fresh was a stretch, since I could smell the refinery odor quite clearly, but it was better than what assaulted us from behind. We pulled over at a stretch of empty ground, and I raced to snatch Henry's leash before he bolted out the door. Poor guy had quite a spell of intestinal distress, and I waited patiently while he went about his business.

"Hey!" hollered a voice coming up quickly behind me.

"Yo, it's the Dude!" cried another one. I turned to find Shaun and Todd pedaling furiously towards me on their bikes.

"Cool car!" shouted Todd, skidding to a stop in the gravel. "Is this yours?" The disbelief that I could have such an awesome machine was apparent. Evan slid out his door, careful to keep Addie in. He looked pleased at the admiration of the eyes examining his car. Who cared that they were kids? Obviously, they were smart kids.

"Cool car!" they both shouted at him.

"Awesome!"

"I'll bet it's fast!" They launched into a car discussion with Evan about V6s versus GTs, horsepower, torque and other things I had no interest in and I tuned out. Henry finished and began walking back, but quickly changed his mind and returned to circling. I drifted to the break-in at my house and tried to figure out, once again, what that person had been searching for. I was almost positive it had been Lonnie. What would I have that Lonnie would be willing to break into my house for? Somehow Dayna had screwed them over, as Cherilynn had stated at the memorial service, and yet Lonnie had gotten angry at her for bringing that up in public. So how did those two items tie? I still didn't know if anything had been taken from my house. Perhaps he found what he was looking for, and I didn't even know it.

"Oh, dude," said one of the boys. "That is gnarly." Shaun had turned away from the car discussion and had caught sight of Henry.

"Aww, dude!" echoed Todd. "What's wrong with the little guy?" Henry, suddenly aware of his audience, hunched a little lower to the ground and tried to inch away.

"He got upset coming back here," I said, trying to draw their gazes away from the embarrassed dog.

"Why'd ya bring him back here, then?" Todd asked, rightly so.

"We were just driving around. Somehow we ended up here."

They exchanged a glance, then looked away in separate directions. Todd brushed the long dark hair out of his eyes and turned back.

"It's real good you took him," he said. "That Mr. Lott guy is loco. He came looking for you the day you took Little Dude."

"Did he know I took him?" I asked, fingers of fear running up my neck.

"He knew someone took him. He wrecked our place in the woods that night."

"Were you there?" I asked, fear extending on behalf of these two kids.

They exchanged glances again. "Todd was," said Shaun. "He was waiting for me. I was supposed to meet him, but my Dad came home early and made me go to the Home Depot with him to pick up some stuff he needed to fix my granny's front door. He wouldn't even let me go tell Todd I couldn't come."

I shifted my gaze to Todd. "It was no big deal, really. I kinda knew Shaun wasn't coming, so I was just hanging out. But then I heard this crashing through the woods coming from over by the Lotts' way. I knew that wasn't Shaun, so I ducked around some trees, outta the way. Got bit by some red ants too —hurt like a mother!" He rubbed his ankle, reliving the pain.

"Anyway, there I was behind the trees and here comes Lott, kicking through our stuff. I didn't have time to pick up our magazines. And I'd just gotten the latest NASCAR issue," he said, his voice going up several octaves, obviously still distraught at the coming injustice. "We had some cigarettes there too." They both looked sideways at Evan to see if he was going to launch into a lecture on the perils of smoking. He looked blandly back at them. "So, he just, like, goes nuts. Starts kicking everything around."

"Wish I'd a' been there," said Shaun. "We'd have kicked his ass."

Todd tightened his fingers around his bike's hand grips, squeezing hard. "Yeah." He didn't sound convinced. I suspect he had a better appreciation for just how nuts Lonnie was. Shaun had only heard this secondhand.

"So tell 'em what the crazy shit did next," prompted Shaun bouncing up and down on his bicycle seat.

"Well, he kept kicking everything around for a while, cussin' and swearing like nuthin' I've ever heard. I was thinking I needed to get home, but I didn't want him to hear me. So, I stayed where I was.

"Then it goes quiet for a while. I thought maybe he'd left. I was just gonna go see if my magazine was still there when I smelled something and I heard this splashin' goin' on. I popped my head up over the bushes and I see him throwing this liquid all over everything. I knew from how it smelled it was gasoline. And I caught a sight of his face. Dude, that guy really is insane. I mean really crazy, you know?"

He looked at me and I could see the fear welling in his eyes.

"I know he is," I said.

"I thought he was gonna kill me if he found me there. I swear to God, I thought I was dead. I was afraid to move at all in case he saw me. So, I just stood there, real still. He even splashed me with that gasoline—hit my cheek when he was throwing it."

"He threw gasoline on you?" I asked, ready to drag this kid in to the cops right now to make a statement.

"He didn't see me, it just splashed on me while he was flingin' it around. But when he brought out a lighter and started flickin' it—I knew I had to get outta there. So I ran like hell."

"Did he see you then?" I asked.

"I know he heard me, cuz he started hollering 'Who's there?' but I ran out the far way past the Nemers' house. He didn't come after me. I know, cuz I waited behind their garage for like half an hour or somethin'."

Would Lonnie really have set this boy on fire? Was he that dangerous?

Shaun picked up where Todd had left off. "That crazy dude lit the whole woods on fire!"

"Why would he do that?" asked Evan.

"Maybe he thought they had something to do with taking the dog," I said. Maybe they'd angered him some other way, who knew? They didn't have any ideas. "How bad was the fire?" I asked.

"We haven't been back there," said Todd. "And it wasn't like we could go around asking anyone. I didn't want him or anyone to know I was there."

After they rode off, Evan and I got back in the car in silence. Addie, thrilled to have us back, greeted us with wild kisses, and Henry, feeling better, resumed his place by the window.

"I think we should go to the police," said Evan finally.

"With what?" I countered. "Surely they're already looking at him as a suspect. We don't have anything new to add."

"Yeah, we do. He tried to torch that kid!" He started up the car, revving the engine.

We didn't know he'd tried to torch Todd. According to Todd, Lonnie hadn't even known he was there. "Why don't we go by the woods and take a look?" I said. "Maybe there's something there that they could use to link him to arson."

"Forget arson! They need to link him to murder!" He glanced at the brownies on my lap. "Forget about leaving those too."

From the road, the woods looked unscathed. If there had been a fire, it hadn't done a tremendous amount of damage. I told Evan to wait with the dogs in the car while I took a quick look around. No sense in both of us going, especially with Henry as worked up as he was.

Still clutching my plate of brownies, I slid from the car. Even now, I liked the idea of leaving them. Perhaps I could drop them at the Lotts' if there still wasn't anyone home. I followed the same slim path that I had the day I'd kidnapped Henry. Half walking, half jogging, I quickly lost sight of the car as I rounded a small grove of brush and trees. The smell of fire was strong and the acrid taste of the air rasped my tongue. Ahead I could see the burn marks on the trunks of several pines, as well as the skeletal remains of several smaller bushes, their branches black and brittle, a testament to the blaze that roared past. The smell was stronger here, encased by the surrounding brush. The little hillock that had been the back-drop to Todd and Shaun's hideout was burned black, bits of charred debris the only sign that anyone used to hang out here. Against a rock curled a fragile fluff of ash that might or might not have been Todd's new magazine. There was no sign of the cigarettes.

I poked through the ashes with my foot, looking for anything recognizable, but nothing remained. The fire had apparently stopped, or been stopped, before it raced through the underbrush; I guessed that the wet weather we'd had last week helped stop it before it really took off. What had been the point of this?

I crept along the path towards the Lotts' backyard. Had the boys done something specific? Had Lonnie blamed them for the dog's disappearance, or had he just wanted to stop them from hanging out behind his house? I didn't think this was Lonnie's land, but I didn't know that for sure. Maybe it was, and he just didn't want them on his property, so he made sure they had nothing to come back for.

Their hideout was closer to the Lotts' backyard than I'd thought. The first time I'd run this path, it had felt like quite far, but really it couldn't be more than twenty-five yards or so, although the density of the brush, and the twisting of the path, added to the illusion of distance. Peering past a mound of leaves, I gazed at the Lotts' yard. Everything was quiet in the late-afternoon sun. In the distance, I could hear a dog barking and wondered if it was Addie. It sounded like her, but it was too far away to be sure which direction it was coming from.

The shed next to the house drew my attention. If Lonnie had anything to hide, I was willing to bet it was in that shed. Of course, Cherilynn might be privy to everything he was doing, in which case the house would be the place to look. Assuming I was going to look. Straining my ears, I listened for signs of life. Everything was quiet.

A stockpile of drywall rotted in a heap halfway across the small clearing between where I crouched and the shed. The lack of windows in the back of the shed and the angle of the house made it an easy decision, and I hunched into a quick trot to the back of the pile. The wind rustled dried brown leaves on their branches, and the sound of traffic from a distant street swept past. But I heard nothing from the immediate property.

I poked my head up over the top of the pile, feeling like a soldier in enemy territory with a known sniper in a nearby building. I would feel better with a helmet, flak jacket and rifle, but all I had was a wrinkled potty-bag in my pocket and a plate of brownies in my hand. Not much help unless I got hungry, or a sudden urge came on. Then again, as nervous as I was, the potty-bag might come in handy.

The windows along the back of the house seemed dark, although the dirt was so thick I probably wouldn't be able to see in even with the curtains open and all the lights on. The shed had one window on the back, but it had been boarded up and painted over, probably forty-some years ago, judging by the rotting wood and peeling paint. The entire thing looked as if it might fall down in a good stiff wind. I tried to think of the last time I'd had a tetanus shot. If I got scraped by any part of that building, I'd have to make Evan take me to the nearest urgent care clinic.

Piles of junk lay strewn between my current hiding place and the back of the building. I'd have to be careful where I stepped. I picked out my route, past the mound of rusty cans, around the old twisted realtor signs, and straight between the stacks of discarded tires. This was probably a haven for snakes. Yet another reason to run back to the car and be done with it.

Instead, I high-stepped quickly past the junk and rushed to the side of the shed, pulling myself tight against the wall. If anyone was here, they surely would have heard that thundering. I held my breath and listened hard. Still no signs of people. Holding my ear to a crack in the boards, I listened for noises within. Nothing. Leaves piled in heaps along this side of the shed, and I tiptoed farther out, hoping there really weren't any snakes. I'd never believed the adage that snakes are just as afraid of us as we are of them. What does a snake have to be afraid of? All he has to do is show himself and the humans generally run screaming in the opposite direction.

Inching along the edge, I took a deep breath and poked my head around the corner to survey the front. The door to the shed was only four feet away, a homemade plywood mess, hanging heavily on its rusty hinges. The edges of the wood had started to rot and peel back, leaving gaps big enough for squirrels to dart through. My luck, this shed was just another storage spot for junk.

I wanted to go in and check it out, but first I needed to put the brownies at the front door of the house. Hopefully without getting caught. The driveway was still empty, so I held my breath, hunched as low to the ground as I could get, and duck-ran my way across the driveway to the porch. I set the plate of brownies on a ratty, worn welcome mat and made a mad dash back across the opening towards the shed door, hoping it wouldn't be locked. It wasn't. I grabbed the slim metal bar that acted as a door handle and slipped as quietly as I could inside, which wasn't very because the hinges that held it in place were furry with rust. It was dim inside to the point of being dark, and I waited for my eyes to adjust, praying that no one had heard the racket or seen my peculiar run from the house.

The shed wasn't large, maybe nine feet by seven, but it was cluttered to capacity. Large shapes loomed out of the darkness, and as my vision adjusted I was able to make them out. Against the far wall stretched a dirty old cot covered by a scratchy-looking blanket. I wondered if Lonnie slept out here sometimes. The back wall had been converted into a workshop of sorts, and tools hung from the wall while a makeshift bench below constituted the working area. As with the outside, the floor was scattered with bits of metal things that I assumed were car parts, pipes, hubcaps and even a couple of old tires that stuck out from under the cot. An elderly TV balanced on top of a rickety stool behind the door.

Now that I was here, it was exactly like I'd pictured it, and yet disappointment loomed large in my chest. I'd been convinced that this place would hold the smoking gun, so to speak. Somewhere here I would find the evidence the police needed to lock up this lunatic, and in return, I'd get to go back to my normal life. The pre-finding-Dayna-dead life. The one where the most threatening thing I had to deal with was the possibility that I'd get hit with flying poop while watering my flowers, or one of my new dog cookie flavors wouldn't be a hit. I wasn't keen on people breaking into my house and scaring me with crank calls.

Well, I might as well poke around for a few minutes while I had the chance. If Lonnie did have anything to hide, he wouldn't hide it in plain sight. Shuffling my feet along the floor so as not to trip over anything in the gloom, I made my way towards the back, where the cot was. I knelt on the floor to peer underneath, but it was too dark to see anything, and I was too afraid to reach my hand into the darkness to feel for anything in case a snake was coiled up waiting for me. I found a length of pipe and poked it in quick stabbing motions into the blackness. At the farthest end, near the pillow, the pipe hit something with a metallic clank. Risking a bite, I reached my hand under and felt along the filthy floor until I hit a square metal box.

It took two hands to drag it out and I broke a nail in the process on the rough edge, but I was convinced that it held something incriminating. At the very least, maybe it would contain something that could point to a motive. Shifting a broken headlight out of the way, I squatted beside the box and pulled open the metal top, which bulged open from the paper stuffed inside. Dirt crusted the edges, and it looked as if it hadn't been opened in a long while. I tamped down any thoughts that there wouldn't be anything helpful here, telling myself that maybe he'd been waiting to off Dayna for a very long time.

As I pushed back the top, a large black roach shot across the short distance right at me. I fell over backwards onto my butt and scuttled crab-like away, heedless of the racket I was making. Short staccato mini-screams vibrated against my throat as I tried to avoid the bug's fast-moving body as it weaved directly towards me. It finally veered away and disappeared under a greasy white rag. Holding my hand against my mouth, I clambered to my feet, a shudder racking my body. Okay, I'm not good with roaches or snakes.

My heart thudded like a runaway racehorse, but I made a concerted effort to slow my breathing. It was just a roach. They can't hurt you. Although they could run up your leg and send you screaming 'round the bend. I picked up my length of pipe, and approached the box again. Using the pipe, I poked the edge of the box up, displacing the top papers onto the floor. From standing level, feet ready to run, I looked down and tried to make out what they were. They appeared to be auto parts receipts. I pushed the top layer aside with my toe. More auto parts receipts. I poked the pipe down into the box and lifted up more of the same. Good grief, it appeared that the whole box was crammed with auto parts receipts. How many auto parts could one guy buy? Actually, looking around the floor and the yard, I guessed quite a few.

As I scooped the scattered papers back into the box, I heard the rumble of a diesel engine approaching fast. What were the odds that it wasn't Lonnie? Not good, I realized as the truck flew into the drive and nearly into the side of the shed, judging by the sound of tires skidding on the gravel just outside the wall.

CHAPTER NINETEEN

I shoved the box under the cot, kicking the loose papers under as well, and frantically looked around for a back door or a hiding place. The door in front was the only way out, and while I'm not a terribly big person, even a ten-year-old would have had trouble hiding themselves under that cot. I darted from side to side, hoping a plan would pop into my head before Lonnie found me and killed me. The truck door slammed and I froze in place, hoping he would go into the house. Then a second door slammed and I heard Cherilynn's voice whine through the wall. "Where you goin'?"

"I gotta check on something in there," grunted Lonnie. Realizing I was still clutching the pipe, I grabbed it in both hands, readying myself to use it like a baseball bat if I had to.

"Well, I need you to help me carry in these groceries. Whatever you need to check can wait." *Yes, it can wait! Help your wife with the groceries*, I prayed. I didn't hear a response from Lonnie, so I stood rooted to the spot, debating what to do. Without a window, I couldn't tell if they'd gone into the house or not. I slunk towards the door, wishing my hearing was half as good as Addie's. I couldn't hear anything except my heart beating weirdly in my ear, so I leaned down and put my eye towards one of the gaps in the plywood door. It took me a minute to recognize what I was looking at: stained gray coveralls standing directly outside the door. My intestines twisted and I thought of the crumpled potty-bag in my pocket. Lonnie was standing inches from me, separated only by a piece of flimsy wood.

"Lonnie! Help me with these sacks. Don't be thinkin' I'm gonna be your pack mule and carry this all in. I'm sick of havin' to do everything around here. Most of this shit is for you anyway."

Frozen to the spot, I saw the coveralls stiffen. "Damn bitch," he muttered. He stood there as if deciding whether to ignore her, and I held my breath, terrified that the slightest movement on my part would cause him to throw open the door and pin me against the shaky wall. Finally, he moved away, and I watched his backside approach the pickup and pull a couple of bags out of the back of the truck. He walked towards the house and I lost sight of him through my peephole. From the front porch, I heard a small cry.

"Lonnie! Look, someone left us something."

Sweat beaded on my forehead and broke through the protection of my antiperspirant. I counted off the seconds I thought it would take him to reach the front door and go inside, then I darted out the door and ran around the far side of the shed, praying that neither of the Lotts saw me. I paused only a moment before racing across the exposed part of the backyard and towards the woods beyond.

From behind me, I heard the front screen door slam, then Cherilynn shouted, "Hey, what are you doing there?"

I didn't even slow down, I just kept my eyes focused on the woods. Before I hit the tree line, I heard Lonnie shouting after me as well, and I tried to ignore my sore ankle and run faster. Dodging a tree branch, I ducked into the cover of the woods, but they'd seen me. Dammit. Why had I gone in there? I was just supposed to look over Todd and Shaun's burned-out hiding place, and maybe drop the brownies off without being seen. And what had I found? A bunch of auto parts receipts.

Forced to slow down by the thick shrubs, I railed at myself for being so stupid. I hoped Evan still had the car running and was ready to step on it, because behind me I heard the roar of Lonnie's truck engine revving up. For a minute, I was afraid Lonnie was going to drive straight across the yard, into the woods and mow me down, but then I heard him throw it into reverse, tires skidding as he shot onto the street. Double shoot, he was going to drive around the block and cut me off on the other side. A stitch in my right side just below my ribs sent pain shooting fiercely into my abdomen, but I kept running, trying to ignore it. Who needed to breathe? I could catch up on that after I was safely in Evan's car and riding away down the highway.

The smell of the fire assaulted me as I raced past the boys' clearing. I could just see the edge of Evan's car through the bushes and I raced toward it, praying the engine was running. As I got closer, I saw Addie begin to wag when she saw me coming, and Evan turned quickly to see what she was looking at. He must have seen the fear in my face, because he started up the car as soon as he saw me. I flung myself into the front seat and he pulled away before I even shut the door. Without saying a word, Evan gunned the engine and we raced up the street. I quickly realized it wasn't the look on my face motivating him to move, but rather the large black truck bearing down on us from behind.

I alternated between bracing myself against the dashboard, terrified we were going to crash, and whipping my head around to look out the back window, equally terrified that Lonnie was going to catch up to us and ram us. Addie and Henry skidded and slipped across the backseat in a tangle of flying legs and tails as Evan careened around the corner barely touching the brakes. There wasn't anything I could do to steady them, but at some level, my brain worried that one of them might break a leg. Then again, all of us might break more than that if we didn't get away from this lunatic.

The light at the access road turned red as we were still fifty feet away, and cars were beginning to move through the intersection. Every muscle in my neck tensed up as I looked in the passenger-side mirror and saw Lonnie bearing down on us. We could either run the light and try not to hit someone, or slow down and get nailed from behind. Evan jerked the wheel to the right, maneuvering us through a narrow space between moving cars. Horns blared as we cleared the first intersection and continued through a second, heading for the highway. I glanced behind, hoping that Lonnie had gotten stuck behind the moving cars, but the drivers that had almost struck us had stopped and waited for the mayhem to pass. He was right on our tail.

"Oh my God! Oh my God!" When I realized I was shouting out loud, not just screaming in my head, I shut myself up. Evan had enough to worry about without me shrieking in his ear. I clamped my hand over my mouth and watched mesmerized out the windshield. We shot onto I-10, heading west towards the city. It was like living a wild chase video game. Evan's fingers were white against the steering wheel, and splotches of red broke out on his cheeks. His eyes darted from the highway in front of us to the rearview mirror, where presumably he was keeping an eye on Lonnie.

Traffic was light for Houston, meaning we weren't at a standstill. Nevertheless, there were enough cars on the road that I was terrified of how this would end. Lonnie, to his credit, was quite determined, and a better driver than I'd hoped. My arms were moving of their own accord, jerking to the left or right as we came up suddenly on a slower car, and my foot thumped against an imaginary brake pedal.

In the backseat, Henry took refuge on the floor and Addie gave up trying to maintain her balance, instead crouching miserably on the seat. I couldn't tell how fast we were going, but we were passing everyone around us. Looking out the back window, I didn't see the black pickup, and for a moment I thought we'd lost him. Then I caught sight of him out the passenger-side window. He was passing cars on the right-hand shoulder in an effort to catch up with us. Where are the cops when you need them?

Evan still wasn't speaking, his concentration entirely focused on his driving. For a moment, he let up on the gas and I looked forward, only to see a semi poking along in the far-left lane. Didn't that driver know Houston laws? Trucks aren't allowed in the left- hand lane. We passed a sign that stated "No Trucks Left Lane." Evan swerved to the right, cutting between two minivans to get past the truck.

The driver in front of us picked this moment to teach us a lesson and hit his brakes. Evan slammed on his brakes in response and the minivan behind us crashed into the back of us, throwing us forward into the first one.

I screamed as I felt Addie hit the back of my seat and bounce backward. My head jerked back and forth like a tennis ball on a limp rope. That would probably hurt later. The minivan in front of us steered over two lanes, the driver waving his arm at us to follow. He nearly ran into Lonnie, who was still riding the shoulder.

Lonnie swerved into a real lane and began closing the distance between us. Behind us, the second minivan laid on the horn and began chasing us as well. I caught a glimpse of the driver: a woman with long dark hair and a bright pink visor. I guess she thought we were fleeing the scene of an accident. We were. We were also fleeing the scene of an impending double homicide.

I looked over at Evan to see if he was okay, but he was completely engaged in averting total disaster. Seriously, where were the cops? We needed them to come flying to our rescue, sirens blaring, lights flashing. Surely someone in one of the cars around us was dialing 9-1-1 by now. The minivan chasing us took another hit as Lonnie clipped the front bumper, veering suddenly into her lane. She began honking at him and giving him the finger. Lucky for us, she stopped chasing us and set her sights on Lonnie. That was one pissed-off soccer mom. I hoped she didn't have any kids in the car with her.

We flew past the beltway and a slight clearing opened in the traffic. I gave a little sigh of relief as Evan headed for the opening. Seconds later, a crushing blow on the right side sent the back end of the car into a fishtail. Evan screamed, "Dammit!" but managed to get control of the swerving car.

A clanking from the back was followed quickly by a scraping thud as a part of the bumper came loose and flew off the frame. In the side mirror, I saw it roll directly into Lonnie's path. He swerved hard, but still clipped an end with his big tires. The front driver's-side tire blew out and the bumper flew up, crashing into the driver's-side door. The truck veered out of control into the concrete median, sparks flying as it scraped along the side. That was definitely going to leave a mark. Hopefully Lonnie had the parts already available to repair his damage.

Evan took advantage of Lonnie's preoccupation with not losing total control of his truck and floored the gas on the Mustang, shooting us well out of range. The lady in the minivan had given up the chase, finally convinced that this was something more than a case of boorish driving.

Looking back, it was like a scene from a movie: Lonnie's truck slid to a stop in the left lane, while bits of debris littered the highway, causing everyone who wasn't already slowing or stopping to see the action, to slow or stop to miss hitting the car parts. Two more cars, piloted by drivers looking no more than five feet in front of their vehicles, slammed into other cars who had already stopped. I could finally hear police sirens in the distance but we just kept going.

In fact, we really kept going, passing 610, downtown and the Galleria area, heading relentlessly west on I-10. Evan wasn't saying a word, wasn't looking at me, didn't even seem to be aware of what had just transpired. I was afraid to say anything in case I startled him out of whatever place he had retreated. His driving had been tremendous back there, and I hated to scare him into crashing now. Finally, I began talking to the two dogs in the back. Henry was still on the floor, trembling and whimpering softly. He didn't appear to be hurt, but I suspected his carefree car-riding days might be over for a while. He'd probably need doggie therapy before getting willingly into a car again. Addie was lying on her belly, head draped over the seat, panting heavily. I suspected they could both use a potty break.

"You guys okay back there?" I asked, stretching out a hand to pet first one, then the other. Henry made a move to clamber over the console to me, but a quick snap from Addie put him back in his place. "Be nice," I told her, reaching back to lift him over. I never take my dog anywhere without seat-belting her in. And the one day I don't, look what happens. I made a mental note to pick up a seat belt harness for Henry as well.

As we passed the Memorial City Mall, I finally felt Evan lift up a little on the gas pedal. We were probably only doing about seventy-five now.

"Umm, Evan?" We slowed a little more. "You okay?"

He signaled and made his way to the far-right lane, carefully looking over his shoulder to check his blind spot, as if his car wasn't already crushed on that rear panel. But at least he was being careful. We exited, and he made his way to an empty parking lot outside an abandoned strip mall. Rolling to a stop, we sat for a moment in silence. Evan's hands gripped the wheel in the same position they'd been since this ordeal had started back in Channelview. His knuckles were white, and the thought struck me that maybe his hands were cramped, stuck in that position. The red splotches on his cheeks looked as if he'd been hit with a paintball pellet, and his dark hair fell limply over his forehead. He let his head fall forward onto his chest, and his shoulders began to shake.

I reached out and touched his arm. "Evan?" The shaking continued to increase in intensity, as did my concern. "Evan, are you okay?"

Finally, he reached over, opened the door, leaned out and threw up. Frankly, I felt a bit nauseous myself, but I blocked it out of my mind and turned my attention to Henry, who was nestled under my chin. I concentrated on comforting him, trying to get him to stop shaking.

When Evan leaned back into his seat, he turned to me and gave a little shaky laugh. "Holy shit," he said. There wasn't much I could add to that. Setting Henry on the seat, we got out to inspect the damage to Evan's precious Mustang. It didn't look good. Gone was the sleek, powerful machine. In its place was a crumpled, dented beater.

"You know I'll take care of this," I said. My mind whirled around, trying to assess my available accounts, which I was pretty sure were drying up quickly in the pursuit of my new business. Maybe I could get a loan from Frances. "Totally. This was entirely my fault." The thought of the damage to the other cars crept into my head, and I quickly pushed that aside. There was no way we were going to get out of this without the respective insurance companies getting involved. We would be lucky to get out of this without lawsuits being filed.

In my mind, I could hear the sound of metal crashing.

Images flashed through my head, snapshots of the carnage as it happened: the slow-moving car suddenly in front of us; Addie falling across the backseat, Henry huddled on the floor; the grille of Lonnie's truck bearing down on us; my hands bracing against the dashboard. And the crashing. So much damage in so little time. I felt waves of guilt building up in my stomach. Someone could have been killed or maimed. There could have been children in those cars. Innocent victims, merely out on the highway late on a Sunday afternoon. Addie could have been thrown through the windshield. Evan could have been killed. As it was, I'd wrecked his car. Granted, I hadn't been driving, but if I hadn't been so stupid as to go into that shed, Lonnie wouldn't have come after us. Evan had probably saved my life. Without his powerful engine and quick-reacting motor skills, this would have turned out much worse. I sat down on the rough pavement, suddenly too rubber-legged to stand.

Evan didn't say anything, he just kept circling his baby. Occasionally he'd reach out and touch an especially damaged section, running his fingers lightly over it like a parent caressing a boo-boo. The dogs circled the car from the inside with him, noses pressed to the windows, smudging all the way around. They seemed to sense Evan's distress, and a series of whimpers made their way through the windows like a sad score in a tear-jerker movie. After Evan's fourth go around the car, I mentioned that the dogs probably needed a bathroom break, but he didn't seem to hear me; he was too engrossed in the rear end of the car where the bumper had fallen off.

I opened the passenger-side door, which had miraculously suffered no damage, and pulled the seat forward, grabbing leashes as the dogs made their way out. Addie quickly found a broken section of payment and peed on it. Henry I had to walk around so he could mark the light poles and leftover parking stops.

Evan was on his back with his head stuck up under the rear of the car when we returned from our brief walk. Henry took advantage of his vulnerability to scoot under the car near Evan's face, where he pawed at his head and licked any exposed skin he could find. Evan laughed and sat up quickly, trying to protect himself, promptly smashing his forehead on the rough exposed metal. Blood began trickling down his forehead as he scooted out from under the car, scraping both elbows against the pavement in the process.

"Damn," he said finally when he emerged. At least he was looking at me and appeared focused. He scooped Henry up and held him close against his chest while the little dog continued to rain kisses on his face. Addie, not to be left out, assaulted him with kisses from the other side.

We sat recovering and ran through options of what we should do. I thought we should call Officer Wilson and give him an update on what had happened. For all we knew, someone had gotten Evan's license plate number and he was now wanted for fleeing the scene of an accident. He would also be liable for the damage to the minivan we'd hit from behind. The whole thing was shaping up to be an insurance nightmare. At the same time, I wasn't quite sure how to frame the story of what had precipitated the ugly car chase. My little entry into the Lotts' shed was no doubt considered breaking and entering. It was at least entering, if not breaking. *Okay, so maybe we don't call.*

The other pressing issue was the car. While it was drivable, as evidenced by our flight down the highway, I was concerned that maybe it had sustained some damage that would render it undrivable in the near future. Evan insisted on making a few more rounds of the thing, taking it all in. The sky was growing dark and a mild breeze picked up, blowing bits of trash across the empty parking lot. The traffic on the freeway behind us rushed along at a good clip. Addie and Henry had settled down in the dirty gravel, probably wondering what their weird humans were doing. It was time to make a move, whatever it was, although I was reluctant to leave the anonymity of this abandoned parking lot. No one knew where we were. Not Lonnie. Not the police. Not the angry drivers we'd caused to wreck.

Finally, we decided to go to my house if for no other reason than it's more comfortable than a deserted parking lot. I rose stiffly to my feet. My neck was getting sore and the muscles in my lower back were stiffening up as well. Evan said he felt okay, but I saw him rub his neck when he thought I wasn't looking.

By the time we'd retraced our route back towards the city and down to my house, darkness had crept through the streets hiding clarity in its shadows. One of the streetlights closest to my house was burned out, and I suffered an unreasonable sense of dread over that. Streetlights burn out. It didn't mean that someone had shot it out and was waiting in the shadows of my front walkway to wrap a garrote around my throat and cut through my windpipe before anyone could hear my strangled cries. Really, I needed to cut out the few thrillers I read altogether.

My house looked the same as it had when we'd left it less than two hours ago, although I felt like I was returning from an extended journey. Larry's lights were on, which I took as a sign that he might be alive. Evan parked in the driveway and we made our way stiffly up the walk. I realized I still had the pipe from Lonnie's shed, and I tossed it discreetly behind my front shrubs. I'd get rid of it later. No sense in keeping evidence that would tie me to a break-in.

It would have been nice to collapse onto the couch, only it was still perched on the curb. No one had hauled it away; I suspected the smell and the stains had deterred most of the garbage pickers. So we collapsed on the rugless floor, which only put pressure on my sore joints. The dogs raced around the house, sniffing for signs of intruders. Their happy wagging reassured me that no one had been there. Hauling myself to my feet, I headed for the refrigerator.

"Would you like a beer?" I asked Evan's prone figure.

"Maybe six or seven," he grunted. I poured two and carried one over to him. He rolled to an upright position and we sat cross-legged on the floor like a couple of second graders. The blood on his forehead had dried into an L shape.

"Okay, what the hell happened back there?" he finally asked me. His eyes were serious and fixed on me, while his hands idly rolled his glass between them. "I thought his truck wasn't there when we went past."

"It wasn't. He and Cherilynn came home while I was there."

"While you were leaving the brownies?"

"No, I'd already dropped them at the door."

I took a protracted sip of my beer.

"And they pulled up and caught you on the porch?"

"Not exactly. I was looking at the backyard. And there's this shed they have next to the house. It looks like it's a thousand years old. But I get the feeling that if Lonnie has something to hide, he'd hide it in there."

Evan's eyes popped wide in their sockets. "Tell me you did not go in there."

"I did."

We stared wordlessly at each other.

"And that's where he caught you." It was a statement more than a question.

"Almost. Believe it or not, Cherilynn probably saved my life by nagging him to help her bring in the groceries. I saw him through the crack in the door. He was about to open it and find me there. I nearly wet my pants." I giggled in a way that made me think I could be losing it. Apparently, Evan thought so too, because he took another long drag on his beer and didn't say anything.

"Cherilynn caught sight of me running back towards the woods. She yelled at me, which brought him running." My heartbeat picked up a little, just to let me know it remembered the rush.

"Was it worth it?" he asked. I thought about his damaged car, which could be fixed, as well as the legal trouble we would probably be in for leaving the scene of the carnage on the highway, which would be harder to fix, as well as the personal risk he'd taken to get me and the dogs to safety.

"No." I sighed. Exhaustion seeped through my muscles, carrying with it a hint of depression. "That place is a dump. Car parts, receipts for car parts and a roach that would give Henry a run for his money. That's about it."

Addie wandered over and plopped down next to me. I ran a hand along her muscled side, thankful she was safe. It was going to cost me, but I needed to make things right for Evan. He'd only been sucked into this mess because he was my friend. Henry trotted over to Evan, bounced into his lap and threw a front paw on either side of Evan's neck, leaning into what looked like a hug. Evan ruffled his ears affectionately.

"Was there anything weird about the car parts stuff? Like maybe he's running a chop shop or something?"

That was certainly an interesting idea. I tried to think back to the receipts I'd seen. The problem was, I had no idea what chop shop records would look like. "Maybe," I said. "There were car parts all over the floor. You could hardly move at all without running into one. And there was a giant box of receipts hidden away under a cot in the corner. I wondered why one guy would need so many parts."

"Did you get a look at the paperwork? I can't imagine that someone running an illegal business would want a lot of records around, but what do I know?"

"It just seemed like a bunch of loose receipts. I didn't look that close, but when I saw them, I assumed they were for things that Lonnie bought."

"Well, it's an idea. Whether it's a chop shop or something else, maybe he's doing something illegal and Dayna found out about it. I'm not sure which one of those two I'd put my money on in a situation like that."

"I'd have to put my money on Lonnie," I said, thinking of Dayna's lifeless body.

CHAPTER TWENTY

E van left shortly after finishing his beer. He said he was tired and wanted to go home and call his insurance company. I felt guilty, but he assured me that he'd had a really good time. Well, until we felt the first crunch of metal.

As soon as the door shut, I raced upstairs for some clean clothes to take to the Doubletree. Shoot. I hadn't ever made it to Target to pick up new underwear, and I'd already thrown my panties into the garbage. I considered picking out a couple of pairs, but then remembered they'd gone into the bag with the towels that I'd used to try and clean up the living room. I'd just as soon go bare-bottomed.

I love my house and I've always been happy here, but tonight it felt alien and unfriendly. When I was downstairs, I felt as if there was a malevolent presence upstairs, and when I was upstairs, I worried about what was going on downstairs. Addie wasn't helping the situation. Either she was picking up on my nervous energy, or she felt it too, because she was pacing and whining, much like I wanted to do.

Digging through the closet for tomorrow's outfit, I spotted the hamper and realized I still had some old unwashed laundry.

I could grab whatever undies were in there and wash them out in the sink when I got to the Doubletree. I grabbed a duffle bag from the bottom of my closet and made a beeline for the hamper. Poking through the jumbled clothes, I jammed my finger against something hard. Holy cow! The files and the box I'd stolen from Dayna's office. I couldn't believe I'd forgotten that thing. It seemed like three years ago that Evan and I had been digging through Dayna's office.

Pulling the plastic bag to the top, I shook off the socks. A few small bits of limp brown matter fell to the floor with them. Hopefully it was old lettuce from Evan's lunch bag, and not something nastier that had crawled in and died. As I lifted the bag, the folder edges cut through the flimsy plastic, and everything flew to the floor in a heap, sending papers sliding in every direction. I knelt down and carefully slid everything back into what I hoped was its correct folder. Some of these notes didn't have names on them, and without their corresponding folder, I wouldn't know who Dayna had been trashing.

Grabbing my duffle, I shoved the folders into the bottom and topped it off with clothes and a rawhide chew for Addie. We were back at the Doubletree twenty-five minutes later.

I took an extended hot shower, changed into an oversized pair of sweats, washed three pairs of underwear in the sink and ordered a steak, baked potato and grilled asparagus from room service. It felt great to be back in my room, and definitely more secure than my own house. The turned-down bedspread with the chocolate mint on the pillow, the oversized love seat and the soothing decor did much to restore my sense of balance.

I started to spread the files out on the coffee table but decided to wait until room service came. Flipping on the TV, I surfed mindlessly through the endless channels they offered, nothing catching my attention. Finally, I settled on a documentary of the remaking of New Orleans after Hurricane Katrina. Obviously, living in Houston, I'd seen my share of Katrina coverage. Shoot, we'd taken in more refugees than any other city during the aftermath. The news had been filled with little but, for weeks following the disaster. All of that I was familiar with. But this was a different take. This focused on the rebuilding of New Orleans' sex trade.

A woman in a tiny strip of shimmery material that passed as a dress was walking through the French Quarter, speaking into the camera. "Business went to nothing for almost a week," she rasped in a voice that spoke of too many cigarettes and late nights. Her wrinkled face made her look like an AARP spokesperson, but for all I knew she might be thirty. "But you gotta look for the blessing, right? And the blessings came to town! Yes sir, they came!" She gave a throaty chuckle and the camera panned to a scaffolding climbing the side of an historic French Quarter building, where four shabby dust-covered men hung off the sides, swinging hammers with practiced blows.

One of the men raised his head from his work and made a high-pitched cawing sound like a bird in distress. The madam waved her hand appreciatively and shouted back at him, "Love ya boys!"

A knock on the door woke Addie from her nap on the bed, and she charged the short space, barking at top decibel. "Shush, shush," I told her as a second knock sounded. Peering through the peephole, I saw a uniformed Hispanic man holding a tray. I slipped open the door, trying to keep Addie back with my knee as she shoved forward, growling deeply. He raced back several steps, stumbling and almost dropping my steak, which was probably exactly what my dog was hoping for.

"Hold on," I told him as I shoved her back and slipped out the door to sign the charge form, tip him and save my meal. Once he was safely away, I went back into the room, holding the tray high as Addie bounced up and down, trying to get her nose as close to the cover as she could. The smell was fabulous even with my poor human's nose; I could only imagine how good it smelled with her heightened doggie sense.

I settled myself at the desk, trying to ignore the deep brown eyes that stared at me unblinking. Her bowl of dried kibble lay untouched, and her look made clear how insulted she was by it. I turned back to the TV, looking over the top of her head, trying not to feel guilty. But it didn't work. Thoughts of my ransacked house and niggling fears of what could have happened to her if she had been there rushed to the front of my head, and I relented. Addie rarely gets people food, with the exception of a little cheese here and there. But between the break-in and the car wreck and the fact that someone might very likely be trying to kill me, maybe we both deserved a little bit of steak.

Once she was happily settled with a few shavings of beef mixed in with her food, I turned back to my dinner and the documentary playing itself out. I'd pretty much lost interest and was just plowing through my dinner when a voice from the TV caught my attention.

"New Orleans may have been forever changed by Katrina, but some things will never change here." The voice was so familiar, but I couldn't place it. The camera was showing a night scene on Bourbon Street: men being approached by scantily clad young women who attached themselves to the nearest arm. A couple of the more aggressive ones were slipping their hands into pockets that they shouldn't be slipping their hands into.

The voice rolled on in a slow drawling, seductive tone. Like a blast, it hit me—that was Daniel! This must be one of his documentaries! Wow, from everything I had heard, his documentaries were nothing more than glorified home movies shot for his own viewing pleasure, financed by Dayna's money. I guessed he'd gotten lucky and finally sold one. Interesting choice of subjects. The program rolled to a close while I finished my dinner. The filming was edgy and raw and maybe in some circles would be considered artsy. I found it mostly depressing.

I flipped the channel to HGTV to soothe myself. There's nothing like watching people hunt for houses or redecorate drab rooms to lift one's spirits. Gathering the stack of files together, I spread myself out on the bed, careful to remove the bedspread before settling down. I saw a news story once where they flashed a special light around a hotel room, illuminating bodily fluids. I'm really careful about where I sit now. Addie popped up next to me and turned several times in a tight circle, crumpling most of the papers in the process, before plopping herself down.

The collection was an eclectic mix of handwritten notes, copies of personnel records and random bits of spreadsheets sprinkled with meaningless numbers paper-clipped to other arbitrary papers. There were even a few photos mixed in, and I studied those with particular interest. Most of the photos were of people we'd worked with at Astor Oil: a few Christmas party pics, a couple from the company picnic two summers ago, and some taken with people I knew at unidentifiable bars. Most of the subjects looked drunk, and the pictures had a grainy look to them. But aside from being a little embarrassing, I couldn't see that these were any big deal.

I set the work-related photographs aside and turned to the ones I didn't recognize. There were two showing a man I'd never seen, wearing dusty jeans and boots, leaning so far back in a chair to drain his beer bottle that I was sure at some point he must have fallen back and cracked his head on the floor. It was hard to tell anything from those, because his face was mostly obscured. In the second picture, I could just make out the face of a little girl in a dark doorway behind him. Maybe I'd ask Daniel if he recognized the man. Or the little girl, for that matter.

The night flew past as I learned more about my ex-coworkers than I'd ever cared to know. And yet, it was impossible to look away from the pages as I read about affairs, rumored affairs, illness, family illness, drinking problems, drug problems, money problems, who surfed nasty websites at work, who was caught on the security cameras doing nasty things and what was revealed in pre-employment screenings. Who knew Dayna had such a stash of trashy information? I wondered who her informant had been, because a lot of what was recorded was nothing more than office gossip. She had hosted countless after-work happy hours, but the gossip here extended to people who had never attended those gatherings, and frankly, I'd never seen anyone chat it up with Dayna. Everyone had been too terrified of her wrath to risk incurring it.

What had inspired Dayna to collect this type of information about the people who worked for her? Did anyone even know she had this type of information? Judging from the way someone had snuffed the life out of her, I would guess yes, someone was aware of it. Then again, maybe these papers had nothing to do with her murder. Aside from a lot of potentially embarrassing things that no one would want their coworkers to know, there wasn't anything here that I could picture killing someone over.

And yet, it was another example of Dayna's need for power and control, holding these personal embarrassments in her back pocket to pull out and torment her victims with, at the least provocation. It explained how she had been able to stop any opposition to her ideas in meetings. Whenever anyone had dared question her, she always had a quick quip or a sly question that seemed to stop the opposition cold. It hadn't been lucky guesses on her part after all. She'd had all of us scoped out and documented up.

I set the rest of the papers aside, feeling sick and ashamed for having read through them. I felt dirty, like I'd been

snooping through a neighbor's house or peeping through someone's curtains. Glancing at the clock, I was shocked to see it
was already one forty-five. My neck was stiff and my back hurt,
as much from the awkward position I'd been laying in as from
the beating we'd taken in Evan's car this afternoon. I hoisted
myself to my feet and limped to the bathroom to take another
Advil. Addie took the opportunity in the twenty-five seconds I
was gone to rearrange herself in the middle of my pillow.

Too tired to move her, I gathered the papers in a loose pile,
threw them on the table and made my way to the other side of
the bed. Muscles I didn't know I had protested every move,
shooting little aching arrows up my spine. It was too late to
hope a good night's sleep would cure me. I could only hope I
didn't feel worse when I got up. Lying beneath the crisp sheets,
I felt sleep slipping away from me. My body was exhausted, but
my brain wouldn't shut off. Snippets of gossip I'd read raced
through my mind, creating little visual images of people I
knew. Warren in accounting—I'd thought he was just
unfriendly, but according to Dayna's notes, he'd been dealing
with a severely ill child. Visions of red-rimmed eyes that I'd
attributed to staring at countless spreadsheets for long hours,
rearranged themselves into expressions of grief that I should
have been able to read. And Dayna had kept him working late
many nights as she questioned every number. I couldn't
imagine the stress he must have been going through, needing to
be with his child, and yet requiring the job that provided the
critical healthcare.

Sue Giles, who always acted like she hadn't a care in the
world, battled depression and substance abuse. Matt Hurley's
wife had left him, taking both kids with her and accusing him
of abuse. Other things she'd recorded weren't as major, but
they were spiteful. She'd recorded personal things like bad
breath, knock-off clothes and crooked teeth. Car choices, polit-
ical preferences and poor vocabularies also made the list. The

absurdity of this kind of documentation rattled my mind. It felt evil, and I closed my eyes and willed the thoughts away.

Eventually I drifted off, but slept fitfully, aware of Addie's every move, the rattle of the air conditioner and the thumping of feet along the hallway. At seven I gave up and stumbled to the shower, hoping the hot water and steam would soothe my aches and clear my head. I reviewed my list of things I had to get accomplished today. Being that it was Monday, my doggie clients were a top priority. I groaned aloud as I thought of the four-plus hours of walking these aching muscles were going to have to endure with numerous pulling canines on the end of their leashes. Maybe I'd opt for short business-only walks, supplemented by vigorous indoor play.

Next, I needed to find someone to repair or replace my back door. I'm not enough of a home improvement girl to know if it could be fixed or if I'd need to replace it. I hoped it could be fixed because that would be faster than ordering a new door and having the doggie door reinstalled.

My inventory of dog cookies had been totally depleted, and I needed to get baking if I hoped to keep my business alive and well. I'd worked too hard and too long cultivating my cookie buyers and my distributors to let it fall apart now.

An overwhelming desire to go back to my life as it had been before Dayna's murder washed over me.

Dammit. It wasn't my fault I'd found the body. I missed the active days with my clients, full of love and playfulness. The satisfaction I found in baking healthy treats that dogs adored. The friendly chatter and casual friendships I'd forged with the doggie daycare and spa owners who distributed my treats. And the way I had been able to build this business, small but growing. Supporting myself and still loving what I do.

It seemed like the innocence of those days was gone. The cloud of someone breaking into my home left me feeling like I might never feel the same security there that I had before. The phone calls were unnerving, and I was convinced someone wanted to kill me.

I certainly didn't have any information that could nail the killer, other than a healthy fear of Lonnie's short fuse. I thought again of yesterday and debated if I should contact the police. Reason indicated I should, although I still waffled when I thought of admitting to illegally entering private property.

I packed up my measly belongings and checked out of the hotel. With daylight comes courage, and I resolved to stop letting some lunatic drive me out of my house and away from my routine. I also resolved to buy some new underpants today.

We were home before eight, cup of caramel cappuccino double whip steaming in my hand. I seriously had to start making more money if I was planning to support this cup-a-day habit. Addie completed her customary sweep of the house to reassure herself that nothing had changed since her last visit.

The cappuccino flowed sweet magic through my veins, clearing my head and revving me up. I dug a small spiral note-book out of the junk drawer and made my list for the day:

1. get door repaired
2. min. four large batches of dog cookies
3. walk clients
4. buy underwear
5. check with cookie distributors
6. Evan
7. maid service (to make house feel uncontaminated)
8. shooting lessons
9. call police

I scratched out "call police." Then I scratched out "shooting lessons." This was about reclaiming my life. My life effective today had no place for crazy killers or the associated reactions I was having to them.

The door was my number one priority. I didn't want to go back to the hotel tonight, but I needed a little more substance between myself and the outside world than a flimsy piece of cardboard and masking tape. Although if I couldn't get the door fixed today, I could always line the top of my wall with barbed wire. That should take care of anyone getting into my backyard, much less getting anywhere close to the door. Or I could take a lesson from my neighbor and line it with dog poop. Who would want to crawl over dog poop to get into my yard?

The third door company I called said they could get someone out today to see if they could repair it, or take measurements if they couldn't. They couldn't promise they'd be there before I left for my dog-walking rounds, so we made an appointment for four. Item 1: check!

On to number two. Setting two packages of frozen liver under hot water, I gathered all the other ingredients and began assembling them in multiple mixing bowls. I felt energized and organized, and I whirled around the kitchen like Emeril on speed. Bam! There's a little pinch of parsley. Bam! A little bit of wheat germ. The liver was almost thawed when I threw it in the food processor. Pink flesh flew around the bowl spattering the sides. I hummed along tunelessly, drowned out by the noise of the machine.

It wasn't until I noticed Addie racing towards the front door, mouth moving like she was in full bark, that I realized someone was at my front door. I killed the machine, and as the blades wound down I heard a pounding on my front door. My first thought was Larry.

Looking through the peephole, I was surprised to see the top half of Cherilynn's head leaning towards the door as if listening for something other than Addie's barks. Cherilynn was not on my list. I opened the door anyway. She fell forward, catching herself awkwardly against the door frame, then glared at me as if I'd pushed her.

Addie backed up a few steps but braced her front legs and

stiffened her tail while switching to a low-level growl. I felt much the same way. I stood holding the door, not inviting her in, but not slamming it in her face either.

"You gonna invite me in, or what?" she asked, eying Addie with distrust. "And can't you shut that dog up?"

You can be rude to me, but my dog is a whole other matter. "She doesn't seem to like you," I said as mildly as I could. "Funny."

"Where's the one you stole from us?" She strained her neck trying to peer around me into the rest of the house.

"How did you know where I live?"

"I could ask you the same thing," she shot back. I guessed she could, although I was having a hard time believing she and Lonnie were internet wizards. Needing to get back to my dog cookies, I relented and stepped aside, allowing her to enter. Addie stepped aside too, but her tail remained on high alert and her lips quivered with suppressed growls.

Cherilynn propelled herself into my living room, clutching an oversized faux leather handbag with shiny chrome clasps close against her chest as if afraid a band of purse snatchers was going to materialize from behind the corn plant and have a run at her. Her head swiveled from side to side, taking in my living space. I made my way back to the kitchen and turned the food processor on for the final few seconds until the liver was the proper consistency.

Still clutching her purse and giving Addie a wide berth, she made her way to one of the barstools set up along the counter separating the kitchen from my living room. Hoisting her plump bottom onto the seat, she grunted and made a rude gagging sound when she saw my cookie batter.

"What the hell is that?"

"I'm making cookies," I answered. "I still have some left from a prior batch. Would you like one?" She gave an involuntary shudder, her lips moving wordlessly in disgust. "I'll take that as a no," I said, using a spatula to scrape the dark pink mass from the sides of the food processor into a mixing bowl. Stealing a glance at Cherilynn, I started to worry she was going to throw up. I just couldn't take any more of that. "Seriously, it's batter for dog biscuits."

She looked away, gazing at my patched back door and breathing through her mouth. I'd grown accustomed to the smell of the dog cookies, and indeed, I even found it soothing now, but I remembered how disgusting I'd found it the first few times I'd made them. Oh well, I hadn't invited her over. If she didn't like what she was seeing, and smelling, she could go. She didn't.

"So, have the police found who killed your sister yet?" I asked.

"No. They asked us some questions, but I ain't heard anything from them like that they caught the scumbag that did this." She settled her bottom a little more deeply into the cushion and began running a finger along the countertop.

"So, not to be rude, Cherilynn. But I've got a lot to do today. What did you need?"

She stiffened her spine and tried to sit up higher in her chair, but even with that effort, she was sitting below me creating an uneven power shift that she didn't like. She hopped off the chair, but that made it even worse. Finally, placing her purse on the counter, she put her hands on her hips and faced me.

"I came here to give you a chance to pay for all the damage you caused to Lonnie's truck."

Well, that wasn't quite what I expected. I added some parsley to the bowl and mixed it in slowly. "Interesting take on things. I'm pretty sure that Lonnie was the one responsible for a great deal of damage, not only to his own truck but to multiple other cars as well. He could have killed someone." I looked up from my mixing in time to see her eyes narrow into little slits.

"He wouldn't a' been on that road if you hadn't a' broken onto our property. I'm a mind to call the cops and tell them that."

"Why don't you do that? Then maybe they can take some prints from your husband and match them up to the ones they found on my back door there." I nodded towards the broken window. "Breaking and entering. Harassment. Stalking. He'll probably be out in a few years."

"You haven't got no right to say those things, you little bitch! I'm gonna get a lawyer and I'm gonna sue you for defecation of character."

Defecation of character? Oh. It struck me what she meant, and I almost laughed out loud. But I stopped myself when I saw the fury building in her face. Patches of crimson were creeping up from her collar, mottling her neck and the lower half of her face. She puffed her breath hard, and her fists curled into little balls of sausages.

"People like you think you're so much better than everyone else. Well let me tell you something. You ain't no better than my no-good whore sister. She had that same attitude—thinkin' she was better than everyone, and just look at where that got her. She's dead. Maybe you ought to think about that."

I set down my spatula and eyed her warily. What did I know about Cherilynn, really? Her anger at Dayna seemed to match her husband's, and I considered that maybe they'd both been in on the killing. Addie came and stood at my side, a quiet rumbling emanating from her chest.

"Look, Cherilynn, I'm sorry. I didn't mean to upset you. I know this must be a really difficult time for you right now."

"That's just it. You don't know nuthin'." She broke eye contact with me and looked at the back door again. "When did that happen?" she asked.

"Saturday night."

"Were you here?"

A chill ran up my spine at the thought of being here while someone was smashing in my door. Would they have broken in if I had been here? What were they looking for?

"Luckily I wasn't." I watched her for signs that she knew about my break-in. I wasn't sure, but I got the sense that while she hadn't known about it, maybe she had some ideas about it. "I don't know what they were looking for," I prompted, hoping she would take the bait.

"Did they take anything?"

"I'm not entirely certain," I said. "It looked like someone was looking for something because it was pretty well trashed. But I haven't found anything missing."

She surveyed the room behind her. "They take your couch, or something? Looks like a big thing's missing right there," she said, swinging her arm in the direction of my living room.

"No. That was another issue. I had to get rid of my couch and the rug for other reasons." I hadn't seen my couch or rug on the curb when I'd gotten home this morning. Someone must have hauled them off. Bless them.

"Oh." She seemed relieved. Probably thinking that Lonnie couldn't have done this because he hadn't come home hauling a new sofa.

"I really don't have anything valuable," I said. "I mean, I have a TV, a computer, that kind of thing. But they didn't take that stuff. I don't know what else they could have wanted."

She still wasn't talking, but she had calmed down a bit, so I went back to my mixing.

"So why you thinkin' that Lonnie did that?" It came out raspy, as if she'd just woken up.

I weighed my answer carefully. Cherilynn, no doubt, knew more than she was letting on and I needed to get past the antagonism if I was going to ferret anything out of her. "Actually, I don't know who broke in. But I thought maybe he came looking for the dog."

"He don't care about that dog," she snorted. "Leastways he only cared that we might be able to get some money for him. I'm glad he's gone." She looked around the kitchen, belatedly wondering where he was. "He was a whinin' little sack a' shit."

Happily for Henry, he was safely away from the Lotts' reach. I needed to check on him and Evan this morning, make sure they suffered no ill effects from our rough ride yesterday.

"So, you don't happen to have any guesses as to what someone might be looking for here, would you?" I asked, casually stirring my batter and checking the recipe as if I wasn't paying careful attention to our conversation.

"How would I know what someone wants with you?" she said. I ran a finger along the recipe, checking ingredients I knew by heart. The silence stretched between us. Measuring in the wheat germ, I went back to my mixing.

Most people aren't comfortable with silence. I, myself, often babble on about nothing in particular just to fill the dead air, but now I could feel the value of that silence, pressing on Cherilynn's nerves like elastic pinching her bikini line. She would flinch soon.

"You got a nice place. They coulda wanted anything."

"But they didn't take any of the things I would have expected," I said absently, checking the temperature of the oven. I sprayed two cookie sheets with nonstick spray and began forming the batter into little bone shapes. Cherilynn watched my fingers flying with practiced precision, tossing the forms into neat rows.

"When you found Dayna, where was she?" she asked.

"She was in their home office or study or whatever they call it," I said, surprised at the sudden flip-flop of this conversation.

"You didn't take nothing from there, did you?"

My fingers stopped their cookie making and I looked up to

meet her gaze. "Just the dog," I said. "Why? Was there something missing from Dayna's? Has Daniel noticed that something was taken?"

"I don't know. The police haven't told us nothing. I told you that." She sounded peeved, like I hadn't been listening. "And Daniel ain't exactly making tracks to see us now that he don't have to."

"Was there something in particular you thought I might have?" I asked. Maybe she and Lonnie had broken in here and tossed my place together. Maybe they had decided that she should just come back and ask directly for whatever it was.

"No." I went back to my cookie making. "You got that down good," she said somewhat grudgingly.

"Thanks. I make a lot of these. It's my business."

She looked around again as if sizing it up in a new light. "You got this place by makin' that shit?"

"Well, not entirely," I said. Actually, not at all. At last check, while I was making a small profit, it wasn't enough to buy the good-looking dog bed from the Orvis catalog I'd had my eye on, much less a house. "I worked at Astor Oil for several years." *And my grandmother paid off my mortgage when I quit there to start my real life,* I thought.

"Yeah. Dayna made a lot of money there too. But God, she was selfish with it. You seen where she lived and you seen where we live. Not the same, is it?" She folded her arms across her ample chest. "Could she get Lonnie a job? No! She didn't want any a' her business ass-o-ciates knowin' what kinda people she came from. We wasn't good enough to present to her hifalutin society."

Same story, slightly different version than she'd told me before.

"And that's still not enough for her." She was working herself into a true state of agitation. She paced back and forth across the kitchen tiles, squeezing her arms tighter and tighter across her chest until her breasts began popping up from the pressure. "Nothing's ever enough. Wasn't enough that she had everything she wanted. No! She had to try and take away what little bit we had."

I held my breath, trying to disappear into the scenery. Now we were getting somewhere. A motive danced just out of reach. I could feel it. *Keep going,* I thought as hard as I could, willing my brain waves into her head. *Keep going.*

"Damn bitch. She couldn't just leave well enough alone. She never did anything for Aunt Edith when she was alive. I did everything for her, right up till she died. Dayna didn't do nuthin' for her. But she couldn't stand it that she didn't get what little bit that poor woman had. And trickin' me that way about the will…" She trailed off, suddenly aware of what she was saying.

Feigning nonchalance, I piped up encouragingly, "Oh, I know! Family wills are the worst. It's just hard to believe how some people can be in those situations. You don't have to tell me. And frankly, if Dayna was involved, it must have been horrible." I popped the cookie trays in the oven, set the timer and washed my hands, all the while not looking directly at Cherilynn. *Keep going,* I willed.

"Yeah, well let's just say it wasn't good," she said in a subdued tone.

"Can I get you something to drink?" I asked, belatedly turning into a good hostess. The thing I hadn't put on my list was "find out who killed Dayna and get him/her off my back." Suddenly it seemed like this unexpected visit from her sister might just help me get there.

"Nah, I gotta get going," she said, picking up her purse. "If you're not gonna help pay for Lonnie's damage, then I'm just wastin' my time."

"Well, but maybe you could tell me what Dayna was

tricking you over regarding the will. My father's a lawyer and I could ask him what you should do."

Her eyes squinted into slits as she stared at me, weighing my offer.

"Nah, I better not say nuthin' more without talking to Lonnie." She shuffled towards the front door, staring at my bookcases and wall decorations as she went. I followed in her trail, desperately trying to think of some way to get her to spill her guts. This was it. I just knew it. It had to be.

At the door, she turned and looked me square in the eye. "I'd 'preciate it if you didn't mention this here visit to my husband," she said.

"Oh, don't worry," I told her. "I have no intention of getting close enough to your husband to have any conversation at all."

CHAPTER TWENTY-ONE

I t was dark before I finally plopped into a chair with a defrosted plate of vegetable lasagna and a small salad. Aside from the unexpected visit from Cherilynn, I'd pretty much been able to stick to my list for the day. The repairman said I needed a new door, but he had boarded up the broken pane more securely while exposing the other panes so that my kitchen no longer appeared cave-like.

Evan had been quite surly when I'd called him, worn out from a day of fighting with his insurance company. I offered again to pay for his damages, which only served to increase his irritation. We didn't talk long. I didn't even tell him about Cherilynn showing up at my door.

But on the bright side, I had baked and packaged four batches of cookies, which filled enough of my striped paper packages to make me feel like my business wasn't in shambles. I still needed to set aside a good hunk of time tomorrow to keep at it if I wanted to resupply my distributors' happily dwindling inventories.

I watched the news while I ate, wondering again if the police had any leads on Dayna's murder. The news repeats daily, the same stories involving new contestants in slightly altered circumstances. Two more people were killed in traffic accidents. Another apartment building burned down. An elderly woman was mugged in her house. Chance of rain tomorrow afternoon. I was pretty sure I'd seen this same broadcast last week.

Halfway through dinner, the phone rang. There had been multiple hang-ups on my machine when I had gotten back from my dog-walking rounds, all identified as Unknown Caller. Maybe my anonymous caller was at it again. Glancing at the caller ID, I was surprised to see it was Daniel Burke.

"Hello?"

"Hi, is this Jessie?" he asked in his sexy, gravelly voice.

"Yes, it is," I said in my most formal tone.

"This is Daniel Burke." He paused as if waiting for me to shriek in delight like a schoolgirl. I waited. My silence seemed to unnerve him.

Two more beats and he started rambling. He wanted to check to see how I was doing. He couldn't imagine how terrible it must have been for me to find his wife dead. He wondered whether I was seeing someone to talk about it, and so forth and so on for several minutes. He apologized again for putting me on the spot at the memorial service. I propped the phone against my shoulder and continued on with my dinner, since he didn't appear to need much participation from my side.

Once he talked himself out of the caring, sensitive chitchat, he finally said something that caught my attention. "Someone broke into my house today."

I set my plate on the coffee table. "Really? Did they take anything?" This had to be related to Dayna's murder and my break in.

"I can't tell yet. The whole house is a mess."

"But, like, electronics—that's usually what burglars want. Did they take anything like that?"

There was a pause, like he was surveying his immediate area. "I don't think so. We've got a new TV and computer, they're both untouched. It seems like whoever broke in spent most of their time in the study." Where Dayna was when she was killed. I wondered if she had come home and interrupted a burglary. If so, they obviously hadn't found what they were looking for and had come back for another go-round.

"Were you at work?" I asked, thinking being gone might have just saved Daniel's life. Then again, where does a self-employed documentary maker work?

"I was at the studio, editing a piece for my next film," he said. "I actually spent the night there last night and didn't get home until early this afternoon." I wondered if that was true or if he was with a woman. It wouldn't exactly put him in a favorable light if he was seeing someone within a week of his wife's murder. Although, no one I knew had assumed his and Dayna's marriage was airtight.

"You're probably lucky you weren't home," I said. "You know, my house was broken into Saturday night."

He was shocked to hear about my break-in and also skeptical about it being a coincidence. He suggested we meet for a drink the next night to "put our heads together and see if we could figure out what was going on here." Surprisingly, I agreed. I didn't really want to see Daniel, but I most definitely wanted to get to the bottom of this so I could get back to my life. I made a note to buy some pepper spray tomorrow to take along. Not that I really thought Daniel had killed his wife, but I could see him putting some unwanted, persistent moves on me and it was not appealing. Better to be prepared for any contingency.

My neck was aching again after we hung up, and I retrieved my ice bag and settled into my easy chair. Arranging the ice pack on the back of my neck, I leaned my head against the soft cushion and closed my eyes. Bits of information floated around my head. Somehow, they all fit together, I was sure of it, but what fit where? Start at the beginning. Dayna had been killed in their study, paper piles scattered every-where. Someone had broken into my house and hadn't taken anything but had made a mess as if they were looking for something. Paper piles everywhere. Now back to the Burkes—more break-ins more paper piles. What was so critical that it was worth killing for?

I started to drift, and other random thoughts mixed into my pattern. Damn, I'd forgotten to buy underwear again. I was going to have to do a quick wash of the ones I was wearing. I could scratch Evan off the list I'd made, but everything else was still open. The cold of the ice pack flowed soothing relief to my aching muscles. I needed to finish going through Dayna's work files.

My eyes flew open. "Did you take anything from the house?"

"Just the dog."

And it was just the dog, but I had taken paper piles from Dayna's office. Whatever her killer was looking for could easily be in the pile I'd taken from her office. And when they'd searched my house, the papers had been stuffed in my hamper.

Throwing the ice pack back in the freezer, I grabbed my bag from the floor, where I'd left it when I'd gotten home this morning, and pulled the now wrinkled stack of paper from the bottom. Shuffling through, I separated them into the ones I had looked through and the ones I hadn't. I couldn't take the time to read through as carefully as I had last night. Surely someone wasn't killing over a snidely written comment regarding personal drama or cleanliness habits.

There was much of the same that I'd seen last night. The gossip didn't hold my interest this time, and I quickly raced through, glancing at each sheet and moving on to the next. A sudden thump from outside caught my attention, and I paused to listen. Nothing followed, probably a neighbor slamming a door.

Almost at the bottom of the pile, a crisp white sheet with legal letterhead caught my eye. I did a quick scan. Oh. Wow. This necessitated a slower reading. Drawn up by an attorney I'd never heard of, it appeared to transfer the rights and responsibilities as executor of the last will and testament of one Edith Schmull from Cherilynn Lott to Dayna Burke. That would explain Cherilynn's remark about being tricked over a will. I didn't know much about estate law, but I did know that the executor receives a sum as recompense for the work they put into ensuring the deceased's lasts wishes are carried out. I couldn't imagine that we were talking about a great deal of money if this was the aunt that had lived next door to the Lotts.

Another thump outside sent Addie racing to battle position at the front door. Her ability to wake in an instant and charge immediately into action impressed me every time. It didn't sound like a car door this time, but I couldn't place what it was. Based on the events of the past week, I set the paper down and went to check out the noise. Pushing Addie aside, I peered through the peephole in the door, but the only thing I could see was a light from the house across the street. I hushed my dog as much as possible, and we stood side by side, listening. Her ears pricked forward and her mouth closed as she quieted her breathing in order to listen harder. I stopped breathing as well in the hopes of hearing better, but my pitiful human ears couldn't make out anything more. After a couple silent minutes, she retreated to her spot in the kitchen and I went back to the letter.

The tingle on my neck convinced me this document was important. Maybe even important enough to kill for. What could the aunt have that was so valuable? I closed my eyes and tried to picture the dusty, run-down house next door to the

Lotts'. I hadn't paid that much attention to it, but even using an enhanced airbrush in my memory, it needed a great deal of work. Not being a real estate expert, I couldn't even hazard a guess as to its worth. And unless it was sitting on its own little oil well, the land probably wasn't worth that much either.

Maybe she'd kept stacks of money stashed under her mattress. But Cherilynn and Lonnie could have just quietly appropriated those without anyone being the wiser. Maybe she had original bearer bonds from General Electric. Whatever the prize, Lonnie was clearly irritated over Dayna filching the executorship away from his wife. Was he irritated enough to kill Dayna? Judging from the fact he'd tried to run over Evan and me yesterday, I would guess yes. Was Cherilynn angry enough to kill her own sister? It didn't make sense that Cherilynn would sign that document and then change her mind so completely that she'd be willing to kill.

Maybe this had nothing to do with anything, but I didn't believe that for a minute. It had everything to do with it. Someone was looking through stacks of papers. At Dayna's house and at my house. Cherilynn had wanted to know if I'd taken anything from Dayna's house. Daniel had had another break-in.

So now what? I should contact the police, and yet I felt a certain reluctance. Explaining where I'd gotten this could only get Evan and me in trouble. Could we slip it back into her office, where the police would find it themselves? I would check with Evan, but my guess was the police were long finished with her office. I could mail it, but would they get the significance of it? It was more than I could decide today.

Exhaustion dragged me quickly into a realm of dark dreams, populated by menacing figures that I couldn't quite make out in the shadows. Their presence enveloped me in a cold dread, but every lighted place in which I sought refuge faded away as I approached, leaving the danger ever closer. I woke with a start, jerking to a sitting position and fighting to free my legs from the tangled sheets that bound them. Addie tensed beside me, her head up, ears pricked to a sound I couldn't hear.

Glancing at the clock, I was startled to see it was only ten thirty. My limbs felt heavy and stiff as if I'd been sleeping for hours. Bunching my pillow under my cheek, I flopped down, determined to get back to sleep, hopefully to more peaceful dreams than the ones I'd just escaped. A loud clattering and crashing sound from just outside sent Addie flying off the bed towards the top of the stairs, hackles on end and barking as loud as I'd ever heard her bark.

I leaped out of bed hard on her heels, struggling to identify the sound I was hearing. The clattering continued, and in the micro pauses between Addie's barks, I could make out the sound of a man shouting unintelligible words. At the front door, the noise was louder, but I couldn't see anything through the peephole. I paused only long enough to grab my trusty skillet, slip on Addie's leash and run out in my bare feet. Surely with all that racket, every neighbor up and down the street would be dialing 9-1-1 and running out to see what was happening.

On the small plot of grass in front of Larry's house, Lonnie Lott was flinging himself in wild circles, trying to extricate himself from what appeared to be long rows of aluminum cans strung together with wire. The more he struggled, the more entangled and enraged he became. The clattering was deafening, and Addie pressed her ears back hard against her head. I wished I had the same ability. A spotlight on the front of Larry's house suddenly flew on, flooding the whole surreal scene with enough wattage to light up Minute Maid Field. I held my skillet up to shield myself from the blinding light and tried to make sense of what was going on.

More cans crashed down from the branches of a small live

oak near the curb and wound their way towards Lonnie like snakes slithering towards their prey. The front door of Larry's house flew open and he raced out, wearing only a pair of dingy gray boxers. He was holding what looked like a bright yellow potty-bag and screaming, "I caught you! I caught you! That'll teach you to sneak around leaving your dog crap on my grass!"

Lonnie stopped thrashing long enough to take in Larry and his waving potty-bag before gathering his angry, hulking self and charging straight at him with a wordless scream of rage. I saw the look of surprise and sudden fear flit across Larry's face before Lonnie was on him, aluminum cans rattling along with his every move. Lonnie tackled him to the ground and began systematically beating Larry's head against the ground. I could hear the thud every time it hit the grass, and small staccato bursts of pain erupted from Larry.

If I didn't do something, Lonnie was going to kill him. Where were my other neighbors? Where were the police? I put Addie in a sit and stay and ran towards the struggling figures. Rows of cans trailed from Lonnie, and I kicked my way through them until I was just behind his thrashing form. Pulling my skillet back, I gave him a sharp tap on the back of the skull with the flat end. He swung a hand back and swatted at me as if I was nothing more than an annoying gnat. So much for trying not to really hurt him.

I swung my skillet using two hands this time and connected with the back of his head hard enough to knock him out. He fell forward onto Larry, knocking whatever air was left in my neighbor out with a whoosh. I stepped back in a crouch, ready to swing again. I'd seen too many horror flicks to know that the bad guy always plays dead just long enough to get you to put your ankle in the reach of his hairy hand.

But he wasn't moving. Larry began to struggle under him, and I leaned forward, still alert, and gave Lonnie a shove, trying to get his dead weight off Larry. Larry managed to slip himself out from under the prone form, but his underwear slipped down around his knees in the process. I looked away. This had been a bad enough night as it was without being exposed to that.

Addie was still sitting very upright where I'd left her, with a look that said people were weird. By the time I looked back, Larry had righted himself and was panting heavily, grasping at his neck and head, where Lonnie's big hands had pummeled him.

"Are you all right?" I asked. He was still staring at Lonnie with a look that said he'd seen the same scary movies I had and was just waiting for Lonnie to make a grab at his leg.

His hands massaged the back of his head, and I hoped he wasn't going to turn around and show me a pulpy mess like a kicked-in melon. He was still panting, throwing in an occasional high-pitched whimper.

I glanced around at the chains of cans that snaked their way around the yard. A couple of small wooden stakes, trailing what looked like fish line tilted out of the corners of the yard. In the bright glare of the spotlight, I could see more cans in the tree. Larry was looking at Lonnie's prone form like a fisherman who'd been hoping for a trout but who had somehow reeled in a great white and now didn't know what to do with it.

"So, uh, Larry? You okay?" I asked again. Maybe he was in shock. I was also starting to worry about Lonnie. What if I'd killed him? I leaned in a little closer to see if he was breathing. A slow rise and fall of his chest assured me that for at least the time being, he was alive. "I think we should call 9-1-1," I said, still afraid to take my eyes off Lonnie lest he leap to his feet to grab one of us by the throat. The memory of red marks around Dayna's neck flashed through my mind, and I inched away. "And what the heck is all this?" I asked, waving an arm around towards the mess of cans.

"I'm sick of them not picking up the shit," Larry said in a

quavering voice. "I thought I'd catch one in the act and scare them so they wouldn't do it anymore." He was staring at Lonnie's inert form, seemingly mesmerized. "But he doesn't have a dog." The inadequacies of his plan were belatedly coming to light in his one-track mind.

In the distance a police siren wailed, growing closer. Hopefully one of our other neighbors had finally made themselves useful and called the police. Larry looked up startled and began gathering strings of cans in his arms.

"Help me," he shouted as he pulled on one of the lines that was still wrapped around Lonnie's leg. The heavy leg moved slightly as Larry jerked and pulled, but in the end, it was too much for the fish line, and the string broke, sending cans cascading in all directions. "Come on!" he shouted as he tried to sweep individual cans into his arms while kicking at the others and trying to corral them closer to his front door.

The siren screamed closer, and Larry went into overdrive like a soccer player on speed. It was a surreal scene. In the blazing spotlight, he danced and gathered his booty, getting himself tangled in several different lines until he was dragging as many cans from his legs as he was carrying in his arms. Lonnie lay prone on the grass, hopefully not dead, and I stood, still clutching my skillet. Addie sat on the sidelines, her mouth open in what looked like a laugh. She seemed to be having the best time.

The officer on duty must have thought he'd pulled up on something too bizarre to handle alone, because when his squad car screamed to a stop next to us, I could see him lift his radio to his mouth before he even opened the door. I dropped my skillet on the grass, and it bounced once before hitting the driveway with a crash.

The cop had his gun out of the holster faster than I'd have thought possible, and Larry and I threw our hands up in unison. The cans he'd been holding rained down on Lonnie, who rolled onto his side and began moaning.

"Down on the ground!" the officer screamed at us.

I hit the driveway belly first, arms spread wide on the concrete. Addie, unsure of this maneuver, rushed to my side and began licking my face frantically.

Larry was still standing, and actually still kicking cans across the yard as if that request didn't apply to him. One of the cans bounced off Lonnie's face.

"I said down on the ground!" screamed the officer, fingering his trigger. I clapped my hands across my ears and turned my face away, reluctant to see Larry get blown away.

"Down," I hissed to Addie, who promptly dropped by my side, still amused at this latest game.

Larry fell with a clatter in a heap and began moaning about his head. Lonnie was coming to, and when he rolled sideways, he caught a glimpse of Larry lying just feet away. With a roar, he launched himself at Larry, who squeaked like an injured chipmunk. I scrunched my eyes closed and pressed down on my ears. I didn't see what happened next, but an unfamiliar noise filtered through my hands, sounding like an electric mosquito zapper, and suddenly there was silence.

I took my hands off my ears and shifted my gaze to the right. Lonnie's mountainous body quietly convulsed with short jerky movements, his head cradled in Larry's prone lap. Larry began to squirm as if trying to pry himself out from under an overturned car.

"Stay down, sir!"

"What the hell! Get this maniac off me. I'm not staying down, he's drooling on my crotch. Oh my God, that's disgusting," he shrieked.

"Sir, do you need to be tasered?!"

With a final pull, Larry slipped out from under Lonnie, his drawers slipping down once again. He collapsed in the grass, careful to move away from Lonnie's twitching body. Rolling onto his stomach and flopping forward, he twitched his underwear back up, threw his arms out and rubbed his thighs against the lawn. It looked obscene.

My neck muscles were getting sorer by the moment and I shifted sideways.

"Everyone stay down! Don't move!"

He didn't need to tell me twice. I folded one arm and rested my head to relieve the pressure. I slipped the other hand out to Addie and ran a finger across the ridge of her head just behind her ears. She settled her head on snowy-white front paws.

A second patrol car pulled up and two more police officers raced out. Their feet thundered and crunched against my driveway as they ran towards us. I assumed they had their guns drawn and I flattened myself as much as possible against the ground bracing myself for a volley of shots.

"Everyone stay down," shouted one of the newcomers. I grasped Addie's collar and told her to stay in case she was considering breaking away and making a run for it.

"That one's tasered," said the original officer, doubtless gesturing towards Lonnie. "Looked like the big one was going to kill the smaller one." I felt eyes turn towards me. "I don't know about her."

"I hit the big one in the head with my skillet," I volunteered.

"What the hell is all this shit?" asked one of the cops. "A party or something?" They started kicking their way through the cans as they approached.

"Cuff the men until we get this sorted."

I stayed politely out of the conversation, holding tightly to Addie's collar as she began to squirm and wag in preparation for a big greeting for the new cops.

"Ma'am?"

I raised my head a few inches, blinking against the glare of the spotlight. I could only make out a dark shadow looming over me.

"Yes, sir?" I plunked my head back down, eyes watering from the assault of light.

"Can you tell us what's going on here?"

I shifted my hand, trying to shield my eyes from the light.

"Can I sit up?" I asked after determining that I wasn't going to be able to hold my head at that angle. Pushing my way to a sitting position, I pulled Addie close to me and glanced over at Larry and Lonnie. Lonnie had stopped twitching, but Larry was still gyrating against the grass.

"I'm not exactly sure where to start." Here was my opportunity to spill everything I knew about Lonnie's involvement with Dayna's death, but how could I distill this down to a short, manageable story? I launched into as succinct a tale as I could muster while one of the cops took copious notes.

"Hey," shouted Larry from his facedown position on the grass. "You *know* this guy?"

"It's not like we're friends," I snapped back at him. "I think he may have killed my old boss. Not that she was so fabulous herself," I added before considering how that would sound in the record. "Anyway, I think he was here to break into my house again. I found a document that he might have been trying to get back." I explained about the document shifting power of executor from Lonnie's wife to Dayna. Luckily my story was convoluted enough that no one thought to ask me where I'd gotten the document.

"What's with all the cans?" one of the other cops asked.

I looked at Larry.

"I'm protecting my property," he said defensively. "You can't tell me I don't have a right to protect my property."

The cops looked at each other. They'd probably never encountered anything like this before.

"Are you two married?"

"No!" we both shouted in unison.

"I live next door," I said, horrified at the idea that anyone could think I would marry a slob like Larry. I gave a shudder.

"You knew this guy was stalking your neighbor, so you strung these cans together as a warning system?"

An obstinate silence emanated from Larry. Trying to decide what would put him in a better light was obviously taking its toll on his brain.

"That just sort of turned out to be a bonus," he finally said.

"So, if you weren't trying to catch him, who were you trying to catch?"

"The damn dog walkers who won't clean up the shit!" he exploded. "I'm sick of it. Shit here, shit there, and can they bother to pick it up? No! It's their dog, it's their dog shit, right?"

One of the cops muttered, "Amen, brother."

"I thought that if they got caught red-handed, with all the noise and lights, they'd stop using my yard as a dog dumping area." He lapsed into a sullen silence, straining against his handcuffs with an ill-tempered jerk. "And dammit, I can smell more. Can't you guys do anything? Write some tickets or arrest someone?"

"We might be able to arrange an arrest," said the cop who was taking notes.

"Really?" asked Larry hopefully.

"Yeah, right. We've got nothing better to do."

Lonnie twisted suddenly in the grass, groaning and thrashing and coming back to life with a vengeance. A meaty leg shot out and kicked Larry hard in the thigh, eliciting a frightened yelp. Hard to tell if it was a final convulsion from the Taser or a precision shot, but Larry humped like a clumsy worm away across the grass as fast as he could.

"Hey," shouted one of the cops. Two of them converged

on Lonnie and pulled the mass of dead weight to his feet. "Let's take a ride to the station, shall we?"

He stumbled along between them, catching my eye as he passed. The malevolence in his eyes hit me like a blow, and in spite of the handcuffs and armed escort, fear shot along my nerve endings. Addie tensed beside me and pulled back her lips in a soundless growl. Her bravado was shadowed by the tremor I felt run along her muscles. She was as frightened of him as I was.

Carefully holding his head, just like on TV, they loaded him into the back of one of the squad cars. His bulk filled the small space and he leaned forward, turning sideways and resting against the grille separating the backseat from the front. His dark eyes continued to bore into me and I was thankful when they slammed the door and drove him away.

"What's going to happen to him?" I asked.

"They'll take him down to the station and book him on assault charges." He unlocked Larry's handcuffs and reattached them to his belt. "We'll need you to come down and file a statement if you're going to press charges. Do you need medical attention?"

Larry's shoulders slumped against the grass and he rubbed the back of his head. He looked as deflated as I felt. "I don't think so." His hand ran up the back of his head again as if conducting a more thorough investigation of the question. "What happens if I press charges? How long will he be locked up for? That guy looked crazy. I'm afraid he'll come back here and kill me!"

I was afraid of that too.

"We just arrest them, sir. It's up to the judge to decide what to do with them." He offered Larry a hand as he heaved himself to his feet. Thankfully his drawers stayed up this time, although the fly flapped open in the breeze.

The officer consulted his notes and told me that he'd turn

the information I'd given him over to the detective in charge of Dayna's case. I took that as a dismissal, and after I retrieved my skillet, Addie and I made our way back inside.

The timer on my downstairs light had shut off already, so I shuffled to the kitchen, trying to avoid the dog toys and bones strewn across my path. Weariness seeped through me like fog through a screen. Every last fiber was saturated with exhaustion, and it was an effort to lift my pan into the sink. I seriously considered whether I'd be able to drag myself up the stairs, but since my sofa was gone, unless I wanted to sleep on the floor, I didn't have a choice.

Relief that Lonnie was in police custody was only marginal. I had no way of knowing how long they would hold him or what he would do when he got out. The look in his eyes as he'd stared at me from the police car would haunt my dreams for at least tonight, if not for ever. That was assuming I could get to sleep.

I turned the water on and reached for the Comet. I'd let the skillet soak overnight and then still probably throw it out tomorrow. At the rate I was going, I would need a whole new set of furniture, dishes and clothes if my life didn't settle down soon. Several strands of Lonnie's pale hair clung to the edge of the skillet, like a token of evil infiltrating my home. I picked up the whole thing and tossed it out the door into the garage.

I checked and double-checked all the window and door locks. Then I tilted a kitchen chair under the handle of the door to the garage, put the cover on Addie's doggie door, and wedged a saucer-shaped rubber Kong against the back door and another against the front door before dragging myself to bed.

When Addie was settled on the bed, and before I joined her, I dragged my chest of drawers in front of my bedroom door. Only then was I able to rest.

CHAPTER TWENTY-TWO

I had wanted to meet Daniel at a restaurant, but at the last minute he'd called and asked if I could swing by and pick him up. Apparently, his car had broken down on the way home from the police station this afternoon. Ambivalence at seeing him gave way to curiosity about what the police had told him about Lonnie's arrest, and he was smart enough, or wily enough, to keep me hanging until I got to his house.

The sun had slipped just below the horizon and a cool breeze rustled dead leaves along the gutters of Daniel's street as I drove slowly along the block. There weren't many people out, just a young couple ambling along behind an elderly Lab. The construction crews had knocked off for the night, taking their rumbling diesel engine trucks with them. This part of town wasn't the big truck bastion of that most of Houston was. Instead, the street was lined with late-model Volvos sporting environmental bumper stickers, older-model subcompacts with peeling bumper stickers, and a fleet of small SUVs that were easy to park on these narrow streets.

Daniel's house was lit up like the Vegas strip. I pulled into an empty space along the curb and killed the engine. He'd sounded almost giddy when he's called me this afternoon, and I had to guess that they'd nailed Lonnie for Dayna's murder. I kicked my way through the covering of dried leaves that lined the front walk and made my way to the front door. A niggling feeling tickled my brain, and I realized that I'd forgotten to pick up some pepper spray. Surely, he wouldn't try anything. And if Lonnie had indeed been arrested for killing Dayna, then all I had to worry about with Daniel was some potentially unwanted advances.

The smell of fried chicken wafted my way as I rang the front door, and my stomach growled in appreciation. Images of running through this door after Henry flitted through my head, and I pushed them away. Going down that road would only lead me to the vision of Dayna's dead face, and I'd been working hard at pushing that particular memory deeper into the recesses of my brain. Daniel threw open the front door and the smell of fried chicken grew stronger and mixed with other savory scents. Nothing like the smell of good food to tamp down my defenses.

"Something smells fabulous," I said as he flashed his even white teeth at me in greeting.

"I hope you don't mind, I decided to cook tonight. It's one of the things I love to do, I just haven't had much opportunity lately." He stepped back, absently adjusting an apron that covered the front of his crisp white shirt and faded jeans.

I followed him down the hallway towards the back of the house and into the kitchen. The specters that I'd anticipated, failed to materialize, no doubt driven away by the bright lights and cheerful cooking. A plate of fried chicken shed its excess grease onto neatly folded paper towels next to a tray piled high with stuffed mushrooms, squares of phyllo-wrapped spinach, rows of olives and columns of neatly sliced cheese. Fresh grape tomatoes added a splash of color, as did a few strategically placed orange and yellow strips of bell peppers. Ramekins of dip were nestled amongst the bounty.

My mouth watered like Addie confronted with an unexpected bit of cheese.

Daniel took a moment to poke his head into the oven. Satisfied with what he saw, he withdrew and smiled at me again.

"Can I get you something to drink?" A bottle of white wine was submerged in icy water in a wine bucket, and another bottle of red stood at attention on the counter. "I wasn't sure what you liked. I have wine, beer. I could make you a martini if you'd like?"

"A glass of white wine would be nice."

He uncorked the bottle with an expert touch and poured us each a glass. He'd kicked up his charm level several notches, but I hadn't forgotten how he'd been during Dayna's memorial service. Charm or not, I didn't trust this man.

We clinked our glasses and took a sip, and he went back to bustling around the kitchen. Lifting a pot off the stove, he gave it a quick stir and a shot of salt and moved quickly to the refrigerator. Bending low, he rummaged around, glancing surreptitiously backwards to see if I was admiring that particular view of his backside. I took my wine and moved into the family room, cursing myself for forgetting the pepper spray.

"So, what did the police have to say?" I asked. Might as well cut to the chase and get the information I wanted just in case I had to make a quick getaway. Although the food was really tempting me. The man, not so much, but I am a sucker for a fabulous meal, and this looked as good as it smelled.

He stood up and closed the refrigerator door, disappointed with my failure to fully appreciate his butt. "We've got plenty of time for that later. Let's just enjoy our wine and the company, shall we?"

He gave me another full-grille smile, picked up his wineglass and slithered over to my side. His charm was actively bouncing off me now like hailstones off a trampoline. Taking my elbow, he led me to the sofa in the family room and sank down beside me, slipping an arm along the back of the couch behind my shoulders. I scooted over under the guise of adjusting my skirt, managing to widen the gap between us by almost a foot. He shot me an injured look and removed his arm.

"If I recall, I understand you have a new business now?" he asked.

"I do. I make gourmet dog treats." His failure to ask even once how his dead wife's dog was hung between us.

"That's nice." He hopped up, returning quickly with the tray of appetizers and two small plates. "How's business?" He set the plates down and resumed his place next to me, settling himself once more up against my leg. Unfortunately, there was no more room for me to scoot over without landing on the floor.

"Business is good. Most people love their dogs and are willing to buy high-quality, healthy treats for them." I picked up a stuffed mushroom and popped it in my mouth. It was incredible. "And I love it. Way more than what I was doing before."

"You mean when you were working for Dayna."

Well, yes, but it didn't seem very polite to say so. I picked up a piece of cheese.

"I think I'm better suited to having my own business." The cheese was lovely, a nice smooth camembert. "I would think you could relate. You work for yourself, don't you, making documentaries?"

The smarmy predator look in his eyes softened. "It doesn't seem like work to me. It's more like a calling." He sipped his wine. "I know that probably sounds pretentious, but I'll get an idea that fascinates me, and I have to chase it to see where it goes."

I flashed to the New Orleans documentary I'd seen at the Doubletree. And also to the handheld video camera he'd pushed in people's faces at Dayna's memorial service. I'd be willing to bet his themes didn't run much towards puppies and children.

"What kind of films do you make?"

"Whatever fuels my imagination at the time." He ran his tongue along the lip of his wineglass and checked to see if I'd noticed. Oh, yes, I'd noticed. The same muscles that contract and make me shiver and scream when I see a roach were doing their thing. My shoulders twitched and I grabbed my own wineglass, taking an unladylike slug.

"Are you chilled?" he asked, leaning closer. "I could get you a blanket."

"No. No, I'm fine," I said. I leaned away, the arm of the sofa pressing into my back. "You're actually a bit in my space. I have some space issues and, uh, you're kind of encroaching."

By the look on his face, I could guess he'd never had someone tell him that before. He shot up off the couch and headed for the kitchen. "Sorry," he said, sounding like a truculent six-year old. He no doubt meant for me to feel bad, but he didn't realize that I'd learned long ago not to let others make me feel bad for asserting myself.

"No problem," I said, following him to the kitchen. Having a large center island between us definitely suited me better. "Tell me about what you're working on now."

He lifted the lid off the pot on the stove and gave it a vicious stir, banging the spoon against the side when he was finished. His anger surprised me. Clearly here was a man that didn't take rejection well in any form or fashion. Had I underestimated him? Had Dayna decided to divorce him and he'd snapped and killed her? I glanced around the kitchen, looking for dangerous items that I could use to defend myself, or that I needed to watch out for. There was a wood block set of kitchen knives on the far counter, some butter knives on the table (which was set for two, complete with candles waiting to be lit), a heavy cut-glass vase perched on the counter filled with a heady bouquet of orange lilies and leafy green fronds, and of course the pot simmering away on the stove.

After slamming the oven door shut, Daniel turned back towards me. "What am I working on now?" he echoed. His tone was still churlish, but he obviously wanted to talk about his latest project. "I'm doing a piece on the homeless in Houston."

"Really?" I must have sounded as surprised as I felt, because he gave me a wry grin.

"Does that surprise you? And before you go attributing some vague altruistic munificence to me, perhaps you should wait to see the final product before deciding if I'm doing a noble thing or not."

I had no idea what that could mean, and I wasn't sure I wanted to know. What I really wanted was to hear what the police said and be on my way. Preferably with a couple pieces of that mouthwatering chicken that Daniel was patting gently with a paper towel to remove the last traces of grease. He transferred the pieces to a glass dish and slipped them into the oven. Rats. I'd hoped we were going to be eating shortly.

"That really looks good," I said, hoping he'd pull the dish back out and serve it right up.

"Thanks. My grandmother taught me how to cook."

"Really? My grandmother taught me how to cook too."

He lifted the dripping wine bottle from the bucket and refilled my glass, which had gotten decidedly empty. A slight buzz was warming my cheeks, and a vague tingle ran through me as my muscles began to relax. I should probably stop, or at least slow down my drinking. I definitely needed to keep my wits about me with this character around.

We backtracked into the niceties normally found at a social dinner. What dishes did we enjoy cooking the most, favorite wines, restaurants, music, the common topics that most people can pleasantly converse about without threatening anyone else's sensibilities. I was surprised when I got to the bottom of another glass of wine, although I tried to temper the buzz by eating more of the fabulous appetizers.

Daniel busied himself around the kitchen while we chatted, quickly getting over his previous snit. Maybe he just had a moody, artistic temperament. By the time he lit the candles and brought all the steaming dishes to the table, I was well past any hard feelings myself. How could you stay irritated with someone that could cook this well and look so good in those faded jeans? *Whoa, stop in your tracks*, I told myself. *That was definitely the wine talking. No more wine.*

The chicken was delicious, crispy and spicy without a hint of grease, served with creamy mashed sweet potatoes and a delicate corn soufflé that melted on your tongue. Forgetting all manners, I shoveled food like a teamster coming off a long shift. Daniel ate more slowly, savoring each bite. Maybe the food would help soak up the excess wine that seemed to be muddling my brain.

By the time I was halfway through seconds, I found myself rambling on about my childhood and the boarding school I'd attended. Daniel hadn't attended boarding school, but he did come from money and he had spent his senior year abroad. Maybe his family money explained how he financed his films.

"You know, Dayna never let me meet her family until the day of the wedding," Daniel said, pushing away his plate. "And I don't think she would have even invited them to that, but I insisted."

Picturing Cherilynn and Lonnie, I couldn't say I blamed her. "Did she just have the one sister?" I asked.

"Yes. Cherilynn was married already, so it was just her and Lonnie and their aunt Edith who came to our wedding. She was a very sweet woman," he said. "She pretty much raised them after their mother left." He refilled our glasses before I had the chance to say no. "You know Dayna was incredibly ashamed of her background. I tried to tell her that I loved who she was, and she was who she was in part because of where she came from."

"When I met Cherilynn, I have to say I couldn't believe they were sisters. I mean, Dayna didn't even have an accent."

"Dayna was smart, and she studied how to sound, how to look, how to act. It's just that once she decided what was 'right,' she despised anyone that wasn't that."

I lifted my wineglass, then pushed it away. A small headache was forming behind my eyes, and I realized that Daniel was looking vaguely fuzzy around the edges.

"From what the police told me this afternoon, that had a lot to do with why she was killed."

I pushed the fuzziness away and tried to focus. "What had a lot to do with it?" I thought maybe I'd drifted.

"Lonnie confessed this afternoon." He looked excited, and a thrill ran through me as I realized that if Lonnie had confessed, then he was still locked up and would go to prison and my life would get back to normal.

"That's great!" I said. "Well, it's not great. But you know what I mean."

He locked eyes with me. "I know what you mean."

"Did they say why he did it?" As if Lonnie had to have any more reason than you looked cross-eyed at him or set a toe across his property line.

"Dayna and Cherilynn's aunt Edith died a couple of

months ago. She owned both the house where the girls were raised, which is where Cherilynn and Lonnie live now, and the house next door, where she lived."

My head buzzed with the document I'd found. I knew Lonnie had been after it.

"Seems that Edith left Cherilynn the house where she and Lonnie live. When Edith got older and started having health problems, Cherilynn took care of her. So, Edith wanted her to have their house outright. And to make sure that Dayna couldn't ruin that plan, because obviously, having raised my wife, she knew her fairly well, she made Cherilynn the executor."

He stood up and began clearing the table as he talked. I picked up my plate and followed him over to the sink.

"Only she underestimated my wife." A bitter note crept in. "It seems that Dayna told Cherilynn that you have to have a college degree in order to be the executor of a will."

"No, you don't," I said.

"Of course you don't," he said, piling the dishes in the sink. "But Cherilynn didn't know that. She always felt inadequate around Dayna, and Dayna liked to make her feel stupid. So she convinced Cherilynn to sign the executorship over to her." He stopped the water and faced me. "Then *my wife* put the Lotts' house up for sale."

"Could she do that?"

"Legally, I don't think so. But she made Lonnie and Cherilynn think she could. In fact, she called in a realtor and had it put on the market."

"Again, could she do that?" Even as I asked, I knew that was a stupid question. Dayna did anything Dayna wanted.

"Probably not. But you know how she was. If she said something was gospel, she made you believe it was. If Lonnie and Cherilynn had gotten an attorney, they could have put a stop to it, but they didn't have money for that, and frankly, they're not well educated. They probably thought it was a done deal."

I wondered if Daniel had known what was going on.

"Then Lonnie killed her because she was selling his house out from under him?"

"Well, according to the police, he came over here looking for the document where Cherilynn had signed the executorship over to Dayna. He and Cherilynn thought if they could destroy that, everything would be okay."

"That doesn't make sense. Wouldn't the attorneys have had the original and Dayna a copy?" I tried to think if the thing I'd seen was an original.

Daniel had started the water running again and began loading the dishes into the dishwasher. "I told you they were uneducated. In Lonnie's mind, that document held the key to his future. If he could get it back and destroy it, everything would be fine.

"Once he'd found out that Cherilynn had signed away the rights to Edith's estate, he contacted Dayna and demanded she return it." He gave me a wry look. "You can probably guess how well that went."

No doubt I could. I'd seen her crush people in meetings, out of meetings, in her office, in the hallway. She'd mastered the art of cutting someone's confidence to shreds in under a minute. She'd almost made me start doubting myself. Who was I kidding? She'd convinced me that I was too stupid to work in the glorious world of oil and gas unless it was in a menial capacity, preferably cleaning the restrooms.

"Apparently, he came over after work, thinking he could find it here and take it. He broke in, which set off the alarm. The alarm company called Dayna at work and told her an alarm was going off." He paused and took a deep breath. "For whatever reason, we'll never know, she told them not to send the police. She came home and found Lonnie going through the office. He hasn't said what was said between them, or if he has, the police aren't telling me. But I guess whatever it was, it was enough to enrage him, and he killed her."

I thought of all the times she'd made me furious at work. Furious enough that I could have happily smacked her smug face. And I'm pretty stable. Lonnie didn't have a chance against that attitude, and as smart as Dayna thought she was, she couldn't really have been. Waving a red flag in front of a bull like Lonnie wasn't the same as degrading a white-collar drone at the office.

Daniel must have read something in my look. "I know," he said. "Sometimes she pushed me too. But I just left."

"I did too," I said. Waves of relief were beginning to build as I realized that tomorrow I could get my door replaced, go back to baking my gourmet doggie treats, back to my sweet dog-walking clients, back to my post-Dayna life.

"There's something I didn't tell the police," he said. "I guess it's not important now." He rubbed his brow. "I think I know why she told the alarm company not to send the cops."

Daniel's outline was getting blurrier for me as I tried to focus. "Why?"

"We had had a fight a couple of nights before, and I left. She had the locks changed on the doors, and she probably thought it was me getting home and breaking in when I found out my key didn't work."

"And it wasn't. It was Lonnie."

He ran his hands up and down his face like he was rubbing away frostbite. "It was Lonnie. It should have been me. If I would have come home, this never would have happened."

"Daniel, you can't think that. This was not your fault. You didn't tell her to take over Edith's will. You didn't tell her to try and sell Lonnie's house out from under him. If anyone should have known better, she should have." I patted him awkwardly on the shoulder like a stranger confronted with a crying child on the sidewalk.

"Thanks for that," he said, making an effort to smile and bring back his jovial side from earlier in the evening. He excused himself, and I wandered through the kitchen, squinting against the lights that had seemed so warm and cheerful earlier but now seemed overly bright and harsh. Trying to remember where I'd put my purse, I wondered for a minute if I was okay to drive home. I had to drive home. Staying here was not an option. For all his current emotion at the loss of Dayna, he still had a predatory air about him, and I had no doubt if he sensed any weakness on my part, he'd be right there ready to make a move on me.

I found my purse where I had tucked it next to a decorative jug on the fireplace hearth. When Daniel came back, I had my keys in my hand and was ready to make my departure.

"You're not going yet, are you?" he asked, a boyish look of devastation on his face.

"Yeah, I really need to be going. It's getting late and I have to get up early tomorrow."

"But we haven't had dessert yet."

"I know. That's okay. I really couldn't eat another thing." I turned and headed for the hall to the front door.

"Well, at least let me pack you up some dessert to go. I made some espresso brownies that I thought you'd like."

That stopped me in my tracks. Brownies and espresso. A winning combination in my mind, although better suited for breakfast than this time of night. "Sounds good," I told him. "I'll have them for breakfast."

I was rewarded with a wide, warm smile. I glanced at my watch while he packed up my brownies. Holy cow, it was almost eleven already. I was definitely going to be tired and probably hungover in the morning. I'd take an aspirin when I got home, and if I had any willpower at all, I'd toss the brownies. No sense in starting the day with a pure sugar-and-caffeine breakfast. Then again, sometimes you have to treat yourself.

The street was quiet as we stepped out the door. Short gusts of winds whipped fallen leaves into tiny tornados along the sidewalk and batted at the end of my ponytail. Daniel appeared intent on walking me to my car, and tension built in my head as I wondered if he'd try and kiss me. Halfway down the walk, my cell phone began bleating in my purse. Who would be calling me at this time of night? I thought of Frances and a surge of worry shot through me. *Stop it*, I told myself. *Every unexpected phone call does not mean something bad has happened.*

I tucked the package of brownies under my arm and began rummaging around in my purse. Just as I found the phone, it stopped ringing. Daniel hesitated next to me.

"Do you want to come back inside and check your voice mail?" he asked. "It's getting pretty chilly out here."

He was right. It was getting chilly out here, but having escaped the house, I now just wanted to be home, tucked away in my own bed with Addie curled comfortably at my feet. I could check my voice mail from the car.

"Thanks, but no. I need to be going."

He walked me to my car, held me by my shoulders and gave me a Latin-style kiss on both cheeks. Okay, that worked. I'd just tossed the brownies onto the passenger seat when my phone rang again. This time I had it in my hand, and I hit answer before they could hang up again.

"Hello?" I said rather more loudly than I intended.

"Sure you don't want to come back inside?" Daniel mouthed at me.

I waved him away, trying to indicate that it was fine for him to go back inside while at the same time trying to focus on my call. He reluctantly wandered up the front walk, pausing on the steps.

"Thanks for dinner," I shouted at him, then waved him inside, shouting "Hello" into the phone one more time. A faint "Hello" answered me. I couldn't tell if it was a bad connection or if the other person was whispering. A chill crept up my spine, and I slid quickly into the driver's seat, slamming the door shut behind me. I batted at the lock, wondering why I'd been so hasty in sending Daniel inside. I waited in the dark, holding the phone to my ear. Listening.

I watched the lights flick off on the porch and I felt increasingly alone. Was that breathing I heard coming over the line, or had the person already hung up? I waited another minute, listening to nothing. Ending the call, I tossed the phone on the passenger seat next to the brownies and poked the key into the ignition. My head was reeling from too much wine, and exhaustion was sucking what little strength I had left. I started the car, anxious to be home. A feeling that I was missing something taunted me. Lonnie was locked up, he'd confessed to killing Dayna, so everything should go back to normal now. Right?

Pulling away from the curb, I glanced at the brownies beside me. Brownies. Had Lonnie left the poisoned brownies at my house, or rather at Larry's house? Surely he knew where I lived, because he'd broken in looking for Cherilynn's legal document. So why had he put the brownies in front of the wrong door? Then again, the brownies were before the break-in. Maybe he'd figured out his mistake. But what if it wasn't Lonnie? What if Daniel had left them? I was feeling paranoid about the foil-wrapped package and vowed to throw them away as soon as I got home. I couldn't think of a reason why Daniel would try to poison me, but then again, I wasn't thinking that clearly right now.

It took me a minute to register that something was wrong

with my car. I bumped along the street, listening to a thudding noise coming from the back of my car. I pulled to a stop less than a block from where I'd started and got out to check the rear passenger-side wheel. It was flat like a deflated balloon. Probably due to the small silver knife protruding from the edge.

CHAPTER TWENTY-THREE

I stood for a moment staring stupidly at the knife, trying to imagine how it had gotten there. A cat raced across the sidewalk behind me, and I glanced around, aware of how dark the street was. Out of the corner of my eye, I caught a glimpse of movement, a flash of pale arm reaching towards me, and I ran.

For a second, I considered that I was imaging this. I was running down the street like a crazy woman for no reason. But then I heard the sound of feet pounding heavily behind me. I wasn't imaging it. The sidewalk was dark and jagged, and I knew if I fell, I was dead. I darted onto the empty street and turned at the next block, trying to increase the distance between myself and my pursuer. Who was behind me? Instinct kept me moving. I was running away from Daniel's house rather than towards it, but I wasn't willing to risk turning around now. My breath was ragged and the large meal was sitting heavy in my stomach. I wouldn't be able to run far.

Just ahead of me, an abandoned house loomed, its open door beckoning towards darkened hiding places. Something about it was familiar, but there was no time to think about that now. The footsteps were fainter, and I took a chance that the person chasing me hadn't made it around the corner yet. I darted across the junk-strewn lawn, high-stepping past broken boards and bottles, and slipped as quietly as I could into the narrow gap between the side of the house and a rickety fence separating the house next door. Maybe I should just start screaming and alert the neighbors, but I was afraid that no one would actually come to my rescue. Most people, if they heard me at all, would probably just roll over and pull the pillow tighter against their ears, or check to make sure the front door was bolted.

I crouched into a dark recess and listened. The only thing I could hear clearly was my thudding heart. It was beating so loud I was afraid it would give me away. Holding my breath, I inched along in the darkness, sliding farther away from the streetlight. A faint rustling near my feet nearly made me scream out loud. Dear Lord, if a rat ran up my leg, I'd take my chances with the maniac in the street. I kicked towards the darkness, hoping to scare off whatever might be there. I didn't hear any more rustling, but that didn't mean the rat, possum or oversized roach wasn't just biding its time.

Sweat popped out in a line along my forehead and pooled under my arms. The lack of footsteps passing by was as ominous as if they were racing right towards me. Stepping daintily along the ragged ground, I inched farther along towards the backyard. Maybe I could cut through the backyard to the street behind and get back to Daniel's.

The air was thick with the smell of cat urine and mold. Odd as it was, the smell gave me comfort. If there were cats around, there shouldn't be too many rats. I pushed farther, alternating between squinting into the darkness ahead and rotating my head back around to check the alley behind me.

The skin on the back of my neck was tingling with fear. I was also having a killer case of the heebie-jeebies. It took everything I had not to swat at the imaginary spiders crawling along my skin. At least I hoped they were imaginary.

Barely eight feet from the backyard, a sneeze welled up in the back of my nose. I pushed frantically at my upper lip with my index finger, trying to quell it, but it was a monster sneeze that wouldn't be denied. Damn, probably the mold. I pressed my face into my forearm and tried to sneeze as quietly as possible. Turned out, it wasn't possible at all. The "choo" part of the sneeze ripped into the quiet of the night. I stood stock-still for a moment, hoping that the unknown follower was already well down the street.

Within seconds, I heard footsteps scrape on the loose gravel of the street as if someone had come to an abrupt stop. Then with a clumsy thump, thump, thump, they started coming closer.

No time to lose. What just moments ago had felt like a good hiding place now seemed like a death trap. The footsteps were on the street in front, so I made a break for the back, crashing along like an adolescent moose. I raced around the back of the house, looking for a way out onto the next block. Screams were welling at the back of my throat, but fear stifled them before they could escape.

Even in the dark, I could see the fence that separated this run-down shack from its newer neighbor behind. Dammit, I couldn't get out; I'd trapped myself. Like a pigeon trapped by a box, I flitted side to side while my heart fluttered in small wild beats in my chest. Footsteps combined with heavy breathing from the side of the house. I only had a second to hide.

I raced through a gaping hole in the back of the house that had once been a back door. The little light from the street didn't extend inside, and by squinting hard, I could just make out shades of gray. I raced-walked, waving my arms out in front of me towards a darker gray rectangle that I hoped was a door or hallway that led to the front of the house. If I could cut through the house and out the front, maybe I could survive till the cops came, by running and screaming down the street.

Intent on not running into a wall, I entirely missed the loose boards that were haphazardly propped across the floor of the threshold. My left foot caught and I went down hard, cracking my head on something as I fell. The air shot out of my lungs with a loud woof as I hit the ground. I hardly noticed the pain in my head; that was obliterated by the sting in my right hand. I clutched the hand against my chest, feeling a warm oozing coming from a gash that I could feel open under my fingers. For the second time in as many days, I tried to remember the last time I'd had a tetanus shot.

"Jessie." It was a whisper in the dark. I probably wouldn't need to worry about tetanus setting in. I'd be long dead before that.

"I know you're in here." The whisper was raspy and androgynous, making the blood freeze in my veins. Who the hell was that? A dark shape loomed against the lighter gray of the back door. A buzzing wooziness was creeping into my head and I feared I'd pass out. I lay perfectly still, afraid to even breathe, which wasn't helping the lightheadedness.

With my left hand, I started feeling along the floor, hoping to find something I could use as a weapon. My fingers brushed up against something that scuttled away as I touched it and a whimper escaped my throat.

"Oh, there you are." The voice stopped whispering and changed to normal conversational tones. Woman. The bulky shape stepped nearer. As she got nearer, I could make out the bulk of a long skirt draping stocky legs, and a frizz of pale hair shimmered in the dark. Naomi. What? Why was Naomi chasing me?

"Naomi?" I asked the dark shape that was slowly coming

closer. "Is that you?" A feeling of relief washed over me. It was just Naomi.

An eerie laugh echoed off the empty walls, and my relief quickly gave way to bone-chilling horror at the insanity of the sound. "Of course it's me. Who were you expecting? Daniel?" She gave a throaty laugh. "Looks like you two are getting pretty friendly."

Tears pricked my eyes, and I shook my head, trying to chase away the buzz of wine that was slowing my reflexes. I needed my wits about me, and the fear that I might be slightly impaired from the wine was causing great heaving sobs to form in my throat. Or maybe that was unrestrained fear. I'd never been more afraid than I was right now.

"Daniel and I aren't really friendly at all," I babbled. What did she want with me? I slipped my hand along the floor next to me. Furry, scurrying thing or not, I needed a weapon. Something with hard edges lay about a foot away. I couldn't tell if it was a brick or a board. If it was a board, I might not be able to swing it or throw it freely.

"What are you doing?" she barked, her tone moving quickly from conversational to menacing. I needed to keep her level, but how to do that?

"Nothing," I said in my most sane, chatty tone. "I thought there was a spider." I gave a little laugh that even to my ears bordered on hysteria. "I'm really afraid of spiders."

Her shadow moved a few feet backwards. "I don't like them either," she said, suddenly empathetic. "I know they're God's creatures and we're to love all of God's creatures, but some are easier to love than others."

My heart hammered in my ears. *Keep her talking. Keep her relating.* A giggle escaped my throat that was as much sob as laugh. What was wrong with me? Naomi seemed to relax and she gave a little laugh with me. Just a couple of girls having a fun night out. I was stymied as to what to do now.

I could hear traffic noises coming from Montrose and Naomi's heavy nasal breathing. Otherwise the night was quiet. My eyes were adjusting to the dark, but even so I couldn't really make out anything around me in the blackness. I thought about trying to scoot along the floor towards the front, but my guess was that the floor was littered with debris, and Naomi would hear me.

"I know. I know!" she said, suddenly sounding as if she were speaking between clenched teeth. "Be quiet! I know!"

A new surge of adrenaline shot through my veins. If I'd had any doubt about her level of sanity, those doubts were quickly fading. I shifted backwards, trying to silently change my position.

"It won't help, you know," she said sounding relatively sane again. Sounding sane and being sane, clearly two different things.

"What won't help?" I asked, hoping to get the conversation rolling again.

"Trying to get away. I have to do this. If you would have just eaten the brownies, you could have been spared this." So, Naomi had brought the brownies. "Why didn't you eat them? I remember you always liked brownies when you worked at Astor. In fact, gluttonous is what I thought about you whenever someone brought them into the office. Gluttony is a sin, you know."

If I wasn't terrified for my life, I would have been insulted. I wasn't gluttonous. Okay, if someone brought in brownies or cookies, I would usually have one, but so would everyone else.

"You left the brownies in front of my neighbor's house."

"Did I?" She genuinely sounded surprised. "Oh. Those houses all looked the same to me. But I had your name on the box. He should have never eaten them when they were addressed to you. Did he die?"

"No. He was pretty sick, though."

"God spared him." No matter that she'd nearly killed the wrong person. Her breathing was coming heavier and more labored. I could only hope she was having an asthma attack, or better yet a heart attack.

Through the fog of fear, the question of why Naomi wanted to kill me popped up.

"Naomi? Can I ask you something?"

"Ours is not to question God's will!" she thundered at me. I shrank against the wall. I wasn't questioning God's will, I was questioning the will of this nutcase. In fact, I was hoping that the good Lord would step in here and help me out.

"I would never question God's will," I said in my most placating voice. "I, um, just wanted to ask you what we're doing here?" Maybe she wasn't planning on killing me, and although all signs pointed that way, she hadn't specifically said that was the plan.

"I have to kill you. It's right and just." Okay, that was specific.

"But why? What did I do?" My voice wavered with fear and I tried to control it. I'd read somewhere that some killers got off on seeing the fear of their victims. Oh, my God, had Naomi killed Dayna? Had I been wrong about Lonnie? But he'd confessed. Why would he confess if he hadn't done it?

"You're trying to get Walter arrested. I can't let that happen. Everyone makes mistakes, and I've forgiven him his mistakes."

Was she talking about forgiving him for what he'd done with Dayna? I was confused, but that probably didn't count for much.

"I'm not trying to get Walter arrested. Er, what he did wasn't exactly illegal." If it was, there surely wouldn't be enough jail cells to ever go around.

"I know that he did what he had to do in order to atone for

his sins. He killed that demon to save our marriage. We're happy again! I won't let you spoil his selfless act of attrition!"

"Walter didn't kill Dayna," I nearly shrieked at her. I stopped myself from calling her an idiot just at the last minute. Geez. *Just my luck, I'm going to be murdered for all the wrong reasons.*

"He killed the demon," she said, her voice sounding slightly uncertain. I'd knocked her a little off course. I needed to keep going.

"No, he didn't. Didn't you hear? The police arrested Dayna's brother-in-law today. He confessed to killing her because she was trying to sell his house out from under him." I started pushing myself up to a standing position, but was startled by a sudden glint off an ugly-looking carving knife in Naomi's hand. "Uh, whoa there, Naomi." My knees went wobbly and I leaned, half crouching against the wall.

"Don't you lie to me," she hissed in a suddenly deep whisper. "I shall not tolerate your falsehoods."

"Seriously, Lonnie was arrested today for killing Dayna." The darkness had swallowed the knife again, and my eyes searched frantically for signs of it. Naomi was perfectly still. Even her breathing had quieted. I could feel the grit from the filthy wall sticking to my bloody hand. I was going to have to make a break for it. Unfortunately, I didn't know if the hall was clear to the front door, or even if I could get out the front door. My luck it was nailed shut.

Just as I was about to take my chances with the hallway, Naomi seemed to gather herself, and with a primal scream that froze the marrow in my bones, she charged at me, arm lifted high over her head. I ducked to the side as she slashed downwards towards my chest. The knife missed me, but her meaty elbow caught my shoulder with a sideways blow and knocked me off balance. I fell to one knee and scuttled along the floor, oblivious to any pain. Feeling along the floor, I prayed for a board. Or a brick. Or a chest protector that would stop an eight-inch knife from cutting through my breastbone.

It was too late to run; I couldn't risk taking my eyes off her. In the dark, she seemed to be gathering herself for another strike, and I skittered away backwards in an ungainly crab-walk. I could hear her sharp intake of breath as she raised the knife once again. I braced myself against the floor and prepared to kick upwards at her chest, but before I could, something sliced through the air and caught Naomi's head with a resounding thwop, almost like a wooden bat against a softball. She dropped like a sandbag.

I could barely hear the sudden stillness over the thundering heartbeat in my ears. A dark shape eased out of the shadows, holding what looked to be a two-by-four.

"You okay?" asked a rusty voice. It sounded familiar to me, but my brain was too far gone to process where.

"I think so," I whispered. I was transfixed by the heap that was Naomi. In spite of the crack she'd taken to her skull, I was still frightened. Cliché or not, she'd tried to kill me. With a giant, hair-raising knife, she'd tried to kill me. Where was the knife? "Where's the knife?" My voice shook and I tried to stand, but my knees were shaking so badly I could only pull myself up and lean against the wall.

"Good point." The shadow moved closer, still brandishing the board like a bat. He wasn't much bigger than me, and I prayed he'd knocked her out cold, because I wasn't sure the two of us could stop her together if she roared back to life. He pushed the end of the board against her neck just under her chin and pushed down slightly as if holding her in place. She didn't move. "Do ya see it?" he asked.

Gathering my nerve, I inched closer, taking my eyes off her face to scan the ground near her hands. To my horror, it was still resting in her grasp, loosely to be sure, but still in her hand.

"Ooohhh," I whimpered. "She's still got it."

He put a little more pressure on the board. "Maybe you could just reach in there and get it?" I glanced at his face. Small, black and wrinkled. It was Hudson. First, he'd saved Henry, now he'd saved me.

"Hudson!" I wanted to grab him and hug him.

"Yes, miss. I'm here. But maybe you could go ahead and get that knife from this lady?"

I looked back to the knife. "Yes, of course." *Of course. Let me just take the knife out the hand of this crazy person who may or may not be faking unconsciousness.* I leaned forward, my hand reaching towards the blade. Naomi's fingers gave a sudden twitch, and I jerked back with a scream of fright. Faster than a cat scratch, Hudson hauled the board back and gave Naomi a hit upside the head that would have made a high school All-American field hockey player proud. Naomi's head jerked sideways with the blow.

"Whoops," he said. "Ya scared me."

Hysterical laughter bubbled up my throat. Hudson shot a look at me as if deciding whether I warranted a swat on the side of my head as well. "Sorry," I said. "I'm a little on edge here, I guess." Perhaps a bit of an understatement. I reached in and snatched the knife with two fingers, flicking it about three feet away, still not entirely sure that Naomi wasn't faking. Only after the knife was safely out of reach did I start to breathe a little more normally.

"Thank God you were here," I said to Hudson, who was holding his post with a steady determination. Although I guessed he was shaken, since even in the dark I could see his legs wobbling.

"Yes, miss. I guess it was lucky for you that I was."

My ears picked up the faint sound of a siren wailing to life in the distance. I hoped they were coming here.

"This is the second time you saved me," I said. "I really owe you." My brain started focusing on ways I could thank

Hudson without hurting his pride. It was a happier path to go down than to keep hearing Naomi's animal cry that was eerier than anything I'd ever heard. There had to be a way I could get Hudson off the streets. Maybe help him find a job, a place to live. Make his life easier, since he'd literally just saved mine.

"It was my pleasure, miss. It was truly my pleasure."

CHAPTER TWENTY-FOUR

E van shifted in his chair, squirming like a five-year-old at the opera. I halfway expected him to slide onto the floor and begin kicking his feet. It was a dreary day, and we were sitting in Frances's kitchen, warm cups of tea steaming on the table in front of us. Evan's tea was untouched, but he'd eaten most of the shortbread cookies from the plate Frances had put out.

I'd given her a watered-down version of the events, leaving out large chunks of the story, which made the whole thing sound rather convoluted. I'd skipped the part about the poisoned brownies, the break-in at my house, the trip to the Lotts, and the resulting car chase that had nearly gotten us killed.

I also left out the part about Naomi coming after me with a knife. There are certain things you just don't want to relive, in any form or fashion. I still struggled to get the sounds of that night out of my head. Her laughter was the soundtrack of nightmares, and the scream as she tried to kill me, still ricocheted around my brain as I was drifting off to sleep. Instead, I'd merely mentioned that she'd lost her mind, thinking that her husband had killed Dayna, and was now safely locked up in a padded room somewhere. Hopefully somewhere that she could never get out of.

"Why would she think her husband had killed Dayna?" asked Frances, glancing down at Henry, who was nestled contentedly in her lap. His eyes were half-closed, his breathing slow and even. She ran her hand rhythmically along his back, and he gave a loud sigh.

"Well, because Dayna had—" I paused, suddenly realizing you can't blurt out indelicate acts like that to your grand-mother. "Well, um, she had crossed some boundaries with Naomi's husband one night, when he went to the office to pick her up. And I guess she thought killing Dayna was the right atonement for what had happened."

"That sounds very odd," she said.

"Luckily, she and her husband had different ideas," I said, taking a small sip of tea. I wondered if Walter was still visiting his hooker-friend on Westheimer. I wouldn't blame him, really. I mean, he probably had better companionship with her than he'd ever had with Naomi. She'd seemed kind of nice, so long as you didn't try and cut into her territory.

A gust of wind rattled the crepe myrtle outside the window, blowing an avalanche of dead leaves off its branches. Addie, who'd been sleeping next to my chair, raised her head and listened intently. Convinced there was no need for action, she settled back down.

"Oh, I went and saw Melba yesterday," I said, turning towards Evan. "She told me that Cherilynn got a job as an assistant manager at the Discount-A-Rama, and it seems like she's doing well. I imagine Lonnie couldn't have been easy to live with. She's probably glad he's locked up."

Frances stopped her petting long enough to take a sip of tea. Henry raised his head, imploring her to continue. "My word, that poor woman," Frances said, setting her teacup back down.

"Poor woman!" Evan said, his first contribution of the afternoon. "She's horrible. Look how she treated Henry!"

"I know, dear," Frances said gently. "But sometimes people are victims of their circumstances. It sounds like she had a very difficult life. And she obviously didn't know anything about dogs." Her hand went back to Henry's head. He closed his eyes and settled against her lap. "But Henry has you now, and I know you'll take wonderful care of him."

Evan relaxed almost imperceptibly and took another cookie. "Yeah," he said, popping the cookie in his mouth. I reached out and took the last cookie before that too disappeared.

"And Melba said she thinks Cherilynn is going to be able to keep her house and the aunt's house," I continued. "Daniel's lawyer is reviewing everything. I doubt he wants it."

"She should be careful," Frances said. "I don't know the man personally, but from everything you've told me, I would find it hard to believe he wouldn't want that real estate."

"Well, it can't be worth much," I said. "I mean that neighborhood isn't exactly prime."

"Oh, I heard that Dayna had a massive life insurance policy," Evan said, finally looking engaged. "Someone at work told me it was huge, like a couple million dollars, or something. And they said Daniel's already taken off. I heard he's planning on doing a documentary in Aruba. Or maybe it was Fiji." His brows furrowed, and he peered out the window. "No, I think it was Mumbai."

"Those aren't even close to the same thing," I said, rolling my eyes. "But they're all really far away, so I'm happy about it."

"Yeah, me too," Evan said, glancing over at Henry. "Oh, and hey!" he said, "I forgot to tell you. The insurance company called me Friday and they're—ow!" I'd kicked out at him under the table with a shade too much force, and had connected solidly with his shin.

Frances looked over at me, one eyebrow arching up. "Oh, dear. Were you in some kind of accident?" she asked, turning to Evan with concern.

He looked over at me, as I stared unblinking at him, my lips pressed together.

"Oh, it was nothing really," he said, suddenly showing an interest in his tea. He grabbed the cup and took a gulp, sputtering as it went down the wrong pipe. I leaned over and thumped him on the back.

"You okay?" I asked, whacking him a couple more times for good measure. He held up a hand and leaned away from me.

"Yeah, yeah, I'm fine," he said. "Where were we?"

"You were just going to tell me about your accident," said Frances. "Jessica, why don't you get some more cookies? I would get up, but I hate to wake Henry." Henry's head had rolled sideways, and his tongue was lolling out the side of his mouth. His feet began to twitch, and then all four legs began moving in rhythm, as if he was running full speed in his dream.

"It's okay. We don't need any more cookies, we need to get going in a minute."

"I'd like another cookie," Evan said, giving me a look and rubbing at his shin.

I scooted out of my chair, careful not to disturb Addie, and race-walked the five feet to the counter, where the remaining cookies sat. I brought the box and thumped it down on the table, sliding back into my chair.

"What sort of accident did you have, Evan?" Frances asked, clearly unwilling to give this up.

"It was nothing," he mumbled, shifting sideways in his chair and tucking his legs away from me on the far side.

"Someone just ran into me, and there was some confusion as to who was at fault. But luckily, after the insurance company got the police report, they said they're going to take care of everything."

I was guessing by "everything," he meant they were going to replace his car. As for the minivan, Evan had gotten the driver's contact information from the police, and we had reached out to her directly. I felt responsible for the whole mess, and I'd offered to pay for her repairs in cash, so that it wouldn't go against Evan's insurance. Who knew car repairs were so expensive? I'd had to dip into some savings, but at the end of the day, it had felt like the right thing to do.

"Well, I'm glad you're okay," she said. "And as for the rest of this mess, it certainly sounds like things worked out as well as they could after such a dreadful event," said Frances.

"I don't know," Evan said, sighing heavily and looking suddenly depressed. "Dayna might be dead, but Chip's still around. Geez, he's almost as bad as she was." I felt a tingle of relief that I was out of that world. Tomorrow I would get back to building my business, one box of biscuits at a time.